KU-369-498

numerous ... ... g a
nation for the RWA ... ... or *The*
...stmas Stranger. She enjoys featuring her cats (or
...nds' pets) in her stories and always has another book
...he pipeline! She currently lives in Louisiana with her
...sband, one son and three spoiled cats. Contact her via
...r website, bethcornelison.com

Also by K.D. Richards

Pursuit of the Truth
Missing at Christmas
Christmas Data Breach
Shielding Her Son

Also by Beth Cornelison

Mountain Retreat Murder
Kidnapping in Cameron Glen
Colton 911: Secret Alibi
Rancher's Covert Christmas
Rancher's Hostage Rescue
In the Rancher's Protection

Discover more at millsandboon.co.uk

DARK WATER DISAPPEARANCE

K.D. RICHARDS

COLTON'S ULTIMATE TEST

BETH CORNELISON

MILLS & BOON

First Published in Great Britain 2022
by Mills & Boon, an imprint of HarperCollins*Publishers* Ltd
1 London Bridge Street, London, SE1 9GF

www.harpercollins.co.uk

HarperCollins*Publishers*
Macken House, 39/40 Mayor Street Upper,
Dublin 1, D01 C9W8

Dark Water Disappearance © 2022 Kia Dennis
Colton's Ultimate Test © 2022 Harlequin Enterprises ULC

Special thanks and acknowledgement are given to Beth Cornelison for her contribution to *The Coltons of Colorado* series.

ISBN: 978-0-263-30371-1

1222

This book is produced from independently certified FSC™ paper to ensure responsible forest management.

For more information visit: www.harpercollins.co.uk/green

Printed and Bound in Spain using 100% Renewable electricity at CPI Black Print, Barcelona

DARK WATER DISAPPEARANCE

K.D. RICHARDS

For Shara and Kendra

Chapter One

Dominique "Nikki" King turned her Camry onto the familiar road leading to the house that had been her refuge for as long as she could remember. The limbs of the decades-old trees lining either side of the street swayed gently as if waving hello to an old friend. She made a right turn into the horseshoe driveway and got her first look at the modest farmhouse she hadn't seen in years.

Lakewood House. The house had been christened at some point years before her grandfather bought it. The name had stuck.

Her chest tightened. She pulled to a stop and let the car idle.

It was the first time she'd been back to her grandfather's house since he'd passed away a year earlier. It was her house now. Her grandfather had employed the services of a local handyman as a caretaker, and she had kept the man on retainer after she'd inherited the home. But it looked as if the monthly stipend had only extended to the basics. There'd never been much of a lawn. There was too much tree cover for any kind of grass to flourish, and since the house sat on nine acres of land, there weren't any neighbors within sight to complain about the curb appeal. The once bright white wooden siding was dirty, dingy, and several shingles were missing. The black shutters were faded and chipped. The windows themselves desperately needed a good scrubbing, and the pronounced dip in the two stairs leading up to the wraparound porch served as a warning to take care to anyone approaching the front door.

Tread carefully.

A warning she should have heeded more generally in life. Then she might not have found herself back in Carling Lake, New York, unemployed and a pariah among the political world she'd worked so hard to enter.

Just a temporary blip, she told herself for the thousandth time. It had almost become a mantra. She'd been putting off coming back to the house for too long, anyway. There were decisions that needed to be made. Whether to sell the house or keep it and rent it out. Carling Lake was a tourist town, so it wouldn't be too difficult to find renters on a regular basis. But the idea of strangers tromping through the house didn't sit well. Sleeping in her old bedroom. Making a mess of her grandfather's spotless kitchen. She wasn't sure she could stand it.

Well, there was plenty of time to figure all that out. Right now, she just wanted to get unpacked and settled in.

Without a job, she had no way to pay for her Washington, DC, apartment, so she'd broken the lease and put all of her furniture in storage. Two extra large suitcases of clothes, three boxes of knickknacks and miscellaneous items, and her laptop were pretty much all she had to her name at the moment. It was a precipitous fall for the girl voted most likely to become the first Black female president in her senior year of high school. For as long as she could remember, she'd been interested in politics, an interest she'd inherited from her grandfather, who had served on the Carling Lake town council for nearly twenty years.

After years of internships that didn't pay well, if at all, and various entry-level jobs, she'd climbed the ladder and finally landed a position as a policy aide to Thomas Manco, a member of New York's delegation to the House of Representatives. Her dream job working for a man she'd thought was an honest public servant with the sincere desire to help the people he represented.

Oh, how wrong she'd been on that one.

"Hey, you left DC to get away from all that," she said out loud, shaking thoughts of her ruined career from her head just as her phone chirped the receipt of a text message.

You there yet?

Carolyn Montgomery, Nikki's only work friend who hadn't stopped returning her calls and texts. Carolyn was the only person she'd told she was leaving DC for Carling Lake.

Just got here. Will call you tomorrow if I make it through the night. JK.

Nikki tossed the phone back into her purse, shut off the engine and exited the car.

She wheeled her suitcases to the porch stairs and tested that the tread would hold before hauling them, one at a time, to the front door. Last week, when she'd decided to temporarily relocate to Carling Lake, she'd contacted Pete Bonny, the man her grandfather had hired to act as caretaker of Lakewood House when he'd moved to Florida two years earlier. Pete had assured her the property, though a little worse for wear over the years, was perfectly habitable. She hoped he was right. Living in DC wasn't cheap, and what little money she'd managed to save would go quickly, even in Carling Lake, if she had to rent a place.

Luckily, her key turned easily in the lock, and the front door swung open into a living area that looked into the kitchen. The home's layout was unusual, but her grandfather had opened up as many walls as he could to make the home feel as spacious as possible. A small dining room sat adjacent to the kitchen, and tucked into the rear corner of the main floor was her grandfather's study, which was about the same size as the walk-in closet in her apartment back in DC.

The second floor was apportioned into three bedrooms—a tiny guest room and two larger rooms that shared a Jack-and-Jill bath, the only bathroom in the house. A cozy, if oddly configured, space by anyone's standards, but it had been perfect for her and her grandfather.

She got busy pulling the dirty covers off the furniture and bringing in her belongings from the car. She'd just set the last box from her car on the living room sofa when the sound of an engine bloomed outside. She stepped to the open front door and watched as a metallic blue pickup bounced its way toward the house. Hitched to its rear was a boat Nikki recognized even without seeing the lettering on its side.

Annalise. Her grandfather had named the boat after his beloved late wife, Nikki's grandmother, who had died the year before she'd been born.

The truck pulled to a stop behind her red Camry, and Pete Bonny hopped out of the driver's side.

Pete was only ten years older than her thirty-two

years, but hard living had aged him. At just after three in the afternoon, his eyes were already bloodshot, and his thinning brown hair stood up in tufts over his head. His orange-beige skin looked rubbery, as if he'd spent too much time under a tanning light or, more likely, out on Carling Lake without using sunscreen. A sizable beer gut hung over the waistband of his jeans. Still, when he smiled, she could see a hint of the heartthrob the teen-age girls in town had swooned over many years ago.

Pete climbed out of the truck. "Well, aren't you a sight for sore eyes."

Nikki grinned and bounded off the porch. "Hi, Pete."

He pulled her in for a quick hug before stepping back. "Your granddad always bragged about how smart and pretty you were, but I don't think he did you justice." Pete winked.

Her grandfather had been openly affectionate. He'd made sure she knew how proud he was of her. Still, her heart clenched at Pete's words—words she'd never hear directly from her grandfather again.

It had been more than a year since Bernard King had passed on peacefully in the Florida retirement home he'd moved to when the New York winters and the up-keep on his beloved Lakewood House had gotten to be too much for him. But she was still struggling to deal with the loss of the only real parent she'd ever had. Her mother and father had been more interested in call-ing themselves parents than in actually parenting once they were. High-powered careers as US diplomats had taken them all over the world, and caring for their only daughter hadn't been a priority. They'd stuck her in a boarding school when she'd turned six. It had been a point of contention between Grandpa Bernie and his son, her father, for years, but thankfully, she had still been allowed to visit her grandfather on breaks and during the summer. Then, not long after her tenth birthday, her parents had been killed in a car accident. Grandpa Bernie was granted guardianship, and he'd immediately taken her out of the boarding school and brought her to live with him in Carling Lake.

It had been a transition for both of them. Bernard King had spent his lifetime building up his trucking-and-shipping company, King's Trucking. As was tradition at the time, Grandma Annalise had raised their only son. But they were now all the family either of them had, and Grandpa Bernie had been determined to do things differently this time around. And he had, attending every dance recital, basketball game and piano concert that she'd been in. He'd bandaged scraped knees, set curfews and imposed punishments when called for. He'd been the father he hadn't been to his son. The father his son hadn't been in the ten years she'd known him.

She wasn't sure if she'd ever come to terms with never hearing his voice again or simply lounging beside him on the *Annalise* in the middle of Carling Lake again.

She pushed away the tears that threatened to come and focused on Pete.

"…so I figured you might like to have the boat."

"Thank you." She forced a smile. "You didn't have to go through all that trouble."

Pete waved away her words. "No trouble at all. It is your boat after all. Your grandfather allowed me to use it whenever I wanted, part of my compensation for looking after the house, so I primarily kept it at my place. But since you're back now, you should have it."

Pete didn't exactly sound thrilled about having to give up the boat, but he was right that it, as well as everything else her grandfather had owned, was now hers. Maybe she should have told Pete he could keep it, but what was the point of living lakeside if she didn't have a boat to take advantage of the lake.

Pete ducked his head and stepped back toward the truck. "Well, I'll get her docked for you."

Nikki took a step back toward the house. "Let me just put on my boots and I'll come help you."

Pete flashed a smile that didn't reach his eyes. "No, no need. I can handle this alone. You get yourself settled in."

Truth be told, as much as she was happy to have the boat, launching and docking it was the last thing she wanted to deal with at the moment. She was exhausted from the drive from DC, and she wanted to unpack and make a trip to the grocery store before it got dark.

She waved to Pete as he hopped back in the truck and started toward the lake at the back of the house.

Nikki walked through the space, memories rushing her as she did. In the kitchen, she ran a hand over the wooden countertops. A slip of paper on the floor caught her eye. A business card, homemade by the looks of it. There were no words or lettering on the card, only a symbol: a yellow fleur-de-lis. The only person who should have been in the house in the last year was Pete. It must belong to him.

She pocketed the card to ask Pete about it when he returned from launching the boat and focused on the more pressing task at hand.

By the time she'd lugged her two suitcases up to the second floor, she was breathing hard and wondering whether unpacking couldn't wait a little longer.

The first door to the right of the stairs opened into

the tiny bedroom she'd occupied when she was home from college for holidays.

Nikki rolled the suitcases past the room and toward her grandfather's bedroom. Her grandfather had taken anything of value with him when he'd moved to Florida, leaving his room a blank canvas. But that wasn't why she'd chosen this room. It was the bigger of the two rooms that opened into the bathroom, and unlike her tiny room, it had an unobstructed view of Carling Lake.

She might not have remembered the roads in Carling Lake, but she remembered how gorgeous the sun was rising over the water in the mornings.

It was too late to catch the sunrise, but Nikki glanced out of the window anyway. The lake was beautiful at any time of the day.

But it wasn't the lake that caught her attention now.

Pete jogged back toward the house. She was too far away to see the expression on his face, but from his body language, she could tell something was very, very wrong.

Nikki turned and dashed back down the stairs, throwing open the back door of the house as Pete bounded onto the back porch.

"What is it? Are you okay?" she asked, leading Pete to one of the old rocking chairs that lived out there.

"There's…a…body," Pete said between labored breaths.

Nikki turned and squinted toward the water. Her eyes scanned the lakeshore until they landed on something, she wasn't sure what. Red plaid maybe? Whatever it was, it was lying partially submerged in the lake.

She pulled her phone from her back pocket and dialed 911 before handing it to Pete. "When the dispatcher picks up, tell them what's going on. I'm going to take a look."

She ignored Pete's protests and stepped off the porch, walking fast toward the thing she'd seen.

As she got closer, it became clear that the object was a person. A female. And she looked young, late teens or early twenties, but it was hard to tell.

Nikki slowed. She was sure the police wouldn't want her to disturb the scene, but if the woman needed help, she didn't want to wait.

She lay in a prone position, her legs still in the water, dirty reddish-brown hair obscuring her face. Her body, the air around her even, was so motionless, it wasn't really necessary for Nikki to feel for a pulse. She did anyway, reaching for the woman's ashen wrist and pulling away, unsurprised when she didn't find any sign of life. Whoever the poor soul was, she'd been dead for quite some time.

Nikki stepped back, careful to plant her feet in the same soft ground she'd trodden moving forward, in an attempt to disturb the scene as little as possible. Now that the initial shock had worn off, she could see that the stranger was soaked from head to toe.

Maybe she'd fallen overboard and drowned, the currents of the lake washing her up on the property. Nikki said a quick prayer, then hurried back to the house to wait for the police with Pete.

It had been a long, trying day for her, but not nearly as bad a day as it had been for the poor woman lying lakeside.

Chapter Two

Terrence Sutton weaved his way through the streets of Carling Lake. He passed the turn leading to his aunt Charity's house, keeping his car pointed toward the sheriff's department. Good manners dictated his first stop in Carling Lake should be family, but this time, social niceties would have to take a back seat. He wasn't in town for a social visit.

He hadn't heard from his sister, Jill, in a week. While it wasn't unusual for his sister to let his calls and texts languish for a little while if she was caught up in a story, she had never been out of contact for so long. She knew he worried about the chances she took as an investigative reporter, digging up information many people would rather keep hidden. Over the years, they'd worked out a routine of sorts. When he called, she'd get back to him within twenty-four hours even if that response was only a quick text saying she was too busy to talk. And the same went when Jill called and left a message for him. His job as a detective with the Trenton, New Jersey, Police Department had its own set of dangers.

That's why he knew something was wrong. Jill wouldn't be out of touch for this long if there weren't. She wouldn't leave him to worry unnecessarily.

Terrence pulled his car into a parking space in the

small lot adjacent to the sheriff's station and checked his phone again. No messages or texts from Jill. His gut twisted a little tighter.

There had to be something here in Carling Lake that would lead him to his sister. He'd find it and Jill if it was the last thing he did.

First stop, make nice with the town sheriff. He was going to be running his own unofficial missing person investigation whether Sheriff Webb liked it or not, but it wouldn't hurt to grease the wheels if he could. Who knew what he'd find or whether he'd need local help. Best to play nice—at least at first.

Although he'd grown up in Carling Lake, he didn't make it back for visits very often. He recalled meeting Lance Webb some years back on a visit to see Aunt Charity, but he had no idea how the sheriff would react to having a Trenton cop running around town asking questions.

Terrence exited his Toyota Highlander and entered the sheriff's department.

A uniformed clerk sat behind a high desk. The clerk's eyes swept over Terrence, assessing him from head to toe as he approached. "May I help you?"

"I'm Detective Terrence Sutton with the Trenton PD. I'd like to speak with the sheriff, please."

The clerk's expression remained impassive. "Do you have an appointment?"

"I don't, but I'd appreciate it if he has a minute for me."

The clerk stared silently for a moment before raising the phone receiver and punching in four numbers. He turned his chair and lowered his voice so Terrence wasn't able to hear the conversation, but when he hung up the phone, he nodded toward the row of chairs in the lobby. "The sheriff will be out in a moment."

Terrence bypassed the seating area and moved to stand in front of a corkboard with a dozen or so flyers announcing everything from the upcoming Summer Festival to missing pets and a want ad for a babysitter. The board encapsulated Carling Lake—a town dependent upon its festivals and the recreational activities provided to tourists while at the same time being a permanent home to so many people.

From the age of eight until he'd gone away to college, he was one of the people who called Carling Lake home. He and Jill had been raised by Aunt Charity and Uncle Jarrod after their mother had dropped them off on her sister's doorstep one summer day when he was eight and Jill was five. Hope Sutton had begged her sister to watch the kids, saying she just needed a few days' break from being a single mother.

Even at eight years old, he'd known his mother wasn't like the other mothers. Hope couldn't have cared less if he and Jill made it to school on time, and she'd never once checked their homework or planned a nutritious meal. So when a week had turned into a month, he hadn't been all that surprised or concerned. It wasn't the first time his mother had disappeared on him and his sister. At least this time she'd left them with two responsible adults. His aunt always made them home-cooked meals, and Uncle Jarrod had taught him how to skip rocks on the lake. It was a little irritating that even though it was summer and school was out, Aunt Charity insisted they read for a half hour each day. Not being able to do whatever he wanted whenever he wanted had been an adjustment, but it had also felt kind of nice, like a weight he hadn't even realized he'd been carrying had been lifted.

As the weeks continued to tick by though, he'd begun to dread his mother's return. But the closer they got to the end of the summer, the harder it was for Aunt Charity to get her sister on the phone. When she finally did, she gave Hope an ultimatum—clean up her act and be the mother her kids deserved or sign over their guardianship to her and Uncle Jarrod. Five days after her call to her sister, Aunt Charity had the signed papers granting her legal guardianship of him and Jill in hand. His mother had paid extra to have the papers overnighted to her sister. In all his eight years, he'd never seen his mother pay extra for anything.

Hope Sutton had popped up from time to time in the ensuing years, mostly when she needed money. When she'd died from an unexpected aneurysm the year he'd turned twenty, it had fallen to him to make the decisions about her burial as her next of kin, even though the woman who'd given birth to him had never been his mother, not in any real sense of the word.

A loud buzzing noise pulled him out of his head.

A tall Black man wearing a dark brown uniform strode through the metal doors behind the clerk's desk. He and Sheriff Webb had a few notable characteristics in common—they were both Black men in law enforcement—but looks weren't one of them. The six-foot-three sheriff was taller by several inches, with a lithe frame as compared to Terrence's stockier, more muscled physique.

"Detective Sutton," the sheriff said, striding forward with his hand outstretched. "Good to see you again. What can I do for you?"

"Please, call me Terrence. Is there somewhere we can talk in private?"

"Let's go to my office. And you can call me Lance," the sheriff said before turning and leading him into the inner sanctum of the station.

Lance kicked off the conversation once they'd both settled in his office. "I take it you're not in Carling Lake just visiting Miss Charity."

"No. My aunt doesn't even know I'm in town yet."

One of Lance's eyebrows quirked up, along with the ends of his mouth. "You think so?"

The internet had nothing on Carling Lake's gossip network, so it was entirely possible his aunt already knew about his arrival in town.

"I'll rephrase. I haven't seen my aunt yet. But she is my next stop."

Lance leaned back in his chair, a curious expression on his face. "Well, whatever made you risk the wrath of Miss Charity and come here before you stopped by her place must be important."

"It is," he said. The anxiousness and fear currently lodged in his chest had become all too familiar in the last several days. "I'm here trying to track down my sister, Jill."

"As far as I know, Miss Charity doesn't have any visitors at the moment. What makes you think your sister is in Carling Lake?"

"I'm not sure Jill is in town to visit Aunt Charity. Or that she's here at all. I haven't been able to get in touch with her in a week. It's not like her to ignore me."

Lance's expression turned thoughtful. "A week is not that long."

"Maybe not for some people, but it is for Jill and me. Or rather it is a long time for her not to acknowledge my calls and texts at all. Since we are both single, live alone and have jobs that put us in the line of fire at times, we agreed that we'd respond to each other within twenty-four hours. I'll admit we usually don't actually engage in conversation more than once a month, if that, but we are in frequent contact via text."

"And Jill has ceased that contact." Lance's face finally took on a concerned expression.

He nodded. "No response to several calls and texts. It took me a little while to realize Jill hadn't responded to my last call within our agreed-upon twenty-four hours."

Terrence's stomach rolled as a wave of guilt hit. He should have noticed, but he'd been wrapped up in what was supposed to have been a major drug operation and had gotten distracted. All for naught, as it turned out. The bust had been a bust, and three days had gone by before he'd realized he hadn't heard from Jill. Three days when his career had rapidly gone into the toilet, and who knew what had happened to his sister?

"Okay," Lance said, the wheels almost visibly turning in his head. "I take it it's safe to assume you've called all her friends. You talked to her coworkers. Been by her place."

Terrence nodded. "Yes to all of that. Jill is an investigative journalist. I spoke to her editor at the newspaper she works for and several of her coworkers. They all said they hadn't heard from her. And her neighbors haven't seen her in days, although they all said that wasn't unusual. I also spoke to her best friend, but she hasn't spoken to Jill in a couple of weeks."

Lance tapped a pen on his desk blotter. "And her apartment?"

"She travels a lot for work, but she has a small place in DC. I drove there yesterday to check things out. Everything looked normal, except I found this." He pulled a plastic bag from his jacket pocket. Inside was a piece of paper with Carling Lake written on it and circled several times. Underneath was a drawing that looked like a fancy flower of some sort. "The handwriting is Jill's. I had a friend in the Philly PD dust it for fingerprints, but he only found Jill's prints on it."

"Okay, I mean, I get why you're concerned, but you don't have much to go on." Lance handed the plastic-encased paper back across the desk.

Frustration bubbled in Terrence's chest. "I know, but I can't shake the feeling that something is wrong."

"And she's your sister and you're not going to let it go until you know for sure she's okay. I get it. What can I do?"

Relief flooded through Terrence. He'd have gone it alone if he'd had to but having the sheriff on his side would be a big help if, as he feared, Jill had gotten herself in over her head.

"Right now, I'm not sure. I hadn't thought much past getting to Carling Lake and seeing if Jill was here or if she had been here."

Lance exhaled. "Well, as I said, I haven't heard she was in town, but I may have missed the latest news. Your aunt Charity though…nothing gets past that woman. If Jill is here or was here, she'd be the one to know."

The phone on the sheriff's desk buzzed before Terrence could respond. Lance picked up the receiver.

His face darkened as the person on the other end of the line spoke.

Terrence couldn't hear what was being said, but it was clearly not good.

Lance ended the call, rising as he did. "I've got to go. Someone's found a body."

Terrence rose as well. "In Carling Lake?" His heart thundered in his chest. *Jill*. "Have you got an ID on the body?"

Lance stopped his march toward the door. Silence hung thick in the room while he visibly contemplated whether to answer.

"I'm not trying to horn in on your case, Sheriff. It's just…" He couldn't bring himself to say what he was thinking. That the body could be his sister. But from the softening look on Lance's face, he didn't need to. Webb knew what was on his mind.

"Don't have an ID yet." Lance reached to open the office door.

"Do you know if the body is male or female?"

"It's female," Lance answered soberly.

Terrence's stomach churned, but he fell in step next to the sheriff. "I'm going with you."

Chapter Three

Nikki remembered Pete as a man of few words and was grateful that he hadn't seemed to have changed over the years. They'd moved to the front porch to wait for the police. Pete cradled a glass of water but still looked as if he might lose his lunch at any moment. The man was undeniably shaken and she couldn't blame him. She wasn't sure she'd ever get the sight of that poor woman out of her mind.

Pete cocked his head, and she heard the sound of an approaching vehicle. A black SUV with the Carling Lake sheriff's department logo on the side pulled to a stop alongside her Camry.

She'd met the previous sheriff briefly on one of her trips to Carling Lake before her grandfather moved to Florida. The man who hopped out of the driver's side of the SUV looked familiar, but she was sure she'd never been properly introduced to the new sheriff. He affixed his sheriff's cap on his head as he exited the car. The passenger door of the SUV swung open as Sheriff Webb rounded the hood.

All the breath rushed from her lungs when she saw the man who stepped from the car.

Terrence.

Her emotions boiled like water in a scalding hot pot. Anger. Elation. Remorse. Longing.

They'd once been inseparable, best friends on the edge of being much more. But all that had changed in what had seemed like an instant when they were seventeen.

Terrence gave no sign of having seen her or Pete on the porch. He leaped from the SUV, his face set in a determined expression.

The sheriff caught hold of Terrence's arm. "You need to stay here. This is a potential crime scene."

Terrence shook free of the sheriff's grasp. "I'm a cop."

"Not on my force." The two men stared at each other with dark expressions for a long moment before the sheriff added more softly, "It might not be something you want to see."

It was clear something was going on between Terrence and the sheriff. But at the moment, Nikki had a more pressing question. "Terrence."

He spun around. His hickory-brown eyes widened in shock when they landed on her. At least the feeling was mutual.

She strode down the porch steps and came to a stop in front of him.

"Nikki." The sound of her name in his deep baritone still sent a delicious chill down her spine. "What are you doing here?"

"Grandpa left the house to me, and as of today, I live here."

The expression on his face softened. "I heard he passed away. I'm sorry for your loss."

She was surprised to hear sincerity in his tone given

how he'd felt about her grandfather when he was alive. "Thank you. What are you doing here?"

Terrence's expression didn't change, and had she not known him so well, she would have missed his reaction. Surprise that quickly turned to displeasure. "I was with the sheriff when the call came in about a body. I'm in town looking for Jill…"

Her heart leaped into her throat. "Jill? What's wrong with Jill?"

Although her relationship with Terrence had been left in tatters as a result of the fraud between her grandfather and his uncle, she and Jill had managed to keep in touch and had become pretty good friends, since they'd both grown up in Carling Lake and lived in DC.

"No one has heard from her in more than a week, and I have reason to believe she might be in Carling Lake. I was in Sheriff Webb's office when the call came in that the body of a female had been found…" He swallowed hard.

His obvious torment at not knowing whether Jill was safe tempered some of her annoyance at his surprise appearance. She hadn't seen a lot of the body, but she'd seen enough to know it wasn't Jill.

"It's not Jill, Terrence."

"How can you…?"

Without thinking, Nikki reached out and took his hand. "I saw the body, checked for a pulse. And I had dinner with Jill three weeks ago when she was in DC for a story. It's not her down there."

He let out an audible breath.

The sheriff, who'd hung back, moved forward now. "I'm glad our victim isn't your sister, but she is somebody, and I need to get this investigation moving. It's my understanding that Pete Bonny made the call to the sheriff's office."

Nikki dropped Terrence's hand and stepped back, inclining her head toward the porch where Pete still sat. "He's a bit shaken up."

The sheriff nodded. "Understandable. I want to take a look at the scene. All three of you need to stay here."

The sheriff shot a look at Terrence that he ignored, if he noticed it at all. His gaze hadn't wavered from Nikki's face, but his expression had morphed into something unreadable once she had assured him Jill wasn't lying by the lake.

She couldn't see the body clearly from where she stood at the front of the house, but she watched the sheriff stride across the lawn and stop and bow his head before crouching.

"I thought you were working for some political muckety-muck in DC," Terrence said.

Nikki frowned, although she wasn't surprised by the contempt she heard in his voice. He'd always been the type of person who saw the world in black-and-white. Good or bad. Compromise and diplomacy weren't in his makeup.

She ignored his question and asked one of her own. "Why do you think Jill is in trouble?"

"I didn't say I thought she was in trouble."

"You didn't have to. You're in Carling Lake, a place you rarely visit. And you're here at Lakewood House, a place you swore you'd never set foot on again. That's more than enough to tell me how concerned you are about Jill."

Once upon a time, Grandpa Bernie and Terrence's uncle Jarrod had been best friends. Charity and Jarrod Jackson had been a source of support when Grandpa

Bernie had suddenly become the guardian of his griev-
ing, sullen, more-than-a-little-angry ten-year-old or-
phaned granddaughter.

The two nontraditional families had been close for
many years. So close that Nikki thought of Charity as
her aunt too growing up. But that had all changed when
the automotive plant outside of town had closed and
Jarrod lost his job. The Jacksons had fallen behind on
their mortgage and were in danger of losing Lakewood
House and everything they'd worked for. With Nikki
set to leave for college the next year and Grandpa Bernie wanting to downsize from the five-bedroom colo-
nial he owned on the other side of town, he'd offered
to buy the Jacksons' property at market price, allowing
them to pay off their mortgage and have a little extra
money to start over.

It seemed as if the sale had been a win-win, but
cracks in the friendship emerged soon after the papers
had been signed. Jarrod Jackson came to resent Nikki's grandfather and began accusing Grandpa Bernie
of tricking him into selling Lakewood House. Jarrod's
hostility quickly trickled down to his nephew.

During their senior year of high school, Nikki had
found herself looking at Terrence Sutton in a whole new
way. For seven years, he'd just been her friend. The guy
she swam in the lake with. Went fishing with. Kidded
around with. But she suddenly noticed how his muscles rippled when he tossed Jill off the dock and into
the lake. And how his brown eyes twinkled and how
devastatingly handsome the dimple in his left cheek
made him when he smiled. She'd seen that other girls
were eyeing him anew as well. And she didn't like that
one bit.

Fortunately for her, it seemed like whatever budding

feelings she was having for Terrence were reciprocated. Their long walks and moonlight chats by the lake had taken on a decidedly romantic tone. At the end of that summer, they'd promised to keep in frequent touch via email, and then Terrence had leaned over and kissed her softly. She'd nearly floated back to school.

By the time she'd returned to Carling Lake for Christmas break, Terrence's emails had turned terse, when he bothered to email at all. She'd thought—hoped—it was because he was focused on his college classes. They'd gotten into a huge argument on Nikki's first day back in town, with Terrence venting all his frustration about her grandfather having stolen his family's home and legacy. There had been no reasoning with him, and she'd soon lost her temper. They hadn't spoken for the rest of her visit. Nikki was grateful that Charity and Jill didn't seem to feel the same way as Jarrod and Terrence. But, like the elder men in their lives, their friendship had fractured right down the middle. Maybe irrevocably.

"You don't have to worry about my sister. I can handle whatever is going on with her myself."

"Oh, for goodness' sake." Nikki dragged her cell from her pocket and pulled up the contact for Jill Sutton.

"What are you doing?"

"Calling Jill."

"Told you she hasn't been answering her phone."

"Not when *you've* called her, and based on spending just five minutes with you, I can see why she might not want to."

Jill's phone rang then clicked over to voice mail. The message box was full. She slid her cell back into her pocket.

"I told you." Terrence scowled.

She planted a hand on her hip, worry clenched in her chest. Terrence wasn't her favorite person by far, but he adored his sister. If he was worried, that was enough for her to be worried as well. "What's your plan?"

"Look, I appreciate your concern…"

"No, you look. You and I may not care for each other, but Jill is my friend. If she's in trouble, I want to help her."

Terrence glared at her for a moment before holding up both hands in surrender. "Fine. If you want to help, tell me about your dinner with Jill. How did she seem? Was she worried or anxious about anything or anyone?"

Nikki shook her head. "The opposite actually. She was excited about a new story she'd just gotten a tip on."

Lines formed on Terrence's forehead. "A new story? What about?"

She shook her head again. "I have no idea. She wouldn't go into specifics. She just said that if her lead panned out, the article could be a career maker."

"I talked to her editor at the paper. He didn't mention any big story."

"Maybe she hadn't pitched it yet." She thought back on her dinner with Jill. "She did say that there was a lot of work to be done. That's why she didn't want to say too much right then."

"Did she say anything else? Give any hint who or what the story was about?"

"I'm sorry, Terrence. She didn't."

He fisted his hands at his sides, the frustration he was feeling evident on his face.

"I'm afraid I'm declaring this a suspicious death," the sheriff said. "An area of the property will be off-limits until further notice."

"How much of the property?" Nikki shot a look at

the house. She could probably get a room at the local bed-and-breakfast, but her bank account really didn't need the extra stress. Saving money, after all, was the primary reason she'd decided to return to Carling Lake and figure out her next step. The thought of going back to DC and bunking on a friend's sofa indefinitely was too humiliating to contemplate.

The sheriff appeared to pick up on her concern. "As long as it doesn't appear that the victim was ever inside the house, it should be all right for you to stay tonight. Would you consent to a search of the house and property?"

"Absolutely," Nikki agreed immediately. "I can tell you that the house was locked up tight when I arrived. It didn't look like anyone had been inside in weeks."

The sheriff turned to Pete, who still sat in a rocking chair on the porch. "What about it, Pete? When was the last time you were here to check on the property?"

Pete's face reddened. He was supposed to look in on the property at least once a week per the agreement with her grandfather. But from the guilt etched across his face at the moment, it appeared he hadn't been keeping up his end of the deal.

"Oh, well, I might not get out here as much as I used to. I'm not as spry as I once was."

From the looks on the sheriff's and Terrence's faces, they weren't buying what Pete was selling, and neither was Nikki. Pete hadn't batted an eye at launching the boat all by his lonesome.

"I guess I was out here a week and a half ago. Maybe a little more," Pete finally answered.

The sound of sirens cut through the air.

"That'll be my deputies and the forensics crew." Looking from Nikki to Pete, the sheriff said, "I'm going to have a deputy take your statements. Just sit tight and, please, have patience."

The sheriff strode away to the approaching cruisers.

Nikki snuck a glance at Terrence. His gaze trailed after the sheriff.

Have patience. Something told her that request was going to be easier said than done.

TERRENCE TRIED TO focus on taking in as much information as he could from the crime scene, but he couldn't stop his gaze from tracking to Lakewood House. It was the house that Aunt Charity and Uncle Jarrod had been living in when his mother dumped him and Jill off on them. And it was the house where he'd learned what it meant to really be part of a family. Until the fall of his freshman year of college, it had been the only home he'd ever known. And it should still be Aunt Charity's home, would still be if Bernie King, once his uncle's closest friend, hadn't swooped in and bought Lakewood House out from under his family when they'd hit a rough patch financially.

His uncle had learned the hard way that Bernie was no friend at all. Their friendship hadn't been the only casualty though. He and Nikki had begun dating during their senior year in high school, and despite going off to different colleges, they'd managed to keep their relationship fires burning those first few months away. Until the sale. Nikki just couldn't—or wouldn't—see how her grandfather's actions had been a betrayal. Then, during the spring semester of his freshman year, Uncle Jarrod had died of a sudden massive heart attack. He was convinced that the shame of losing his family home and having been stabbed in the back by his closest friend had led to Uncle Jarrod's death.

He studied the house now. After Lance had taken Nikki's statement, he'd searched the house and given the all clear. Nikki had disappeared inside without giving him a second glance. It was probably for the best. Their last conversation had taken place fourteen years ago, but it had left plenty of unpleasant memories. And he wasn't in Carling Lake to rehash the past.

Deputy Clarke Bridges had taken Terrence's official statement and was now taking video of the crime scene. A second deputy in waders searched the bank of the lake for evidence. Neither of them questioned Terrence's presence, and he tried to remain unassuming and unnoticed as he circled the body, the smell of decay wafting on the breeze.

The woman lay face down in the sand, her legs still floating in the water. Her dark hair was matted and tangled, and her light brown skin was mottled and gray from having been in the water. She wore black jeans and a short-sleeve shirt that exposed her arms. He couldn't see her features, but he suspected she was Hispanic or maybe Indigenous.

"I thought I told you to stay out front," Lance said, coming to a stop at his side.

Terrence ignored the question and pointed to the woman's wrist. "Did you notice this? It looks like a bruise."

Lance squatted next to the body. "There's one on the other wrist too. Looks like she might have been bound."

"Or handcuffed." He pointed higher on her arm this time. "And look at her upper arm here and here. More bruises."

"And a few burns." Lance looked at Terrence with anger in his eyes. "This woman was tortured."

Terrence wished he could disagree. "You'll probably find more bruises on other parts of her body."

Lance exhaled heavily. "I'll make sure the medical examiner documents them all and looks for signs of sexual assault."

They both fell silent for a long moment. The body bobbed with a ripple of the lake.

"I'm sure you've seen the bruising around her neck too."

Lance shot him a look. "Of course. But again, the medical examiner will have to tell us whether strangulation is the cause of death. Especially given the other bruising on her body, strangling her could have been part of the torture but not the cause of death."

His jaw tensed. "Someone put her through the wringer. It's possible she just drowned trying to get away from whoever did this to her."

Lance frowned. "Possible. But as far as I'm concerned, that still makes them responsible for her death."

Terrence couldn't agree more. He scanned the shore. Lakewood House was the only home in view. Privacy and seclusion were two of the perks of purchasing property in Carling Lake. Especially lakeside property. Most of the lots were several acres, and it was possible not to see a neighbor for days on end unless one made an effort to do so. "Any ideas where she could have gone into the water?"

"No idea. We'll do our best to figure it out, but it might not be possible. Especially if she went in off the side of a boat."

"Someone in Carling Lake must know her. It's a small town." He could feel his frustration level rising. First, Jill goes missing, and now a young woman turns up at the lakeshore dead. Things like this just didn't happen in Carling Lake. Certainly not without anyone knowing anything.

"I've got men canvassing now. We'll talk to everyone we can. If someone in this town knows her, we'll find out soon." Lance signaled for the deputy with the video camera to come closer. "Help me turn her over, will you?"

Terrence did as requested. They gripped the woman from opposite sides and gently pulled her onto dry land while the deputy documented their every move.

Lance patted the victim's back pockets. "No identification there."

The water had done extensive damage to the body, and it looked as if the animals in the water had also gotten to it.

"Do you recognize her?" Terrence asked.

Lance shook his head. "No. Never seen her."

"Any missing persons reports recently?"

Another headshake. "Not in Carling Lake or any of the surrounding towns. I'll put a call out of course, but it might take some time to track down an identity."

"Any idea how long she's been in the water?" He'd been on the police force for eleven years and a detective for almost five of those years, but he'd primarily worked in the narcotics division.

"The body is bloated, so at least a few days. The medical examiner will be able to be more exact." Lance's chin jutted in the direction of the white van that was coming up the driveway. The medical examiner had arrived.

Terrence straightened to his full height. "This woman is young. If she's been in the water for days, why hasn't anyone been looking for her? Parents. Friends. Someone. She must have been missed by now."

"I don't know, man," Lance said as they walked toward the medical examiner's van. "But I will get to the bottom of how she died. You just remember that you have no authority here. You're a private citizen in Carling Lake." Lance shot him another pointed look.

"I hear you, and I have more than enough on my plate trying to find my sister." He stopped walking. "I just…" He glanced at the house. He couldn't see Nikki through the window, but he knew she was inside. "Work fast, okay? It feels like something very dark might have slithered into town. And I don't think it will be safe for anyone until you get to the bottom of it."

Chapter Four

Terrence left soon after the medical examiner's arrival. He stopped by his aunt's house after leaving Lakewood House and discovered she already knew he was in town. He couldn't lie to her about Jill's disappearance, but he did his best not to show her how worried he truly was. She seemed to buy it, but he knew that wouldn't last if he didn't find Jill soon. He stayed for dinner, but Aunt Charity had moved into a tiny one-room cabin a few years earlier that wasn't conducive to guests.

He'd had the foresight to make a reservation at the Carling Lake Hotel, but they could only guarantee him one night. With the Spring Festival beginning, they were booked up for the week.

He'd checked in exhausted from the day's travel and the emotional toll, but he'd rallied enough to spend a few hours calling around to Jill's friends again, checking to see if anyone had heard from her, but to no avail. When he'd finally hit a wall and had lain down to get some sleep, he'd found it wouldn't come.

At half past six, he gave up. Showered and dressed, he went downstairs to the hotel's restaurant and, finding their breakfast menu wanting, headed for the one place in town that had never disappointed him. Lakeside Diner was a mainstay in the community, a place where Carling Lake residents and tourists congregated.

He wasn't surprised to find the diner nearly full when he entered just before seven. He caught the eye of Deputy Bridges, who sat with another man and a young boy at a table near the window. Sheriff's deputies had still been searching Lakewood House and combing the property for clues when he'd left there the previous evening, which explained why the large cup of coffee in the deputy's hand seemed to be doing little to chase away the exhaustion on the man's face.

Terrence nodded hello and took a seat at the counter on one of the few stools not already occupied.

Rosie Whitmer, the proprietor of Lakeside Diner, strode over. Her face broke out into a joyful grin when her eyes landed on him. "Well, will wonders never cease? Terrence Sutton, the long-lost son of Carling Lake, is back in town."

Terrence grinned at the woman who'd owned the diner for as long as he'd been alive. Since his trips to Carling Lake had mostly been limited to major holidays and only for a day or two at most, he hadn't had Rosie's food in years.

Rosie's tightly curled orange coif was now all gray, and her figure was fuller than he remembered, but her bright smile and gregarious personality appeared not to have changed at all.

"I don't know about 'long-lost,'" he replied, leaning forward over the counter to place a kiss on the cheek Rosie presented him. "How have you been, Rosie?"

"Fit as a fiddle and twice as spry. Your aunt Charity didn't mention you were coming to town."

"It was a spur-of-the-moment decision."

"Let's start with what I can get you to eat. Then you

can tell me what you've been up to since I've seen you last?" Rosie asked.

"Oh, I think you know exactly what I want." He grinned. "The breakfast platter with your world-famous blueberry pancakes, please. And I haven't been up to much except working longer than I care to admit. I'm afraid my life isn't interesting enough for the Carling Lake gossip circuit."

"We'll just see about that," she said, writing out his order then turning her back to put it on a spindle for the cook.

"Hey, Rosie, I'm just wondering, when was the last time you saw my sister?"

Rosie turned back to face him. "Jill? Huh, it must have been Christmastime. *She* came home to visit her aunt, like a good niece."

"I know, I know, I've heard it all from Aunt Charity. But if single guys like me didn't take the holiday shifts, the cops with families wouldn't be able to spend Christmas with their kids. You wouldn't want that, now would you?"

"Oh, you're really laying it on thick, you know." Rosie chuckled.

"I learned from the best."

The bell over the diner's door jangled and Rosie's face lit up again. Terrence glanced over his shoulder to see who'd garnered such a reaction and saw Nikki striding into the diner. Her eyes skimmed over him quickly, her smile dimming noticeably before she focused her gaze on Rosie.

"Now it really is like old times around here." Rosie came around the counter and enveloped Nikki in a bear hug that included a half minute of rocking from side to side. "I heard you were back in town and about that unfortunate business at Lakewood House. You doing okay, hon?"

It seemed like the town grapevine hadn't slowed any in the years since he'd moved away. Nor had Rosie's affection for Nikki dimmed. Maybe it was because Nikki lacked a mother figure, and Rosie had a naturally motherly personality, but she'd taken a young Nikki under her wing and had even given Nikki her first real job bussing tables the summer she'd turned fourteen. The two of them had a relationship nearly as close as mother and daughter, and it appeared that hadn't changed at all.

Nikki gently pulled free of the hug and beamed at Rosie. To anyone who didn't know her as well as he did, she looked to be taking the previous day's chaos in stride. But he saw the tiny lines creasing the skin under her eyes.

Nikki wasn't his concern. He was only in Carling Lake to track down Jill. His tumultuous relationship with Nikki was…something he didn't have time to ponder.

"It was a shock, finding that poor girl, but I'm fine. Sad for her family, but I'm sure the sheriff will identify her and get her body back to her family so they can lay her to rest."

"Sheriff Webb is the best there is. He'll get to the bottom of things, I have no doubt. Are you back in town to finally deal with Lakewood House?"

Nikki nodded. "It's time. I have to make some decisions about what I want to do with it. Sell it. Rent it… It was kind of a last-minute decision, so I figured I'd just show up and surprise you."

Rosie slid a sly look from Nikki to Terrence. "Last minute, huh? A lot of that is going around, or so I hear."

The bell over the diner door tinkled, drawing Rosie's attention.

Rosie groaned. "Oh, good grief."

Terrence turned toward the door.

It had been over a decade since he'd seen Melinda Hanes, but the woman hadn't changed much in the intervening years. She swept into the diner in an emerald green pantsuit and kitten heels. She'd drawn her auburn hair into a tight bun at the nape of her neck, and her makeup was impeccable. She made a beeline for the men sitting at the table nearest to the entrance, a beauty pageant smile fixed on her face.

"That woman is insufferable," Rosie said. "She comes in two or three mornings chatting up my guests and scouting for votes."

Terrence turned back to Rosie and Nikki. "Votes?"

"You know what happened with our last mayor?" Rosie's gaze tripped between him and Nikki.

Terrence nodded. His trips back to Carling Lake had been short and few in the last several years, but he did subscribe to the *Carling Lake Weekly* online, so he was well aware of the prior mayor's arrest for fraud, corruption and a host of other crimes.

"Well, Melinda apparently wants to step into her brother's shoes," Rosie said. "At least, with respect to running for mayor. And it seems like she has a pretty good shot."

Nikki tilted her head, her expression skeptical. "Really? It might not be entirely fair, but I'd think voters would be hesitant to vote for her given her brother's actions."

Rosie laughed dryly. "Oh, the voters of Carling Lake

are plenty hesitant, but as of right now, she's the only person who has indicated an interest in the position. I think that's why the town council has been dragging its feet about setting the date for the election, hoping someone else might step up, but they won't be able to hold off for much longer."

Terrence shot a glance over his shoulder. Melinda had moved on to another table, chatting with a man and a woman.

"You know, now that you're back in Carling Lake and with your degree, you'd make a terrific candidate for mayor."

Nikki laughed. "You're kidding, right? I've only been in town for a day."

"Nonsense." Rosie waved away Nikki's statement. "You're a hometown girl. You've got way more political experience than Melinda, and you actually care about the whole town. Melinda only cares about her family's business. And I guarantee some people will vote for you just because you're not Melinda. Tell her, Terrence. She'd be great, right?"

He had no doubt Nikki would be great at whatever she did. She always had been. But he doubted she wanted to hear that from him, so he said nothing.

Rosie frowned at his silence.

Nikki shook her head. "That's good to know, but I'm not your girl."

"Well, sit yourself down and let me get you something to eat." She slapped the stool next to Terrence with the rag from her shoulder.

Nikki quickly assessed the seating situation and chose to sit two stools away instead of next to him.

Rosie slid behind the counter. "Can I get you the special too, hon?"

"Sounds like heaven," Nikki answered.

"Coming right up." Rosie put the order in and grabbed the coffeepot. She flipped over the white mugs at his and Nikki's place settings and filled them nearly to the top. "I've got to make the rounds. Be right back."

The hum of the other diners' conversations and the clink of silverware against porcelain filled the silence between Terrence and Nikki. He snuck a glance at the woman who had once been his best friend and more.

Nikki had always been pretty, but in the years since he'd last seen her she had turned into a bona fide knock-out. Her short blondish-brown hair was cut in a bob that framed her face and accentuated a long, graceful neck. From the lines etched into the caramel-colored skin around her eyes, he guessed she'd gotten about as much sleep as he had. But her dark brown eyes were still sharp and lit with intelligence.

Terrence sipped black coffee while Nikki still dumped four creams into hers. Next came three spoonfuls of sugar. Some things never changed.

"Have you heard anything about Jill?" Nikki asked, pulling him from the past.

"No." His gut clenched with the answer. "I spent half the night calling anyone I could think of and reaching out to my law enforcement contacts."

"What about the DC police? Have they opened an investigation?"

"Not as such." The words came out as a growl.

Despite his best efforts, the DC police had refused to formally begin a search for Jill. Nothing was out of place at her apartment. The only things missing had been a small travel bag and some clothes, which supported the cops' belief that Jill had just gone off for work or maybe a vacation and had forgotten to tell friends and family. No amount of explaining that Jill would never do anything so careless would move the lieutenant he'd spoken to. Which was why he'd put in to use some of the considerable amount of leave he'd banked over the years and set out to find her himself.

As a cop, he understood on some level where the DC police were coming from. There was always more work than there were people, and every force had to prioritize. Most adults who were reported missing turned up unharmed at some point.

But he knew Jill. She would not disappear without a word.

"Well, I meant what I said yesterday. Jill is my friend, and our…relationship aside, anything I can do to help, just let me know."

"I've got it under control but thank you."

Silence landed between them again. Rosie was still circling the diner with a coffeepot, stopping at each table to top off cups and chat up the locals and tourists. A server set a plate of steaming blueberry pancakes in front of Terrence before hurrying off with his arms laden with plates of someone else's breakfast.

A small crowd had grown near the door, patrons lined up, waiting for an open table, but no one attempted to claim the empty seat between Nikki and Terrence. The server swept back through, sliding a plate overflowing with food in front of Nikki before gliding away again. She dug in.

"You never answered my question yesterday." Terrence swiveled so his body was angled toward her.

Nikki gave him a look that said she was searching her memory. "What question?"

"Why aren't you in DC?"

"I need to deal with Lakewood House."

"Curious timing. I happen to know that Congress is in session right now, which usually means aides are swamped."

Surprise spread across Nikki's face.

"What? I'm an informed citizen." He grabbed a fork and speared a clump of eggs from her plate, bringing them to his lips with a grin.

Her shoulders tensed. "I'm taking some time off." She put another bite of food in her mouth and avoided looking at him.

He didn't need to be an expert at reading body language to know there was something more to the "time off" excuse than she was saying. It wasn't his business, but he wasn't the type to let a mystery go unsolved, which was why he had the highest case closure rate of any detective in his precinct.

"I'm surprised you hung on to the house. I would have guessed you'd have sold it, considering you live in DC."

Nikki swallowed the bite she'd been chewing. "I thought about it. I'm still thinking about it. There are so many memories there."

He grunted derisively. "Yeah, I can see how it might suck to have someone else living in the house you loved."

She let her fork hit her plate with a clank and turned a heated gaze on him. "Come on, Terrence. Don't you think you're being more than a little immature at this point?"

He knew he was being a jerk. Whatever her grandfather had done, she'd had no hand in it, she'd been little more than a kid, just like him. But seeing her on property that should have been Aunt Charity's still hurt.

"Immature? You just won't ever get what that house

meant to my uncle, will you? What losing it did to him and my aunt."

"I get that it was hard for your family to sell the property—"

"Hard? That's an understatement if I ever heard one. Yes, it was hard for my uncle to face the fact that his best friend was buying his home out from under him. Making him look like a failure."

"No one bought Lakewood House out from under your aunt and uncle. It was a fair deal that your uncle agreed to."

"That's because he didn't realize—"

Rosie appeared in front of them, a deep frown creasing her face. "All right now. I love both of you, but y'all need to take this conversation out of my diner. You're disturbing my customers."

Terrence blinked and glanced around the diner. He hadn't realized how loud their argument had gotten. Every eye in the place was turned their way.

Nikki flushed pink. She dropped a twenty-dollar bill on the counter next to her nearly full plate before hopping off her stool and hurrying for the exit without another word.

The door closed behind her and the chatter picked up again.

Terrence turned back to his food and found Rosie scowling at him on the other side of the counter.

"You too." She picked up his plate, leaving him holding his fork midair. "Get on out of here."

"But I'm not finished yet."

"You're finished enough. And if you're not, well maybe you ought to think twice about coming into my place and making a spectacle of yourself."

"Look, I'm sorry."

"Out!" Rosie pointed to the door.

He'd seen that look on Rosie's face when they were younger. No amount of reasoning or begging and pleading would change her mind once she got it set.

He stood, grumbling some choice words about customer service, and laid down enough money to cover his bill.

Nikki's Camry was making a left turn onto Main Street through town when he pushed through the diner's doors into the parking lot.

He hadn't made much headway on finding Jill, but his gut told him Carling Lake had something to do with his sister's disappearance. He might be in town for a while. He couldn't permit his feelings about the past to interfere with locating Jill.

That meant clearing the air with Nikki. Whether she liked it or not.

Hopping into his Highlander, he drove the familiar roads to Lakewood House. Aunt Charity had always admonished him about his lead foot, but in this case, he was grateful. He pulled his car to a stop behind Nikki's Camry as she was getting out of the driver's side.

"Are you kidding me?" she said, stalking toward his car as he exited. "You followed me home?"

"It looks like both of us might be in town for a little while, and we can't keep making a scene. We need to clear the air."

"I don't have any air to clear. It's you who's been acting like an idiot for the past fourteen years, blaming my grandfather and me for slights that only exist in your head."

His jaw tightened. "You know full well that's not true. Your grandfather knew exactly—"

The rest of his statement was choked off by the sudden onslaught of shock and fear that bloomed in Nikki's eyes.

His right hand instinctively went for the gun on his hip before he remembered that he wasn't on duty. His weapon was locked in the glove compartment of the Highlander. Still, he angled his body so Nikki was behind him and turned to see what it was that had garnered her attention.

His heartbeat kicked up a notch when he saw the message that had been spray-painted on the detached two-car garage next to the house. It wasn't the most original, but it was still extremely effective.

LEAVE OR YOU'LL DISAPPEAR TOO.

Chapter Five

Nikki stood for a moment, breathing deeply, fighting to get control of her raging emotions. Shock. A small bubble of fear. Who would do something like this? The words were splashed across the faded black of the garage doors in white paint.

The vandalism itself wasn't that big a deal. A couple coats of primer and paint, and the doors would be like new. But the message—*Leave or you'll disappear too*—was obviously intended to scare her off. Why? And even more chilling, what did the vandal mean by "you'll disappear too"? Was that a reference to the body of the poor woman they'd found yesterday? Jill's sudden disappearance? Or was there someone else out there missing?

In a flash, the shock and fear she was feeling was joined by another emotion: rage.

Terrence wasn't the only one attached to the house. Despite its purchase having led to the loss of his friendship, Grandpa Bernie had fallen in love with Lakewood House. For that reason alone, Nikki was hesitant to sell. But she had her reasons as well. Years of fond memories of when the Suttons and Kings were close, and both families had gotten together for weekend picnics and holidays. She'd spent a lot of time playing with Terrence in this house when it had been owned by his aunt and uncle before her grandfather had purchased it.

She moved closer to Terrence. He pulled her toward his car and opened the passenger-side door, all but shoving her inside. "Give me your key to the house."

She already had it in her hand since it was on the same ring as her car key. She handed it over without question.

Popping the glove compartment open, Terrence pulled a holstered gun from inside. "Lock the door and call the sheriff." He snapped the holster onto his belt and unsheathed the weapon before slamming the door closed and heading for the house.

Part of her wanted to follow him. It was her house after all, but her rational mind said he was right. They didn't know if whoever had done this was still on the property, and she wasn't trained to confront criminals. The best thing she could do right now was to call Sheriff Webb and get Terrence backup in case he needed it.

She hit the button for the electronic locks and dialed the sheriff's office. She explained the situation, and the dispatcher assured her that someone was on their way and kept her on the line.

Carling Lake was a small town, but most of the homes, especially those on lakeside property, were spread quite a distance apart. Lakewood House was within walking distance of the downtown area, at least by Carling Lake standards, but it was still nearly a ten-minute drive from the sheriff's department.

Those minutes felt like an eternity. Terrence hadn't reappeared out of the house, and Nikki was just beginning to wonder if she should go inside and make sure he was okay when a sheriff's department SUV swung into the driveway with its siren off but its red-and-blue overhead lights flashing.

Seconds later, Terrence appeared from around the back of the house, his gun still in his hand but held low down by his thigh.

She watched in the rearview mirror as the sheriff pulled to a stop behind Terrence's car and stepped out, his gaze sweeping quickly over Lakewood House, his hand on his weapon.

"All clear," Terrence called out as he approached, holstering his gun.

Nikki let the dispatcher know that the sheriff had arrived and disconnected the emergency call before hopping out of the Highlander and joining the two men in front of the garage door.

"Looks like someone did a number on your garage," Sheriff Webb said.

She sighed. "Something like that."

They gave the sheriff a quick rundown on the events of the morning: having run into each other at Rosie's diner, getting into an argument and Rosie throwing them out, then returning to Lakewood House and finding the message scrawled on the garage door.

"This has to be connected to Jill's disappearance," Terrence said.

It was slight, but Nikki heard the tremor in his voice and knew that the graffiti had affected him as much as it had affected her. Maybe more so.

Sheriff Webb gave Terrence a sharp look. "We don't know that for sure." He circled Terrence and got an unobstructed look at the garage.

Terrence scowled. "What do you think 'leave or you'll disappear too' means then? As far as we know, Jill is the only person in Carling Lake who has disappeared."

The sheriff turned his back to the garage and faced Terrence. "We don't know if your sister was ever here in Carling Lake or if she was even ever headed here. The reference to disappearing could just as easily be related to the body of the woman we found on this property yesterday."

"Except she didn't disappear," Terrence growled.

The sheriff's eyes narrowed even further. "She likely disappeared from somewhere before her body washed up here. But more to the point, your jumping to conclusions is only going to hinder the investigation into where your sister is, as well as the investigation into this woman's death, and I don't need that."

Terrence took a step forward, into the sheriff's personal space. "You don't need—"

Sheriff Webb stiffened but held his ground.

The display of testosterone overload was simultaneously unhelpful and annoying. Nikki clapped her hands and pushed her way between the two men. "Alrighty then. This has been…something, but can we get back on track? The message is somewhat ambiguous but obviously meant to be threatening. I'm sure there's something you need to do to document it for the record, Sheriff?"

Sheriff Webb and Terrence glared at each other for several more seconds until Nikki sighed heavily.

The sheriff glanced at her, his face softening, which only seemed to make Terrence's glower harden.

"I'll get started," he said, stepping back from the male pissing contest with Terrence and heading for his SUV.

She pulled Terrence away from the garage so they could talk with some privacy. "What are you doing?"

Terrence jutted his chin in Sheriff Webb's direction. "He's not taking Jill's disappearance seriously."

"I don't get that at all. I think he's taking Jill's disappearance very seriously, but he's not her brother."

Terrence met her gaze, his eyes flashing in anger. "What is that supposed to mean?"

"It means he can be more objective than you can. Or even I can. He doesn't see everything that's happening in Carling Lake through the lens of a missing sister or friend. But that doesn't mean he isn't doing his best to locate Jill. And you need him. You have no jurisdiction here and having the sheriff's help is not something you want to just cast aside."

She watched him. He knew she was right, but he didn't like it. After a moment, the hard line of his jaw softened. She nodded and walked back to the detached garage where the sheriff was already taking photographs of the vandalized doors.

He lowered the camera, letting it hang from the strap around his neck as Nikki and Terrence approached.

"What's next?" she asked.

"Well, I know Terrence checked inside, but I want to do a quick walk-through with you, Ms. King, and make sure nothing was taken or disturbed in any way. I also think it's best for you to stay somewhere else, at least until we get a handle on what is happening out here."

She was already shaking her head. It wasn't just that she had to watch every penny now that she didn't have a job or any current prospects for one. Plain old pride and stubbornness wouldn't let her be run out of her grandfather's home. "I'll be fine."

Both men looked at her with displeasure now. At least she'd given them something to agree upon.

"Those locks are a joke," Terrence said. "Anyone who wants in is coming in."

"And I'm concerned that you weren't gone that long, right? You were at Rosie's for what? Forty minutes from the sound of it?"

"About that, give or take a few minutes," Nikki conceded.

"Yet someone managed to vandalize the property at the exact time you weren't home?"

Terrence took a protective step closer to her, and she wondered if he even realized he'd done so. "You think someone is watching Lakewood House?"

"Maybe." Sheriff Webb dipped his head. "Or, there's a lot of property here. Someone could be camping out. Living on the land. It's hard to say. That's why I think it's best that Ms. King stay somewhere else until we can sort it all out."

She shook her head firmly. Even if she'd had the money to pay for a hotel—which she didn't—she wouldn't go. "No. This is my property. I'm not letting anyone run me off. Come on, it's Carling Lake. It's not like the hotel and bed-and-breakfast here have top-of-the-line security."

Sheriff Webb tilted his head, his expression thoughtful. "Actually, I do know one place. A new B and B that just opened. With the Spring Festival so close, every available room is filling up fast, but—"

Nikki held up her hand to stop whatever was coming next. "It doesn't matter. I'm not leaving. I know how to protect myself if I need to."

The look Terrence gave her said he was dubious of her claim.

"I don't like guns, but Grandpa was concerned with me living in a big city. He bought me a pistol when I

moved to DC, and he made sure I knew how to use it."
She could tell that Terrence and the sheriff remained
unconvinced, but she wasn't about to back down. "So,
like I said, what's next?"

Sheriff Webb sighed. "I'll write up a report. You'll
need it to make a claim to your insurance. You can pick
it up later today. I'll also increase the frequency of pa-
trols in this area."

"That's it?" Terrence said sharply.

"I'm open to hearing your suggestions," the sheriff
shot back just as sharply. "That's what I thought," he
said when Terrence remained silent. "You know how
something like this goes. We'll keep an eye out, but it's
not easy to catch vandals unless they keep vandalizing.
Maybe this is just teens not wanting to lose their favorite hangout and hookup spot."

Nikki flinched at the idea that kids were hooking up
in her grandfather's house.

The sheriff chuckled lightly. "Sorry for putting that
image in your head, but empty house…small-town teenagers." He shrugged. "I'm sure you remember what it
was like being that age."

She felt her cheeks heat because she could remember
how she felt when they'd dated as teens, and Terrence
and his family had lived at Lakewood House. Meeting
him by the lake on warm starry nights. Or sneaking up
to Terrence's room to make out for a few minutes before his aunt and uncle got home from work and brib-
ing Jill not to tell. Or just sitting out on the back porch
in the white Adirondack chairs that Terrence and Uncle
Jarrod touched up every spring. Holding his hand on a
warm summer evening.

Her gaze slid to Terrence's face, and she knew he

was recalling the same memories. She looked away quickly, focusing all her attention back on the sheriff.

"Okay. I'll come by later this afternoon," Nikki told the sheriff.

Terrence stayed at her side, and they watched the sheriff pack his gear away.

He turned to her as the sheriff's SUV backed out of the driveway. "I think you should listen to the sheriff and find somewhere else to stay."

She waved away the comment and started for the house. "You're not going to change my mind."

He scowled. "This is serious, Nik. We have no idea what's going on, but Lakewood House seems to have something to do with it. What if whoever did this isn't happy with you ignoring them and comes back?"

"I can take care of myself," she repeated, and continued walking.

He followed her, his scowl deepening. "I didn't say you couldn't." At the front door, they both stopped. He exhaled, running a hand over his short hair. "Will you just make sure all the doors and windows are locked? And be careful."

The look he turned on her stole her breath for a moment. "I will," she said once she was able to speak. "I have to go. I have a work conference call I can't miss."

That part was true at least. Carolyn had texted last night saying she thought she might have a line on a job. They'd agreed to sketch out a plan of attack. *Attack* because she was sure it was going to take a lot of convincing to get someone to hire her at the moment.

"Okay," Terrence said. "I'll wait for you to get inside."

She rolled her eyes, but a little part of her was comforted by the gesture. More than a little part of her. Despite how their romance had ended, she realized she still cared about Terrence, and she couldn't deny that it pleased her to see that he might still care about her.

Nikki went into the house, flipped the lock on the door and watched from the adjacent window as Terrence got in his car and pulled away.

Chapter Six

After leaving Nikki, Terrence focused on reaching out to anyone Jill might have been in contact with in Carling Lake. Several of her friends from high school still lived in or near town. Unfortunately, none of them had heard from or spoken to Jill recently. Frustration had him climbing the walls.

He stepped out of Lakeside Books, where a former classmate of Jill's now worked, and onto Main Street, the sign for Laureano's Hardware catching his eye. His investigation into Jill's whereabouts was at a standstill until he could think of a new avenue to pursue, but he knew one person in Carling Lake he could help, though she might not want it.

He crossed the street and entered the hardware store. Thirty minutes later, he hefted the gallon cans of primer and black paint into the back of his car and closed the rear door.

What was he doing?

Looking for a reason to go to Lakewood House and check in on her was what he was doing. Despite himself, he couldn't seem to stop worrying about Nikki being alone at Lakewood House. Which was why, even though she'd been clear that she didn't want his help, he'd just spent eighty bucks on paint and supplies for her garage.

You're a fool and a glutton, Uncle Jarrod's voice resounded in his head.

Maybe. He'd cared deeply for Nikki, and that hadn't stopped after her grandfather stole his family home as much as he'd tried to will it to. Even now, it seemed he couldn't stop himself from feeling…something for her.

Who was he kidding? He'd fallen in love with Dominique King at age fifteen, and she'd ruined him for all other women. No matter how hard he'd tried over the years, he'd always seemed to unconsciously compare every woman he'd dated to Nikki, and they'd always been found wanting. At some point, he'd realized how unfair he was being to these women, so now he kept all his relationships casual. It wasn't their fault he was stuck on a woman he could never have and shouldn't want. They didn't deserve to get hurt because of it.

But what did he deserve?

He pushed the question aside and turned the Highlander onto the Lakewood House driveway.

His head knew that Lakewood House belonged to Nikki now, but in his heart, it would always be Aunt Charity and Uncle Jarrod's place. He could almost see himself at various ages, like little ghost boys, running around the yard. Playing keep-away with Jill and Nikki. Uncle Jarrod teaching him to ride a bike on the then dirt driveway. Long summer afternoons down by the lake, swimming and lazing out under the sun. This place was part of his past. It had meant something to him once upon a time. It still did if he was honest with himself.

His and Jill's early childhood had been rough. Their mother, Hope Sutton, was unstable on her best day, chasing dreams of…he didn't know what, but they certainly weren't dreams of a stable home for her two children. Abandoning them with her sister and brother-in-law, ironically, was the most motherly thing Hope had ever done. They'd finally had a home and people who cared for them and allowed them to be children.

Until Bernard King snatched that safety and security away.

Then what are you doing here?

That was an excellent question but another one he pushed from his mind as he put the Highlander in Park and climbed out.

He was stacking the paint cans in front of the garage when the door to Lakewood House swung open and Nikki stepped out onto the porch.

"What are you doing?" She eyed him warily.

"Helping you clean up this mess."

"I told you I didn't need your help."

He fisted his hands on his hips and glared at her. "You want me to take it all back then?"

She drew in a deep breath and let it out slowly. "No. Sorry. Thank you."

It was a begrudging apology, but an apology nonetheless. He'd take it. "I'm going to get started unless you have any other objections."

In spite of himself, he couldn't help finding the slight scowl she shot at him cute, maybe even a little sexy. "No objections. Give me a minute to change and I'll help you."

Nikki disappeared back into the house.

The garage wasn't as old as the house itself, but it was old enough that it hadn't had automatic doors when he lived there. Bernard must have had an automatic lifting system installed because when he went to pull the handle to release the doors, he found that he couldn't raise them.

He walked around to the side and tried the side door.

When he'd lived at Lakewood House with his aunt and uncle, the door to the garage had been wonky. No matter what Uncle Jarrod did, the door never quite hung properly, which meant that it never locked properly either. If he jiggled the handle just right...yep, whatever the problem was, Bernard King had never fixed it.

He let himself in and grabbed an empty bucket, some all-purpose cleaner and a few rags to wash the doors down before painting.

He'd just finished filling the bucket when Nikki joined him outside. It was only early May, not quite summer yet technically, but you couldn't tell Mother Nature that. At two in the afternoon, the sun was high enough that its heat broke through the tree cover and warmed Carling Lake enough that Nikki had donned an old Carling Lake High T-shirt and a pair of ratty gray shorts. The T-shirt he recognized as one he'd given her oh-so-many years ago. Was wearing it now some sort of message? A reminder of what they'd once been to each other? Or maybe she was trying to tell him his gift meant so little to her now that she'd wear it to do grunt work, like painting.

Or it was simply the first shirt she'd found in her dresser, his rational mind chimed in.

It didn't matter, he thought, turning away from Nikki as she neared, but not before he caught the way her hips swayed as she walked. Carling Lake High and fifteen-year-old Nikki and Terrence were in the past, where they should stay. This wasn't about that. He was just helping someone who needed it.

He wiped down the doors while she stirred the primer using the long painter's stick he'd gotten from the hardware store. They each took a door and got started covering the message.

They worked in silence, but despite their earlier sniping, it was a comfortable, familiar silence.

Nikki had about a quarter of her door covered when she let out a chuckle. "This feels like déjà vu."

"Déjà vu?"

She looked at him with a smile that made his heart stutter. She was so beautiful. "You don't remember doing this once before? When we were fourteen?"

The memory burst into the forefront of his mind. He couldn't believe he'd forgotten it. "Oh yeah," he said with a groan.

She was laughing now. "I thought your uncle Jarrod was going to lose it for real."

"He did lose it." He grimaced, remembering how long and loudly his uncle had yelled.

"What in the world possessed you to take that car out?"

He bent to get more primer onto his roller. The answer to that question was complex. His uncle's prized silver Mustang GT had always been forbidden fruit. Uncle Jarrod rarely let him ride in the car, reserving that treat for special occasions, but drive it? No one, not even Aunt Charity, drove the 'Stang but Jarrod. That would have been enough to entice him to take the car for a spin, eventually. Moving in with his aunt and uncle had given him much-needed discipline and stability, but he'd inherited his mother's temper and propensity for risk-taking. But what had pushed him over the edge that particular day was Nikki. Or rather the desire to impress Nikki, the girl he'd recently realized he liked as more than just as a friend.

"Oh, you know. Fourteen-year-old boys who live in small towns with nothing at all going on tend to come up with very stupid ideas."

"It was a humdinger," she said, laughing. "You started out all right, though. Almost as if you knew what you were doing."

He smiled at the memory. "Yeah, I did not."

"Oh, I figured that out when you put the car in Reverse instead of Drive," she said, laughing harder now. "When you backed into the garage, I thought the whole thing was going to come down on your head."

"You could have tried to stop me," he said, giving her a wry look.

She shrugged, still laughing. "I guess I could have, but fourteen-year-old girls who live in small towns with nothing at all going on tend to rely on fourteen-year-old boys with stupid ideas for entertainment."

"How'd that work out for you?" He laughed now because they both knew how it had worked out.

She cringed. "Not great. We were relegated to doing grunt work for anyone in town who could scare up something for us to do that summer to pay for the new garage doors. That was not a fun summer."

They were both laughing now.

"Look on the bright side," he said, gesturing to the door, "we learned how to paint a garage door, a skill which has come in handy once again."

"That's a way to look at it." Nikki's phone beeped. His gaze followed her hand to where her cell peeked out of her back pocket. He pulled his eyes away when he realized he was staring at her ass, but not before she shot him a look that said she'd noticed.

He smiled boyishly before going back to painting the door.

She set her roller in the paint tray at her feet and looked at the phone, her smile falling away.

"Damn."

The word was little more than a whisper, but the look on her face had him setting his roller aside and stepping toward her.

"Everything okay?" He studied her face, not liking what he saw there. Not anger exactly. More disappointment.

"Everything is fine." She slid the phone back into her pocket. "Actually, it's not, but there's nothing anyone can do about it."

"You want to talk about it?"

She looked at him for a long moment, obviously considering it.

There was a time when they'd told each other everything. They'd been best friends. And even when their relationship had begun to veer into more-than-just-friends territory, their friendship hadn't suffered. If anything, it had grown deeper, like roots burrowing into the soil.

But now he wasn't sure if those roots still existed, and from the looks of it, neither was she.

Finally, she spoke. "I'm in Carling Lake because I was fired from my job."

He wasn't sure what he expected to hear, but it wasn't that. "You? Fired? What happened?"

He knew she worked as an aide for New York Representative Tom Manco. He wasn't much for politics, but he knew that a job like that was a great stepping-stone for someone who wanted to be in the political world like Nikki. She was politically savvy, diplomatic and legitimately one of the smartest people in any room she walked into, so he couldn't fathom her getting fired.

"Me. You know I believed in Tom. I mean, it's why I agreed to work on his campaign when he was a long shot." She paced a short line in front of him. "But going to Washington, DC, changed him. Or maybe it revealed who he really was. Isn't that what Michelle Obama said? Gaining power doesn't change you—it reveals who you are."

"Something like that," Terrence chimed in, but he wasn't sure Nikki heard him.

"Tom became all about keeping his seat. Fundraising. Hobnobbing with lobbyists. I mean, I'm not a neophyte. I get that that stuff has to be done if you want to have the space and network to get the really important legislation passed, but that's not why Tom was doing it, you know."

She looked at him for confirmation. He didn't know, but nodded.

"Anyway, I was disillusioned and thinking about moving on when I discovered discrepancies in the campaign's fundraising reports." She stopped pacing to look him in the eye. "I honestly thought they were just that, discrepancies. At least at first. I brought them to the chief of staff's attention, and she said she'd take care of it. Weeks passed, and no amendment was made, so I brought it up again. This time she told me to drop it, and I knew that it wasn't a mistake. Tom was misusing campaign funds. Paying his car note. Mortgage. Vacations." She looked down at the ground. "I reported it. Tom said it was a misunderstanding. Made the corrections. Put the money back into the accounts and fired me." She laughed, but it was without mirth. "Fired me and blackballed me. Nobody in DC will hire me."

Terrence stepped closer and used a finger to lift her chin. "I have never been more proud of you. You did the right thing. You hold your head up and own it."

A sizzle of electricity whipped through him, and he tried to read the look in her eyes. Every nerve in his body tingled.

The desire to kiss her at that moment was almost overpowering, and if he'd had to guess, he'd bet good money that she was feeling the same longing.

That's why he nearly cursed when the sound of a car's tire crunching over the gravel drive ruined the moment.

Nikki hesitated before taking three giant steps backward.

He sighed and turned toward the interloper. "Are you expecting someone?"

"No."

The man who stepped out of the car wasn't familiar. Short and stocky, he wore a well-cut brown suit despite the heat and had thinning blond hair that revealed the shiny white skin atop his head.

Terrence shifted so he stood between Nikki and the stranger.

"Good morning." The man's expression was polite, his smile open and practiced. Had it been a different decade, Terrence would have prepared for a spiel about encyclopedias or Tupperware. "Ms. King?" The man locked his gaze on Nikki.

"Yes. And you are?"

"Albert Chester, attorney-at-law."

Terrence glanced at Nikki to see if the name meant anything to her. She shrugged, indicating that it didn't.

"What can we do for you today, Mr. Chester?" Terrence said. Nikki would probably be unhappy with him for taking over the conversation, but given the recent events, he wasn't taking any chances with uninvited visitors.

Chester's smile dimmed a little. "I was hoping to speak to Ms. King about a very pressing matter I've taken on for a client. A private matter."

Nikki stepped from behind him, lightly hip-checking him out of the way. Yeah, she wasn't happy with him. What else was new?

"What kind of pressing, private matter?" she asked.

Chester's eyes darted between Nikki and Terrence, seemingly deciding whether to press the point.

There was no way he was leaving Nikki alone with a stranger.

Chester must have picked up on that. "My client has authorized me to make an offer on this property."

Nikki's brow rose in surprise. "Someone wants to buy Lakewood House?"

"That's right." Chester pulled a slim envelope from the inside pocket of his suit jacket and held it out to Nikki. "I think you'll find the offer more than generous."

Nikki didn't reach for the envelope. "Lakewood House is not for sale."

"I realize you haven't put the property on the market, but I think if you consider the offer my client is making—"

"Who is your client?" When Nikki still didn't make a move to take the envelope, Terrence took it from Chester's outstretched hand.

Chester frowned. "Well, that I can't share."

Terrence shot another glance at Nikki. "I guess it doesn't matter since, as I said, Lakewood House isn't for sale. I'd like you to leave now, Mr. Chester."

"Now, Ms. King, I'm sure the house holds a lot of fond memories for you—"

Terrence cut him off. "The lady asked you to leave. You're officially trespassing now."

Chester's brow furrowed, and Terrence could almost see the thoughts rolling through the man's mind. Had

Chester really thought he'd come by and make a deal to purchase Lakewood House in what…a few minutes? Maybe because the house had been sitting empty for so long, he or his client had gotten the impression that Nikki didn't want the house.

But something about the whole thing stunk. Lakewood House had been empty for several years. Why was this offer to buy it coming up now? Had Nikki's return to Carling Lake set off some kind of chain reaction? Did Jill's disappearance fit in somewhere?

Something was going on, and Terrence didn't like not knowing what it was.

"Maybe after you take a look at the offer, you'll have a change of heart. My card is inside. Please call with any questions. Day or night." Chester shot them another car salesman–like smile before slinking back to his car.

"What was that about?" Nikki asked as they watched Chester's car retreat away from the house.

"I don't know. But I'm going to find out."

Chapter Seven

"You're going to find out?" Nikki asked. It was bad enough he'd interjected himself in the conversation with Albert Chester as if he owned the place or she needed protection. But now he was what? Launching his own investigation into the strange goings-on at Lakewood House?

Terrence frowned. "You can't think that everything that has happened here in the last couple of days is just coincidence."

"Of course not." She brought her hands to her hips. "But Lakewood House is my responsibility."

Terrence's frown deepened. "And Jill is my sister. All of this is connected. I feel it in my gut. If I figure out what's going on here, I think I'll find Jill."

She studied him for a moment. "Okay. Then we—" she emphasized the word by wagging her finger between the two of them "—will look into things together."

He shook his head. "No way. I have no idea what's going on. It could be dangerous. It probably is if Jill's disappearance is any indication."

She smiled what she knew was a cold smile. "It's cute how you think I was asking your permission." Not. Arrogant was more accurate. A pity he hadn't grown out of that unattractive character trait. "I wasn't. I'm in this whether you like it or not." She moved away from him, tossing the envelope from the lawyer onto the pavers leading to the house, picking up her paint roller and starting in on the garage door again.

Terrence trailed behind her but made no move to continue painting. "You're as stubborn as ever even though you have no training to deal with whatever this might turn out to be."

"That's why working together is the perfect solution. Your police training may come in handy, but you have absolutely no diplomatic skills whatsoever, if your tête-à-tête with the sheriff earlier was any indication. Together we're perfect." Heat flamed in her cheeks. "I mean we make the perfect team for finding Jill and getting to the bottom of whatever is going on here at Lakewood House."

She shot him a sidelong glance to see if he was at all affected by her saying they were perfect together; she'd been close to kissing him before Albert Chester had shown up. At least the lawyer's unbidden appearance had stopped her from making that mistake.

Terrence grabbed the roller from his paint tray, aggressively covering the last few spots of faded black paint.

He might not like what she'd said, but she suspected he knew she had a point. They'd always made a good team, his strengths and weaknesses complementing hers. But he always had to come around to seeing things her way in his own time. More importantly, there was nothing he could do to stop her from investigating, so they may as well do it together. If he *was* correct about the vandalism having a connection to Jill's disappearance—and she believed he was—she had just as much an interest in getting to the bottom of things as he did.

She shot him another sidelong glance. She didn't think it would take him long to see the wisdom in teaming up.

Five minutes later, he put the roller down again and faced her. "If we are going to work together, we have to trust each other. No running off without telling the other where we're going." Something in his eyes beseeched her. "I don't know what's going on here exactly, but I have a really bad feeling."

"Agreed." She held out her right hand. The warmth of his hand burned through her, and the scent of his woodsy cologne tickled her nose. "And for the record, I never stopped trusting you."

He held her gaze for one intense moment before the sound of yet another car turning onto the gravel drive had her snatching her hand away.

Terrence's brow rose. "Lakewood House is party central today."

"Sure seems that way," she mumbled.

Sheriff Webb pulled to a stop behind Terrence's car and got out.

Nikki took the opportunity to put some distance between her and Terrence and walked toward the sheriff. "I was headed to the station right after I grabbed a shower."

"I thought I'd save you a trip." Sheriff Webb thrust a brown envelope in her direction.

She took a peek inside and found the incident report for the vandalism on the garage. "Thanks. Any word on who the poor girl we found yesterday is? Was." She corrected herself.

The sheriff grimaced. "Not yet. The medical exam-

iner was able to say that the cause of death was strangulation, which makes this a homicide. She puts the
time of death at about twenty-four hours before you
found her."

"She can't be any more specific?" Terrence said.

"She's working on it. The water makes things more
difficult."

"We'd at least have somewhere to start if we could
identify her, but I've searched through the county's
missing person reports for the last two years, and nothing matches."

"She could be from anywhere," Terrence offered
with a sad shake of his head.

"That is unfortunately true. Too many females disappear every year." Lance sighed heavily. "And it's why
I'm concerned about you staying at Lakewood House
alone, Nikki. This property is isolated and has direct
access to the lake, which makes it easy for someone to
sneak onto the property."

She sighed. "I've already been through this with Terrence."

"You should listen to him," Sheriff Webb said.

A pleased-as-punch smirk crawled across Terrence's face. Of course, the two cops would agree. But
she wasn't a defenseless damsel in distress, and she
wouldn't be acting like one.

"I've been turning something else over in my head
since we found the threat painted on the garage doors,"
Terrence said after a moment. "The access to the lake
doesn't just make it easy for someone to sneak onto the
property. It's also ideal for anyone who wants to sneak
off the property."

"Sneak off the property?" she asked, unsure what
he was getting at.

Terrence nodded. "Say someone who's been using the lake access here for criminal activity, like transporting illegal contraband. Opioids and other drugs have been ravaging small rural towns like Carling Lake for years, even though the media and politicians seem to have just begun to take notice. I know you're the sheriff, but it would be foolish to think that Carling Lake has escaped these kinds of problems."

Sheriff Webb nodded sadly. "No, you're right. We have our fair share of drug-related crime and incidents. They've been increasing over the years, but it's hard for me to fathom that someone could have regularly been moving drugs through this town, and I haven't caught a whiff of it."

"Maybe it's not regular enough for you to have noticed yet. And maybe it's not drugs," Terrence said. "I'll tell you what though. If Jill heard about something like this—an organized criminal operation in the town where she grew up—she'd be all over it."

Nikki could see the idea had already taken root with him.

Sheriff Webb's expression darkened. "And if her nose is better than mine, she might have found herself in a world of trouble."

"That's why we have to find Jill soon."

"We're doing everything we can," the sheriff reiterated before changing the subject. "I didn't just come out here for Nikki. I was also looking for you."

"Well, you found me," Terrence said. "Although I'd like to know how you knew I'd be at Lakewood House."

The sheriff smirked. "It wasn't hard to deduce. I heard from Vincent Laureano that you'd been in his hardware store earlier buying paint and paint supplies."

Terrence's eyes rolled. "Of course. Too many years

of living in a city. I'd forgotten how much everyone is in everyone else's business in this town."

"Just part of our small-town charm," Sheriff Webb said with a grin. "Anyway, I wanted to let you know that I ran that symbol you showed me through the system, but it came up with nothing."

Nikki looked from one man to the other. "Symbol?"

"When Jill stopped answering my calls and texts, I searched her apartment for some indication of where she might have gone. I found this." Terrence pulled his phone from his pocket and called up a photo before passing it to Nikki. "A piece of paper with Carling Lake and some kind of symbol or flower on it."

"I've seen this before." Nikki used two fingers to make the part of the paper with the drawing bigger. "I found a business card on the kitchen floor the day I arrived at Lakewood House with this fleur-de-lis and nothing else on it."

Frown lines burrowed into the sheriff's forehead. "Fleur-de-lis?"

"It's what this is called. It's a symbol that's been used in politics, religion, architecture—you name it—for thousands of years and across cultures. It's fairly common, especially in places with French influences like New Orleans, where it's part of the official city flag."

"Okay, so why was Jill doodling it on this paper, and why has it shown up at Lakewood House?" Terrence said.

"All fine questions." Sheriff Webb stroked his chin. "Do you still have the card?"

"I think so." Nikki turned and jogged toward the house. Terrence and the sheriff followed at only a slightly slower pace.

Inside, she scanned the island counter where she'd

first seen the card, then the rest of the kitchen. Nothing. She closed her eyes for a moment, walking through what she'd done after she'd found the card the previous day. She remembered Pete had been there with her grandfather's boat. She'd taken her bags upstairs, then seen Pete running back toward the house after finding that poor girl's body.

What had she done with the card before all that?

She rewound through her memories. Coming into Lakewood House for the first time. Finding the card on the counter.

"I put it in my pocket." She spun toward the staircase and dashed upstairs.

The slacks she'd worn yesterday were in the middle of the pile of laundry growing in the corner of the room. She found the business card, a little worse for wear, in the pocket and brought it back downstairs. "This is it."

Sheriff Webb reached for it, but Terrence was closer. He took the card from her hand, handling it along its edges. "Not much to it. Just the fleur-de-lis symbol. No name, address, phone number."

He took a photo of it with his phone before holding it out to the sheriff.

"There's probably no point in looking for fingerprints, but I'll give it a shot," Sheriff Webb said, taking the card by the edges himself and sliding it into a plastic baggie he'd taken from his coat pocket. "I'm also going to widen the search beyond the county borders, but the results might take a little while to come in. Especially with the Spring Festival starting up in a few days. I won't have anyone to spare."

Terrence's hands clenched into fists. "This is more important than the festival. Jill could be in real trouble here."

"I understand that, and my department is doing everything it can to locate your sister," the sheriff reiterated through gritted teeth. "But it can't be our only focus, which is why I have a suggestion."

Nikki could read the thoughts passing through Terrence's mind on his face. Exactly where Sheriff Webb could shove his suggestion. "What do you suggest we do, Sheriff?" she interjected before Terrence could say what he was thinking.

The sheriff's gaze swung to her face, his brow rising at her use of the word *we*. "I think you should go talk to Carling Lake's newest resident, James West. He owns the art gallery on Main Street. Shares the building with the *Carling Lake Weekly* newspaper."

"Your suggestion is that I speak to an art dealer?" Terrence grumbled. "How is that going to help me find Jill?"

"James West is not your typical gallery owner," the sheriff said angrily. "Trust me. Go talk to him."

Terrence looked like his temper was about to blow. Nikki placed a hand on his arm and gave a minute shake of her head before turning back to Sheriff Webb. "Thanks for the suggestion. We'll go see him this afternoon."

The sheriff headed for the door, ignoring Terrence's grumbling about wasting time.

Truthfully, she couldn't see how an art dealer could help them, but if the sheriff was suggesting they talk to James West, there had to be a reason. And at this point, they had nothing else to go on and nothing to lose in finding out.

Chapter Eight

The stone-and-brick structure that housed the offices of the *Carling Lake Weekly* had endured. Over the years, the *Weekly* had shared the building with a host of other businesses, but Terrence was pretty sure this was the first art gallery. Carling Lake was getting a taste of the cosmopolitan.

The building sat on an entire Main Street block. He parked in a nearby lot, then he and Nikki rounded the building, passed the pair of large double glass doors of the newspaper and headed toward the more modest entry for the gallery at the other end of the block. A discreet sign announced this was the entry for The West Gallery in elegant gold lettering.

The space inside was a sweeping two-story expanse with support columns dotted throughout the open space and a set of curved stairs in the left rear corner. The lighting was subdued, but with the large picture windows along the front wall and the peaked skylight overhead, there was more than enough natural light flooding the space and accentuating the art lining the walls.

Nearly a dozen pieces hung on each side, with several more displayed on the temporary walls that had been erected in the open space.

From where he stood, Terrence could see that the

artwork had been done in various media—some ink drawings, some watercolors, other oils—but all done with a skill, talent and unique style that showed through in each canvas.

He and Nikki stopped in front of the piece near the entrance. A woman and young child beamed at them from the canvas so vivid and lifelike that had the small plaque next to it not stated it was an ink drawing, he'd have thought it was a photograph. What he didn't need to read to know was that whoever this woman and child were, they meant a great deal to the artist.

"This is…amazing," Nikki said, the awe in her voice palpable.

"Thank you." The Black man descending the circular staircase looked nothing like what Terrence had imagined of an artist. For one, he was large. Over six feet tall and wide with muscle tone that even his very well-cut slacks and tailored collared shirt couldn't disguise. He wore a pleasant enough smile, but his eyes reflected a worldliness and experience—not necessarily all good—that said he was a man not to be underestimated. Terrence didn't need to ask to know that this man had been in the military. Everything about the man screamed order, honor and sacrifice. "My wife and son."

Terrence and Nikki moved toward the man, meeting him roughly in the center of the gallery space.

Terrence extended his hand. "Detective Terrence Sutton. I don't know much about art, but even I can tell you are extremely talented."

The man shook his hand and gave a self-effacing smile. "James West. And thank you. That particular piece is one of my best, though not for sale, of course."

"Nikki King." She extended her hand now. "Your love for your family shines through in it."

"They are my everything." James gave her hand a quick shake before dropping it and turning back to Terrence. "Lance told me you might be stopping by."

Terrence couldn't stop the frown twisting his mouth downward. "Yes, well, I don't know how much he's told you about the reason I'm in Carling Lake. No disrespect, but I'm not sure how an artist can help me find my sister."

Nikki slapped his bicep lightly and gave him an exasperated look.

Yes, he was a bull in a china shop. It was a criticism he'd gotten a lot from his coworkers and several of the higher-ups on the force. And it was probably the reason he hadn't yet been promoted beyond the rank of detective. But it was also one of the reasons he had the best closure rate of all the detectives in the department. It might not look pretty, but he got answers.

James's smile grew. "I think Lance sent you to me because of my other business. Or rather, because of my family business. Why don't we go upstairs to my office? You can fill me in on all the particulars, and I can see if we can help."

He and Nikki followed James to a long narrow office. The side of the room with windows facing Main Street would have rivaled any top CEO's suite. A large executive desk and high back leather chair dominated the space. But that wasn't the most impressive thing about the office. On the other end of the space was a U-shaped table with three computer monitors, a laptop and several other electronics that Terrence wasn't familiar with.

"Whoa! This is quite the setup. Not what I'd expect in an artist's office," Terrence said.

"My studio is on the other side of the floor. It probably looks exactly how you'd imagine." James motioned them toward the comfortable-looking seating area that separated the two different parts of the office. Terrence settled in next to Nikki on one of the beige sofas while James took a seat on the matching sofa opposite them. "This is where I run the business side of the gallery and do a little bit of side work for my family's business, West Security and Investigations."

The name struck a chord. He hadn't immediately made a connection between James West and the elite security and private investigations firm. Lance's suggestion that he speak to the gallery owner made a lot more sense now. "West Investigations. I've heard of you guys."

"It's my brothers' business now, but I still dabble here and there. Mostly where it concerns the safety of my wife and son."

Terrence cocked his head to the side wondering why James West's wife needed the services of a security firm like West Investigations. But since it wasn't his concern, he refrained from asking.

James studied him as if he could read the thoughts rolling through Terrence's mind.

Nikki cleared her throat. "So, you are a private investigator?"

"Not me, no. It's why I dabble. Any work I do is under the supervision of one of my younger brothers. They just love that," James added wryly. "But Carling Lake is my home now and if, as Lance suggested, there's something nefarious going on, I want to know about it." His eyes went to slits. "And stop it."

Terrence had been around enough dangerous men to know one when he saw one, but for now, if James was willing to put the resources of West Investigations behind finding Jill, he was more than willing to accept that help.

He glanced at Nikki. She gave a slight, almost imperceptible nod, letting him know that she was on board.

Terrence slid to the edge of the sofa. "I'm looking for my sister, Jill." He told James about not hearing from Jill for days, going to her apartment and finding the scrap of paper with Carling Lake written on it and the fleur-de-lis doodle. Nikki picked up the story then, explaining the body of the woman they'd found on her property, the threatening message written on her garage doors and the business card with the same fleur-de-lis symbol.

With each passing minute, James's expression grew darker, the worry in his eyes deepening.

When he and Nikki finished speaking, the threesome sat in silence for several moments, turning over the sequence of events, trying to make the pieces fit into a logical, sensible scene.

James finally spoke. "There's definitely something unusual going on. Let's call my brothers." He stood. "See what they think our first steps should be."

And just like that, their ragtag investigation got some very real firepower behind it.

A minute later James initiated a video call on the largest of the three computer screens on his desk.

A man's face filled the screen when the call connected. He was younger than James but with enough similarities that no one would doubt that they were brothers. He too appeared to be sitting in an office surrounded by computer monitors similar to James's.

"Hey, bro." The younger man's smile reflected genuine happiness. "I've been trying to reach you."

"I know. Sorry about not calling back. I've been swamped with this gallery show coming up."

The younger man's smile grew even wider. "Nadia is so excited. Sean and Addy too. I'm sorry we can't get up there earlier to help you set up and all, but we will be there for your show."

James waved his brother off. "No worries. Erika's on the job, and there is nobody better at organizing an event than my wife. That's not why I'm calling though." He shot a glance at Terrence and Nikki and adjusted the computer monitor so they could be seen more fully by the wide lens camera projecting their images at the bottom of the screen. "Ryan, meet Nikki King and Detective Terrence Sutton. They need our help."

James quickly filled his brother in on the particulars of the situation. Just like James moments earlier, Ryan's expression darkened the longer James spoke. "How can we help?" he asked once James was done with his explanation.

"I've filed a missing person report with the DC police since Jill is officially a resident of DC, although she travels so much she's rarely at her apartment. They've gone above and beyond what they would do normally since I'm a fellow cop, but she's an adult and there are no signs of foul play—"

"But their hands are tied," Ryan chimed in.

"Right," Terrence said. "So they can't pull her phone records or try to find her using the GPS."

Ryan typed on the keyboard in front of him. "It's not exactly legal on our end either, but I'll see what I can do."

"Thanks." Terrence rattled off his sister's cell phone number and the name of her carrier.

"I might be able to help with that too, now that you

mention the carrier's name," Nikki said, biting her lower lip as if she wasn't quite sure about the truth of her statement. "I know someone who works there. Their policies about giving out information are pretty strict, but you can talk to him."

All three men looked at her with a question in their eyes. "My boss—my former boss—was on the Communications and Technology subcommittee. I met a lot of corporate bureaucrats and lobbyists in the field."

"I'll take whatever contacts I can get," Ryan said.

Nikki drew her phone from her purse and rattled off the number of her contact for Ryan.

"There's one more thing," Terrence began to say as Nikki put her phone away. "The fleur-de-lis symbol. Its appearance in Carling Lake and in Jill's apartment can't be a coincidence. The sheriff ran it through his system and got no hits. I'm guessing you may be able to do a wider search. Maybe it's a calling card of some sort. If so, it would at least point us in the direction of where to start."

"It could."

Based on Ryan's tone, Terrence could tell he wasn't convinced. "Jill is an investigative reporter. She digs into powerful people's secrets and deceptions. Her last big piece broke up a large opioid ring and took down a handful of county council members in West Virginia who, at the very least, were looking the other way while these drugs ravaged their residents. She has a habit of getting under the skin of the wrong people. Lance is good at his job, but anyone doing something criminal in this town is going to take pains to keep it from him. But someone has to know about it."

"I'll put out feelers, but something like that could take some time," Ryan said.

"I'll also see what I can dig up," James offered. "People might be more willing to talk to a local, not that you two aren't from Carling Lake, but it's been a while since you've lived here according to the town scuttlebutt."

Ryan smirked. "You haven't lived in Carling Lake for a whole year yet. Have you so thoroughly charmed everyone that they already think of you as a home-town boy?"

James beamed at his brother. "What can I say? I'm a charming guy."

A smile played at Nikki's mouth. "We'll take all the help we can get. Thank you."

Ryan focused his attention back on Terrence, all business again. "I'm sure you don't plan to sit around and wait. What's your next step?"

Terrence nodded. "You're right. My gut is telling me Jill can't afford for us to take a wait-and-see posture. It's been a week." He left the rest of what he was thinking unsaid. That it could already be too late. He wouldn't let himself think that way. He couldn't. "I'm sure that whatever Jill was working on brought her here to Carling Lake. I've checked in with my aunt, who hasn't seen her, and Jill's friends, so I'm going to start scouring the rest of the town. Someone has to have seen her. Talked to her. Something. I'll go door-to-door if I have to."

Resolve flooded his body. He'd talk to everyone in this town and search every house if that's what it took.

Nikki placed a hand on his. "Half the town knows you're here looking for Jill, and the other half will know by the end of the day. Anyone who knew anything about Jill's whereabouts and wanted to help would have come to you."

Surprised, he turned to look at Nikki. "What are you saying? You don't think Jill made it to Carling Lake?"

If she didn't believe they'd find Jill, why had she insisted on helping him?

She shook her head. "That's not what I'm saying."

James spoke softly. "I think what Nikki is getting at is that whoever your sister came to see in Carling Lake doesn't want you to know she was here. If you find that person, you'll be a lot closer to finding your sister."

Chapter Nine

"Well, that wasn't at all what I expected," Nikki said as she and Terrence stepped out onto the sidewalk. She hadn't known what to think when Sheriff Webb sent them to an art gallery, but it definitely hadn't been the former sniper/security specialist/artist that was James West.

Terrence donned a faux shocked expression. "What? You mean to tell me the gallery owners in DC don't look like they could bench-press a minivan and have connections to elite private security firms?"

Nikki laughed. "I don't know any gallery owners in DC, but I'm going to go out on a limb and say no." The city was full of culture and art, but her job had left her precious little time to take advantage of any of it.

"Yeah." He let himself smile. "That's probably a good assumption. I have a feeling James West is one of a kind, but I'm glad he's on our side."

They turned toward the parking lot where Terrence had parked the Highlander.

"Where to next?" Nikki asked, walking slightly faster than usual to keep up with his long stride.

"I want to speak to Lakewood House's caretaker, Pete Bonny. Maybe he's noticed something out of the ordinary going on at or around Lakewood House."

"That sounds like a good idea. I need to talk to him about getting Grandpa's boat to the house. Sheriff Webb wouldn't let him dock it the other day because of the crime scene, but now that I've got the all clear, I really would like to take the *Annalise* out on the lake again."

They approached the Highlander. Terrence reached for the passenger door and held it open for her to slide inside.

"We had some good times on that boat. Do you remember the time my uncle and your grandfather took us fishing and we caught that huge bass?"

She shot him an incredulous look. "Um…we? If I recall correctly, *I* was the one who snagged that beauty."

He leaned forward into the space created by the open door. "And if I recall correctly, you would have never gotten it on the boat if I hadn't helped you reel it in." His brown eyes sparkled in amusement.

"I think your memory is faulty. You should have that checked out."

Memories of a time when it had been so easy for them to be in each other's presence—when that was all either of them needed to be happy and content—flooded through her. At the moment, with Terrence standing so close, it was hard to remember how or why it had all gone so wrong. How they'd let it go so wrong. Maybe they could fix it? Get back what they'd lost. His uncle and her grandfather were gone. Maybe she and Terrence could find a way back to each other.

She guessed that some of what she was thinking had been reflected on her face. He had always been able to read her so easily.

The amusement that had been in his eyes moments before was gone, replaced now by unmistakable desire.

She leaned toward him, the urge to be closer, both physically and emotionally, too strong to resist.

Terrence stepped back, the charge in the air dissipating. "We should get going." He shut the door.

She took several deep breaths in an attempt to slow her racing heart and stem the embarrassment of his rejection. He'd felt the frisson of attraction between them, she was sure of it. And his reaction made it clear he had no intention of giving in to it. Fine. She wasn't about to throw herself at any man.

She'd recovered a modicum of dignity by the time he rounded the car and got into the driver's seat. She pulled her phone from her purse while he started the engine and put the Highlander in Drive. "I'm going to give Pete a call and let him know we're coming."

"No problem, but don't mention the plan to question him. Just let him think our visit is all about the boat. I have a tow hitch, so I can haul the *Annalise* back to Lakewood House and help you launch it."

"Okay."

He continued to outline his plan, seemingly unaffected by the intensity of the prior moment. "And maybe you can ask for a glass of water or to use the restroom? Some excuse to get inside the house and poke around?"

She shot a skeptical look across the car. "Pete's kind of curmudgeonly."

"It's worth a try. All he can say is no. I'd do it, but I think he'd be more likely to let you inside."

"You don't really think Pete has anything to do with Jill's disappearance or that girl's death, do you?"

Terrence looked thoughtful. "I don't know. But he had access to Lakewood, which puts him on the suspect list as far as I'm concerned."

She wasn't comfortable invading Pete's privacy, but

if he'd been using her grandfather's home for criminal activity or—God forbid—to commit murder, she'd make sure he paid for it.

"Okay. I'll try."

Terrence shot a smile across the car. "Great. And while you do that, I'll try to find out if he's seen anything suspicious at Lakewood House or anywhere else in Carling Lake lately."

She felt her forehead crease with frown lines. "Like I said, Pete might not take too well to being ambushed with questions."

Terrence frowned but kept his focus on the road as he turned out of the parking lot. "Don't worry. I've dealt with my fair share of curmudgeons."

She made the call. Pete hadn't sounded happy to be getting visitors but said he'd have the boat ready for them when they got there.

The Bonny family had owned several hundred acres of land high up in the Carling Lake Mountains for longer than most current residents could remember. Despite being longtime residents, the Bonny family, or what was left of them, were peripheral members of the community at best. She didn't recall them having ever participated in Carling Lake social events, and they were unlike other residents who made a point of shopping as much as possible in town. She knew from her grandfather's updates that Pete preferred to drive thirty miles west and patronize the big-box stores. The more generous-minded folks in town noted that taking care of Lakewood House and a few of the other seasonal cabins in the area was Pete's only source of income and that maybe he could only afford to buy in bulk. Those with a more begrudging attitude toward the man took umbrage at his failure to shop at local businesses.

Pete Bonny probably wouldn't have been her choice to watch after Lakewood House, but Grandpa Bernie had always felt strongly about supporting everyone in the Carling Lake community, so Nikki wasn't surprised when he'd told her he'd enlisted Pete's help with the family home.

They turned off the highway and onto a narrow back road that wound its way into the densely wooded area. A few miles later, Terrence took a right turn onto an unpaved road, the Highlander's tires kicking up a cloud of dirt that followed them to their destination.

Terrence pulled his car to a stop between Pete's pickup and a large maple tree with No Trespassing and Keep Out signs nailed to its trunk. The trees cast shadows over the dilapidated state of the small prefabricated home that had enough junk strewed around the surrounding yard that the property could have been mistaken for a scrapyard. Amongst the detritus, still on its trailer, was Grandpa Bernie's boat.

Nikki hopped out of the car, wariness flowing through her.

Pete stepped out of the house onto the small front porch as Terrence rounded his car and stopped beside her.

"You okay?" he asked.

She nodded. "Yes. Fine." She didn't know what it was about Pete, but he'd always made her uncomfortable. She'd only been to Pete's property once when she was younger, and she'd been with her grandfather then, who'd always made her feel safe no matter what the situation.

Nikki glanced at Terrence. Grandpa Bernie hadn't been the only person who'd made her feel safe when she was younger.

"Got the boat all ready for ya." Pete's voice broke into her thoughts.

"Great. Thanks so much, Pete. Um…sorry to impose upon you, but could I possibly use your restroom?"

The wrinkles on Pete's face deepened with his frown. "Yeah, I guess so," he answered after a moment.

The interior of the home was grim, sparse and impersonal. A small eat-in kitchen opened onto a living area where a worn and faded gray sofa faced a television set. Pete had formed a makeshift end table out of two milk crates and a piece of cardboard. A dirty bread plate and an empty beer bottle sat on top.

Nikki's eyes roamed the space, looking for any sign of Jill—a scrap of clothing, her phone, anything that might indicate she'd been in the house—but found nothing.

Off to one side was a short hallway. She walked past the kitchen and to the first door. A bathroom with no sign that anyone but Pete had used it in a while.

She headed for the second door in the hall but hesitated. Taking note of what was out in plain view after being allowed inside the house was one thing, but going into his room would most definitely cross a line into snooping. She wasn't as convinced as Terrence that Pete knew anything about Jill's disappearance, the poor girl they'd found or why anyone would want her to leave Lakewood House. But if she was wrong and there was a clue to Jill's whereabouts in this house?

It was enough to have her pushing the door to the room open. The decor was just as sparse in this room as it was in the main living area of the home. A bed and a dresser were the only pieces of furniture. She searched under the bed and in each of the drawers, careful not to disturb anything, and again found nothing.

Terrence might not be happy to hear it, but as far as she could tell, nothing in this house indicated that Jill had ever been inside.

She rejoined Terrence and Pete outside. Terrence had moved his car, backing it up to the trailer so it could be hitched.

"Nothing at all unusual?" Terrence's voice carried across the yard as Nikki approached the men. Terrence crouched on one side of the boat, attaching the safety chains and brake line.

Pete stood on the other side, glaring. "I already told you, I ain't seen nothing funny. I just do the job I was hired to do."

"And I really do appreciate everything you've done," Nikki said, coming to a stop beside Terrence. He looked up at her expectantly.

She gave a little shake of her head to indicate that she hadn't found anything useful inside the house. Terrence donned a frown to match the one on Pete's face.

Pete turned his glare on her. "I guess you won't be needing me anymore since you're moving into the place?"

She hadn't thought about it before now, but he was right. She didn't need him to keep an eye on the house, but she suspected he needed the stipend he'd been getting for caretaking at Lakewood House.

"Well, I don't need a caretaker per se, but Lakewood House is old, and it hasn't been occupied for a while. I'm sure there's a bunch of stuff that I'll need to take care of. Why don't you give me a little bit of time to settle in, and then I'll call you?"

Pete didn't exactly look happy about the offer, but he gave a gruff nod of acceptance.

Terrence straightened. "We're all done here."

"You ain't done till you check the brake lights work and walk around the entire rig, son. I've seen more'n one person lose their boat on the highway 'cause they failed to do a simple walk around."

Terrence's shoulders stiffened at the admonishment. "You're right. It's been a while since I trailered a boat."

Pete jerked his head at Nikki. "Hop in the cab and tap the brakes, will ya?"

She did as requested while Terrence and Pete walked around the boat, their paths crossing at the back of the rig and each ending on the opposite side from where they'd begun.

She hopped out of the car and joined Pete now at the rear driver's side of the Highlander. "Looks good?"

Pete patted the bow of the boat, his face softening. "Looks good."

"You know if you ever want to take her out, just let me know," Nikki said.

Pete gave her a small smile. "I just might."

Terrence joined them. "Look, I know you said you hadn't seen anything odd at Lakewood House, but what about this." He held out his phone. The photo of the business card with the fleur-de-lis was on-screen.

Pete leaned toward the phone, his eyes squinted. For a moment, Nikki thought she saw recognition in his eyes, but a second later, they were back to a flat emptiness. "What is it?"

"It's a business card I found in the kitchen at Lakewood House," Nikki offered. "Have you ever seen it before?"

"Can't say that I have. Kinda funny for a business card. What kinda business is it for?"

"We don't know." Terrence swiped the screen, and the photo of Jill's note came up. "But I found this piece of paper at my sister's apartment—Jill. You might remember her."

Pete shrugged, which Nikki interpreted as a no.

"She's a reporter, and she's gone missing," Terrence said. "I think she came here to Carling Lake, maybe following a story that has something to do with this fleur-de-lis symbol."

"Fleur-de-what?" Confusion clouded Pete's expression, but Nikki couldn't tell if it was genuine or faked.

"Fleur-de-lis. That's what it's called," Terrence said, frustration tingeing his words. "Look again. Are you sure you've never seen a card like this or the symbol before?"

Pete didn't glance down at the phone's screen this time. "I told ya. I ain't ever seen nothing like this floor-de-liz before." He took several steps toward the house. "You got your boat hitched up. It's time for y'all to get on now. I got things to do."

Pete stalked back to the house. The front door closed with a slam.

She and Terrence got into the Highlander.

"He recognized the fleur-de-lis," Terrence said.

"I thought so, but it's hard to tell for sure given Pete's sour attitude."

He put his car in Drive and began easing it forward slowly. The Highlander could handle the rough dirt path without a problem, but the boat and trailer might not. "I think he recognized it," he confirmed without taking his eyes off the road in front of him. "Whether he knows what it means, if anything, is another question."

She studied his face, finding determination and something else she couldn't quite name there. "You didn't push him on it though?"

"No, I didn't."

His voice had fallen to just above a whisper. The expression she hadn't been able to name before came to her then. He looked haunted.

"Why not?"

He remained silent for so long she assumed he wasn't going to answer.

"There was a missing eight-year-old boy a couple of years ago. I was the lead on the case. We got lucky, got a description of the kidnapper early and found a guy who matched it living in the boy's neighborhood. He had a record of domestic abuse against his wife and child. An arrest for assault against a prior girlfriend that had gone nowhere when she refused to testify. Another for lewd behavior. My gut told me he was our guy. I questioned him for hours, but this guy knew the system. I didn't have enough to hold him, so we let him go. We assigned a man to watch him, but wires got crossed somewhere. By the time we figured it out, he was running. He didn't get far. Patrol pulled him over before he got out of state. The boy was in the trunk, but it was too late."

A heaviness fell over the interior of the car, weighing on Nikki's chest. She reached across the space between them and put a hand on his arm. "I am so sorry."

"Maybe if I hadn't pushed. What did you say earlier? I lacked diplomacy? Maybe if I had been more diplomatic, taken a softer approach—"

"This guy sounds like he was a psychopath. Nothing you did or didn't do could have stopped him from doing what he did. He's the one responsible—the only one responsible—for that child's death." She squeezed his arm.

Terrence gave his head a shake as if he were freeing himself from the horror of his memories. "Yeah, well, I'm not taking any chances with Jill's life. We need more information. If Pete recognized the fleur-de-lis, someone else in Carling Lake would too. We just have to find them."

Chapter Ten

Terrence had no idea why he'd told Nikki about Brian Malroy's kidnapping case. It had been nearly three years now, and he still thought about the eight-year-old every single day. His captain had forced him to see the department psychologist when it had become obvious that his way of dealing with the loss of the little boy was to fall into a bottle of rum every night. His shrink said it was normal to feel guilty but that he needed to forgive himself if he wanted to be of use to all the other people who needed his help. That had been enough to get him to lay off the booze, but forgiving himself? He hadn't yet figured out how to do that.

He shot a glance across the car at Nikki. They'd been riding in silence for the past several minutes. He wondered if his confession had brought back memories of all the times they'd commiserated with each other as teenagers. Worrying over failed tests, tough teachers and college admissions woes seemed outright ludicrous in the face of the adult problems they both faced now.

And yet, despite the odds, here they were some fifteen years later, still leaning on each other for support. Not to mention the moment they'd shared after leaving The West Gallery. He had no idea where that had come from. No, that wasn't true. He'd felt it the moment he'd laid eyes on Nikki at Lakewood House. The attraction between them was still there and as strong as ever. Maybe stronger. But that didn't mean they had to give in to it. None of the things that had pushed them apart fourteen years ago had changed. They'd only called a temporary truce in order to help Jill. Nothing could change the fact that Bernie King had stolen his aunt and uncle's home right out from under them—and that he'd never forgive the man for having done so.

But should the granddaughter be held responsible for the sins of her grandfather? The thought pressed down on him.

He pushed it away as he turned onto the Lakewood House property. He had bigger fish to fry right now, like figuring out the next step in the search for Jill.

Nikki jumped out of the car and guided him as he turned it around carefully in the driveway and backed the boat up slowly toward the lake. Just as he was beginning to worry that he was getting too close to the water, she called out for him to stop.

He put the car in Park, set the emergency brake and got out.

She'd already released the straps and was reaching for the boat crank.

"I can do that," he said.

"It's not a problem. I've done it thousands of times when Grandpa and I used to take the boat out on the water."

"You sure? That was a long time ago."

She shot him a look. "You do a lot of boating in Trenton?"

He didn't try to stop the smile that spread across his face. "Touché."

Her return smile made his heart stutter.

The boat slid into the water, making a small wave.

"If you want to help," Nikki said while keeping hold of the line at the front of the bow, "you can release the hook for me."

He did and wound it back up while she tethered the boat. "I guess DC hasn't knocked all of Carling Lake out of you."

"Ha ha." She hip-checked him and, for a moment, it felt like they were fifteen again.

The smile on his face fell away as something over Nikki's shoulder caught his attention.

Smoke. Coming from a window in Lakewood House.

His sudden change in demeanor registered with Nikki. "What?" She turned and followed his line of sight. "Oh no!"

She took off in a sprint toward the house.

"Nikki, wait!"

She didn't slow down. "We've got to try to stop it," she called over her shoulder.

He cursed under his breath and picked up his pace, running after her.

Carling Lake's fire department was all volunteer. It would take time to get everyone mobilized. Time Lakewood House might not have. Whatever their differences, they both loved Lakewood House. He was no more willing to let the home burn down than she was.

He caught up to Nikki just as she was about to push through the back door. "Wait a minute." He grabbed her wrist, pulling her to a stop.

If looks could kill, he'd be on his way six feet under.

"You have to test the handle and make sure it's not hot. And we need to stand off to the side when we open the door. The oxygen from the outside could fuel the fire if we're not careful."

"Okay, let's do it then."

His phone was still in the Highlander. "Do you have your phone?"

"No, it's in my purse in the car."

"You should get it and call 911." And it would get her out of the line of fire, literally.

He knew the answer before she spoke though. "No way. I know where the fire extinguisher is. You need my help."

He thought about pointing out that she could just tell him where to find it but arguing with her now only wasted time.

He placed his hand on the doorknob. It was cool. That was a good sign. The smoke seemed to be coming from a window on the side of the house near the front. The space Bernie King had used as an office if memory served. If the fire was contained to that room, it was probably okay to enter.

He gestured for Nikki to stand back from the door, then opened it.

A haze of smoke filled the home. He pulled his jacket collar to cover as much of his face as he could and stepped into the home.

Nikki did the same, veering off toward the kitchen. "Grandpa kept a fire extinguisher under the sink."

Terrence turned toward the front of the house. He was right that the origin of the fire appeared to be in the small office. The smoke was thicker there, although thankfully, he didn't see any flames. He walked toward the room carefully.

The door to the office was open. It took a moment for his eyes to adjust, but when they did, he could see that the fire seemed to have been started in a wastepaper basket and was now climbing the nearby curtains.

He shrugged out of his jacket and beat at the flames shooting out of the trash can. The fire caught the hem of his coat and raced upward, catching his sleeve. He dropped the jacket and stepped back, pain searing his skin.

Nikki rushed into the room, pushing him aside. "Move."

She pulled the pin, pointed the extinguisher at the fire and squeezed the handle, sending a stream of white foam shooting out at the base of the inferno. She worked her way up the window until all the flames were snuffed out.

They stumbled from the office, still thick with smoke, and out onto the porch. The burn radiated pain throughout his arm.

Nikki's eyes filled with concern. "Oh my God, you're hurt." She crossed the porch to him.

"I'm okay," he said through gritted teeth.

"No, you're not. That burn looks serious. Stay here." She hopped off the porch and ran around the side of the house. She returned less than a minute later, her cell phone to her ear.

"Yes, Lakewood House. The fire is out, but we need an ambulance."

"It's not that bad."

The look she shot at him was quelling. "And the sheriff. I don't think this was an accident."

He heard the dispatcher's promise that help was on the way before Nikki ended the call.

"I don't need an ambulance." The second after he'd spoken, a lightning bolt of pain zinged up his arm, making him cringe and putting a lie to the statement.

"Yeah, I can see that." Soot marked Nikki's face, and they both smelled like smoke. Their clothing was probably a lost cause. "I'm pretty sure you'll need to go to the hospital to have this cleaned and bandaged. Don't argue." She cut off his protest before he got started. "You need to be in one piece if you're going to help Jill."

The sound of sirens cut off any further protests.

His evening had just taken a noticeably downward turn. Nikki's statement to the 911 dispatcher played through his head as he watched the ambulance shriek toward them, followed closely by the sheriff's SUV.

"You told the dispatcher that you didn't think the fire was accidental."

She pulled her gaze from the emergency vehicles to look at him. "You do?"

"No, I agree with you. This wasn't an accident." He'd known that the moment he'd seen the flames shooting out of the trash can. He doubted very much Nikki would have thrown a lit match or another incendiary device away carelessly. But he almost wished he could believe she had. Because if this wasn't an accident… "Somebody wants you out of Lakewood House, and it looks like they are willing to go to the extreme to make it happen."

And that scared him more than he wanted to admit.

Chapter Eleven

The EMTs insisted on transporting Terrence to the hospital. As a silent nod to just how much the burns to his arm must have hurt, he hadn't put up a fight. Nikki followed in her car, arriving just behind the ambulance to a relatively quiet clinic. There was only one other patient in the waiting room, and he appeared to be struggling with a spring flu.

Terrence was whisked into an exam room immediately. Nikki followed, shooting a look that turned the nurse who attempted to stop her's march past the admissions desk to stone.

As the doctor examined Terrence, she worked to chase away the tremor of fear that hadn't stopped running through her since she'd noticed Terrence's injury. She'd felt a level of terror she'd never felt before and hoped to never feel again when she'd run into the office and spotted fire crawling up the sleeve of Terrence's shirt.

She drew in a shuddering breath and pushed the images away. He was going to be fine.

As if reading her thoughts, the doctor spoke. "You were very lucky. These burns aren't nearly as bad as they could have been. I'm going to clean the wound and dress it with a bandage. You'll have to repeat the process at home while it heals, but I'll leave you with a sheet of instructions. I'll also write you a script for a pain reliever."

"I'll be fine with a couple of aspirin," Terrence replied.

The doctor, an older man who had gone mostly gray and had eyes that looked as if they'd seen it all, raised his eyes from the burn on Terrence's arm. "Burns can be tricky injuries, Mr. Sutton. Follow my instructions and yours should heal without any permanent damage." The tone of the doctor's voice made apparent what he'd left unsaid—don't follow my instructions at your own risk.

Terrence nodded. "Don't worry, doc. I'll do what you tell me. I have no desire to see you again. No offense."

The doctor smiled. "None taken. I wish more of my patients would follow your lead." He tucked the tablet he'd been tapping notes into under his arm. "Give me a couple of minutes to get everything I'll need together, and I'll be right back to take care of that wound for you."

The doctor started for the door, stopped to greet Sheriff Webb and stood aside to let him into the room before disappearing into the hall.

"How are you doing?" the sheriff asked, coming to stand next to the bed. From the swing of his gaze from her to Terrence, then back to her, she knew the question was directed at both of them. Her emotions swirled and twisted inside of her to the point that she wasn't sure how to answer his question, so she let Terrence answer first.

"The doc says the burns aren't that bad. He's going to bandage them up, and I should be out of here any minute."

"That's good to hear." The sheriff's eyes swung to Nikki's face.

"I'm fine. Not a scratch on me." She tried for a reassuring smile, but from the look on Sheriff Webb's face, she was pretty sure she'd failed.

"You should get checked out while you're here," he said.

"That's not a bad idea," Terrence seconded. His concern for her was also written all over his face.

She doubted there was anything the doctor could do for her, and she no longer had medical insurance to cover a hospital stay anyway. Physically, she wasn't hurt, but mentally and emotionally, she felt like she was treading on thin ice.

She shrugged in answer.

After a moment, the sheriff moved the conversation in a different direction. "The fire marshal has declared the fire arson, but I doubt that comes as any surprise."

"The flames leaping from the trash can kind of gave it away," Nikki deadpanned.

Sheriff Webb held up his hands in a don't-shoot-the-messenger motion. "We got a print off the wastepaper basket. Maybe we'll get a hit. The good news is, thanks to your quick action, the damage was confined to the office. You'll need to have some work done in there, but the remainder of the house is sound. As much as it pains me to say this, there's no structural reason you can't stay there. That said, I think you should consider finding another place to stay until we get to the bottom of whatever is going on."

"Not happening." If anything, the attack on the house had increased her resolve to stay. She needed to be there if Lakewood House was attacked again to protect it and, hopefully, to get a glimpse of whoever was targeting her home.

Sheriff Webb sighed heavily and shook his head, a

look of resignation on his face. "The medical examiner also finished the autopsy and got back toxicology results. It looks like our Jane Doe was a heroin user, but it had no hand in her death, according to the medical examiner. Doc sticks by the strangulation call and puts her age at nineteen or thereabouts. I've got an officer searching the missing person reports in the area again with a revised age range."

"That poor girl," Nikki said, thinking about the tragic loss of such a young life. A look at the anger on Terrence's face told her he was thinking the same thing.

"We met James West and spoke with his brother Ryan. They've agreed to see if they can find out more about the fleur-de-lis symbol and see if it connects to anyone or anything in or around Carling Lake."

Sheriff Webb grinned. "I'm glad you listened to me."

Terrence pushed himself up straighter in the hospital bed. "You could have told us why you wanted us to speak to him. I've heard of West Investigations, but the name didn't click for me when you sent us his way."

"They are good people to have on your side."

"True." Terrence nodded. "And hopefully they turn up something for us."

"We also showed Pete the fleur-de-lis and asked him if he knew anything about it." Terrence shot her a look she ignored. "We thought he recognized it, but he pretended that he didn't."

"I'm not surprised," the sheriff said. "Pete's picture is right there next to *ornery* in the dictionary. The man can be downright mean when he gets a few drinks in him, although nowhere near as nasty a piece of work as his nephew."

Nikki searched her memories. "I don't remember Pete having a nephew."

"Dana," Terrence offered the name. "He was a few years younger than us. In Jill's class, or maybe a year behind her. Pete's older brother's boy, I think."

"His parents named him Dana Bonny?"

"Yeah, he got a lot of ribbing for it too until the other kids realized, as Lance said, he was a nasty piece of work. The teasing stopped right fast after that. He was basically your typical bully. Picked on the younger, weaker kids. Lied. Cheated. Stole. Got away with a lot of it because his father was an even nastier piece of work, and no one wanted to confront him about his son."

Nikki tried again to pull up an image of Dana in her mind and failed. "I don't remember him at all."

"You're the better for it. I caught Dana hassling Jill once. Put the fear of God in him. Like most bullies, he's a coward at heart, but I wouldn't turn my back on him." Terrence shifted his attention to the sheriff. "Do you know where he is now?"

Sheriff Webb gave him a questioning look. "No. When he's not in my jail cell, I never know exactly what Dana is up to, but I can guess it's probably not good. Why?"

"I want to talk to him. Maybe he'll tell us what Pete wouldn't."

Sheriff Webb shook his head slowly. "You said it yourself. Dana Bonny is a man you want to steer clear of."

Terrence's eyes narrowed. "I wasn't afraid of Dana when we were kids, and I'm not afraid of him now. And if he knows something that could help me find Jill, he's going to tell me."

A commotion in the hall grabbed all their attention, forestalling any response from the sheriff.

Charity Jackson burst into the room, a mini tornado

of a woman, the scent of White Diamonds by Elizabeth Taylor swirling in her wake. "Oh my goodness. Terrence, are you okay? I came as soon as I heard you'd been hurt. What did the doctor say? You better have a darn good reason for not calling me, boy." She threw her arms around him even as she shot questions at him faster than he could have possibly responded.

"I'm fine, Aunt Charity. It's just a minor burn. I didn't call because I didn't want to worry you."

She took a step back and slapped him lightly on the arm that wasn't injured. "I worried because you didn't call." She slapped his arm again.

"Maybe you shouldn't assault the patient," Sheriff Webb interjected.

Nikki remembered it being difficult to raise Charity's ire, but once she was worked up, it was best to stand back and let her temper run its course. This was apparently something the sheriff hadn't yet learned.

Charity shot him a look over her shoulder that had him taking two steps back. "And why didn't you call me? Isn't it standard police procedure to notify the next of kin?"

"I'm not dead, Aunt Charity," Terrence said, exasperated. "Here, sit." He motioned toward the rolling stool in the corner where Nikki stood out of the way of Charity's wrath.

She grabbed the stool and rolled it over to where Charity waited next to Terrence's bed.

"Thank you, sweetheart," she said. "It's good to see you even if it is under trying circumstances."

"It's good to see you too, Charity," Nikki responded.

Charity turned back to her nephew, wringing her hands. "First Jill, now you. Have you heard from your sister at all since we last spoke?"

"Not yet."

"I know you don't want me to worry, but I am be-ginning to. Jill has always been unpredictable, but she's never out of touch this long. And it's obvious you think something is wrong." The hand wringing sped up.

"Aunt Charity, now don't you worry. I'm looking for Jill and so is the sheriff." Terrence nodded toward him. "I'm sure we'll find her, and she'll tell us we are all overprotective and overreacted." He paused. "I hope you didn't drive in the state you're in."

"I drove her."

All eyes in the room turned toward the door. A young, slim Black woman stood in the threshold. Nikki mentally ran through the girls she'd known in Carling Lake who this could have been but came up short.

"Yes, Talia came by the house to drop off your bags from the hotel and offered her well wishes for your speedy recovery. Imagine my surprise."

"Sorry." Talia looked as if she'd rather be anywhere in the world except in this exam room. "Miss Melinda packed up your things from your room and sent me to deliver them to your aunt's house since we'd heard about the fire and you getting injured and all. She says she's sorry she can't extend your stay, but the hotel is booked."

Nikki assumed that the Miss Melinda Talia referred to was Melinda Hanes, and that Talia worked for her.

"Nothing to be sorry for," Terrence said, smiling over his aunt's head at the woman hovering in the doorway. "I'm sorry you had to go out of your way."

"That was very nice of you," Sheriff Webb said. Talia blushed.

"I'll just leave your things." She dropped the bag near the closet by the door and backed out of the room.

"Thank you," Terrence called after the fleeing woman.

The sheriff headed for the door. "It's dark outside, and I'm just going to make sure she gets to her car safely."

Charity tsked. "If that man doesn't ask her out soon, I just might do it for him. Those two have been circling each other for months now."

Terrence shook his head. "Lance is a grown man. I'm sure he can get his own dates."

Aunt Charity rolled her eyes. "Yeah, he seems to be just about as good at getting and keeping a woman by his side as you are." Her gaze landed pointedly on Nikki, sending heat crawling up the back of her neck.

"Aunt Charity," Terrence snapped, then stopped, taking in a deep breath and letting it out slowly. "Listen, could I stay with you? As you heard, the hotel could only give me the one night."

"I'm sorry, Terrence." Charity shook her head, but she didn't look sorry. "You know how small my place is. It's why you and Jill stay at the hotel or the B and B when you come to visit."

"Yeah, of course, you're right," Terrence said, frustration tingeing his words. "Don't worry about it. I'll figure something out."

"You should stay at Lakewood House." Nikki thought she saw a hint of a smile on Charity's face.

"I'm not sure that's a good idea." Terrence shot a questioning glance at Nikki.

Sure, she and Terrence had only called a temporary truce, which was delicate at best. But if she was brutally honest with herself, the message on the garage and the fire had scared her. She didn't want to let whoever was behind these attacks run her out of Lakewood House, but she wasn't totally comfortable staying there alone anymore. Letting Terrence have the guest room could solve both their problems. Of course, given the feelings he'd awakened in her, it might also create a host of new issues, but it was something she was prepared to risk at this point.

"I think it's a good idea," she said before she could change her mind.

Charity and Terrence looked at her with surprise written across their faces. "I've got the spare room at Lakewood House, and if the hotel is full, the B and Bs in town are probably full as well. There isn't another option."

"See, it's perfect." Charity smiled.

"I appreciate the offer, but…" Terrence stared at her for a long moment.

"Oh, come on, Terrence. It isn't safe for Nikki to stay at Lakewood House alone, not with a vandal and arsonist on the loose. This way, you can make sure Nikki is safe."

"Well, I can take care of myself," Nikki interjected before Charity turned her into a damsel in distress, "but we do have to figure out a game plan for finding and talking to Dana. This way we can strategize, and I can make sure you get some rest."

"Are you talking about Dana Bonny?" Charity asked.

Terrence turned back to his aunt. "Yes. You know him?"

"Everybody knows him. There's no mystery about where he'll be. He inherited his father's place just outside of town, but at least three to four nights a week, you can find him saddled up to the bar at Whistler's over in Stunnersville."

Stunnersville was about fifteen miles west of Carling Lake. Whistler's was a dive bar sometimes populated by the bikers in the area and always a place that attracted people looking for trouble. Which were apparently Dana's kind of people.

If Charity knew that Dana frequented Whistler's, it was a sure bet that the sheriff knew as well. Maybe he'd thought it best not to encourage them to seek Dana out, especially not at Whistler's, but his keeping this information from them rankled Nikki. From the look on Terrence's face, he'd come to the same conclusion and felt the same way.

"I'll head over there as soon as the doctor lets me out of this place." Terrence swung his legs so they hung over the side of the bed.

"Not today, you won't." Charity pressed her palm firmly against Terrence's chest, holding him down.

"Aunt Charity, I know you're worried about me, but I'm fine. I promise. We don't know what's going on with Jill, and I don't want to lose any more time."

"I am worried about you, but even if I wasn't, Dana won't be at Whistler's tonight, for sure. Whistler's is closed on Mondays."

Terrence let out a curse.

Charity shot him the same look she'd given to them as teens when one of them cursed in front of her.

"Sorry," he said, looking very much like a chastened teenager under his aunt's glare.

"Tonight you'll rest at Lakewood House. If Jill hasn't turned up by tomorrow, you can track down Dana and ask your questions." Charity patted Terrence's thigh as if everything had been settled.

"Really, I'm fine with you staying in the guest room." It cut against Nikki's grain to admit weakness, but after the events of the day, she didn't want to stay at Lakewood House alone. "I'd really appreciate it if you did."

He gave Nikki a searching look. "Okay. Thank you for the offer."

"Of course."

She let out a breath of relief. It was settled. Tomorrow night, they'd face whatever potential dangers lurked at Whistler's.

And tonight at Lakewood House, they'd face a wholly different kind of threat—sleeping under the same roof.

Chapter Twelve

The white cotton bandage covering most of his forearm struck Terrence as a bit much, but he kept his thoughts to himself. Anything to get out of this hospital.

"Okay. I'm all done here. I'll be back in a moment with your prescription and discharge orders." The doctor pulled the blue nitrile gloves off his hands and tossed them in the trash before striding from the room.

"Are you really okay? Maybe the doctor should keep you here overnight for observation?" Aunt Charity pressed the back of her hand to his forehead, just like she'd done when he was sick as a little boy.

"I'm fine, Aunt Charity." He reached for his aunt's hand and squeezed. "The burns aren't that bad, and the doctor said there should be no permanent damage."

Nikki patted his aunt's shoulder as a ringtone sounded. "I'll make sure he rests tonight." She fished her phone out of her purse and frowned at its screen. "I'm sorry, I have to take this." She walked from the room.

"Promise me you'll take it easy," Aunt Charity said, pulling Terrence's attention from Nikki as she retreated to the hallway to take her call.

He hesitated. His gut was telling him that time was

of the essence if he was going to find Jill unharmed. "I'll take it easy tonight."

She pulled a sour face. "I guess I'll have to be content with that. I'm sure Nikki will take good care of you."

"I wish you hadn't pushed her into offering to let me stay at Lakewood House. I'm not sure that it's a good idea."

"Of course it's a good idea. I think you're reading the situation all wrong, dear. That girl is terrified. Having someone else in the house will be a comfort."

Was his aunt right? There was a time when he'd known Nikki's moods better than she had. But no more.

"Aunt Charity, you have to understand. Nikki and I have agreed to work together to find Jill, but I wouldn't call us friends."

"Of course you are friends. You've been friends since you were both knee-high to a grasshopper. And a little more than friends for a while there if this old memory serves."

"Whatever we were fifteen years ago, we certainly aren't now." A frown twisted his lips. "Too much has happened. Too much has been lost."

His aunt sighed heavily, her shoulders slumping. "I've let this go on for far too long, but you and your uncle are so much alike. Stubborn and pigheaded."

"Aunt Charity, what are you talking about?" He felt the frown lines deepen around his mouth.

"I'm talking about the anger Jarrod and you have toward Bernie King and, by extension, Nikki."

"Uncle Jarrod had a right to be angry. So do I. Bernard King stole our family home."

"No. No, he didn't."

"What are you saying, Aunt Charity? I was there. Bernie King was supposed to be your and Uncle Jarrod's friend, but when he saw the opportunity to grab Lakewood House out from under you, he took it."

"You were there, but you don't know everything."

"I don't understand."

"Bernie bought Lakewood House from your uncle and me because we asked him to."

His aunt's words stunned him. "You what?"

"Your uncle loved that house and the surrounding land. His grandfather built it and his mother inherited it from him. It was Jarrod's dream to pass it down to you and Jill when the time came. But the upkeep on the house and the land was so costly. It was always a struggle. Several times we considered selling part of the land off, but Jarrod was adamantly opposed, and somehow we always found a way. Until your uncle lost his job at the auto manufacturing plant."

"I remember. That's when Uncle Jarrod started working for King's Trucking."

"Bernie gave your uncle a job when we were at our lowest, but it wasn't enough. Your uncle had been a manager at the auto plant, and trucking just didn't pay the same. And we'd taken a second mortgage out on the house and property a few years earlier to cover Jarrod's mother's hospice care. The bank was threatening to foreclose. We *asked* Bernie to purchase the house so at least it wouldn't fall into the hands of developers. He'd always admired the property, and your uncle and I figured, at least if Lakewood House couldn't be ours, it would go to someone who'd love it and was a friend."

As his aunt spoke, he mentally pictured a puzzle scrambling and reforming to create a totally different picture than what it had looked like moments before. "So Bernie bought Lakewood House to help you?"

A lock of hair fell from the messy bun Aunt Charity had thrown atop her head as she nodded. "He did, and paid enough for it that we paid off the second mortgage and had a bit of money to get you off to college."

"I really don't understand then. Why was Uncle Jarrod so angry that Bernie bought Lakewood House?"

His aunt patted his hand gingerly. "Your uncle was a proud, proud man. He took losing the family home hard, even though he'd agreed it was best to sell it. Harder than either of us could have anticipated. I think it just became easier for him to blame Bernie than it was to blame himself."

"Well, Bernie could have still let us live at Lakewood House. Pay rent."

Aunt Charity snort laughed. "Paying rent for the house he'd owned a year earlier. Your uncle never would have agreed to it. No. We did the right thing by selling, and I think your uncle knew that even if he didn't want to face it."

Terrence felt like he was coming out of a fog. "Why didn't Bernie ever say anything? Tell the world that Uncle Jarrod's version of things wasn't what actually happened."

"Because he was Jarrod's friend, even if Jarrod couldn't see that."

"So, all this time I've been angry at Bernie King? And at Nikki for defending her grandfather's actions—"

Aunt Charity looked at him with sad eyes. "Neither of them deserved it."

"But why didn't Nikki ever tell me the truth?"

"My guess? I don't think she knew the truth. For the same reason, Bernie didn't tell anyone else what had really happened. He didn't want it to get out and cause Jarrod any more pain."

It felt like a chunk of lead had taken root in his stomach. All this time, Nikki had been right. "Nikki always defended her grandfather."

"Maybe that was enough for him."

"I owe Nikki an apology." He hoped she accepted it, although he wouldn't blame her if she didn't.

"You do and so do I. And I owe you an apology. I should have stopped your uncle from infecting you with his anger and told you the truth about all this a long time ago. Maybe then you and Nikki would have remained friends or even—"

"None of this is your fault, Aunt Charity."

"No, I bear some responsibility. Your uncle, well, he was who he was, but I should have intervened with you. I thought the whole thing would eventually blow over, but it didn't. And then Jarrod left us so suddenly. It just got harder and harder to tell you the truth. You and Nikki had both left Carling Lake and were getting on with your lives. It just seemed best to leave well enough alone. But now with the two of you back in Carling Lake, I can see that I was wrong not to have said something sooner."

Part of him was angry with his aunt, but another part understood she'd done what she thought was best at the time. His uncle Jarrod had been so angry, and he'd adopted that anger as his own. That was no one's fault but his.

"It's okay, Aunt Charity. I understand." He leaned over and wrapped his arms around his aunt. Over her shoulder, he could see Nikki pacing outside the door of the exam room, still on her call, her facial expression serious.

How would she react when he told her the truth about the sale of Lakewood House? After years of accusing her grandfather of stealing his family's home, would she be able to find it in her heart to forgive him?

"You know. Despite everything, I've always held out hope that Lakewood House might one day be back in the family."

His gaze moved back to his aunt. "I wouldn't hold my breath if I were you. Nikki loves that place and frankly, I can't see Jill or I ever being able to afford to buy it back."

She made a half turn, looking from him to Nikki and back. "We shall see. It doesn't hurt for an old lady to hold out hope."

"I TALKED TO my friend working on Lyon's campaign," Carolyn said.

Nikki skirted out of the way of a nurse as she waited for the punch line from Carolyn. "And?"

"He didn't say no."

She let out a sigh of disappointment. "Great." She turned to start the loop she'd been pacing again. Charity stepped out of Terrence's room, followed by Terrence carrying his overnight bag. Charity kissed his cheek and headed down the hall in the opposite direction from the exit.

"We knew it might not be easy to find you a new job with Manco bad-mouthing you behind the scenes. My friend said to send him your résumé. That's good, because no one has credentials like you. Since Lyon is running as an outsider with the knowledge and courage to fight corruption and the big donors, I decided not to shy away from the fact that you stood up to Manco and did the right thing at great cost to your career. I think he liked that, so don't give up hope."

"Right, and if this job doesn't work out, I can always run for mayor," Nikki said, bitterness tingeing her voice.

"Come again?"

She exhaled, rubbing at the headache growing behind her left temple. "Nothing. It's just something a friend here said to me. That the election for mayor is coming up and I should run."

There was a beat of silence on the other side of the phone line. "Maybe you should."

"Come on, Carolyn. Get serious."

"What? Why not? That's the goal, right? Elected office."

It was no secret to her colleagues that she had plans to run for elected office at some point, but she'd envisioned taking that step years from now. "Yes, of course, in, like, ten, fifteen years."

"Why wait? The opportunity is presenting itself now. And plenty of big-name politicians have started their careers as small-town mayors. Michael Bloomberg. Pete Buttigieg. Grover Cleveland."

Nikki chuckled. "Grover Cleveland?"

"Hey, he was the mayor of my hometown of Buffalo before winning the New York governor's office and then the presidency, so don't knock old Grover."

She turned to see Terrence headed for her. "Yes, here I go. Literally. I have to get off the phone. Hey, Carolyn—thank you. I can't tell you how much I appreciate all your help."

"Don't sweat it. We have to watch each other's backs. I'm emailing you my friend's contact info. Don't forget to send him your résumé ASAP."

"Everything okay?" Terrence said as she ended the call.

"Great." The last thing she wanted to do right now

was get into a conversation about the sad state of her career. She scanned the hall beyond his shoulder. "Where's Charity? I figured we'd drop her off at her place before heading to Lakewood House."

"Sy Martin from Aunt Charity's church came in to the ER a little while ago. The doctor thinks she's just got a touch of indigestion, but Aunt Charity wants to stay with her until they get the all clear. She'll catch a ride home from Sy when she's released."

"Okay then. We should get going." Nikki reached out and took his duffel bag from his hand and hooked it over her shoulder, ignoring the irritated look Terrence shot her as she did. "It's been an awful day, and I still have to see the damage at the house."

"Lance gave the okay for you to occupy Lakewood House still, so it probably looks worse than it is," he said as they headed for the exit.

"I hope you're right."

The automatic doors at the front of the clinic slid open on their approach, and they stepped out into the cool night air.

The clinic shared a single-level commercial building with a dollar store and a bakery, both of which had long since closed.

She led Terrence to the second row of the parking lot, where she'd haphazardly parked her car earlier. Thankfully, there were more than enough empty spaces so that her atrocious parking shouldn't have been too much of an inconvenience to anyone.

"I don't have the money for remodeling or redecorating, and at this point, even the insurance deductible might be out of reach." She used her key fob to unlock the car and opened the passenger door, holding it for Terrence to slip into the seat.

He smiled wryly, sliding his bag off her shoulder. "You know I'm fine. Perfectly capable of opening my own door and carrying my own bag."

"I promised your aunt I'd make sure you rest, and I keep my promises, so get in the car."

"Yes, ma'am." He gave a mock salute. She didn't want to encourage him, but she couldn't hold back the smile that turned up the corners of her mouth. His levity was a welcome respite from the stresses of the day at the moment.

She closed the door and hustled around to the driver's side of the Camry.

Twenty minutes later, they arrived at Lakewood House.

Nikki hit the light switch on the wall next to the door, illuminating the space. The door to the office was closed. The only sign of the fire visible from outside the room was soot marks around the door and frame.

"It looks different than I remember it." His eyes roamed over the living room, dining area and kitchen.

"Grandpa Bernie had most of the walls taken down on this floor and had the kitchen updated."

"It's different but nice."

"Well, you already know where everything is." She sat his duffel bag down by the stairs, then headed for the kitchen and opened the door to the fridge. "I still haven't been to the market, but I have the fixings for a bacon, lettuce and tomato sandwich if you're hungry."

He leaned against the newel post at the bottom of the staircase. Exhaustion appeared to be catching up with him.

"I'm not hungry. As much as I hate to admit it, what I'd like most right now is to climb into bed and sleep for eight hours straight."

Nikki closed the fridge and crossed back to the stairs. She squinted her eyes at him when he scooped his bag from the floor before she could get to it. "Come on. I'll show you to the guest room." It also happened to be his old bedroom when his family had lived at Lakewood House, which led to another feeling of déjà vu. She wondered if he felt it too, but if he did, he showed no signs.

She led him up the stairs and to the bedroom on the other side of the Jack-and-Jill bathroom.

"Let me just put some clean linens on the bed."

"You don't have to put yourself out. I'm okay on the couch if that's easier."

But she had already stepped into the bathroom and grabbed clean sheets from the linen closet.

She worked quickly, changing the bed linens while Terrence moved to the window overlooking the lake.

"This used to be my room," Terrence said quietly.

Nikki looked up from smoothing the sheets. "I know. I always slept in the small room across the hall when I came to visit because I always thought of this one as yours, even after Grandpa Bernie moved in."

"You remember when we used to climb out of this window and sit on the roof of the back porch in the summer?"

The memory brought a smile to her face. "Of course. We used to think we were so cool. Hanging out on the roof." They'd had their first kiss on that roof.

After making the bed, she came to stand next to him at the window. The night sky was clear enough to see all the way across the lake to Carling Island.

"I remember sneaking out of the house and rowing over to the island."

"Yeah, I do too." That was something a lot of the teenagers used to do. To make out and…more. It was thinking about the *more* part with Terrence that was making her body tingle at the moment.

She wasn't sure which of them moved first, but she was very aware of the moment his lips covered hers. Red-hot desire coursed through her, banishing all rational thought beyond one. She wanted Terrence. She opened to him, deepening the kiss and steering them closer to completely losing control.

It felt as if someone had doused her with ice-cold water when Terrence broke off the kiss and stepped back abruptly. "I have to tell you something."

"What is it?" Her heart beat wildly, both from the heat of the kiss they'd just shared and from the feeling of foreboding that had sprung into her chest.

Terrence took another step back, putting more distance between them. "While we were at the clinic earlier, Aunt Charity told me that she and Uncle Jarrod *asked* your grandfather to buy Lakewood House from them."

Nikki shook her head, trying to clear it. "I don't understand. Your uncle loved this place."

"He did, but apparently, the upkeep of the house got to be too much for them and the bank was going to foreclose. My aunt and uncle didn't want the property falling into the hands of a developer so they asked your grandfather to buy it."

"But your uncle was so angry at Grandpa Bernie?"

"I know. Apparently, Uncle Jarrod took the loss of Lakewood House harder than he thought he would. Losing the family home, everything he and his parents and grandparents had worked for, it was too much of a slap to his pride. At least, that's what Aunt Charity thinks. He needed someone to blame, and your grandfather became that someone."

"Why didn't your aunt say something? Why didn't Grandpa Bernie?" She felt as if she were riding an emotional seesaw. A moment ago, she'd been high on the need to be with Terrence. But now? She wasn't sure what she was feeling beyond shock and confusion. Nothing he was saying made sense, except that it did. Wasn't he just saying what she'd always believed to be true? That her grandfather was the man she'd known him to be all along.

"Aunt Charity says she thinks your grandfather saw that my uncle was hurting and embarrassed, and he didn't want to add to that. She thought my uncle Jarrod would eventually come to his senses, but there wasn't time for him to come around."

Jarrod Jackson had passed away from a heart attack six months after selling Lakewood House. It was an immense loss for Terrence's family, as well as the town. It had also been the death knell for any chance of reviving her and Terrence's relationship. Terrence had wanted nothing to do with the man whose actions he felt had contributed to his uncle's death. Or his granddaughter.

She stared at Terrence, trying to take in everything he'd said. His words felt like a kick to the gut. For years, he'd believed the worst about her grandfather and destroyed their friendship and budding romance as a result. Even when she'd called and texted, tried to reason with him, he'd ignored her, going so far as to block her on his phone and on his social media.

"Look, I know I've been an idiot and I'm so sorry."

"Sorry just isn't going to cut it." She fought back angry tears. "You blamed my grandfather for years for something he didn't do. You wouldn't even listen to me when I tried to tell you that Grandpa Bernie would never steal Lakewood House from your aunt and uncle."

"I know. I was stupid. So stupid. But Uncle Jarrod was so angry, and if I'm honest, I was pretty angry about having to leave the first place that felt like a real home."

She felt sick. Her guts twisted with regret and remorse. Grandpa Bernie had died knowing that Terrence, someone he'd once cared for like a son, hated him for something he hadn't done. She didn't know if she could ever forgive Terrence for that.

"I don't know what to say. I need time to think." She started for the door.

"I can't say enough how sorry I am for what I did to us. For hurting you. I just hope you can find it in yourself to forgive me."

Nikki paused at the door and looked at him over her shoulder. "Honestly, I'm not sure if I can."

Chapter Thirteen

The sun had just begun to top the mountains when Nikki rose for the day. Sleep had been elusive, so it hadn't been difficult to rise before Terrence stirred. She'd done as she'd promised Carolyn and submitted her résumé for the position with the Lyon campaign after leaving Terrence's room the night before. Either Carolyn's friend owed her a big favor or the campaign was desperate, because less than five hours later, she already had an email asking to set up a time for a phone interview. It might not go anywhere, but the glimmer of hope was enough for now.

With everything that had happened since she'd returned to Carling Lake, she hadn't found the time for grocery shopping. She headed for the diner. Despite the early hour, there were already patrons seated in the diner.

The frown on Rosie's face as Nikki approached made it clear that Rosie had neither forgotten nor forgiven the scene that Nikki and Terrence made the last time they were at the diner.

"I'm sorry," Nikki said, sliding onto a stool at the counter. "My behavior was way out of line."

Rosie's frown stayed fixed on her face. "You two put on quite the show."

Guilt shot through her. "I know and I am truly sorry, and it will never happen again. I promise."

Rosie sighed. "I remember a time when the two of you were inseparable. Best friends."

"That was a long time ago." And somehow the last several hours had made it feel even longer.

"Not that long. Don't you think it's time to let this feud between your grandpa and Jarrod go?"

It was sage advice and for a while, she'd thought that's exactly where she and Terrence were headed. But now? She wasn't sure if that would ever be in the cards. She wasn't about to discuss it with Rosie, at least not until she worked out what she wanted to do about Terrence's revelation.

"Can I get two of the breakfast specials?" It wasn't a subtle change of subject.

Rosie sighed again. "Coming up." She called the order through the cutout in the wall separating the dining area from the kitchen before focusing on Nikki again. "You must be awfully hungry this morning."

"It's not just for me." Nikki cleared her throat awkwardly. "I'm sure you heard about the fire at Lakewood House."

Rosie nodded. "Yes, of course. I'm so glad you're okay, and I heard there wasn't too much damage."

"No, there wasn't, thankfully. But Terrence was hurt."

Alarm flashed in Rosie's eyes.

"Not badly. Minor burns, but he needed a place to stay, and he had been hurt helping me, so he stayed in the guest room at Lakewood House last night."

Rosie quirked an eyebrow, a small smile starting. "Is that so?"

"Rosie, don't go thinking—"

The bell over the diner door tinkled, drawing Rosie's attention before Nikki could set the record straight.

Melinda swept into the diner. "Good morning, Rosie. Could I get a coffee, please? Nikki!" Melinda leaned forward and placed an air kiss on each of Nikki's cheeks. "I didn't get to chat with you the last time you were here at the diner. It's so lovely to have you back in town."

"Thanks, Melinda. It's nice to see you again as well. How are you?"

"I'm great." Melinda flipped her hair, which flowed in gentle waves today, over her shoulder. "You probably heard I'm thinking about throwing my hat into the ring and running for mayor."

Nikki smiled tightly. "I have heard. Good luck."

"Oh, well, thank you so much, but I don't think I'll be needing luck. I hope I can count on your vote, if you're planning on staying in town, that is."

"I don't really know what my plan is at—"

Melinda cut her off, dropping her voice to a whisper. "I heard about your little professional setback. I'm sure you'll find something. You know, if you're up for it, my campaign will be looking for volunteers soon." Her words dripped with condescension.

"Actually, I'm thinking about running for mayor myself." The words popped out of her mouth, surprising her and Melinda from the stunned look on the other woman's face.

"You're running for mayor?"

The rational part of her brain screamed no, but pride wouldn't let her back down in front of Melinda. "Maybe. I'm considering it."

"You can't possibly believe you'd win."

"Of course she could win," Rosie said, sliding a to-go

cup at Melinda. "She grew up here, and she has political experience."

Melinda frowned. "She hasn't lived here for what? A decade? Come on, Nikki. You don't know the town, the community, like I do."

"I think I know the community very well. And I care about the people in it."

Melinda pulled a few dollar bills from her purse and set them on the counter. "That's all well and good, but do you even meet the qualifications? You have to be a resident of Carling Lake."

"I've moved back into Lakewood House, so that shouldn't be a problem if I choose to run."

Melinda grabbed her coffee, her face scrunched as if she'd smelled something foul. "Well, may the best woman win." She didn't wait for a response before flouncing out of the diner.

"Looks like you may have just made an enemy there, Madam Mayor." Rosie laughed her way into the kitchen.

TERRENCE WASN'T SURE when he'd fallen asleep after having spent most of the night trying to work out if there had been a better way to tell Nikki the truth about their families' feud. Not kissing her before dropping the bomb that he'd blown up their friendship and beginning relationship based on a lie would have probably been a good start. But an inexplicably primal urge had come over him at that moment. He hadn't been able to stop himself. And based on the hurt in her eyes when she'd left his room the night before, that may just be the last time he ever did. His gut clenched at the thought.

He showered and dressed before descending the stairs and padding into the kitchen. Nikki stood in front of the coffee maker, spooning sugar into a steaming coffee mug.

"Good morning."

Her shoulders stiffened. "Morning." She scooped one more spoonful of sugar into the mug and stirred vigorously. "I haven't had a chance to go grocery shopping, so I went by the diner and picked up breakfast."

She pointed to the cardboard carton in the middle of the island, then sat at the other side in front of her own breakfast. It didn't go unnoticed that she'd put as much distance as possible between the two of them while staying in the kitchen.

"Thanks." He grabbed a mug from an overhead cabinet and poured himself a cup, ignoring the sugar and cream Nikki had set out. She'd gotten him pancakes and home fries with a side of bacon and toast. A more decadent and fattening breakfast than the coffee and bagel he was used to, but his stomach was already growling, so he dug in.

A labored silence fell between them as she ardently avoided looking at or speaking to him.

He sighed. "Thanks for letting me stay the night, but I think it's best if I find another place."

Nikki set her coffee cup down on the counter so hard he was amazed it didn't shatter. "So you're going to bail on me again."

"I'm not bailing on you. You're obviously upset with me, and with good reason. I just wanted to give you space."

"I didn't ask for space. Not now. Not then."

"What do you want?"

"I want you to keep your part of our agreement. We work to find Jill and to figure out who is targeting Lakewood House together."

He studied her. Her body language screamed that she was still angry with him, which was bound to be problematic. But the desire to be near her, to prove to her that he really was sorry, was overriding his concerns. That and he wasn't at all sure she was safe on her own. "Okay."

"Okay."

They both returned to sipping their coffee silently for a moment.

"After you left my room last night, I had trouble falling asleep, and I remembered that there were a couple of structures out on Carling Island. Do you remember them?"

Lines formed between her eyebrows. "I think so. A house and a smaller shed or something."

"Yeah, well, I think we should go out there and take a look. Jill could have gone to the island for some reason, and if she hurt herself out there, she'd have no way of calling for help. I do remember there was no cell phone reception on the island."

He could tell before she spoke that he hadn't convinced her. "Last I heard, even the local teens don't go out to that island anymore. And Jill would have needed to borrow or rent a boat to get out there. Even if she drove over by herself, whoever she got the boat from would have raised a red flag when she didn't bring it back."

"Maybe," he answered, annoyed by her pushing back on his plan. Everything she was saying made sense, but he wasn't about to leave any stone unturned when it came to finding his sister. "But maybe she rowed out. Aunt Charity still had the old canoe in her garage the last time I visited."

"We should ask her if it's still there."

"I will, but either way, I want to check out the island. We can't go to Whistler's to track down Dana until later tonight, and I haven't gotten anything from the guys at West Investigations yet, so boots-on-the-ground investigation is all we have left."

"It's a good thing we got the boat from Pete yesterday. We can use it to get to the island."

"Just give me twenty minutes, and I'll be ready to go."

Twenty minutes later, he'd laced up his sturdiest boots and holstered his gun at his hip. He didn't expect trouble on a deserted island, but with the strange goings-on recently, he wanted to be ready for it if it appeared.

He found Nikki on the dock behind Lakewood House. She was already on the boat and had donned a life jacket. "There's a vest for you." She pointed to the bright orange preserver resting against a seat. "I've already done the safety checks, so we're ready to go when you are."

He fastened himself into the vest while Nikki started the boat's engine. She slowly navigated them away from the dock and out onto Carling Lake.

The journey from Lakewood House to Carling Island took nearly a half hour when traveling by canoe, which was how they'd made their way to the island as teens. The *Annalise* got them there in a fraction of the time.

Nikki brought the boat close to the island's dock. It was older than either of them, but surprisingly, it looked to still be in pretty good shape.

He tied the boat off and glanced over at Nikki when she came to stand next to him as he studied the island for the first time in nearly fifteen years. It was still early enough in the morning for a light fog. Carling Island was a big rock in the middle of the lake with a small pebble-strewn shoreline. At the top of a hill at the center of the island stood a time-and storm-ravaged old house. The house had stood unoccupied at least since he and Nikki were kids. Back then, the rumor had been that the house was owned by a New York City banker who'd loved the place almost as much as he'd loved the mistress who he kept hidden away in it. When his wife had found out about the affair and the house, she'd made sure she'd gotten it in the divorce and had let it rot away out of spite. To this day, he had no idea if the story was true or not, but whoever owned the home certainly didn't care about it much.

"There's no other boat docked here," Nikki said. "Not even a canoe."

He'd noticed. Even though he'd known finding Jill on the island was a long shot, he couldn't help but hope that the answer to her disappearance was something as simple as she'd made her way out here and gotten stuck somehow.

"There's another dock on the other side. Maybe her boat is there." It was possible but unlikely that Jill would have had to circle the island to dock there, which wouldn't have made much sense.

From the look on Nikki's face, she was thinking the same thing, but she said nothing.

"Well, we're here now, so let's have a look." He hopped onto the dock, then extended a hand to help Nikki off the boat. She ignored it, making her way without his assistance.

He bit back a curse and fell in step beside her. The breeze followed them up the hill to the house.

All the windows had been covered with plywood

boarding, and they found a new-looking lock on the front door.

"Huh," Nikki said, eyeing the lock. "It seems like someone is keeping up with the property after all."

He inspected the plywood covering the nearest window. It had been through a few storms, but no way had it been there more than a few months. "Yeah, I've been wondering about that since we pulled up to the dock. Someone has clearly been taking care of it, although it could still use some work. It's serviceable though, which would be unlikely if no one had been coming to the island for years."

Lines creased Nikki's forehead. "That is a little weird."

Terrence stepped off the small front porch and headed around the side of the house.

"Where are you going?" Nikki asked, following.

"I want to see if there's another way in."

"Don't you think you might be getting a little bit obsessed with this? I mean, it's pretty obvious Jill isn't here."

He stopped and turned. "You can go wait on the boat. Actually, that might be a good idea. I don't like the feel of this place."

Nikki's expression darkened. "I'm not going to wait for you on the boat. And that feeling you have might just be your internal alarm warning you away from breaking and entering."

"Look, I'm going into this house. You can do whatever you want." He turned and stormed toward the back of the house.

This alliance of theirs was breaking down fast. He knew he was mostly to blame for that, but regardless of responsibility, if they were going to continue working together, they'd have to hash out the past and come to some understanding going forward. He'd wait until they got back to Lakewood House before bringing it up, but they'd have to deal with this. Soon.

The dock at the back of the house was in better shape than the one at the front, increasing the number of concerns and questions he had regarding exactly what was happening on this island. Unfortunately, the rear dock was also noticeably empty of any vessels.

A new lock had also been installed on the rear door of the house. However, whoever had installed the plywood over the windows hadn't done as good of a job back here. One of the pieces of wood had come loose from a rear window and now lay forlorn in the yard near the house. Luckily, the window it had come from was on the first floor. He grabbed the window sash and, with a bit of effort, got it open far enough that he and Nikki could both slide through.

The interior was dark and empty except for animal droppings and copious amounts of trash that appeared to span several decades.

Once they were both inside, he eased the window closed, then jumped as something scurried over his foot.

"We're disturbing the rats," Nikki said, turning on the flashlight on her phone.

He did the same and led the way through the first floor, spying nothing of interest.

"We could split up. One of us searches upstairs while the other searches downstairs. It will make things go faster," he said.

Nikki looked at him as if he'd grown two heads. "Um, I don't even want to be in this creepy house. I'm definitely not going exploring on my own."

"We stick together then."

They headed toward the front of the house. The large two-story entryway opened onto a circular staircase leading to the second floor. He climbed the stairs, taking each step gingerly. Four doors branched off the hallway. They checked each of the rooms, finding more trash covered in a thick layer of dirt and grime.

They crept back down the stairs. Off the foyer was a single door. He opened it and found that it led to a set of stairs to the basement. They headed down with their cell phones, providing only a small circle of light around their immediate area. The basement was so dark it was difficult to make out anything. They could have been walking into a trap or a completely empty space. It was impossible to know.

The staircase ended at a dirt floor. He held the phone out, moving it in a slow circular motion, illuminating the space in front of him.

The basement was utterly empty. Even the decades-old detritus and animal droppings they'd found upstairs were absent from the space, which immediately put him on alert. Someone had cleaned up down here, that much was obvious. But why clean the basement and not the main floor?

"What is that?" Nikki took several steps forward, shining the light from her phone toward one corner of the room.

He grabbed her arm and pulled her back. "Hang on. Let me go first." He wasn't sure what he was looking at, but he wasn't going to take any chances. He held the phone out in one hand and hovered his other hand at the gun on his hip.

He stepped forward slowly, conscious that Nikki was at his back, letting his brain process what he was seeing.

Handcuffs. No, that wasn't accurate. Shackles. Four

metal cuffs attached to chains attached to metal loops bolted to the concrete wall in what he estimated to be six-feet intervals.

"Dear God," Nikki whispered from behind him. "It's like a prison."

More like a dungeon. His mind flashed onto a picture of the young girl they'd found at Lakewood House. He had a strong suspicion who had been held here. They needed to get out of this house now.

He turned to face Nikki and relay that urgent message, but before he could get it out, a sharp creak sounded above them, followed by footsteps.

Someone else was in the house.

They were trapped.

Chapter Fourteen

Nikki's heart pounded frantically. Terrence raised a finger to his lips and shut off the light on his phone. She did the same with her own phone. There was no way out of the house without going back upstairs, and she doubted very much whoever was up there now was friendly. She glanced at the shackles on the ground and shuddered. Definitely not friendly.

"We have to get out of here," Terrence whispered. "Follow me, and on my signal, run for the boat as fast as you can. I'll be right behind you." He paused before speaking again. "But if I'm not, don't wait for me. Go. Get to Lance."

She shook her head. "I'm not leaving you. We came to this island together and we're leaving together."

She held his gaze until he finally gave a short nod.

He took her hand, and they started up the stairs slowly, making their footsteps as soft and quiet as possible. They stopped at the top of the stairs. The door was still firmly closed, but the voices on the other side of it were loud enough to hear most of what was being said.

"What are we going to do?" The voice was deep and male.

A different male, one with a higher voice, responded, "...moved the goods...okay for now but...it's only temporary." Nikki hadn't caught the entire response, but the part she had made it clear whatever the men were doing in this house, it wasn't on the right side of legal.

It did appear as if she and Terrence had gotten lucky on one front, however. The voices sounded as if they were coming from the rear of the house, where the men must have docked their boat. That would explain why they hadn't seen the *Annalise* and why they appeared to be oblivious to the presence of anyone else on the island with them—at least so far. That could change in an instant if either of the men came downstairs or went outside to the front of the house.

"What do we do about our other problem?"

"Why are you asking me so many questions? I don't know. I'll figure it out. I just need some time, okay." Footsteps pounded on the old wood floors.

Terrence brought his mouth to her ear. "I think they're at the back of the house. As quickly but as quietly as you can, head for the front door and the boat."

She nodded her agreement and held her breath as Terrence pushed the basement door open. She followed him into the small hall, then eased by him toward the front door. There was no sign of the men. They'd either stopped talking or moved into a room where they couldn't be heard from the hall.

Nikki did as Terrence had instructed and moved as quickly and quietly to the front door as she could. The door squeaked when she pulled it open. She didn't stop to see if the men had heard. As soon as her foot hit the front porch, she began to run.

The hill hadn't seemed steep or treacherous when she and Terrence had climbed up to the house, but running at top speed had her concerned about falling and possibly breaking a bone. Or her neck. Fear of falling kept her from glancing over her shoulder to see if Terrence was behind her as he'd promised. She said a quick prayer he was and kept moving.

She made it to the dock, adrenaline giving her an extra boost as she leaped onto the boat. She went straight for the rope tied to the dock.

Her heart went into her throat when the boat rocked and she felt the presence of another person on board. She was relieved to see Terrence scrambling for the steering wheel.

The relief was short-lived.

The men from the house had spotted them. They ran down the hill toward the dock, guns raised.

The noise from the engine starting almost covered the sound of gunshots. Almost. Bullets pelted the water on either side of the boat as Terrence pulled away from the dock at a speed much faster than was safe.

"Get down," he yelled, ducking as much as he could himself.

She did as he said and felt the boat lurch forward as he pushed the *Annalise* to go even faster.

The men were running on the dock, still firing. But the boat was too far away now for the bullets from their handguns to have a chance.

Nikki raised her head above the side of the boat to get a look at their pursuers. Both were white men who appeared to be in their late twenties or early thirties. One was stocky, and though it was hard to gauge how tall he was, given the distance between them now, he was taller than the second man by a couple of inches. Both were dressed in work boots, jeans and dark windbreakers. The stocky man had dark hair while the shorter guy had a lighter, though not quite blond, mane. The boat careened around a corner, and she lost sight of them.

She rose and went to Terrence's side.

"I'm not taking us back to Lakewood House," he said without looking at her. "Just in case."

Her heart was still beating a mile a minute, and the grave expression on Terrence's face did nothing to slow it. "Just in case of what?"

His expression grew darker, and he didn't respond.

Her thoughts whirled with possibilities until one pushed its way to the forefront of her mind. "Oh, God. Do you think they are headed for the house?"

"The public access is closer to the sheriff's station. I'll dock us there. Lance needs to know about this as soon as possible, and I won't be able to get cell service this far out on the water."

"You didn't answer my question."

He shot her a glance but remained quiet for the rest of the short ride to the dock.

At the dock, she tied up the boat. Terrence had his phone out and was calling the sheriff before they'd stepped off the boat.

Nikki's phone vibrated as they headed for the sheriff's office. Ryan West had sent an email with the information he'd promised and copied Sheriff Webb and Terrence.

Minutes later, they were in a small conference room with the sheriff sitting across from them, taking notes as they recounted their ordeal. He'd already sent two deputies out to Carling Island with a promise to follow up as soon as he got the details from Nikki and Terrence.

"Shackles?" Sheriff Webb's brows went up to his hairline.

"Bolted to the wall. Four of them side by side." Nikki shuddered at the memory. "It was like some medieval prison."

"Not *like* a prison. It *was* a prison for someone—multiple someones," Terrence said gravely.

The sheriff tapped his pen against his notepad. "You have a theory?"

"Unfortunately, I do."

Dread twisted into a knot in Nikki's stomach. Instinctively, she knew whatever Terrence's theory was, she wasn't going to like it. Though she supposed a basement full of shackles was never going to lead to anything good.

"I think the men who shot at us are part of a human trafficking ring. The dead woman we found was probably one of their victims," Terrence said.

"Human trafficking in Carling Lake?" The disbelief in Sheriff Webb's voice was palpable.

Terrence frowned. "No one thinks it could happen in their town, but trafficking is far more widespread than people know or want to admit."

"I know all that but..." the sheriff started.

"Listen, those shackles were in that house for a reason. And you can't deny the extensive abuse that woman we found suffered. Carling Lake has easy access to the interstate, and if those guys have been hiding women on the island, who would know?"

Nikki could see Sheriff Webb gearing up to defend his hometown, and while she understood the sentiment, she'd been raised in Carling Lake, and she still thought of it as her home. Terrence had made good points, but there were holes in his logic.

She held up her hand. "Terrence's theory has some merit, but I don't see how anyone could transport people back and forth to the island without someone noticing. I mean, on any given day, there are fishermen, day cruises and any number of other people out on the lake."

"Carling Lake might just be a pass through on the way to wherever the final destination is," Terrence said. "One of many, probably. That's most likely, actually. It's a tourist town, so locals will be used to seeing unfamiliar faces. Traffickers generally have several different routes mapped out for moving their victims around the country. Even out of the country. They switch up their routes to better avoid detection. These guys might only bring their victims through Carling Lake once a month or once every couple of months. And if they are working under the cover of night, it's more than possible no one has noticed. Or someone has noticed but didn't know what they were seeing or didn't think anything of it."

Nikki sat beside Terrence at the table, but she turned to face him head-on now. "How does Lakewood House figure into your theory?" Because she knew it did somehow. The vandalism. The fire. Finding the woman's body on the property. His refusal to take them back to Lakewood House after those guys shot at them.

Terrence looked her in the eye. "If you're a bad guy and you need access to the private lake, what better place than an empty house with a dock?"

Nikki swallowed hard. Somewhere inside, she knew that he'd hit the nail on the head, but she wasn't ready to accept it. "You're saying you think human traffickers have been using Lakewood House to smuggle women?"

Terrence nodded.

Nikki lurched forward, putting her head between her legs in an attempt to stop the bile rising in her throat.

Sheriff Webb pushed to his feet and went to the small fridge in the corner of his office. "Take it easy. This is only a theory."

Terrence rubbed her back in small circles. "Breathe.

That's it. Look, even if I'm right, there's nothing you could have done to stop this. You aren't responsible."

She accepted the cold bottle of water from the sheriff without lifting her head. "How can I not be responsible? I own Lakewood House. I should have known what was going on there. I should have installed a security system, video cameras, an alarm, something."

Terrence stopped rubbing her back. "You hired Pete Bonny to be the caretaker."

She sensed more than saw the look that passed between the two men. She straightened. "You think Pete has something to do with human…this?" She couldn't bring herself to say the words in relation to the man she knew. Pete was a difficult person, but preying on vulnerable women? He'd have to be a monster.

Sheriff Webb's jaw twitched. "I'm definitely going to have a talk with him. If he's not involved, he might have seen something."

Terrence stood. "Maybe I should go—"

The sheriff held out a hand. "Absolutely not." Terrence shot him a death glare. "You know how these investigations go. There is a protocol. You have no jurisdiction here."

Terrence glanced at Sheriff Webb. "I think Jill stumbled on this human trafficking ring, and she came up here to investigate. If Pete or somebody else involved realized she knew about what they were doing and grabbed her…" Emotion filled Terrence's voice.

Nikki took his hand in her own. "We don't know that's what happened."

He looked at her. "When those guys were talking back at the house, they said they'd 'moved the goods.' I think they were talking about moving their victims to another place where they'd be less likely to be found.

One also asked what they should do about 'their other problem.' I think they were talking about Jill. What else could 'the other problem' be?"

The sheriff put a hand on Terrence's shoulder. "A lot of things. Don't let your imagination run away with you, man. It won't help. Work with what you know. Good, solid investigative work is what's going to help us find your sister."

"Sheriff Webb is right. West Investigations sent us what they found on the fleur-de-lis." She'd recalled seeing the email while Terrence spoke to the sheriff after they'd docked the boat. "Let's comb through that and see if we can find any connections that will help us find Jill while the sheriff pursues this."

She could tell he wasn't happy about it, but Terrence finally nodded. "Okay."

Some of the tension in Sheriff Webb's shoulders eased. "I'll have a deputy accompany you back to Lakewood House. Those guys are probably on their way out of town as we speak, but I'm not taking any chances. My deputies have taken the department boat out to Carling Island. Nikki, would you mind if I borrowed your boat?"

"Of course not."

The sheriff looked between Nikki and Terrence. "This situation just got infinitely more serious. I think both of you may be in more danger than you realize. My advice? Get as far away from Carling Lake as you can."

Chapter Fifteen

Terrence had no intention of taking Lance's advice, and although he did wish Nikki would, he knew it would be a waste of time to broach the topic with her. Lance had Deputy Bridges drive them back to Lakewood House with instructions that the deputy should stay and keep watch over the house until Lance returned with Nikki's boat.

They rode in silence until Deputy Bridges said, "So, Nikki, I heard you're running for mayor."

Terrence's eyebrows rose. "You are? You've been back for what, a day? Two?"

Nikki frowned. "I know this town as well as anyone. I grew up here, and unlike you, I came home regularly."

"I didn't say you didn't. I'm just surprised you'd want to take on such a big responsibility so soon after moving back."

"I didn't say I was running for mayor, just that I was considering it, and I only said that much because I let Melinda Hanes get under my skin."

"Ah, well, you're not alone in that. That woman could rub the pope the wrong way," Deputy Bridges said with a wry smile.

"I think you'd make a great mayor," Terrence said. And he did. She'd always cared about people. And she had more integrity than any person he'd ever met.

Nikki shot him a look from the other side of the car. "Two seconds ago, you sounded mortified by the idea."

"I was surprised, but the more I think about it, the better it sounds. You love this town. You love politics, obviously, and you're a great leader."

She studied him like she wasn't quite sure what to make of his compliment for a moment. "Well, then thank you. But like I said, I don't know if I'm really running. I've got a line on a job back in DC, and if that pans out, it makes a lot more sense than running for mayor."

"I'm sure you'll make the right decision for you," Terrence said as Bridges turned the cruiser onto Lakewood House's driveway.

The deputy remained idling in the driveway when Terrence and Nikki got out of the car and went into the house.

Terrence pulled out his phone as he headed up the stairs to his room.

"What are you doing now?" Nikki asked.

He turned back halfway up the stairs. "I need to call Jill's editor. If Jill was onto a trafficking ring here in Carling Lake, he would know. I talked to him when I couldn't get a hold of Jill, but he blew me off. Told me not to worry, Jill would turn up, and he wouldn't tell me anything about what she was working on."

"And you think you can get him to tell you now?"

Terrence's eyes lit with fire. "Oh, I know he will."

Colby Marquez's gravelly voice came over the line after the second ring. "Marquez."

"Mr. Marquez, this is Terrence Sutton. Jill Sutton's brother."

"Oh, Mr. Sutton. How are you? Has Jill been in touch?"

"She has not, and I'm more concerned than ever."

"Well, as I told you before, I can't share anything about what your sister was working on."

"Law enforcement talks. What do you think your sources on the DC force would think about an editor who's unwilling to help an officer find his missing sister?"

"You're blackmailing me?"

"No. But I will if that's what it takes to find my sister. When I'm done, no cop in the tristate area will talk to your reporters. Is that what you want?"

"Come on, Jill is a professional. She can handle herself."

"I have reason to believe Jill learned of a human trafficking ring operating in our hometown of Carling Lake. I can't prove it yet, but I think she came here and either asked someone the wrong question or saw something she shouldn't have. Now she's disappeared. If anything happens to her because you didn't tell me everything you know, losing sources will be the least of your troubles. I'll make sure of it."

"Hang on." Marquez's voice rose.

"No, you hang on. There's no way Jill would have chased a story this big without talking to you about it first."

A loud sigh came from the other side of the line. "Okay, okay. Jill did bring me a story about a possible human trafficking ring. But her sources were spurious at best. A woman contacted her saying that her sister, who'd run away several years earlier, had been in touch asking for help. The woman wouldn't give her name or any details at all, but she said that she'd been able to track the call through her cell phone provider as having come from Carling Lake."

"Did the woman say anything else?"

"Not that Jill mentioned."

"Nothing about a fleur-de-lis?"

"A fleur…no. I told you everything that Jill told me. And I told her it wasn't enough to warrant pursuing, considering her other assignments."

"Is there anything else at all you can tell me that might help me find Jill?"

"No, nothing. Do you… Do you really think she is onto a human trafficking ring?"

Terrence ignored the question. "Is there anyone else Jill would have spoken to about this?"

"You know Jill. She keeps her cards close to her vest. She barely tells me anything." Marquez paused. "So you really think Jill is in trouble?"

"I really do." Terrence let out a breath. "Call me if you or anyone at the paper hears from her, okay?"

He ended the call and glanced out the window, looking onto the front yard at Lakewood House. The sheriff's department cruiser was still parked in the driveway. The call to Jill's editor had all but confirmed his suspicions about why Jill had come to Carling Lake. And it had sent the fear he felt for his sister into the stratosphere.

Despite the persuasiveness of Lance and Nikki's argument for why he should let Lance handle the investigation, he couldn't help but feel he should also be out on the island, looking for any clues that might lead them to Jill's whereabouts. Or better yet, tracking down Pete Bonny. He was sure now that Pete had recognized the fleur-de-lis and was kicking himself for not pressing the issue with the man. Lance had promised to send a deputy to question Pete, but whether he had already done so and what had come of it, Terrence didn't yet know. There was no point in calling Lance either. He said he'd bring the *Annalise* back to Lakewood House when he finished his investigation, and there was no cell service on the island.

He'd have to wait, not his strong suit in the best of circumstances, and this certainly wasn't the best of circumstances.

Terrence retrieved his laptop and headed back downstairs as Nikki emerged from the fire-ravaged office with a .22 and an ankle holster in her hand.

"You sure it's safe to be in there?" he asked.

"Safe enough." She placed the gun next to her laptop on the coffee table in front of the couch, then sat, lifting her leg and strapping on the ankle holster.

"I thought you didn't like guns." He sat down next to her.

"I don't. But we're talking about potential human traffickers here who have already shot at us." She snapped the gun into the holster and covered it with the cuff of her pant leg. "So, how should we do this? Split up the information West sent us?" She pulled her laptop onto her lap.

"That's probably the fastest way. There are only a few files. Why don't you take the last three attachments, and I'll work through the first three? Then we can summarize them for each other or point out anything we think the other should read for themselves."

"Sounds like a plan."

The first of the three files he was supposed to read was a Word document. A report that looked to have been prepared by West that combined a variety of source information about a criminal enterprise being run out of the southwest states. What had once been a loose partnership between various gangs with territory along the border in Texas, New Mexico and Arizona had in recent years gotten more organized. Based on the information he was reading, these guys were a nasty bunch of creeps known to be involved in drugs, gunrunning, identity theft and smuggling people over the border for exorbitant sums. Just the kind of people who wouldn't think twice about branching out into human trafficking. The truly interesting part, though, was that members of the gang each had a tattoo of a symbol that resembled a fleur-de-lis, the same fleur-de-lis that Nikki had found on the business card at Lakewood.

Ding ding ding! They had a winner. These had to be the guys they were looking for.

"I think I've got something." He shifted closer to Nikki on the sofa. The scent of her lilac perfume tickled his nose, reminding him of their kiss the previous night. He shook off the memory and forced himself to focus. "This report is about a gang out of the southwest that uses the fleur-de-lis symbol to self-identify."

Nikki's eyes scanned his screen. "Not a very scary symbol for guys involved in all this." She pointed to the computer.

"No, but if you're trying to fly under the radar, it's less suspicious than a skull and crossbones. Most importantly, if they are already involved in smuggling desperate people across the border, they have the means and opportunity to make the leap into trafficking."

Nikki looked away from the screen and out the window. "You know, as much as I don't want to believe something so vile could be taking place in Carling Lake, it seems more and more likely that you're right about what's been going on here."

"I don't want to believe it either, but—"

The rest of his sentence was cut off by the sound of an approaching car outside.

He went to the window and immediately recognized the lawyer's car from yesterday.

"That lawyer, Chester, is back."

"Why is it some people can't take no for an answer?"

"Do you want me to deal with him?" He opened the door.

Nikki grabbed his wrist, stopping him. "No, I got this."

She moved past him and out onto the porch. He followed her outside.

The deputy was already approaching the car.

"It's okay, Deputy. I know this man." Nikki walked from the porch toward the car.

Terrence wouldn't have gone that far. They didn't know anything about Chester, but he planned to remedy that as soon as possible. He'd all but forgotten about the lawyer's offer to buy Lakewood House, but now he couldn't help but wonder whether the offer on Lakewood House wasn't a coincidence.

"Ms. King," Chester said, eyeing the deputy as he retreated back to his cruiser. "I was hoping you had time to give some thought to my client's offer."

"I'm sorry if I didn't make myself clear when you visited the first time, but I'm not selling."

"Now let's not be hasty. My client understands it can be emotional to part with a home. We are willing to increase our offer by a substantial amount to ease your transition from the home."

He recognized the suspicion in Nikki's eyes. "A substantial amount?"

Chester's smile was cocksure. "Fifty thousand dollars. But my client is very anxious to close this deal and take possession of the house, so we'd need an answer in forty-eight hours."

"Well, I've already given you my answer. Lakewood House is not now, nor will it ever be, for sale."

Chester's smile fell.

"I do have a question for you though. Why is your client so interested in purchasing Lakewood House?"

"I'm afraid I can't share that with you," he said with irritation in his voice.

"Then I don't think we have anything else to talk about. I'd like you off my property."

Chester glared. "Ms. King—"

Terrence took a small step forward. "The lady asked you to leave."

The two men scowled at each other for a moment before Chester shifted his markedly chillier gaze back to Nikki. "My client is willing to wait another forty-eight hours. I suggest you use that time to seriously consider their offer. I assure you, it's in your best interest to do so."

"Did that sound like a threat to you?" Nikki asked as they watched Chester back out of the driveway.

There was no doubt in Terrence's mind it was a threat. And Chester and his client were about to discover he didn't take kindly to his friends being threatened.

Chapter Sixteen

Deputy Bridges resumed his watch, and Terrence followed Nikki back inside the house.

"I'm going to take this upstairs to my room. I'll let you know if I find anything." Nikki grabbed her laptop and hurried up the stairs.

He didn't try to stop her. He needed to make a call that he didn't want her to overhear, anyway. Moments later, he was on the line with Ryan West.

"I have a favor to ask," Terrence said once they'd gotten through the initial pleasantries.

"Shoot."

He gave Ryan the truncated version of the events that had taken place in the last couple of days, as well as his theory about the possibility that the gang Ryan had sent them information on had ventured into human trafficking.

"That's some pretty heavy stuff, but that crew is nasty enough to be involved."

"And if they are, they're more dangerous than I imagined. Nikki's home is isolated and without any security at all. I'm wondering if you can't help me out with a recommendation for a system. Something I can get locally and fast."

"Of course. I'll look into it today and get back to you ASAP."

"Thanks."

Terrence spent the next two hours calling his law enforcement contacts in the southwest to dig up the information that never made it into the official reports or news articles. Anything at all on suspected gang members or crimes that the cops were sure the gang pulled but couldn't prove. The unofficial files all cops kept in their heads or in old notebooks. Theories, gut feelings, rumors that couldn't be used in a court of law or even to bring a person in for questioning.

Lance returned Nikki's boat in the late afternoon. He'd found the dungeon basement and copious amounts of trash, but not much else. He had been able to pull several fingerprints from the shackles and was hopeful something would pop there. He left with Deputy Bridges as dusk began to fall.

When Terrence finally stopped for dinner—spaghetti marinara Nikki prepared while he'd been on the calls—he was surprised to find that she had done some calling of her own.

She slid handwritten notes across the table toward him. "Cops aren't the only ones with sources. I called a couple of reporters I know in Texas and Arizona. That's what they know about the gang."

It was the most she'd said to him since they'd gotten back from the sheriff's office. Despite their harrowing experience earlier in the day, it was clear she was still angry with him. He still thought they needed to sit down and hash things out so they could move forward as friends, or maybe more. Being shot at by a couple of thugs had put one thing in perspective, and that was that he still cared about Nikki. He'd regret for the rest of his life having let his pride come between them. And if he could make it right? Get them back on the track they'd been on before he'd blown up their burgeoning relationship? He was open to it if she was.

But now was not the time for that discussion. Especially when there was another, more pressing discussion they needed to have.

He'd finished his dinner in record time, hungrier than he'd realized. He set his fork across the now empty plate and spoke. "I want to head over to Whistler's at nine. It's a little early for that crowd, but I want to make sure I don't miss Dana if he shows up tonight."

Nikki wiped her mouth with a napkin. "Okay, I can be ready to go at nine."

"About that."

She held up a hand and glared across the table at him. "I'm going."

"Whistler's is no place for a lady. Hell, it's no place for a man. The people who frequent that place are volatile when they aren't drunk. I think it would be best if you stay here and let me go alone."

"You've been telling me for days that staying at Lakewood House alone wasn't safe for me. Now it is?"

He gritted his teeth. "You know that's different. I can call Lance and have him send another deputy."

"That won't be necessary. If it's safe enough for you to go, it's safe enough for me to go." She rose and carried her plate to the sink before striding from the kitchen.

He sighed, resigned. "I guess we're both going then."

Nikki was waiting for him by the front door at nine. They made the twenty-minute drive to Whistler's in silence. The bar was housed in a one-story building with a gravel parking lot and glitchy pink-and-yellow neon Open sign over the door.

The lot was already half-full when they pulled in. A couple of motorcycles, two or three muscle cars and a handful of pickups ranging in newness were parked in haphazard rows.

Terrence backed the Highlander into a spot at the very end of the lot nearest to the exit. He'd have preferred parking closer to the door in case they needed to beat a hasty retreat, but this was the only area of the gravel lot where he couldn't be blocked in by another vehicle. It would have to do. Hopefully, Dana would be inside and be willing to answer a few questions. Even though he had the thought, he couldn't bring himself to believe it.

Two men loitered outside the door. Given that it wasn't the kind of bar that strictly enforced the laws about smoking inside, Terrence could only imagine what sort of business had necessitated the men stepping outside.

He shut off the engine and turned to Nikki. "Are you sure you want to do this?"

She rolled her eyes at him and reached for the door handle. "Yes. Now come on. Let's go."

He got out and walked around to her side of the Highlander. The men at the door eyed them suspiciously but moved farther away from the entrance, disappearing around the side of the building as they approached.

He took a steadying breath, then held the door open for Nikki to enter. Only half the heads in the bar turned toward them when they entered. Although this was his first time inside, Whistler's had been around since he and Nikki were kids, and its reputation hadn't changed much over the years. If anything, it had gotten worse. It was the kind of place that attracted people who didn't want to know your name. Or anything else about anybody who frequented Whistler's.

A couple of really rough-looking guys sat at a table at the rear of the bar, their heads huddled together. A table in the middle of the space hosted four men clad in leather. Two of them had scantily clad women, also in leather, sitting on their laps. At a booth near the door, a man who looked like he'd seen better days nursed a beer and stared sightlessly at the television over the bar, although there was no way he could have possibly heard it over the music blaring from the overhead speaker and the chatter of the other patrons.

They grabbed two empty stools on the far side of the bar. Terrence took the stool next to the wall and turned so his back was to it. He wasn't about to put his back to anyone in this place.

He scanned the people in the bar. They'd all gone back to whatever they'd been doing before he and Nikki walked in. None of the men in the bar looked remotely familiar.

He held up two fingers when the bartender sidled over, and said, "Jack on the rocks." One of Nikki's brows went up when the bartender turned his back. "Trust me, you would not want to sample the wine selection in a place like this."

The corners of her mouth crept up and his stomach did a flip-flop.

Terrence had his phone out when the bartender returned with their drinks. "Have you seen this woman? She's my sister and she's been missing for a few days." He thrust the phone at the bartender before the man had the chance to walk away, hoping to tug at his heart-strings a bit. The bartender was an older man, slightly stooped over and balding, who looked to be in his seventies, although Terrence suspected he was quite a bit younger and hard living had just taken its toll.

Nikki looked at him with a question in her eyes. They were at Whistler's to find Dana, but it wouldn't hurt to ask about Jill as well.

The bartender gave Jill's photo a long look. "Can't say that I have. Sorry."

Terrence bit back a curse. He'd been hoping to find some concrete evidence that he was on the right track with the theory that Jill had found out about the trafficking ring and begun her own investigation.

The bartender's eyes slid over to Nikki. She gave him a smile, and after shooting a quick, wary gaze at Terrence, he turned back to her with a tentative one of his own.

Jealousy tangled a knot in his stomach. He narrowed hard eyes on the bartender.

"How about this symbol?" Nikki elbowed him lightly and motioned to his phone. He swiped to the photo of the fleur-de-lis, then turned the screen so the bartender could see it.

He didn't look as long this time. "Nope. Sorry."

It was a long shot, but Terrence was still disappointed.

Two strikes. If Dana didn't show up, the night would be a complete bust.

"Thanks anyway." Nikki's smile for the bartender grew brighter.

"Your next drink is on the house." He winked.

Terrence tossed back his whiskey and tried to reason with the green-eyed monster clawing at his insides. If a bit of flirting got the information, it was more than worth it for him to play the silent sidekick.

"That's kind of you." Nikki shifted on her stool and leaned closer to the bar. "You know, I grew up in Carling Lake. An old friend of mine actually recommended this place. Said he comes in here a lot. I was kinda hoping to see him tonight. Dana Bonny."

"Yeah, Dana. He's over there at his regular table." The bartender jerked his head toward the table with the tough-looking guys, and Terrence saw what he hadn't when they'd first walked in. Another smaller table in the dark corner behind them with a single man hunched over a glass. "He showed up early tonight, already three sheets to the wind."

Nikki turned in the direction the bartender indicated. Her eyes went wide, and she grabbed his arm, squeezing tightly enough to make him wince. "Terrence, that's one of the guys who shot at us earlier today."

He shifted a bit, trying to get a better look at the man in the corner. He'd been too busy getting them away from Carling Island to get a good look at the men who'd shot at them, and although the man in the corner did fit the description of the shorter man Nikki described to Lance, he looked nothing like the Dana of fifteen years ago.

"Stay here," Terrence said in a voice that brooked no disagreement.

He pushed away from the bar, and once again became the focus of several of the patrons.

Dana looked up.

Terrence may not have recognized Dana, but Dana seemed to have no trouble recognizing him. He was out of his seat in an instant, launching the half-full glass that had been on the table in front of him a moment earlier through the air.

Unfortunately, Dana had the aim of a drunk. The

glass went wide, hitting a very large man with a scar trisecting his cheek in the back of his head.

The mood in the bar shifted in a flash.

Terrence held up his hands in a surrender pose as Scarface turned in his direction. "Hey, my friend is drunk. He's sorry, man." He didn't dare take his eyes off Scarface to see where Dana had gone.

The apology had no effect. Scarface stepped forward and threw a punch that landed on Terrence's face.

His head snapped back, but he recovered quickly and came up swinging. Scarface was big but slow and untrained. Terrence threw another punch and sent him flying backward over a table.

Another man from the table charged. The next several minutes was chaos, with patrons of the bar either throwing punches, dodging blows or scrambling to get out of the bar. He mentally kicked himself for having brought Nikki along and hoped she'd taken cover.

He glanced at the bar where she'd been sitting, but a hard right hook kept him from determining whether she was still there. He drove a fist into the stomach of the man who'd just hit him, then threw an elbow at another man who'd jumped into the fray.

The sheriff would no doubt have already gotten a call about the melee and was on the way, so he could expect to have a black eye and get an earful all in one night.

And all for nothing, since he hadn't gotten to question Dana, who'd somehow managed to disappear in the mayhem.

He pushed through the bodies toward the bar. Nikki was crouched between the two seats they'd been sitting in before the fighting started. He grabbed her and pulled her toward the swinging door that led to the kitchen. He stayed close behind as they fled out of the door leading from the kitchen outside, apparently not being the first to take this route since the door stood wide open.

They rounded the building and ran toward the Highlander. He pulled out of the parking lot and pointed them toward Carling Lake just as the first sirens sounded behind them.

Nikki turned in the passenger seat. He glanced at the rearview mirror. Three sheriff's cruisers turned into the parking lot behind them.

Nikki faced forward. "I guess Dana didn't want to talk."

"No, I guess he didn't."

Dana may have gotten away, but now that he was sure Pete's nephew was involved in whatever was going on in Carling Lake, he wouldn't let Dana slip away so easily the next time.

Chapter Seventeen

Despite the chilly night, Nikki put the car window down and let the breeze wash over her. Adrenaline raced, still pumped through her veins. She'd never been in a bar fight before, but if she ever was again, she wanted Terrence by her side. He was amazing.

"You okay?" Terrence asked.

She was still shaking, but she didn't think he could see that in the dark interior of the car. She took a deep breath and let it out. "Yeah, I'm… I'm fine." At least she hoped she would be by the time they got back to Lakewood House.

The look on his face said he didn't believe her.

She peered at him. "I should be the one asking you if you're okay. You got it worse than I did." She reached across the car and touched the cut above his right eye.

He winced and she drew her hand back. "I'll be okay. A few bumps and bruises. They'll heal in a couple of days."

Nikki was glad she wasn't driving. She couldn't have recounted the route they took to get home, but suddenly they were pulling to a stop in front of the house.

They entered the house, and Nikki switched on the lights.

Terrence's eyes narrowed, and he swore. "You're

bleeding." He ran the pad of his thumb lightly over her cheek.

She hadn't felt a thing, but when she turned to look at herself in the mirror next to the door, there was a bright red slash along her right cheek. As if acknowledging the injury had somehow made it real, she could suddenly feel the throbbing pain in her cheek.

"Come on." Terrence led her upstairs, easing her down to sit on his bed, then marched into the bathroom connecting their rooms.

He returned with a handful of cotton balls and a bottle of hydrogen peroxide. "I should have never let you go into that bar. I'm so sorry I put you in danger." He sat next to her and soaked a cotton ball in peroxide.

"It's just a scratch," she said, flinching as he gently swabbed the cotton ball over her cheek. "And I wanted to go with you. I wanted to help you."

"I'm not sure I deserve your help." Terrence didn't look at her as he spoke, focusing on wetting another cotton ball.

She took the cotton from his hand and drew it over the cut over his eye.

He flinched but didn't look up. She placed a finger under his chin and lifted his face until his gaze met hers. "You deserve it and you have it."

His mouth was inches from hers. She wasn't sure who leaned in, but in a moment her lips were on his, the time and emotional distance that had been between them forgotten in a wave of blinding arousal. She felt his hands on her face, a gentle feathery touch that slid down her arms and to her waist. He pulled her onto his lap, taking their kiss from soft and tentative to hungry. She met his desire with her own fiery need.

His lips moved from her mouth to her throat while

his hands roamed beneath her cotton top. "Are you sure about this?"

She was sure she wanted this. Wanted him. But warning bells were going off in her brain. She knew she should heed them, but she also knew she wouldn't. Tonight was tonight. It didn't have to be anything more than that. One night. And tomorrow? To paraphrase Scarlett O'Hara, tomorrow was another day. She'd deal with whatever the fallout was then. Based on the way Terrence's hands felt roaming over her back, cupping her backside and pulling her even closer to him, it was a night that would be well worth it.

She arched her back, pressing her core into his throbbing erection. "I'm sure."

Terrence groaned, then shifted so that seconds later, she was on her back on the bed. Terrence eased his body over hers.

Need crackled between them. He found her mouth again, and they kissed, molding their bodies, one to fit the other, even as their clothes became an increasingly intolerable barrier.

Her fingers went to the waistband of his jeans. He shed his clothing quickly, then stripped her.

His hands and lips traveled over her with abandon. She loved the feeling of him. The hard curves of his body. The smell of his aftershave. The softness of his lips.

Their kisses became more tender even as their urgency to couple grew exponentially. She loved what his touch was doing to her, his hot kisses on her most intimate places eliciting sensations in her that she'd never felt before. There'd been other men, but none of them had ever made her feel the way Terrence was making her feel at this moment.

Her body throbbed for him. "Terrence, please."

He pulled away long enough to grab a condom and sheath himself.

Her eyes were trained on his face as he slid inside her. Raw emotion, emotion she saw reflected in Terrence's eyes, ricocheted through her. They moved together, spiraling ever closer to ecstasy. The magnitude of the sensations swirling deep inside her made her shudder. She ran her fingers over his broad chest and shifted to bring him in deeper.

"You feel so good." He dropped his head to her breast, almost as if in prayer. When he lifted his head again, his eyes were hazy with desire. He kissed her hard, a kiss she greedily returned.

Sparks shot through her, heat permeating her entire being. She wanted more, needed more, even as each shock of pleasure had her wondering if she could stand more. Energy pulsed between them, tethering her to Terrence in a way she'd never felt before.

A way she was sure in that moment she could never feel with anyone else.

When she finally tumbled over, Terrence was right there with her.

Afterward, neither of them moved or even spoke. Nikki rested her head against Terrence's chest and listened to his heartbeat, content to lie entwined for however long this lasted.

She wasn't sure what had passed between them, but it was real and powerful.

And it had the potential to break her heart all over again.

NIKKI STARED AT the man sleeping beside her. They'd been little more than kids when they'd dated back in high school and college. He'd been her first lover, and for a time, she'd thought he would be her only lover. Although they'd never explicitly discussed a long-term future, it's where she'd thought their relationship was headed back then. It wasn't meant to be, but she'd never forgotten how making love with Terrence had felt. As if she were safe. Adored. Home. The way it felt last night. And maybe that was why she felt a little ill at the thought that sleeping with him couldn't happen again.

Terrence opened his eyes, a smile spreading across his lips. "Good morning."

"Good morning."

"What time is it?"

"Quarter to nine."

He yawned. "It's early." He reached for her. "Especially given our late night."

Nikki slid from his grip, grabbing Terrence's shirt from the floor and shrugging into it. She turned back to face Terrence, who'd pushed up into a sitting position. "We need to talk."

"Words a man never likes to hear the morning after."

She released a deep breath. "Last night was incredible, but I don't think it should happen again."

"Last night was incredible, and that's exactly why I think it should happen again. I'd be thrilled if it happened again right now."

Despite her attempt not to, her eyes fell to his lap. He wasn't exaggerating. He was more than ready for a repeat of last night's exploits. Her sex began to throb in response. She dragged her focus back to his face before she gave in to the desire that was building inside her.

"I'm serious, Terrence."

He gave her a lascivious smile. "I've never been more serious in my life."

"Terrence."

"Nikki, come back to bed." He patted the spot next to him that she'd vacated.

"Last night was great, but it doesn't change anything that's happened between us. There's still years of hurt and anger that I'm not sure we can get past."

"And I think we can. We were friends once. More than friends. And we can be again."

"That was a long time ago."

"Not that long." He leaned forward, and the sheet around his waist slid dangerously low. He didn't seem to notice, or if he did, he ignored it. "I am so sorry for not listening to you. For blindly following in my uncle's anger. If I could go back and do it again, I'd do it all differently."

"But we can't go back."

"No, but we can start again. Right here. Now."

The sound of a car approaching the house interrupted their conversation.

Terrence grabbed his pants from the floor and got out of the bed. He pulled them on and strode to the window. "It's James West."

"I'll go get dressed."

"Nikki. I hear what you're saying. But just so we're clear, I'm going to do my best to prove to you that we have something special. Something worth fighting for."

Nikki turned and hurried to her room.

With guests literally on her doorstep, she didn't have time to consider how she felt about Terrence's declaration.

She took the fastest, coldest shower ever and dressed in jeans and a sweater.

Terrence had made coffee and was pouring cups for

James and the pretty woman who sat next to him at the kitchen table.

"You remember James," Terrence said. "And this is his wife, Erika."

"Nice to meet you, Erika. Good to see you again, James."

Erika tilted her head and smiled, a twinkle in her eye.

"Sorry about bursting in on you so early, but I knew Terrence was anxious to get some sort of security set up for the house. I got a recommendation from Ryan, and he had a system couriered overnight."

She shot an annoyed glare at Terrence. He hadn't mentioned getting a security system for her house.

"You got a home security system for Lakewood House."

"I did."

His calmness spiked her ire. She knew her irritation wasn't all about the security system. Her feelings for Terrence were in turmoil, the lines between them more blurred than ever, and she didn't like it one bit. "Without discussing it with me. I can't afford a security system."

"Don't worry about the cost. I'll take care of it."

"I am worried about the cost, and you won't take care of it. Lakewood House is my responsibility."

"It may be your responsibility, but I care about it too. And you. You need a security system."

"Listen," James said. "The system was a gift."

"I can't accept a gift from you."

"Come on, Nikki." Terrence ran a hand over his head. "It's just a couple of cameras and an alarm."

"It's not just a couple of cameras and an alarm. It's you making decisions without consulting me."

He held his hands up in surrender. "Look, I'm sorry.

I should have asked you first. But this is about your safety. Please."

"Okay," she said, annoyed, "but a couple of cameras and an alarm. That's all."

"That's all." Terrence grabbed his jacket from the back of the sofa and faced James. "Let me show you around the exterior of the property."

"I'm sorry if we caused a problem between you two," Erika said. "I told James we should call before we came over. But if it makes up for bursting in on you two, I made scones." She held up a plastic Tupperware container.

"It more than makes up for it. And I'm the one who should be apologizing for arguing in front of company." Nikki grabbed a serving plate from the cabinet. "Things between Terrence and I have been tense lately. Well, more than just lately. More like for the last fourteen years."

Erika whistled. "That's a long time to be tense."

Nikki laughed. "You're telling me." She opened the Tupperware container and transferred the scones onto the serving plate. "Terrence and I were friends for a long time. And then we weren't friends for a long time and now… I don't know what we are. He's been holding a grudge against my family and me for years for something I told him my grandfather didn't do."

"And I take it he didn't believe you." Erika moved to the sink and rinsed the now empty Tupperware container.

"He did not." Nikki slid onto a bar stool. She gave Erika a quick summary of her history with Terrence, the feud between her grandfather and his uncle, and how it had killed their relationship. "And I realize I did the same thing, letting this thing between him and Jarrod drive a wedge between Terrence and me. He sided with his uncle, and I sided with my grandfather, but neither of us knew the truth."

"But you're still angry at him."

"I know it doesn't make any sense, and I don't know why I'm dumping all this on you. You probably think I'm crazy."

"Not crazy. I think you need someone to talk to. Someone to listen. I'm happy to be that person."

Nikki smiled. "Thank you."

"You're welcome." Erika returned the smile. "Can I offer you one piece of advice though?"

Nikki extended a hand. "Please."

"Life is too short to hold grudges and nurture feuds. You and Terrence clearly still care about each other. If there is any way for you two to get back your friendship, don't waste time with anger."

Was that what she was doing? Wasting time? She still couldn't deny she cared about Terrence. Maybe even more than that. In a little more than a year, she'd lost her grandfather and her job, which had taught her that life was unpredictable and not to take anything for granted.

The sound of tires on the gravel driveway put an end to their conversation.

Erika looked out of the kitchen window. "The sheriff is here."

A minute later, all three men strode into the house.

"Sorry to barge in on you when you're entertaining," Sheriff Webb said.

"No worries. Erika and James dropped by to welcome me to the neighborhood with scones and a home security system."

The sheriff smiled warily. "Not a bad welcome."

"Would you like a scone?" Nikki motioned to the platter. "I can make more coffee."

"No, no thanks. I've been subsisting on coffee since yesterday. An early morning call from Terrence telling me that you'd been able to identify Dana Bonny as one of the men that shot at you didn't help me get any beauty sleep."

Nikki turned to Terrence, surprised. "You called Lance?"

"While you were asleep. I wanted to let him know about Dana."

"Are you still contending you don't know anything about the brawl at Whistler's last night?" Lance's gaze moved between Terrence and Nikki.

"Not a thing," Terrence said straight-faced.

"Well, it looks like your face might have been there unless Nikki did that to your eye," the sheriff said.

Terrence smiled. "I tripped."

"Yeah, right. I'll go with that for now." Sheriff Webb shot a look at Nikki.

She gave a tight-lipped smile. The sheriff obviously knew they'd been at Whistler's last night, but if he and Terrence were going to pretend he didn't, she was happy to go along with them.

James's and Erika's expressions said they weren't buying the excuse either.

"We were finally able to identify the woman we found on your property," Lance said. "Her name is Anna Fernandez Alcalá. She disappeared from a women's shelter in McAllen, Texas, last year."

"And no one was concerned?" Nikki said.

There were thousands of vulnerable women out there, but it was hard to believe that in this day and age, anyone could disappear without notice.

"A counselor at the shelter filed the missing person report, but it wasn't unusual for women to move out of the shelter without notifying the staff."

She shook her head in disgust. "Just the kind of vulnerable young woman monsters prey upon."

"Unfortunately, yes," the sheriff said.

"Texas. That tracks with the information on the gang that West sent us."

"I noticed that as well," the sheriff said.

James's face had darkened as the conversation went on. Now he looked ready to spit nails. "I think I speak for my brothers when I say anything West can do to assist your investigation, Sheriff, you just let us know."

"I appreciate that. Right now, we're trying to track Ms. Alcalá's movements after she ran away from the homeless shelter. I expect it will be slow going. She was nineteen but didn't have a driver's license, bank account or credit cards. No cell phone that we know of. We can't use any of our usual means to trace her."

"So, what's the next step?" Terrence asked.

Sheriff Webb sighed. "Based on your identification of Dana as one of the men who shot at you, we were able to get a warrant for his arrest, but we haven't found him yet."

"What about Pete?" Terrence asked.

Lance shook his head. "We don't have probable cause for a warrant or to formally bring him in, or any evidence he's committed a crime."

"Pete definitely wasn't the second guy shooting at us," Nikki offered.

"I've sent a deputy to his place to see if he'd voluntarily come to the station for questioning, but it appears as if he's disappeared," the sheriff said.

Now it was Terrence who looked ready to spit nails. He let out a curse.

Nikki shared in his frustrations. It seemed that for every step forward, they took two steps back. "The Bonny family used to own a pretty large swath of land. Even though they sold most of it off years ago, Pete and probably Dana know these mountains better than anyone. If they want to get lost, it's going to take time to find them."

"What about the other guy who shot at us?" Terrence asked.

"Still working on an ID."

"So you're nowhere." Terrence's frustration filled the room.

Sheriff Webb slapped his palm against his thigh. "Investigations take—"

"Time. Yes, I know," Terrence spat.

"Look, we're doing everything we can." The sheriff moved to the front door, and they all followed.

Sheriff Webb opened the door and stepped out onto the front porch before turning back. "Just sit tight. Why don't you take another look at that information that West Investigations sent you? Maybe something will pop out at you that didn't before."

Nikki and Terrence watched through the open front door as their visitors got into their cars and drove away. "You're not going to listen to him, are you?"

"Wasn't planning on it," Terrence said, turning to look at her. "Why?"

"Because I have an idea."

Chapter Eighteen

The drive to Albert Chester's office took a little over an hour. Terrence hadn't protested when Nikki explained that she wanted to talk to the lawyer, which convinced her that he suspected the attorney might be connected to everything that had happened in the last several days, just like she was. She couldn't picture the mild-mannered lawyer involved with human trafficking, but anything was possible. At the very least, he knew who his client was, and that person might be involved. She wanted that name and she thought she knew how to get it.

The law firm occupied a multifloor cookie-cutter building and stood amongst other multifloor cookie-cutter buildings. The receptionist, a young brunette woman, greeted them when they entered the law firm's lobby.

"May I help you?" The woman gave a tight smile.

"My name is Dominique King. I'd like to see Mr. Chester, please?"

"Do you have an appointment?"

"I do not, but I'm sure he will find the time to meet with me."

The woman's smile tightened, and she picked up the phone on her desk.

"You still haven't said how you plan to make Chester tell you who his client is," Terrence said, keeping his voice low.

"I'm going to use the thing he wants against him."

"You're in luck," the receptionist said, replacing the phone's receiver on its chassis. "Mr. Chester has some time now. He'll be right out."

The lawyer appeared behind the glass doors separating the reception area from the offices less than a minute later. He pushed through the doors with a flourish, a bright smile on his face.

"Ms. King, what a lovely surprise. Can I take this unexpected meeting to mean you come bearing good news?"

"I have been thinking about your offer a great deal." Not a lie exactly. She had been thinking about the offer on Lakewood House. Who was behind it and why? If a little manipulation was what it took to get the information she wanted, she was okay with that.

"Well, all right then. Let's go to my office and discuss this further."

She and Terrence followed Chester, and she ignored the wary look Terrence shot at her.

Once they were seated in Chester's large corner office, the attorney got right to business. "So, as I mentioned, my client would like to move quickly to close the deal but is willing to pay a substantial bonus to compensate you for the inconvenience."

"Before we get to that, I want to know who I'd be selling to." Nikki crossed her legs and leaned back in the silk upholstered chair.

Chester's smile dimmed. "As I've explained, I don't have the authority to do that."

"Then we have no deal." Nikki stood and Terrence followed suit.

Chester pushed to his feet. "Hang on there. Are you saying that if I give you the buyer's name, you'll sell?"

"I'm telling you that the only way I'll sell is if you tell me your client's name."

He hesitated for a long moment. "Let me make a call. If you would wait outside, it will just take a moment."

Nikki and Terrence stepped out of the office together.

"He's calling his client," Terrence said.

"I hope so." She could see Chester on the phone through the long vertical glass window next to his office door.

Terrence looked at her with shrewd eyes. "But you have no intention of selling Lakewood House, right?"

She pulled Terrence farther away from Chester's office. She couldn't hear him inside with the door closed, but she wasn't taking any chances. "Of course not. But I've been thinking about it, and what if the person offering to buy Lakewood House is also involved in the trafficking ring? It would make sense. Now that I'm back in Carling Lake, they'd lose access to the private dock. But if they bought Lakewood House, their problem would be solved. The vandalism and arson could all just be a way to push me toward selling."

"I don't know." Terrence seemed unconvinced. "It makes some sense, and while I don't hold lawyers in great esteem, Chester works for what passes for a reputable law firm. I don't know if they'd be involved with traffickers and arsonists."

"What lawyer knows everything their client is up to?"

"Good point."

Chester's office door opened. "Thank you for waiting. Please, come in and have a seat." His expression was solemn. "My client wasn't happy about your condition, but she did give me permission to reveal who she was."

"She?" Nikki couldn't help the punch of surprise she felt. It was probably sexist, but she hadn't even considered a woman could be behind all this.

"Melinda Hanes is the buyer on behalf of her family corporation, Hanes Hospitality Services."

"Melinda Hanes," Nikki repeated.

"Yes. I believe being from Carling Lake, you're familiar with the Hanes family hotel and B and B."

Of course she was. But that didn't explain Melinda's offer.

"Why would Melinda Hanes want to buy Lakewood House?"

Chester sighed. "As Carling Lake becomes more of a tourist destination, the need for guest accommodations has increased. Several new B and Bs have cropped up in the area and the Haneses want to make sure they retain their market share. Lakewood House is uniquely situated."

"You mean the property Lakewood House is on is uniquely situated. Lakewood House itself is far too small to convert into a B and B."

"Well, that is true." Chester shifted in his chair and looked uncomfortable. "Of course, the offer is for the entire property, and once you sell, Ms. Hanes is free to do with it as she chooses. But the property is perfect for her plans."

Which was to tear down Lakewood House. If Nikki had been inclined to sell before, she definitely wouldn't have been now that she knew Melinda's plans for the property. Lakewood House meant too much to too many people for her to ever let anyone tear it down.

Nikki stood again. "Thank you for your time, Mr. Chester."

"Where are you going? You said—"

"I said I would consider selling if I knew who the buyer was. I have considered it and my answer is a resounding no."

Chester rounded his desk and stalked toward Nikki. "Now wait just a darn minute."

Terrence stood, putting his body between her and Chester. "The lady gave you her answer."

The attorney's glare was venomous. "The lady lied about her intentions."

Nikki shrugged. "You win some, you lose some. Tell your client I won't ever sell to her or anyone else who plans to knock down Lakewood House."

She strode from the office with Terrence at her side. She was pretty sure that Melinda's offer hadn't been motivated solely by business, at least not once Nikki had mentioned the possibility of running for mayor. Melinda had probably figured she could kill two birds with one stone by buying Lakewood House—getting rid of a potential rival for the mayorship and picking up a coveted property for her family's business. Well, she couldn't say she was sorry to disappoint the conniving businesswoman turned wannabe politician.

"You might have just made an enemy."

"I've been doing that a lot lately," Nikki said, thinking about her former boss. "Melinda Hanes will have to just get in line."

Chapter Nineteen

"Well, I guess that was a waste of time." Nikki sounded despondent.

"Not necessarily." Terrence changed lanes and merged onto the interstate.

Nikki glanced over at him. "What do you mean?"

"Now we know the person trying to buy Lakewood House doesn't have anything to do with the trafficking ring." He changed lanes again and pushed the Highlander to go faster. He was relieved at least to have an answer to one mystery, but it didn't help him at all when it came to finding Jill.

Nikki made a sour face. "Melinda could still be behind the vandalism and arson."

His gut said no. "I don't think so. Surreptitiously trying to buy Lakewood House is one thing, but arson?" He shook his head in disbelief. "It's not really the Haneses' style."

"You know Ellis Hanes is in jail."

"For fraud. That's a lot different than arson."

"Maybe."

They rode in silence for several miles. He was sure Melinda was nothing more than an opportunist. Dana Bonny, however, was a key player in whatever was going on.

"Are you up for a detour?"

"Depends. Where to?"

"Dana Bonny's place. We still need to talk to him, and maybe we'll have better luck if we find him at home."

"You know where he lives?"

He merged onto the exit off the highway that led back to Carling Lake. "Aunt Charity said he inherited his father's place. Thaddeus Bonny had a farm off old Route 20."

"Okay. Let's see if Dana is more willing to talk today."

Dana wasn't the only person he wanted to talk to. "Speaking of talking. We never finished discussing what happened last night between us."

Nikki stared out of the front window. "I think I was pretty clear earlier. Last night was great, but it can't happen again."

"Why not?" He turned off the interstate and onto Route 20. Once a main thoroughfare, it was primarily used by the handful of homeowners who lived off the road now.

"Why? Until a few days ago, we hadn't spoken in over fourteen years."

"Exactly. We've already wasted so much time. Let's not waste any more."

Nikki looked across the car now. "We can't just move from not speaking for years to—what? I don't even know what it is you want. Do you?"

He knew what he wanted. He looked over at Nikki. "You. I want you." He held her gaze for a moment longer before shifting his eyes back to the road.

She let out a shaky breath but otherwise didn't respond to his declaration.

Her silence stung, but he reminded himself that he had several years of hurt to make up for. It made sense that she didn't believe him when he said he wanted to pick up where they'd left off. Well, not where they left off exactly. They were adults now, and he was ready for a committed adult relationship. And if he had to work to prove that to her, he was up for the challenge.

He turned the Highlander off the main road onto a long driveway that ended in front of a rundown two-story home. Several junker cars in various states of disrepair littered what should have been the front yard. Once a working farm, the expansive plot of land lay fallow and desolate now. An unpainted barn with a rusted metal door sat twenty yards behind the house, the only other structure in sight for miles.

Terrence and Nikki got out of the car and went to the door. No one answered their knock. He peered through the front windows. They were unadorned by blinds or curtains, but the grime and dirt made it difficult to tell if there was anyone inside.

"Maybe he's in the barn?" Nikki said, pointing beyond the house.

They trooped through the tall grass toward the barn. He waved to Nikki to stand aside as they approached. He tried the door. It was heavy. He pushed harder. It squeezed and groaned but began to move.

He finally got it open enough to see inside. Then froze.

"What is it?" Nikki moved to his side.

The red Prius was parked in the middle of the barn, a thin veneer of dust and dirt covering it.

"Jill's car."

LANCE PULLED TERRENCE aside while Deputy Bridges took Nikki's statement. "What do you think you're doing?"

"I think I'm searching for my sister. And finding her

car on Dana Bonny's property gives you all the probable cause you need to search his house."

"I'm surprised you didn't take it upon yourself to search the house," Lance said, exasperated.

"Come on! I did what I had to do, and now we've got a solid lead connecting Bonny to Jill's disappearance."

A deep-seated chill had settled into his bones the moment he'd recognized Jill's car in Dana's barn. He hadn't been able to bring himself to open the trunk of the car, the fear of what he might find inside overriding all of his police training. But when Lance had informed him that the car was empty, except for a suitcase, he'd nearly fallen to his knees with relief. Jill wasn't inside.

"And if he gets a halfway decent lawyer, he could get whatever case we make against him thrown out of court—"

"I don't care about the court," Terrence yelled. "I care about finding my sister."

Lance held out both hands. "Okay, okay. But you dragged Nikki out here without knowing what or who you might find. It was reckless, and either one of you could have been hurt."

"I'd never do anything to hurt Nikki."

"No? You two have already been shot at by Bonny. Now you bring her here. Look, I don't know either of you that well, and I understand your desire to find your sister. I do. But you're a cop. You know how to handle yourself. Nikki isn't. I know there's nothing I can do to stop you from rushing headlong into danger, but, man, if you care about this woman, don't drag her along with you."

Lance stalked away without giving him a chance to respond.

When Lance finally let them go, Nikki had insisted

on driving them back to Lakewood House, not trusting him to drive.

He stayed silent the entire way.

"Are you okay?" Nikki asked once they were back at the house.

He fell onto the sofa, emotionally exhausted. "Okay? I don't know. When I saw that car, I thought..." Tears threatened to spill from his eyes. "Nikki, I don't know what I'm going to do if..."

She wrapped her arms around him. "Hey, there is still hope."

"Is there?" he said, his face tucked into her shoulder. "The longer a person is missing, the less likely it becomes that they'll be found. I don't even know exactly when Jill disappeared."

Nikki cupped his cheek and leaned back until she could look into his deep brown eyes. "We'll find her." She pulled him closer, placing a kiss on one corner of his mouth. "We'll find her." She kissed the other corner.

He pulled away just enough to look at her face. Desire shimmered in her eyes. The same desire he felt bubbling inside. He wanted her. Needed her now.

He leaned forward slowly, giving her the chance to back away.

Ever so lightly, she caressed his jaw with her thumb, and met his heated kiss with matching fervor. Her hands slid around his neck, her lips curling into a smile even as they continued their kiss.

He deepened their kiss, and she shifted, swinging one leg across him so that she straddled him. He groaned. It was all he could do not to throw her down and ravage her like some caveman. There was nothing in the world he wanted more than to make love to her again. To make love to her every day for the rest of his life, of that he was sure, although he knew it was too early to share that thought with her. But she'd been adamant that sleeping together had been a mistake. He didn't want her to do anything she'd regret. Damned conscience.

He broke off the kiss, panting. "Wait."

She shook her head and lowered her lips to his neck. "No. No more waiting."

He groaned again, his head becoming fuzzy as the blood rushed to other parts of his body. "I don't want you to regret…"

She leaned back so her gaze locked with his. "The only thing I'd regret is not being with you. Not having you inside me right now. I want this. I want you to stop thinking and start doing."

He couldn't control the erotic shiver that raced through him at her words.

Nikki tugged his head down so that his lips met hers again.

He wrapped an arm around her waist and surged upward, holding her against him. She wrapped her legs around him. His erection pressed into her center. God help him. He wasn't sure they'd make it to the bed.

Mine. Mine. Mine. The word was part chant, part prayer marching across his brain as he carried Nikki up the stairs and sat her gently on the bed.

He lowered himself down beside her and claimed her mouth again. As much as he burned to be inside of her, the sizzle that flowed through him when their lips met was addictive. She hummed against him, shifting so he was between her legs.

Piece by piece, they shed their clothes, their kisses moving from fiery to sweet and back again.

"You're beautiful," he whispered reverently, staring at her naked form.

She gave him a lust-filled smile, reaching both her arms up to him. "Come here and show me how beautiful you think I am." She arched her hips and the last of his control broke.

He sheathed himself quickly, then found his place at her entrance. Balancing his weight on his elbows, he stared into Nikki's eyes as he entered her slowly.

She felt…perfect. Absolutely perfect.

Fully seated at her core, he shuddered.

Nikki gripped his shoulders and rolled her hips. "More."

He complied, moving slowly and steadily, then faster, driving her close to the edge but careful not to push her over. He entwined their fingers and raised her hands above her head and slowed the tempo, wanting to make this last for as long as possible.

Eyes closed, Nikki chanted his name, nearly overwhelming him. He wouldn't last much longer. He increased his tempo, feeling his orgasm building.

Nikki's legs tightened around him, her eyes flying open and locking on his. "Terrence." She moaned.

He let go of her hands and gripped her hips, tilting her so he could seat himself deeper inside her, and drove them faster, harder, any tenderness lost in the driving need for release.

Eyes closed, she convulsed around him, screaming his name as she came. His head fell back as his own orgasm took him.

He dropped down on the bed next to Nikki, still shuddering. He pulled Nikki in close to his side, and she rested her head against his bare chest. The cut above his eye throbbed, but it was a pain well worth it if it meant sharing Nikki's bed.

He drew small circles on her back as his pulse slowly returned to normal. "How do you feel?"

Nikki chuckled softly and pressed a kiss to his shoulder. "Don't you know how I feel?"

"That's not…not what I meant." He felt heat climb the back of his neck.

Nikki propped herself up on an elbow. "I know what you meant. And I told you, I wanted you to make love to me. I'm fine."

He was happy to hear her refer to what they'd done as making love, as opposed to a cruder term, but it wasn't enough. He wanted more from her, and he needed her to know that.

"I know I hurt you, and I understand that it will take time before you fully trust me again, but I want that. I want you to trust me. I want us to try to make a relationship work."

She slid away from him. "It's not just about the past and our families' feud. We don't really know each other anymore."

"You know that's not true. You know me better than anyone else on this earth and you would, even if we spent the next fifty years apart."

She shook her head. "You live in Trenton, and I live… I don't even know where I live. I don't even have a job."

"Those are just details. We can work all that out." He took her hand in his and drew in a deep breath. "What I'm asking is that we try? Fourteen years ago, we were on our way to something incredible, and I think we can still get there. I think we can get to something even better, because now I understand what's really important—you. Us. We can't change the past, but we can move forward. Together. If you want to."

He held his breath. Time slowed to a near stop. He'd never wanted anything more than to hear Nikki say she wanted to be with him. To try to make a life with him.

"I need time to think."

It wasn't what he wanted to hear, but it wasn't a no. He'd hold on to that for now.

"Take all the time you need. I'm not going anywhere."

Chapter Twenty

Terrence awoke before dawn. Nikki slept curled up next to him. He brushed his fingertips over the soft skin of her shoulder. The burst of sheer satisfaction at the sight of her face, so peaceful in sleep, on the pillow was everything he'd ever wanted even though he hadn't realized it. Or rather, hadn't let himself think about it.

Nikki was the woman he wanted, and Lance was right. He had to do whatever it took to keep her safe.

He started to rise, attempting to slip from the bed without waking her.

Nikki's arm tightened around his waist. "Where do you think you're going?"

He didn't want to start their renewed relationship out with a lie, so he tried deflection. "Shh." He dropped a kiss on her forehead. "I just want to check something out."

Nikki's eyes opened. "Check what out?"

"It's nothing for you to worry about. You should go back to sleep. It's still early."

Nikki sat up and fixed him with a stare. "No keeping secrets. No shutting each other out or pushing each other away. I want to try to get back what we had. Something deeper and truer even, but we can only get there if we're completely honest with each other. Completely, Terrence."

He sighed. "I'm going back to Pete Bonny's place. I'm hoping to catch him at home. He might have some idea where his nephew could be hiding."

"You don't think Sheriff Webb has asked him about that?"

"If he's found him, I'm sure he has, but Lance isn't likely to share that information with me, especially not after yesterday. And now, more than ever, I want to know what Pete didn't tell us when we picked up the boat the other day."

Nikki swung her feet over the side of the bed and started for the bathroom. "Okay, give me a minute to get dressed."

"No."

She turned back around to look at him. "What?"

"I can't let you go with me."

She scowled. "This again?"

He crossed the room and took her hands in his. "It's not like before. We're dealing with some very dangerous and potentially desperate people who have shot at us. And then finding Jill's car. I may already be too late to save her—"

Nikki squeezed his hands. "You can't think that way."

"Not thinking it doesn't make it any less true. I may have to face the worst. But I couldn't take it if my actions got you hurt. I just got you back. I can't risk losing you."

Nikki slipped her arms around his neck and drew him close. "You aren't going to lose me. And you're crazy if you think I'm going to let you investigate without me."

"Nikki—"

"No, you listen to me now. If we're going to do this, we're going to be full partners. You've got my back and I've got yours. Always." Her words were impassioned. Her eyes were full of sincerity and full-hearted. He had no doubt that she meant every word.

"Always."

While she showered, Terrence got coffee started. There was still little in the house to eat, so he made them both egg sandwiches and ate his while Nikki got dressed. Then he took a quick shower, and they were off as dawn began to crest. As far as he knew, Lance and his deputies still hadn't yet caught up with Pete to talk. But Terrence figured he might have better luck if he approached the man early.

"Are you sure this is a good idea?" Nikki asked as he drove them toward Pete Bonny's property.

The cop in him mentally answered with a resounding no. It wasn't clear whether Pete knew or had a hand in the criminal activity of his nephew, but the fact that Lance hadn't been able to track him down wasn't a good sign. "It's better than sitting at Lakewood House waiting for something to happen."

He pulled to a stop in front of Pete's home. They'd only taken a few steps toward the door when he saw that it was cracked open. "The door is open. Stay behind me."

They crept toward the door together. It didn't look as if the door had been forced. Maybe Pete had simply gone out and forgotten to close it all the way. Since the deputy Lance had sent out to speak with Pete would have certainly noticed the open door, he could assume Pete had been home in the last twenty-four hours. Was he here now?

"Pete?" No response. "It's Terrence Sutton and Nikki King. Are you in there?" He stepped to the door with Nikki at his side. "Pete? Hello? Your door is wide open."

There was nothing but silence from within the house.

The hairs on the back of his neck stood up. Something was wrong.

He peered around the open door. "Pete, are you in there?"

He crossed the threshold, Nikki behind him.

A plate sat on the kitchen table, the uneaten crusts of a sandwich and crumbs still on it. One cabinet door was open, and a chair had been overturned on its side. He and Nikki crept through the house to the bedroom. Three of the four dresser drawers were open, their contents strewed on the bed and the floor. The fourth and lowest drawer had been pulled completely free. It rested next to the dresser, the shirts inside seemingly undisturbed. The closet door stood open with several empty hangers askew.

"There's no one here," he said.

"I don't know if that's a good thing or a bad thing. This place looks like it's been ransacked," Nikki said.

He turned and led her from the bedroom back into the living area. "Yeah, the question is, who did it?"

She looked at him with curiosity in her eyes. "What do you mean?"

"I don't think the place has been ransacked as much as someone decided to leave in a hurry."

Her gaze swept around the room again. "Really? How can you tell?"

"Take the kitchen, for instance. There's only a single cabinet door open, which suggests that someone was looking for something specific and expected to find it in that cabinet. The chair is overturned, but that could have been done in the rush. Clothing is thrown about in the bedroom, but the bed is undisturbed, as were the nightstands. I'd say someone packed in a hurry rather than searched the place."

"Someone. You mean Pete. You think he's running," she said.

Terrence turned in a slow circle, taking in every inch of the space. "I think it's possible. Maybe even likely."

Nikki shook her head, a look of disbelief on her face. "I can't believe Pete would have anything to do with a human trafficking ring."

He'd seen enough as a detective that people rarely surprised him anymore. Soccer moms who ran hundred-thousand-dollar-a-year drug operations. Little old ladies who regularly stole for sport. Kids not old enough to vote leading organized gangs. People had a seemingly infinite capacity for crime, especially when it was profitable.

Something caught his eye. A piece of paper stuck out from under the sofa. He crossed the living space and bent to pick it up. "He might not have, at least not directly."

"What is that?" Nikki looked over his shoulder.

"It looks like the list of homes Pete has been hired as caretaker for and his schedule for checking up on them. He's got three places he takes care of in addition to Lakewood House."

"This is the address for the old Pierce place." Nikki pointed to the first address on the list. "And this one here is Ricky Tanner's place." She pointed at the last address. "But I don't recognize this one here."

It was familiar to him. He didn't know who owned the house, but the address wasn't that far from Aunt Charity's cabin. "I think it's that new all-glass modern place some financier or hedge fund person is building not far from Aunt Charity's place. She drove me past the property the last time I was in town to visit." A thought struck him. "I can't believe I didn't realize this earlier." Terrence shook his head, mentally flogging himself.

Nikki cocked her head to one side. "Realize what?"

"Pete has access to at least four homes that he knows will be empty at any given time." He shook the paper in his hand. "These three houses and Lakewood House. If you wanted to move women through town without anyone noticing, they'd be the perfect hiding places."

Nikki reached into her purse. "We should call the sheriff."

He shook his head. "All we have is conjecture. There's not a judge in the state who would give Lance a warrant to search any of the three houses based on what we have."

"But I'm guessing you have a plan."

"I'm going to go check them out myself. As Lance said, I have no jurisdiction in Carling Lake, so I don't need a warrant."

"I don't think that was what Lance meant by pointing out you had no jurisdiction. You can be arrested for trespassing and breaking and entering."

He was already moving toward the door. She followed him. "It's a chance I'm willing to take. Pete and Dana could be holding Jill in one of these places. And other women." He stopped and gave her a long look. "But I understand if it's not a chance you want to take."

"I said we were in this together, and I meant it."

He shot her a smile as they got into the car. And he plugged the first address into his GPS. "I think we should leave the second address for last. It's closest to town and also mostly glass, both of which make it less desirable for hiding someone."

"Okay, so that means the Tanner place is first, then," Nikki said, reading the address he'd punched into the GPS.

He started the engine and pointed them in the direction the GPS directed. "It's the most isolated."

They made it to the house in record time.

His memory had served him well. The house had a rustic feel with a stone and log fronting, but it was large and looked to have been well taken care of in the owner's absence. It also appeared to be vacant. The driveway was empty. There wasn't a hint of movement from inside the house as the car approached.

He got out of the Highlander and met Nikki at the hood. Nikki already had her gun in her hand, and he pulled his.

They tried the front door and found it locked. They rounded the house to the back door and discovered that it, too, was locked. The shades on all the windows were pulled down, so there was no way to see in from the outside.

He was contemplating whether it was worth it to break in and check out the house thoroughly or whether he should just move on to the second house on Pete's list when Nikki grabbed his arm.

"Wait. Do you hear that? It sounds like metal clanging."

He stilled, closed his eyes and listened. After a few seconds, he heard it. It sounded like someone was banging metal on metal. "It's coming from inside." That answered his question about whether it was worth it to go inside. "Stand back."

Nikki moved off to the side of the back door.

He kicked the lock once. Twice. On the third try, the door splintered but held. He gave it one more fierce kick, and the door swung open.

The daylight streaming in from the broken door cast shadows over the spaces. The main level of the house was really just one very large room with pillars setting off designated areas—living room, dining room, kitchen.

He moved into the house with Nikki at his back, her gun as steady as a pro. He tried the light switches on the wall next to the door he'd kicked in. Nothing happened. The electricity appeared to have been shut off.

Nikki laid a hand on his shoulder. "Listen."

They both stilled. The banging had grown louder. It was definitely coming from inside.

"Downstairs." He swept his gaze across the space until it fell on a door under the staircase. He headed that way, opening the door slowly and peering down the stairs. It was too dark to see anything, but using the flashlight from his phone could potentially alert whoever was down there to their presence if kicking in the back door hadn't.

The clanging stopped.

"Help." The word was low and scratchy, as if the person uttering it hadn't had water in a long time. Still, he'd have known that voice anywhere.

Jill.

Forgetting every bit of police training he'd ever had, he rushed down the stairs. "Jill? Jill, it's Terrence. Where are you?"

A whimper came from the far corner of the basement. He pulled his phone from his pocket and engaged the flashlight.

Jill was huddled on the floor. Her hair was matted

with dirt, and her usually glowing medium brown skin
was filthy. An empty food tray sat on the ground at her
side and a ratty wool blanket covered her legs. A metal
chain, much like the ones they'd found at the house on
Carling Island, ran from a hook in the wall and was attached to the cuff around Jill's wrist. Even in the dim
light, he could see where it had cut into her skin, leaving bloody bruises.

More rage than he'd have thought possible flared inside him. And it didn't fade at all when he noticed that
Jill wasn't alone.

Pete Bonny lay on his side next to her. He'd been
shackled to the wall at his ankle, and his hair was matted with dirt and blood at the temple. He was deathly
still.

Terrence's gaze swung back to Jill. She shrunk farther into the corner. Then slowly, her face seemed to
register that he wasn't there to hurt her. To register who
he was. "Terrence."

He holstered his gun and was by her side in two
steps, followed closely by Nikki. He reached for the
chain connecting his sister to the wall and spoke to
Nikki. "Check on Pete, would you?"

Nikki moved to Pete's side, pressing two fingers to
his neck while she slid her gun into her ankle holster.
"There's a pulse, but it's faint. Really faint."

He tapped his phone, bringing up the keypad and
dialing 911. "Just hang on, sweetheart. We're going to
get you out of here."

"Nine-one-one. What's your emergency?" the operator said on the other end of the phone line.

Before he could answer, a different, closer voice
spoke. "Hang up that phone. Now." Terrence whirled,

dropping the phone and reaching for his gun at the same time.

"I would not do that if I were you." Dana Bonny stood by the stairs, holding a gun on them. The tall man who'd been with him on Carling Island stood beside him with his own gun aimed in their direction.

"Throw your gun and the phone over here. Now!" Dana yelled.

Terrence hesitated for a moment, but with Dana holding a gun on them, he had no choice. He slid his gun and the phone across the floor.

"Is everything okay? What is your emerg—"

Dana stomped on the phone, cutting off the voice on the line. They could only hope that the operator was able to get a location for the call and would dispatch law enforcement to check it out.

Jill whimpered.

"Now stand up. Get your hands in the air."

Again, he and Nikki did as told. There wasn't much choice. He couldn't take the chance that they'd start shooting.

Dana smiled an oily gapped-tooth smile. He jerked a nod at his companion. "Well, isn't this a nice parting gift? We only came back here to clean up loose ends." Dana motioned toward Jill and Pete. "But you two—" Dana's expression hardened. "You're the reason why we have to shut down operations in Carling Lake and find a new transport hub. You disrupted my business and cost me money. I'm going to take a lot of pleasure in killing you both."

Chapter Twenty-One

Nikki fought to hide the panic swelling in her chest. "You won't get away with this. The sheriff knows you shot at us on Carling Island and all about the trafficking."

"Oh, does he now? Well, there's a difference between what the sheriff knows and what he can prove," Dana sneered. "And once I get rid of you lot, there will be a lot less so-called proof." He raised the gun in his hand a little higher.

Nikki felt Terrence's body tighten like a coil next to her. She knew him well enough to know he was preparing to do something. Something heroic and incredibly stupid given the two guns trained on them. He'd tossed his gun about two feet away and to the side. Her gun was in its holster hidden beneath her pant leg, but she couldn't get to it without alerting Dana and his minion.

"I don't understand," she blurted. "Why did you attack Pete? Isn't he part of your trafficking ring?"

Dana laughed. "Uncle Pete? He doesn't have guts. I used him to find out when the owners of the homes he took care of wouldn't be there. They were perfect."

"Pete needs medical attention."

"Uncle Pete should have stayed out of my business. There's nothing I can do to help him now."

The man beside Dana scowled. "Let's just get this over with."

"Wait. If you're going to kill us, I think we at least deserve to know exactly why."

"You think you deserve—" Dana laughed derisively.

Nikki ignored his tone. "Yes. I remember you when you were a kid." A lie, but she'd do whatever she had to in order to get Dana to see them as human and not obstacles to him getting away with his crimes. "You were always a risk-taker, but you were never an evil person. How did you get involved in this?"

"What can I say? Small-time risks that led to bigger, more profitable ventures. Isn't that how upward mobility, promotion within an organization, works? Nobody thinks twice about it when it's college-educated criminals climbing the corporate ladder. But I was never going to be a nine-to-five job kind of guy. The opportunity arose, and the money was too good to pass up."

"You kidnap and exploit women," Terrence snapped. "It's not a job. It's a crime."

"You sound just like your sister over there," Dana snarled. "I knew the moment I found out she was snooping around she was going to be trouble."

"So you kidnapped her?" Nikki asked.

"She's too old to make her a part of my business. I needed time to figure out what to do about her, but then you came to town." Dana glared.

"What about the dead girl I found at Lakewood House? Did you kill her?" Nikki asked. As scared as she was, she still wanted to know the whole sordid story.

"My associate here got a little too aggressive when the girl tried to run away. An unfortunate mistake."

Nikki looked at the man beside Dana. He stared back at her with flat, emotionless eyes. He hadn't so much as flinched at having been labeled a murderer. "Who is he?"

Dana slid a sidelong glance at his companion. "A representative of the man in charge."

"The man in charge," Terrence said. "Who would that be?"

"That's none of your concern, especially since you'll never meet him. Or anyone else, for that matter."

"Enough talk," the man beside Dana growled. "What do you want to do with them?"

Terrence slid closer.

"I figure take 'em deep into the woods, put a bullet in them and let the animals feast," Dana said.

"What about the old guy?"

"We'll have to take care of him when we come back to clean up the house so no one ever knows we were here. You heard what she said anyway." Dana jerked his head at Nikki. "He's in bad shape after the beating you gave him. You've got to learn to control yourself." Dana gave his partner a disgruntled look. "We can bury him in the woods and get the hell out of here."

Anger at the callousness with which Dana was talking about his own uncle soared inside her, along with fear of what he had planned for them.

Dana took a key from his pocket and tossed it at Terrence, who caught it. "Unlock your sister and help her up. If you try anything funny, I'll put a bullet in your girlfriend."

Terrence went to Jill, unlocking her wrist from the cuff and lifting her to her feet.

"Now, we're going up those stairs and outside."

Dana and his partner shifted to either side of the stairwell, leaving a large swath of space for them to pass up the stairs.

Terrence helped Jill upstairs and Nikki followed behind them.

At the top of the stairs, Nikki scanned the main floor for a weapon. Dana's partner grabbed her arm and pulled her against him. "Don't get any ideas, huh?"

The two men pushed them out the front door and across the lawn toward the dense trees lining the property. Despite there still being plenty of daylight left, the density of the trees surrounding them left them shrouded in semidarkness. That alone would have made the little hike they were on terrifying enough, but with two stone-cold criminals pointing guns at their backs, it was as if they were caught in a horror movie. One that did not promise a happy ending.

They marched through the woods for nearly a half hour before Dana told them to stop.

"Turn around," Dana commanded.

They did so, Jill still leaning heavily against Terrence. She looked over at Terrence, but his eyes were glued to Dana and the other man with the gun.

They were out of time. If they were going to get out of this, they'd have to do something now.

Dana raised his gun with a smirk. "Any last words?"

THERE WAS NO way Terrence was going to let Dana Bonny and his henchman kill Jill or Nikki. Hiking through the woods half carrying his injured sister wasn't exactly conducive to planning the takedown of two armed human traffickers, but it's the situation he had to work with. He'd managed to whisper to follow his lead as they walked. He was about to find out if Nikki would do the same.

"Any last words?"

"Now!" Terrence screamed, letting go of Jill.

She crumpled to the ground with a dramatic flourish, drawing Dana's gaze her way.

He seized upon Dana's momentary distraction and launched himself at the man. He caught movement out of the corner of his eye and hoped that it was Nikki taking the opportunity to run from the gunmen. There was no time to be sure though.

He grabbed Dana's arm, attempting to twist the gun away from him and toward the ground. Dana was stronger than he looked, but this was a fight not only for his life but for Nikki's and Jill's lives as well. That gave him an extra boost of strength that Dana could never match. Dana swung his free hand, his fist connecting with Terrence's face. The punch sent him reeling back, but he didn't let go of Dana or the gun. The momentum pulled Dana off balance. The two men toppled to the ground, still locked in a battle for the weapon.

Terrence kicked out his legs, throwing Dana off him. As he did, the gun flew from Dana's hand. He dived toward it, but Dana tackled him before he could reach it. A well-placed punch to the nose had him seeing stars. Precious time lost.

Dana crawled toward the gun, his hand wrapping around it just as Jill stumbled into the fray armed with a thick tree branch. The branch came down on Dana's arm with a sickening crunch.

Dana's howl was cut off by another swing of the branch, this one connecting with the side of his head. Dana fell to his stomach in the dirt, stunned but not knocked out. He'd recover in a moment and be madder than ever.

Terrence pushed to his feet. Ten feet from him, Dana's friend had seemingly lost his gun too, but he held

Nikki around the waist in a death grip, attempting to drag her away into the woods.

As the man lifted Nikki's feet from the ground, she bent forward, sinking her teeth into his wrist. He screamed and dropped her.

Next to him, Dana shifted, recovering quickly from Jill's blow to his head. Jill, however, had not recovered as fast. Having used what limited energy she had stored up, she squatted in the dirt next to a nearby tree, still clutching the branch but obviously spent.

If Dana got his gun back, they were all dead.

Terrence scanned the ground, his eyes landing on the gun at the same time as Dana's did. They scrambled toward the weapon, but before either reached it, a gunshot thundered, echoing off the trees.

For a moment, it seemed as if everything froze— from the breeze to the small forest animals scurrying away from the ruckus they were causing. Time stood still.

Then Dana's partner stumbled backward away from Nikki. Both of his hands were pressed against his chest. He took two more steps backward, then fell to his knees before rolling onto his back.

Nikki's eyes were wide and wild. She pointed the gun from her ankle holster at the man.

Terrence took advantage of everyone's momentary shock to scoop Dana's gun from the ground and level it at the man. "Don't move."

Dana glared. "You don't have the guts."

His voice little more than a growl, Terrence said, "One wrong move. Just give me a reason."

The sound of engines broke through the trees.

Terrence tensed, hoping that the sounds were that of the cavalry coming and not Dana's boss.

Moments later, three sheriff's department ATVs cut a path through the brush.

Sheriff Webb jumped off his ATV and pulled his gun, Deputy Bridges and another one close behind. "Terrence, Nikki, are you both okay? We got an emergency call from your cell phone number, and I was able to triangulate your GPS with help from James. What's going on here?"

Terrence filled him in quickly and held Dana at gunpoint while the deputies cuffed him and the other man. Then he passed Dana's gun off to the sheriff and ran to Jill's side.

"I'm okay," she said in a weak voice.

Since it was clear that she was not okay, he called out, "We need EMTs ASAP."

Sheriff Webb and Nikki joined him at Jill's side, and the sheriff radioed for EMTs and more backup while Nikki did her best to help him make Jill as comfortable as possible.

Jill rested her head against his shoulder, exhausted from her ordeal.

Terrence looked across at the woman he was falling in love with again. "Good job back there."

She smiled at him, then shifted her attention to Jill, brushing a strand of matted hair from her face. "We always did make a good team."

He smiled now too. "Yes, yes, we always have."

Chapter Twenty-Two

Jill sat up in the hospital bed, chatting happily with the nurse taking her blood pressure. She had been dehydrated and had several bumps and bruises but was otherwise fine. She'd even felt well enough to argue with the doctor when he'd told her he was keeping her overnight for observation. Terrence had finally done the unthinkable and brought in the big guns to convince her to listen. Aunt Charity had worked her magic and promised that she wouldn't leave Jill's side before she was discharged.

Lance and his men had searched the other properties Pete acted as caretaker for, but so far, they hadn't found any other girls. The FBI was being called in, but with the way trafficking rings operated, one hand often didn't know what the other did in order to make it harder for the authorities to take down the entire operation. The knowledge that other victims were out there was like a gut punch in the midst of his happiness over having found Jill alive.

Nikki stopped next to Terrence outside the hospital room door, wrapping her arms around his waist.

"How'd your call go?" he said.

"Great." Nikki shifted so she could look him in the eye. "I withdrew from consideration for the job."

"You what? Why?"

"This town meant a lot to Grandpa Bernie. And it means a lot to me. I've always known I wanted to run for elected office and do what I could to make life better for people. It's a little sooner than I planned, but I think I'm ready. I'm going to throw my hat in the ring for Carling Lake mayor."

Terrence pulled her into a hug. "Congratulations. This town is lucky to have you."

"I haven't won yet."

"You will." He dropped a kiss on her head.

She looked into his eyes. "I made another decision. I want us. I want to be with you."

A smile bloomed on his face and he crushed his mouth against hers. After a long moment, she pulled back from the kiss.

"Of course, running for mayor means I'll be moving into Lakewood House permanently and staying in Carling Lake."

"We'll figure it out. Trenton isn't that far away, and the most important thing to me is making our relationship work this time."

Nikki pressed a kiss to his mouth. "Me too." She snuggled in closer to his side and glanced into the hospital room. "How's Jill?"

"The doctor says she's fine. He's keeping her overnight but expects she'll be able to go home tomorrow, as long as she promises to rest for a few days."

"That's great." Nikki gave his waist a squeeze. "Of course, she's welcome to stay at Lakewood House if she's not ready to go back to DC just yet." Her voice sounded tentative, as if she weren't sure how he'd feel about the offer.

He gazed down into her dark brown eyes. "Thank you."

"Of course. Jill is my friend."

"I think she's going to need friends and family around her for a while. The doctor feels good about her physical recovery, but he warned Jill that her mental and emotional recovery will probably be much harder. He suggested a psychiatrist, but Jill didn't seem too open to it."

"Give her time. She might change her mind in a few days."

"I hope so. She says that Dana didn't hurt her, but I don't know…"

"Hey. Let's take one step at a time. Jill knows we're here for her, and we will do whatever it takes to help her get through this."

He pulled her closer. "I don't know what I'd do without you."

Nikki pulled back just enough so she could look at him. "It's a good thing you don't need to worry about that then." She hesitated a moment. "You know, talking to someone isn't a bad idea for you either."

He arched his eyebrows.

"You've been through a lot too. Jill going missing, wondering where she was or if she was hurt. Just… think about it."

He nodded.

"Hey, guys. How is Jill doing?"

Terrence turned with Nikki still in his arms. Lance stood behind them. "She's going to be okay."

"Excellent. I'm glad to hear that even if I'm not happy about you two seeking out Dana Bonny on your own." Lance narrowed his gaze at them. "But we can discuss that later."

Terrence was pretty sure that by "discuss," Lance meant telling them off for jumping into a dangerous situation without calling him first. So be it. If that was the price he had to pay for saving his sister, he was more than happy to pay it. "Have you got a name from Dana's partner yet?"

"Yeah, William Weigel. Career criminal."

"Have either of them made a statement?"

Lance shook his head. "Not a word beyond 'I want a lawyer.' But they'll break. Guys like them always do. They're just the foot soldiers though. They might not know that much about the overall operation."

"What about Pete?" Nikki asked.

"He's in bad shape, but he'll survive. Cracked ribs. A couple of broken teeth. He regained consciousness enough to tell me that he'd confronted his nephew after news of you two being shot at made it around town. He denies knowing about the trafficking ring, but he says he knew that Dana sometimes used the houses he acted as caretaker for to party."

"Very professional," Terrence deadpanned.

"You get what you pay for," Lance shot back. "No offense, Nikki."

"None taken." She gave a small smile.

"Do you believe Pete's telling the truth when he says he didn't know about the trafficking?"

Lance threw up his hands. "Who knows? People have an extraordinary capacity for ignoring what they don't want to see."

Terrence couldn't argue with that.

"Do you think your sister is up for making a statement? If I can get some details, I might be able to use them to get those guys to talk."

He and Nikki had already given Lance their statements, but the EMTs had whisked Jill away.

The three of them stepped into Jill's hospital room. Aunt Charity sat beside the bed, holding Jill's hand.

The nurse finished typing on the tablet she held and looked up. "Only three visitors at a time."

Aunt Charity stood. "I'll go grab coffee. Anyone want anything?"

They all declined, and Aunt Charity left with the nurse.

"Ms. Sutton, I'm Sheriff Lance Webb. First, let me just say how relieved I am that you're going to be okay."

"Not more relieved than I am, Sheriff." Jill smiled.

Lance returned her smile. "I'm sure I'm not." He flipped his small notebook open to a clean page. "If you're up for it, I'd like to ask you a few questions."

"I'm up for it. Ask away."

"Okay, well, let's start at the beginning. What brought you to Carling Lake?"

Jill took a deep breath and let it out slowly. "I got a call about a week ago from a woman who said she'd escaped from a trafficking ring but that her friend was still being held captive."

Lance scribbled on the notepad. "Did you get this woman's name?"

Jill shook her head. "She wouldn't give me her name, and the call came from a blocked number."

"Okay. What else did the woman say?"

"She didn't want to tell me too much. She was terrified, as you can imagine. She told me that she'd been promised a job as a live-in nanny for a rich family upstate by a man she'd met in a bar. He was supposed to drive her to her new job, but instead he took her to a warehouse where there were three other women. They were beaten and assaulted, then transported somewhere else. The woman wasn't sure where because she was in and out of consciousness. But she did hear the men talking about Carling Lake. And she remembered they both had the same very distinctive tattoo on their biceps."

Jill paused and took several deep breaths. It was clear that telling the woman's story was taking an emotional toll on her.

"We can take a break if you need one," Lance offered.

"No. No, I'm okay. She said she managed to get away when one of the clients—that's what she said the men who kidnapped her called them, 'clients'—" disgust permeated Jill's tone "—passed out. She grabbed the cash from his wallet and a card with the same symbol the men had tattooed on their arms and ran. She gave me the card when we met up."

"How did she find you?" Nikki asked.

"I have no idea. She said she didn't know what to do or who she could trust. I'm not sure how she decided to trust me, but I'm glad she did."

"So you came to Carling Lake to investigate a possible human trafficking ring on your own," Terrence growled.

Lance shot him a quelling look.

"Yes, Terrence. I came to Carling Lake to investigate on my own because that's what I do. I'm an investigative reporter, or did you forget, big brother?" His sister pinned him with a scowl.

"I haven't forgotten, but—"

Nikki grabbed his arm and squeezed. "Maybe we should just let Jill tell her story for now."

"That would be ideal," Lance said. "What happened when you arrived in Carling Lake, Ms. Sutton?"

"You can call me Jill. I knew I'd need to keep a low profile, so I decided to stay at Lakewood House rather than with Aunt Charity. I knew it was just sitting there empty, and I didn't think you'd mind, Nikki."

"Of course not." Nikki reached for Jill's hand. "I wish you'd told me though."

"I know I should have. I'm sorry. Anyway, the night I arrived, I was exhausted. I dropped my suitcase in your living room and fell asleep in your guest bedroom. I didn't even bother with making the bed up, I was so wiped out. At some point in the night, I woke up, and these two guys were in the room with me. They grabbed me, and I've been locked in the basement of that house ever since. They'd bring me water and a little food once a day."

Terrence's chest burned with fury. Dana Bonny had better thank his lucky stars he was locked away in a prison cell. Instead of imagining ways to seriously hurt him, Terrence pulled his phone from his pocket and scrolled to the photograph of the business card Nikki found in the kitchen at Lakewood House. "Is this the card?"

"Yes. How?"

"You must have dropped it. Nikki found it at Lakewood House."

"And Dana and Weigel both have fleur-de-lis tattoos," Lance said. "Given the interstate nature of this crime, the Feds will probably take over, but it's a good start for connecting them to the trafficking ring.

"That's enough for now." Lance closed his notebook. "I may have to speak to you again, but for now, rest."

Lance headed for the door.

"I'm going to go check on your aunt. Give you and Jill a moment alone together." Nikki raised her lips to his for a kiss before following Lance out of the room.

Terrence sat on the edge of Jill's hospital bed and

took her hand in his. "You gave me the scare of my life, kid."

"I'm sorry about that. I am. But—" Jill's eyes twinkled "—it looks like some good came of all this. You and Nikki?" She wiggled her eyebrows suggestively.

"I'm glad to see your ordeal hasn't dulled your investigative prowess."

"I'm just happy you and Nikki have finally come to your senses. You two belong together."

Terrence smiled at his sister. "You know what? For once, I'm not going to argue with you."

Chapter Twenty-Three

Nikki eyed the pile of clothes on her bed. "I have nothing to wear to this gallery opening. I really don't think I can go."

"Are you kidding me?" Jill reclined on the bed next to the pile. She wore a black jumpsuit with gold chunky jewelry. A butterfly hairpin adorned her short afro. She looked very bohemian chic. "You have more clothes on this bed than I've owned in my entire life. Not to mention the dresses Erika brought over for you to try on."

In the week since Nikki and Terrence had found her in that basement, Jill had regained most of her strength and energy. She'd talked to her editor and started on the first article in what she was planning to be a multiarticle news spread about her investigation into the trafficking ring. Jill had uttered the word *Pulitzer* in an excitedly hushed tone more than once.

"And you should feel free to wear any of them. I have more than enough." Erika pinned a lock of Nikki's hair up. She'd been working on creating an effortless-looking updo for the past half hour. Nikki had to admit, between the makeup that Jill had applied and the hair, she looked pretty great.

"I think you're just all in a tizzy because you and my brother are going on your first date." Jill grinned.

Nikki rolled her eyes at her friend. "It's hardly our first date."

"It's your first date as adults. The first one that really matters."

Even though he and Jill had been staying with her at Lakewood House for the last several days while Jill recuperated, Terrence had made a point of calling her and asking her to attend the gallery opening as his date, very gentlemanly. It had made her feel a little giddy.

"Okay, I'm making an executive decision," Jill said, lifting herself off the bed. "You should wear the red dress."

"No. No way." Nikki stepped away from the mirror.

"Definitely." Erika clapped her hands. "You looked amazing in that dress. Terrence is going to lose his mind when he sees you in it."

"No. It's way too—"

"Sexy," Jill said.

"Alluring," Erika purred.

"Revealing," Nikki responded.

"That's what makes it perfect." Jill giggled.

Nikki gave in and slipped into the dress. The neckline plunged, revealing more cleavage than she usually did, but she loved the vibrant red color and the loose, flowy skirt that fanned out when she twirled. She was a knockout in this dress. There was no doubt about that. While Nikki put the finishing touches on her outfit, Erika transferred her keys, money and identification from her everyday purse to the little red clutch she had brought over with the dress.

Jill came to stand behind Nikki as she looked at herself in the mirror. "Terrence is going to have a stroke when he sees you."

"Let's hope not," Nikki said wryly.

"I've got to get to the gallery." Erika started for the bedroom door. "I'll come by tomorrow and pick up the other dresses, if that's okay."

"Of course." Nikki grabbed the clutch and walked her new friend to the front door of the house, Jill trailing behind.

"I'm going to catch a ride with Erika, so I'm leaving as well." Jill grabbed her coat from the closet next to the front door.

"You don't have to do that. You can ride with Terrence and me."

Now it was Jill who rolled her eyes. "I'm not going to be the third wheel on your date." Jill put a hand on each of Nikki's shoulders. "Don't worry. You and Terrence are perfect together." She bussed Nikki on her cheek and followed Erika out of the house.

Nikki watched her friends drive away. Dusk had begun to fall, and the trees surrounding the house made it even darker than it actually was.

She closed the door and checked out her image in the mirror once again. She did look pretty amazing. And this was Terrence. She'd known him her entire life. Loved him most of it.

All the air whooshed out of her lungs.

She loved him. Despite the years and the petty feud and whatever else, she loved him. And now she knew she always would.

The doorbell rang and she jumped.

Letting out a breath, she did the best she could to still her racing pulse, to no avail.

"Here we go." She pulled open the door.

Terrence stood on the porch holding a dozen red roses and wearing a perfectly cut black suit. He was pretty alluring himself. She let her eyes roam over him from head to toe, appreciating the view.

"You look amazing," he said, stepping into the house and pressing a kiss to her cheek. He'd gone to James's place to get ready, insisting that they'd do this date right with him picking her up at her door.

"So do you."

She took the roses from him and put them into water.

"Should we go?" She grabbed the clutch from the side table under the mirror.

"Not just yet. I have something I want to show you." Terrence took her hand and led her to the door.

"We're going to be late if we don't leave soon."

"Don't worry. These things never get started on time. Anyway, James will understand if we're late. He helped me set this up for you."

"Set what up?"

"You'll see." He led her onto the porch and around the side of the house.

Her boat had been decorated with white twinkle lights. As they drew closer, she could see that a bistro table had been set up on deck, two flutes and a silver bucket at its center with champagne chilling inside.

"What is all this?"

"We'll get to the gallery opening, but I wanted to make sure this date was special. That we got some time together, just the two of us."

"How did you possibly set all this up without me knowing? I've been inside all day."

"It took some planning but having my sister and Erika on my side, distracting you, helped a lot."

Nikki laughed. "They did their job. I didn't suspect a thing."

"Good." Terrence grabbed the open champagne bottle and poured them both a glass. "To us."

Nikki didn't take her eyes off his as she sipped. She set her glass aside, and he did the same as she stepped into his arms.

She sank into their kiss, filling it with all the things she felt for him. When she pulled back, she slid a sidelong glance at the padded bench seats. "I think we're about to be very late to this opening."

A slow, seductive smile slid across Terrence's face. "Honey, there's nowhere else I'd rather be."

* * * * *

COLTON'S ULTIMATE TEST

BETH CORNELISON

For my mom—my once and always biggest fan

Chapter One

Last January

"A toast to th' bir'day girl!"

"To Lorie!" Morgan Colton raised her nearly empty glass, joining her friends in Helen's salute.

"Girl?" Connie asked with a snort. "Lorie hasn't been a girl for a *looong* time. It's *woman*, thank you."

The table of women had been drinking to Lorie, who was turning forty, all night, but what was one more toast? The clink of glasses seemed loud in the now nearly empty bar. With it being closing time on a cold January night, Morgan and her friends had the place almost to themselves.

Morgan leaned over to whisper to her friend Stacy. "Connie gets more feminist when she's drunk, doesn't she?"

Stacy nodded and laughed.

Morgan had never been a frequent customer at the Corner Pocket, the English pub-style billiards bar poised on a choice riverfront location in downtown Blue Larkspur, Colorado. The bar was more her brothers' kind of place. But Helen had arranged the night out and had picked the pub for the celebration, and Morgan approved. The place had a coziness to it. And good food. And plenty of libations. She could see why her brothers like the place. Or maybe that was just the margaritas talking…

"Hey!" Lorie replied with a frown to Connie as all the ladies around the table sipped their drinks. "Are you calling me old?"

Connie paused, gave the black Mylar "Over the Hill" balloon tied to Lorie's chair a meaningful glance and with a wry grin said, "Yep."

Helen raised a hand. "Billy's shift ends at eleven. By midnight I plan to have him naked."

Stacy hooted a laugh. "Way to go, Helen!" Then, rocking her shoulders as if proud of herself, Stacy pointed a manicured finger across the bar to a patron at another table. "I think I'm taking that fine *thang* home with me. He's been watching me since he came in."

Morgan blinked and cast a glance over shoulder at the man in question. "Stacy, are you sure you want to do that? Do you even know him?"

Stacy flapped a hand at her. "Colton, you worry too much. Of course I know him. He's my future husband." Helen cackled and high-fived Stacy.

"I mean, are you—"

She grabbed Morgan's wrist. "I know what y' mean. I appreciate your concern, mama hen. I'm a big girl."

"Woman!" Connie insisted.

"I'll be careful," Stacy said, giving Morgan a smile. "You should try a one-night stand sometime. It's very freeing. No strings. No commitments. No regrets."

Morgan twisted her mouth, considering Stacy's

stance. She'd never felt comfortable assuming the same casualness toward sex as her friend. She wanted what Lorie had. A husband, a home. Permanence. Love.

And, as they'd all been reminded tonight, thanks to Lorie's birthday, she wasn't getting any younger. She'd turn forty next year. She'd let years slip by, put her dreams of a husband and family on hold while she helped raise her brood of brothers and sisters after an accident had claimed their father when the youngest girls were barely six.

Mama hen, Stacy had called her, because of her tendency to extend that motherly nurturing to her friends as well. Chicken soup and cookies when they were sick. A shoulder to cry on when needed. And more than a little advice concerning everything from clothes to business contracts.

She couldn't help it. As the oldest of twelve—well, technically Caleb was ten minutes older—she came by her take-charge, order-and-structure attitude naturally. But the babies of the family, Alexa and Naomi, were strong, competent women with careers who no longer needed her mothering. Maybe it was time—past time— to consider what she wanted her life to look like in the years to come. The law firm she and Caleb owned, Colton and Colton, filled her days, satisfied her professional yearnings. But what about her nights? Her more intimate yearnings? And, yes, her physical needs. Maybe she did need a wild night of no-strings sex to satisfy her—

"Last call, ladies," said a deeply masculine voice from over her shoulder.

Morgan tipped her head to look up...and up. Holy

mackerel, the guy was tall! And dark. And *tattooed*. Her chest tightened. Then the guy wobbled…

Oops, that was her wavering.

Morgan grabbed the edge of the table as she canted too far and nearly tumbled out of her chair. Tall, Dark and Tattooed grabbed her under her arms. "Whoa! Easy there. You all right?"

She nodded and wrenched free of his grasp, sputtering, "Rain as right!"

Beside her, Helen barked a raucous laugh. "What?"

Morgan replayed what she'd said in her head. "I mean, right as rain. I'm just a little—"

"Too drunk to drive," Tall, Dark and Tattooed— whom she quickly recognized as Roman DiMera, the bar's owner—said, holding out his hand. "Car keys?"

She'd met Roman here at the Corner Pocket once when he took over running the place a couple years ago but hadn't exchanged more than niceties with him. Her brothers knew him somewhat, having spent more time at the billiards bar. She'd heard rumors Roman was an ex-con.

She studied him now, up close and personal. Muscles. A firm, square jaw beneath a short black beard. If she concentrated on his rugged face, those dark eyes, she could get swept up in his masculine appeal. She inhaled deeply, certain she could smell the testosterone oozing from him. Or maybe she only thought so because her friends had reminded her how long it had been since she'd had sex.

Roman wiggled his fingers, his hand still out. "Keys? You're not driving."

Morgan opened her mouth to protest but immediately thought better of it. She was far too drunk to drive. "Fine. Will you get us all 'n Uper... *Uber*?"

"Definitely." He cast his gaze around the table to her friends. "How many of you need an Uber to get home?"

Lorie waved a hand. "My husband is pickin' me up at closin'."

"I'm goin' home with 'im," Stacy said, pointing to the same patron as before.

Tall, Dark and Tattooed called to the other man, "Dan, how many drinks have you had?"

"Nada. I'm working tomorrow. Gotta have a clear head," the future Mr. Stacy called back, wiping his mouth and tossing his napkin on a platter of chicken-wing bones.

"You'll see this nice lady home?" Morgan asked.

Dan nodded. "Indeed I will," he said as he pulled a chair from another table and started chatting up Stacy.

Helen pointed to the door, where a burly guy with a baby face had just walked in. "That's my ride. An' then I'm gonna ride him!"

Helen laughed at her own joke, then staggered from the table to tip into her boyfriend's arms. Morgan waited at the table until Lorie's husband arrived, then she gave the birthday girl—woman!—a hug, promising to call her soon for lunch.

Things between Stacy and her conquest seemed to be going well, so Morgan excused herself to the ladies' room, trying to act as if the floor wasn't swaying under her. While in the restroom, she took a moment to reapply her lipstick, smooth her hair and check for food in her teeth. Through the muddle of alcohol pickling her brain, she had the wherewithal to question whom she was primping for. The night was over. Her friends were heading home. Her Uber to take her back to her house would arrive soon.

She squared her shoulders defiantly. She didn't have to be primping for anyone. She just liked to look tidy, professional, put-together. So why were Roman Di-Mera's wide chest and brown eyes burned like an afterimage in her mind? On the heels of that thought, she pictured the tattoos on his arms, wrists...

She clutched the edge of the sink and took a few deep breaths, clawing back memories too harsh to face at the moment. With a cleansing exhale, she straightened her blouse and headed out of the bathroom.

There was a reason she'd never gotten to know Di-Mera beyond greetings and pleasant small talk. They ran in different circles. The men she dated reserved ink for signing contracts, not their skin. In fact, she avoided men with tattoos entirely because of *that* day in college. Her type of man ordered Cristal, not microbrews. She preferred a tailored suit to a snug rock band T-shirt any day of the week. Although...

Her breath caught remembering how Roman's Rolling Stones T-shirt hugged his broad frame and revealed just a hint of the black hair on his chest. Her head swam, and, blaming the last round of margaritas rather than thoughts of Roman DiMera's physique, she marched back out to the bar. Well, sort of marched. The floor was still swaying a bit, which made a confident, purposeful stride rather difficult.

Roman met her halfway across the bar, his brow furrowed. "Local Uber drivers seem to be tied up thanks to the Symphony Guild benefit that's just ended across town. I guess they figure symphony patrons tip better than billiard players."

Morgan lifted her chin. "I go to the symphony!"

Roman raised one eyebrow, silently reminding her the point was moot.

She sighed and flapped a hand. "Forget a rideshare. I'll call one of my siblings. What's the point of having eleven brothers and sisters if you can't wake one of 'em in the middle of the night to drive you home from a bar, hmm?" She frowned as she calculated which of her brothers or sisters owed her a favor. "Not Rachel. She's got the baby…"

She dug in her purse for her phone, finding it hard to keep her balance while she rummaged in the deep shoulder bag. "Did ev'ryone else leave?" She cut a glance past the numerous billiard tables that occupied one side of the bar to their now-empty table. "They all had someone to drive them? I don't want anyone behind th' wheel."

Roman caught her elbow as she teetered on her high heels and guided her to a chair. Heat from his strong fingers seeped through the filmy material of her blouse and made her pulse stumble.

"All of your friends have gone. All safe and squared away. Tell you what," Roman said, peering down at her with serious brown eyes. "Instead of waking one of your family, let me take you home."

Morgan angled a suspicious look at Roman. "You?"

He nodded.

"I live in the Brookhaven subdivision. Is that on your way home?"

A lopsided grin transformed his face. "Hardly. I live upstairs. I have an apartment here, above the bar."

She frowned. "But— Then why…?"

"Give me a minute to get my coat and the bag with the night's deposit. I'll swing by the bank on the way back."

"I, uh…" She was trying to form a response, to decide if letting Roman drive her home was a good idea or not, but before her inebriated brain sorted past *he's an ex-con,* Roman quickly disappeared through the swinging doors to the kitchen.

Ex-con. The term didn't bother her as much as it might some people. If her work with the Truth Foundation, the nonprofit she and Caleb had established to help the wrongfully convicted clear their names, had taught her anything, it was not to judge a person based on the label *convict.* Not everyone in prison was guilty. And not everyone out on the street was innocent.

"Okay," Roman said, emerging from the back of the bar and tossing the barkeeper the keys. "You'll lock up for me, Tim? Check the grill before you go?"

The man behind the bar nodded. "Sure thing, boss."

He bade a waitress good-night as she headed home, then turned to Morgan. "Ready?" he asked as he pulled on a knit hat with a Philadelphia Eagles logo at the front.

Her brothers seemed to like him. They'd spoken well of him on occasion, even holding Roman up as an example of how someone could turn their life around.

Morgan chewed her bottom lip. "Two questions first."

"Okay…" he said, his tone wary. He folded his arms over his chest and narrowed his eyes.

"First, this is Colorado, bub." She pointed at his hat. "Where's your love for the Broncos?"

He twisted his lips as if in thought. "They're okay. But I'm Philly born and bred. The Eagles were my first love."

She scoffed lightly. "Okay. Fair enough. Question two." She held up two fingers like a toddler telling someone how old they were. She stared at her fingers, realized how silly she looked and tucked her hand under her arm as if she could erase the gesture from his memory.

"Yes?"

"Did you do it?" she asked, lifting her chin along with one eyebrow.

His brow furrowed, and his expression dimmed with confusion. "Do what?"

She flapped a hand. "Whatever landed you in jail. Word on the street is you've had a scrape with the law." Belatedly, she realized her question might be considered rude. But her job required her to ask prying, blunt questions of her clients and witnesses in court, so she'd blurted the question without thinking about manners.

His back straightened, and his face darkened. For a moment, he said nothing, then he muttered quietly, "Yeah. I did it."

Morgan blinked, a bit surprised by his confirmation. Typically she heard denials. Protestations of innocence and justifications that tried to excuse dubious behavior. For long seconds, she stared at him, as if waiting for the punch line, the retraction. His ownership impressed her.

Instead, he said, "Ready to go?"

He said it calmly enough, but she heard a challenge

in his tone. He seemed to be daring her to refuse his offer of a ride home based on a prejudice against him for his past. Morgan knew her reputation for not backing down preceded her. What kind of lawyer would she be if she had no backbone, no conviction, no determination? Likewise, she had to put that terrible night twenty years ago behind her and stop looking over her shoulder. Both literally and figuratively.

She met his gaze boldly and rose from her seat. "Sure. Let's go."

Some niggle in her brain gave her pause, but not because of his stint in prison. No, the whisper tickling her thoughts had more to do with the pulse of attraction she felt as he helped her don her coat and make her way through the cold night to his car. An old Corvette, still in excellent condition. *Nice.*

Past boyfriends had driven Mercedes sedans or Volvos. BMWs. All designed to impress and convey the image of success.

Morgan liked the old Corvette better, she decided as she settled in, even if the confines of his front seat felt uncomfortably intimate. Or maybe because of it.

The darkness and late hour added a sense of isolation. No one was on the street. The city was quiet, and the stars winked brightly in the clear night sky. She was alone with Roman. Alone…

She couldn't decide if the twitter in her chest was ill ease…or intrigue. Interest. Tantalizing promise. She swallowed hard.

When she exhaled a sigh, her breath formed a white cloud that smelled of tequila and lime. Cutting a side glance to Roman, she covered her mouth with her hand.

Maybe instead of worrying about her lipstick earlier, she should have considered a breath mint or gum.

As if I was going to be kissing someone tonight...

A dismissive scoff escaped her throat.

"What was that?" Roman said.

"Huh?"

"I thought you said something."

"No, I..." She dug in her purse, looking for something minty or—

She pulled out a cough drop with bits of lint stuck to the wrapper. God knows how old the thing was. What the hell...

The wrapper crinkled as she opened it and popped the lozenge in her mouth. Sickly cherry menthol filled her mouth. "Ugh."

"Here?" Roman asked, and she looked up to see where they were. The Corvette's headlights illuminated the sign at the entry to her subdivision.

"Yeah. Take the first left," she said, pointing.

"Um," Roman said, chuckling. "Are you sure it's a left? You're pointing right."

She wrinkled her forehead, confused for a moment, then scowled at him. "Just...turn here!" She tapped the window as she pointed right more firmly.

"Do you know which house is yours?" he asked, his mouth pulled in a wry grin.

"Of course I do! Don't be a wiseass!"

"Well?"

Morgan aimed a finger over her shoulder. "That one. You just passed it."

His mouth twitched as if trying to muffle a laugh or a cutting comeback as he reversed the Corvette and braked in front of her house. He cut the engine and opened his door.

"What are you doing?" she asked. "I didn't invite you in."

"No, but I'm seeing that you get in and lock up behind me just the same."

He climbed from driver's side and circled to the passenger door before she could fumble her way out. He grasped her arm, and she shook off his assistance. "I'm good. No need."

She crossed her frost-crusted yard, her ankles buckling when her heels slipped. Again DiMera was there, catching her, supporting her until she reached her front door.

She dropped her keys twice before he took them from her and unlocked her door.

"I coulda done that," she grumbled as she pushed through the door.

"I'm sure you could have, love. But I didn't want to be here until morning." He flipped on the foyer light as he followed her inside.

The cherry cough drop was making her stomach heave, so she pulled a Kleenex from her coat pocket and spit the lozenge out. Wadding up the tissue, she dropped it in the nearest wastebasket.

Roman's face reflected a degree of amusement when she turned to tell him goodbye. "What?"

He pointed to where she'd just tossed the tissue. "Isn't that an umbrella stand?"

She glanced back at the corner of her foyer, and heat prickled her cheeks. He was right. *How drunk am I?*

Sheesh! Squaring her shoulders, she faced him. "Don't you need to be going now?"

One black eyebrow flicked up. "Soon. Need help with your coat?"

She buzzed a raspberry at him and fingered the oversize buttons on her wool coat. When her first attempt failed to produce results, she met his brown eyes and huffed. "My fingers are just cold."

"I see." He reached for her hands and pressed one between his. Tingles raced up her arm as he rubbed and chaffed her icy fingers, warming more than her hands with his caress. Heat built in her core and expanded, filled her. His touch should not have tantalized her so much. But as he stared into her eyes, his skilled fingers massaging her palm, stroking warmth into her cold joints, her knees weakened. She zeroed in on his lips, peeking out from his neatly trimmed beard and mustache. She'd never kissed a man with facial hair. What would it be like? Did it tickle?

"Now give those buttons a try," he said, his voice a low rumble that made her belly tremble. And her resolve cracked.

She stepped toward him and lowered the zipper on his suede jacket. "Oh yeah. Much better now."

"Morgan…" he said, but she pressed her lips to his, silencing him.

With her hands sliding under his coat, she shoved the jacket off his shoulders. Roman untangled his arms from the sleeves and let the coat fall to the floor.

He plunged one hand in the thick curtain of her dark hair and caught her nape as he angled his mouth over hers. His beard was softer than it looked, and she was mindful of the velvet glide of his mouth, the nip of his teeth on her bottom lip…the surge of nausea in her gut.

She shoved him back and staggered quickly toward her hall bathroom. Dropping to her knees, she emptied her stomach into the toilet and groaned at the persistent churning of her stomach. Roman materialized behind her, scooping her hair back from her face with both hands as she retched again. Once she felt able, she sat back on her heels and wiped her mouth on a fistful of toilet paper.

"Better?" Roman asked as he wet a washcloth in the sink. He squatted beside her and dabbed the cool rag on the flushed skin of her face and neck.

She hummed a nonanswer, and her gaze was drawn to the Celtic-looking design tattooed on his wrist. Her vision blurred, and a dark memory made her ears buzz as adrenaline kicked inside her. Shaking off the phantom recollection that nipped at her with sharp teeth, Morgan took the washrag from him, muttering, "I can do that."

She buried her face in the damp cloth, willing the haunting images in her head back to the shadowy corners where she kept them locked away. But when she raised her head again and blinked open her eyes, Roman was still hunkered beside her, watching her with concern in his gaze. She averted her own eyes, only to find her attention locked on his muscled shoulders. The sleeves of his T-shirt were short enough that she could see the eagle inked on one of his biceps and the blue barbed-wire band tattooed around the other.

Another flash of chilling memory skittered through her mind, and she shuddered.

"You okay, Colton?" He caught her chin between his finger and thumb, his tone gentle.

She raised a hand to wave him off. "I'm…yeah. Just…tequila seems to allow bad memories to surface."

He cocked his head to the side. "What kind of bad memories?"

"The kind I don't want to talk about…ever."

"Well—" he slid one shoe off her foot, then the other and set the shoes aside "—I'm betting you've had enough tequila that tomorrow you'll have no memories of tonight—good, bad or otherwise."

She groaned. When she tried to struggle to her feet, he helped her up with a firm grasp of her elbow.

"Yeah, so…" He led her out of the bathroom and down the hall to her bedroom. "Let's get you in bed."

She frowned. "Hey! If you think you can take advantage of me—"

He let her flop onto her mattress. He peeled back the covers and tucked them around her. "Wouldn't think of it, princess."

She considered his reply for a beat then scowled. "Wait. What? Why not?"

"Because I'm not that kind of guy. And because I know you have brothers who'd kill me if I did."

Her pillow and blanket cradled her and coaxed her toward sleep like a lullaby. She blinked groggily. Tall, Dark and Tattooed was still standing at the edge of her bed. His face was shadowed in her dark bedroom, but she caught the twist of his lips. His sigh. "And because you and me…would be a mistake."

"Definitely…" she mumbled and let the pull of sleep drag her under.

Chapter Two

Eleven months later.

"I thought you were going out on an errand."

Morgan glanced to the door of her private office, where Caleb leaned against the jamb, holding a cup of coffee. "I am going out. Soon. I just…" She huffed and drummed her fingers on her desk. "Okay, fine. I'm stalling. I know I promised everyone I'd follow up on that potential lead concerning Ronald Spence and how and where he might try to launder that money we think he stole, but…" She buzzed her lips in frustration. "I need another minute or two to gather my courage."

Caleb frowned, and, pushing away from the door, he moved to sit in one of the chairs positioned at angles in front of her desk for client consultations. "Courage? Is this contact you have someone dangerous? Should I go with you?"

Morgan shook her head. "Not dangerous, exactly. But…it's embarrassing…awkward for me."

"Awkward? That doesn't sound like the twin sister and business partner I know and love. What happened to the go-getter, take-no-prisoners attitude?" He took a sip of his coffee and set it on the edge of her desk. "Geez, if helping raise our siblings while you worked your way through college and law school wasn't enough to faze you, why should asking this contact about Spence bother you?"

"I'd...rather not say. Bad enough I have to humble myself to face—" She swallowed the name on her tongue, unwilling to give her brother any more clues about her humiliating night in January. "Well...my contact."

"Or...you could tell me who it is, and I'll go," Caleb offered, splaying his hands. "Nothing says I can't do the follow-up on your—"

"No." Morgan waved a hand and shook her head as she rose from her desk chair. "I need to do this. What kind of coward would I be if I let one drunken night keep me from—"

She stopped when she saw Caleb's eyebrows shoot up. What had she said?

"A drunken night? This is getting juicy. Now I have to know who your mysterious contact is."

Morgan gritted her back teeth and rolled her eyes as she marched to the coat tree and retrieved her coat and purse. "I've said too much already. If I learn anything useful, I'll let you know."

Caleb stood as well, shoving his hands in his pockets. "Be sure to impress upon your contact the urgency of finding Spence ASAP," he said, referring to the man their firm had helped free from prison earlier that year. That same man had gone on to wreak havoc and tragedy on her family and was currently in hiding with a stolen fortune. "If Spence is planning to move that money out of the country, we have at best five days for that money to settle in local accounts before he can transfer—"

"Caleb." Morgan shot her twin an incredulous look. "I know. We went over all this earlier, remember? I know the law. I know the ticking clock."

He held up both hands in apology. "Sorry. I'm just so ready for all of this Spence business to be over and done. You realize this mess, in one respect or another, has been hanging over the family for a year now?"

"Well aware." She buttoned her coat and hiked her purse strap to her shoulder. "I'm ready to put it behind us, too. I'd like to enjoy Christmas without the shadow of Ronald Spence hanging over us all." She stepped forward to give her brother and business partner a quick peck on the cheek. "Back in an hour or so."

"Good luck with your drunken night of embarrassment," he said with a teasing smile. "You know I'm not going to let this go until I hear all the scandalous details."

Morgan glowered at him and headed to the door. "Not going to happen. That secret is going with me to the grave." When she breezed past the desk of the law firm's administrative assistant, the dark-haired older woman glanced up from her computer screen. "I'm running an errand, Rebekah, then grabbing lunch after. Back by one."

"Take your time. Maybe chew your lunch instead of inhaling it on the go today?" Rebekah Hanlan called back. "I'll hold down fort long enough for you to actually enjoy a meal for once."

"No time today," Morgan returned. "But thanks for caring."

Rather than wait for the elevator, Morgan took the stairs. The exercise helped her burn off the jitters that swirled in her gut every time she thought about the task ahead. Not that gathering the needed information on suspected thief and potential money launderer Ronald Spence was anything more than another day at the office for her. But her memories—the few she had—of what happened after Lorie's birthday party at the Corner Pocket made her want to crawl into bed and pull the covers over her head.

She shouldered open the door to the parking lot and shivered as the chill December air blasted her. That January night had been cold, too. She recalled heavy coats…and shoving one off muscled shoulders so she could get at the man inside the coat. Smoldering dark eyes. Fingers in her hair…

She winced. Those same fingers had raked her hair back from her face while she got sick in her bathroom like some college girl at a frat party. She paused at the driver's door of her Lexus sedan, heat stinging her cheeks despite the Colorado chill. *You can do this, Colton. Maybe he won't even remember you.*

She scoffed at herself and climbed in her car. After her mortifying behavior that night in January—had she really kissed him or had she dreamed that?—the odds of Roman DiMera forgetting her were about as good as those that Santa Claus would forget Christmas this year.

Morgan sighed and started her engine. "Damn."

"Scrooge," Gibb McNulty grumbled as he stopped wiping glasses to watch Roman work.

Roman turned carefully on the stepladder where he

was taking down a string of Christmas lights that no longer worked. "Come again?"

Gibb waved a hand toward the lights in Roman's hand. "It's not even Christmas yet, and you're already stripping the place of holiday cheer. When I was a kid, my mom would leave our decorations up until after New Year's." He paused, his expression pensive. "It's one of the things I missed most while in prison. Christmas lights weren't on the approved list for the state pen. Too many ways to use them as a weapon, you know?"

Roman descended the ladder and gave a knowing grunt. "Yeah." He tossed the broken lights in the trash. "Didn't mean to squash your holiday cheer, man. But those lights are broken. Unlit lights aren't a good look any time of year. So…" He motioned to the trash.

Gibb gave him a skeptical look. "If I remember my Dr. Seuss right, that's the same excuse the Grinch gave Cindy Lou Who."

"Yeah, but did the Grinch replace the broken lights with a new string that worked?" Roman pointed to the box on the bar. "Probably the last set in town. I had to go to three stores to find those."

"You really want to make me happy, you could give me a raise. Or a year-end bonus. A couple thousand would help. I'm behind on my rent and have Christmas bills to pay off. I love my kids, but, damn, are they expensive!"

Roman climbed back up the ladder with the new lights and gave Gibb an apologetic look. "I didn't know things had been so tight for you. You're the best bartender I've ever had, man, and I want to help, but… well, the blizzard earlier this month really cut into our business. I'll see what I can do. But if I can work out a bonus, it won't be more than a few hundred at best. Sorry."

He clipped the new string of lights in place, and as he descended the ladder, he heard someone come in the front door of the bar. He hitched his head, signaling Gibb. "You're up. I'll be in my office looking for a way to offer year-end bonuses all around."

Roman returned the ladder to the storage room and headed to his office, a room barely larger than the closet. He'd had just gotten settled at his cluttered desk when he heard a knock on his door and glanced up.

Gibb stood there, drying his hands on a towel. "Hey, boss, there's a lady out here wants to see you. Said her name was Colton."

Colton.

Roman's breath stilled for a moment remembering a sizzling kiss he'd tried all year to forget. He cleared his throat. "Did she say what she wanted?"

"No. Just that it was urgent."

Urgent? He rubbed his beard, puzzling over that. "Okay, I'll talk to her."

Gibb hadn't said which Colton it was. What were the odds it was Morgan Colton? There were several Coltons in town, including Rachel, the local district attorney. Was he or an employee in legal trouble? He'd had quite enough of the legal system and jail cells in his life, thank you. He had no reason to think Morgan had business with him. After all, she hadn't darkened the door of the Corner Pocket since that night in January when…

Roman rubbed his eyes with the pads of his fingers.

Hell, it had been one kiss in the midst of a debacle of an evening. Why couldn't he stop thinking about it?

Because she shook you to your marrow like no other woman has, a niggling voice whispered as he rose from his desk to head out front. *Get over it, DiMera*, another voice shouted to silence the first. *She made it clear that night and every day since by staying far away from you and your bar that she wants nothing to do with you.*

Roman frowned, remembering the disgust that had crossed Morgan's face when she looked at his tattoos, as if they were a billboard advertising his stint in prison. Or maybe it was something more general, like the fact that he was a humble bar owner who wore his love for the Rolling Stones on his T-shirt, while she practiced law in tidy silk suits. He scoffed to himself, hearing her slightly slurred, "I go to the symphony!" as if he'd given offense when he speculated that symphony patrons might tip better than bar patrons. As if she felt compelled to distinguish herself above the riffraff that came to the Corner Pocket, despite having spent the evening swilling drinks at his bar with her friends.

Roman set his jaw as he strode through the kitchen. Forget her dismissive tone. Forget the kiss. Forget her. It probably wasn't even Morgan waiting to see him. The Colton family was large, and it could be any one of—

He stopped as he stepped through the swinging door from the kitchen and spotted the brunette in a slim skirt and high-heeled pumps waiting at the bar. Even with her back to him, her hair wrapped in a tight knot at her nape, Roman recognized her. He studied the school-marm bun as he crossed the floor, deciding he much preferred her hair loose and flowing around her shoulders, as it had been *that night* in January. His hands twitched at his sides, remembering the silky tresses slipping over his fingers when he'd kissed her, when he'd held her hair back in the bathroom. Okay, the last wasn't the most pleasant memory, but her hair… God, he imagined he could still smell the lingering fruity—was it peach?—scent of her shampoo…

She turned, as if she sensed him, and her spine straightened. Her mouth pinched a bit at the corners, and her nostrils flared as if she'd caught a whiff of something rotten. Propping her wrists on the bar in front of her, her hands clutching a pair of leather gloves, she kicked her chin up a notch.

Message received. Whatever she was doing here, she still found him beneath her and her errand today a task to be endured.

"Hello, Mr. DiMera," she said coolly, adding a flicker of a smile that seemed about as real as a ten-dollar Rolex watch.

"Ms. Colton." He bobbed a nod in greeting and assumed a crossed-arms, braced-legs stance. "What can I do for you?"

She took a deep breath before meeting his eyes with her heart-stopping blue gaze. "I…need a favor."

"Another one?"

His reply wiped the fake smile from her face. "Pardon me?"

He lifted a corner of his mouth. "I drove you home a few months back when you were too tipsy to drive safely. Or were you too drunk to remember even that much?"

She blanched but kept her shoulders squared, her

back straight. After a pause, during which her hands
fidgeted with the gloves she held, she angled her head
and flashed the stiff smile again. This time the twitch
of her lips was more a nervous tic than strained polite-
ness. "I, uh…remember a good bit from that night."
She exhaled through pursed lips as her eyebrows rose.
"Unfortunately."

Roman angled his head in question. "Why unfortunately?"

The look she gave him said he was dense for having to ask. "It was hardly my finest moment. I'm certainly not happy that our reintroduction to each other
was colored by… Well, I was…" She waved a hand as
if looking for the right word.

"Snockered? Wasted? Three sheets to the wind?
Hugging the porcelain god?" he supplied, secretly enjoying watching her squirm. A pink flush crept from
her neck to her face. She was even prettier with that
color high in her cheeks.

She took a beat, clearly trying to compose herself,
and an irritated look creased her forehead. "Tact is not
your strong suit, I take it?"

He lifted a shoulder. "I see no need to sugarcoat
the truth. You were drunk. I drove you home. Simple
as that."

She pressed her palm to the top of the bar, apparently
unable to meet his eyes. "Was it…as simple as that?"

Roman pulled out the bar stool next to her and half
sat down, keeping one foot on the floor. "What are you
asking?"

She looked away, her hands moving restlessly across
the bar. "Are you really going to make me spell it out?"

"Yes."

Her wide blue gaze shot up to his, then away again, her mouth tightening.

"I don't like assumptions, Ms. Colton. I'd think as a lawyer you'd prefer to deal in facts as well. Am I right?"

She huffed. "I do. But I appreciate a little diplomacy or savoir faire now and then, too."

He raised a hand to concede the point, and he followed her gaze as it landed on his wrist tattoo and stuck. He recalled how her attention had strayed frequently to his ink back in January. Remembered how her expression had soured each time. Remembered her distinct withdrawal, as if the tattoos were magnets of the same charge pushing her away. His hands fisted, and he folded his arms as he shoved the recollections away. "I'm a busy man, Ms. Colton. Can we quit dancing around our last meeting and get to the reason you wanted to see me today?"

"Of course." She angled her body more fully toward him, and he watched a transformation he'd not have believed if he hadn't witnessed it. She seemed to peel off the skin of the awkward, irritated woman, reminded of a past mistake, and slide into the body of a huntress, a cool, confident professional about to slay her opponent in court. "I need help finding someone."

"Who?"

She sat on a bar stool, crossed her legs and angled her chin up. "His name is Ronald Spence, and we— my family and I—suspect him of having stolen a large amount of money."

A bitter suspicion gnawed Roman's gut, but he kept his face, his tone even. "And you think I know him?"

She shrugged as if she hadn't just implied he ran with criminals, was maybe a lowlife himself. "If you don't know him, then maybe you know where we might find him? We suspect he'll try to launder the money, so we only have a few days to track down—"

"Hold up," he said, lifting both hands in a halting gesture and giving a short, sardonic laugh. "Care to explain why you think I know this thief? Some guy robs your family and your first instinct is to ask *me* about it? That's rather insulting, don't you think?"

"Well, he didn't rob us so much as he stole money that had previously been stolen by my brother's girlfriend's father," she countered, ignoring his protest, "and hidden—"

He interrupted her with a brief, shrill whistle. "Irrelevant. I don't care about the money. But I do take exception to your presumptions about me."

Her jaw worked as if she were trying to find her voice.

He braced an arm on the bar near her and leaned close—which may have been a mistake, because this near her, he could smell her shampoo. The fruity scent was an erotic reminder of that kiss…

Elbowing that thought aside, he asked, "Why did you come to me about this?"

She licked her lips, and a certain vulnerability swam in her pale blue eyes. "Because you—I remembered you saying—"

He drilled her with his stare. "Go on. I want to hear you say it."

She scowled and seemed to find her moxie again. Meeting his challenge with her own, she said, "Because you served time. Because you hire ex-cons. Because I need, at least, a starting place, and we don't have a lot of time to beat the bushes through our regular channels. We've been trying to find Spence for months and have no other leads."

Roman stayed where he was, glaring down at her from mere inches away, close enough that he could feel her agitated breaths on his face. His own respiration had spiked. Having been drawn into her orbit and held there as if by some gravitational force, his entire body tingled, on high alert and aware of her every move, every scent, every sound. An energy pulsed around her that made his own nerves crackle and spark. Lowering his voice to a whisper, he asked, "Why do I scare you?"

Morgan blinked. Scoffed. "You don't scare me."

Her arched an eyebrow. "You sure about that? Your body language says otherwise."

She frowned and leaned back. "Well, you are rather up in my grill at the moment." She planted a hand on his chest and gave him a firm push. When he leaned back a few inches, she continued, "I work daily with people who've had brushes with the law. I've taken on the best lawyers in the state for my clients and won. I grew up with several rough-and-tumble brothers. Honestly, Mr. DiMera, I'm not easily intimidated."

He gave her a look of measuring scrutiny before removing his hand from beside her and straightening. "I'm not convinced, but it doesn't matter. The answer to your question is no. I don't know this Spence person you're looking for. He's never worked for me, and I don't recall our paths having crossed. So…" He jerked a shrug. "Sorry I couldn't help."

Consternation darkened her expression. "You're sure? You barely gave it any thought. Maybe someone you know could help us? We think he's going to launder the money before sending it to foreign accounts."

He lifted an eyebrow. "Why do you think that?"

"It's what I'd do with cash I wanted to hide. Wouldn't you?" she shot back.

He bristled. He'd moved to Colorado for a fresh start, to get away from the prejudices and preconceived notions that had followed him when he was released from prison. "Considering I've put my lawbreaking days behind me, I'd have to say no. I wouldn't. I'm not a thief."

Her shoulders dropped as she exhaled a frustrated-sounding sigh. "But you know how it works—laundering money and moving it to foreign accounts?"

A prickle of suspicion crawled up his back. "Do I? You sound rather sure of yourself."

She closed her eyes and groaned. "Okay, I may have looked into your conviction and the reasons for the time you served in New York."

Roman tensed, fury slamming him like a fist in the gut. "You what?"

"It's a matter of public record," she said, her tone edged with defensiveness. "It's even common knowledge in town that your conviction had to do with finances. When I asked you in January, you said you were guilty of the charges you were sent away for, but not what you'd done." She waved her hand as if the mistakes he'd made years ago, the events that had altered his life trajectory and broken every relationship he'd had, were not worth mentioning. "I wanted the facts.

The truth, not town gossip. So I made a few calls, an online records search…"

"And *why* did you do that?" he asked bitterly. "Of all the connections you have in legal circles and law enforcement, why was *my* past of such great interest to you?"

Awkward, stunned silence answered his question before she cleared her throat and said, "Knowing you were convicted of insider trading…" Guilt was written in the nervous tic at the corner of her eyes. "I thought, surely, if you'd had ill-gotten gains in the past, you must have known a way to clean them."

"Or had the connections to people who could do it for me?" he suggested with a sarcastic smile.

"Well, yeah."

"Do you hear yourself? Can you step outside your frame of reference for a minute and see how this looks to me?" He huffed his exasperation. "I'd have expected better of you, Morgan. Isn't the Truth Foundation about giving people the benefit of the doubt? But for me, once guilty, always guilty?"

She had the courtesy to look chastened. "Mr. Di-Mera, I—"

"And you can stop with the *Mr. DiMera* as if I'm eighty years old and you didn't kiss the hell outta me in January? It's Roman."

He'd have laughed at her shocked expression, the drain of all color from her face when he mentioned the kiss, if he weren't so mad at her. And why did the reminder of their kiss cause her so much distress? His pique ticked up another notch.

"You come into my place of business, asking for

a *favor*, then proceed to tell me you've pried into the darkest time in my past, have made snap judgments about me without all the facts," he said through gritted teeth, one hand flailing in exasperation, "without knowing anything about me except that when a drunk woman makes a pass at me, I have the decency *not* to take advantage of her, even if I'd normally want her in my bed in a hot minute!"

Now her ears turned a bright red, and her eyes flashed with affront. Her mouth opened and closed as she choked, "Then I— We...didn't sleep together?"

"Like I said, I don't take advantage of inebriated women."

He saw relief filter across her face, though she tried to school her expression, and his irritation spiked.

"And while you savor that big ole 'whew!' moment, let's not brush aside the fact that you've insinuated I'm the lowest sort of scumbag," he said, aiming a finger at her. "I'm an ex-con. I hire ex-cons, so *naturally* I know all the murderers, thieves and money cleaners in Blue Larkspur!"

She rubbed her forehead with her fingertips and drew a slow breath. "Mr. DiMera—"

"Roman," he insisted again, tightly.

Her mouth twisted in consternation. "*Roman...*" A humorless laugh scraped from her throat. "Where do I begin?"

"Yes, where?" He folded his arms over his chest again. "Pick a place. I'm listening. How do you think I'm going to feel about doing your *favor*?"

The swinging door to the kitchen swished, and

Penny, one of his waitresses, waltzed in. "Morning, boss. Gibb."

Morgan cut a glance over his shoulder and scowled. "Can we go somewhere more private?"

He looked over his shoulder and found Gibb watching as he restocked the olives and onions for the cocktails. He hitched his head toward the door. "Penny, McNulty, give us the room, huh?"

"Damn," Gibb said, stashing the jar of olives in the mini fridge. "It was just getting interesting, too."

When the door to the kitchen flapped closed behind Gibb and Penny, Morgan met Roman's gaze evenly. "If I appeared relieved at learning we didn't have sex, please be assured it is not a reflection on you."

He snorted. "Right."

She paused to scowl at him in a way that said, *Do you mind?* "And I'm sorry if my actions, my body language, led you to believe I found you lacking in some way."

He wasn't buying her apology, but he kept his mouth shut as she forged on.

"Furthermore, I apologize if my research into your legal history causes you offense, but a good lawyer needs to be prepared, needs know who and what they are up against in court and in business dealings. It behooved me to investigate the circumstances of—"

Roman groaned. "Stop it."

"Excuse me?"

"First, an apology followed by a justification is not an apology. And second, if you did your research on me, you'd know I went to college, Morgan. I graduated with honors and worked on Wall Street for six years with some of the most brilliant minds in the country.

I've heard all the pretentious yammering I can stomach in one lifetime." Pinning her with a no-nonsense look, he asked, "Can we dispense with the stick-up-your-ass double talk and speak to each other like real people?"

She pulled her eyebrows together and frowned at him as if she didn't know what he meant. "Stick up my ass?" she repeated, clearly peeved.

He flipped up a hand. "Okay, that was uncalled for, but I told you earlier, I don't do fake. I don't have time for liars or falseness from anyone."

She stared at him, the blue of her eyes as hard as ice and as clear as a Colorado mountain stream. After a long, pregnant moment, she nodded. "Okay, how's this for honest? I was dreading coming here today to talk to you, because, try as I might, I can't forget some horribly embarrassing moments from that night in January. Worse, I can't remember other parts of what happened, and I'm afraid to ask, because deep down, I'm not sure I want to know the parts I've blanked on." She took a beat to swallow and fidget with a button on her coat with trembling fingers. "I'm mortified and more than a little confused by my memories. But mostly I wish…"

Her voice trembled the tiniest bit, and that sliver of emotion from her cracked something inside him. He gripped the seat of the bar stool so that he wouldn't do something foolish like reach for her.

She cleared her throat and finished, "I wish I could erase that night from my mind…and yours."

"I don't," he said before he could stop himself. He let the words hang between them for a few taut seconds before he added quietly, "It wasn't all bad."

The crease in her brow eased, and she seemed to be

waiting for…what? Confirmation of something unspoken between them?

Fine. He'd lay his cards on the table. "The kiss was nice."

Her breath hitched, and the pink stain returned to her cheeks. "Until I ran for the bathroom to be sick, you mean?"

He nodded in agreement. "Well, I wasn't going to mention that, but…"

She wrapped her arms around herself as if cold, as if she weren't still wearing her coat. She'd transformed again, from warrior lawyer to anxious schoolgirl waiting for a judgment to be passed down. She was quite the chameleon, this one. How much of her mercurial mood was genuine and how much was a ruse? As a rule, he steered clear of manipulative people. He'd been led down one path of destruction thanks to an untrustworthy faux friend, and he'd sworn never to be duped again.

So which Morgan was the real Morgan?

"So…" she said in a near whisper, "I remembered that much correctly then. I've wondered all these months if I imagined the kiss was better than it was because I was tipsy."

He focused on what she'd confessed. She'd enjoyed the kiss, thought about it as he had. *Interesting.*

She wet her lips with a nervous swipe of her tongue, and his attention was drawn to her plum-painted mouth. Intentional? Was she toying with him to soften him up for the favor she wanted?

She met his eyes for a moment before looking away. "You can see why I had to ask whether we'd…" She waved her fingers rather than finish her sentence. "A kiss like the one I remember would typically be followed by sex."

He twisted his mouth into a moue of agreement. "Typically, if we were both sober. But not this time."

She shifted off the stool to her feet. "Right. Well…"

"I've spent a good amount of time wondering if I'd remembered the kiss clearly, too." He took a step toward her, his tone silky. "But of course, there's only one way to know for sure."

Her face snapped up to meet his gaze, her eyes wide with surprise. "What?"

"You heard me." He grasped the lapel of her coat and gently tugged her closer. "Don't you think we owe it to ourselves to set the record straight once and for all? Eleven months is long enough to wonder whether a kiss is really enough to shake you to your foundation and blow your mind, right?"

Her breath snagged again, a sultry little hitch that sent sparks of anticipation crackling through his blood. He ducked his head, leaned in. And waited.

He held himself poised with his lips hovering over hers. He would not force himself on her. She had to want the kiss as much as he did.

"Roman…" The movement of her mouth forming his name had her lips brushing his. The word could have been either an invitation or a refusal.

And so he waited some more…

Finally, on an exhaled breath, she rose on her toes and closed the distance between them. Her fingers clutched at the front of his shirt, and he skimmed his hand along her jaw until he cradled her head at the nape.

His eager fingers disturbed her prim bun, and a coil of her hair unfurled over the back of his hand.

Angling his mouth, he deepened the kiss, drawing on her lips like a thirsty man tapping a well. He wanted more…needed something just beyond his reach…

She broke the kiss as quickly as she had in January, wrenching her mouth from his and taking an unsteady step back. Morgan touched her swollen lips as if they'd been burned, and her fingers shook.

Roman set his shoulders and moved his hands to his pockets, determined to appear casual and impassive. Not at all like a man who'd just had an explosive theory proven true.

He'd never have pictured himself being turned on by a judgmental, snooping, capricious lawyer. Morgan Colton was not his type, and he'd wager the deed to the Corner Pocket he was not her ideal man.

On the surface, they appeared to be oil and water. They should repel each other. But then he remembered what happened if you poured water on a grease fire. Whoosh! Massive conflagration. Scalding steam. Uncontrolled flames.

Was that what Morgan was to him? Water on smoldering oil? Disaster waiting to happen? Or was there more to this intriguing woman than met the eye?

"So…okay," she said with a nervous chuckle. "Definitely as good as I remembered."

She tugged at the front of her coat, flapping it for air as if she were too hot.

"Right. So what are we going to do about it?"

Her face wrinkled with confusion. "Do about it?"

"Well, yeah. Did the first settlers in Colorado find

gold in a stream, then walk away from it? No. If you find something of value, you mine it. Figure out if it was a lone nugget or a vein that's going to make you rich. Aren't you even a little curious what could happen if we explored this—" he flicked a hand back and forth between them "—further?"

"Of course I'm curious. Why do you think I—"

She stopped so abruptly, her expression flashing with guilt, that suspicion tickled Roman's nape. "Why do I think you...what?"

She shook her head. "Forget it." She hiked her purse strap onto her shoulder. "I should go. If you're not willing to help me find Ronald Spence, then there's no point—"

"*Finish what you were going to say,*" he pressed, his tone hard.

Her jaw tightened, and her eyes closed. After a beat, her shoulders drooped. "Fine. The truth is I looked up the details surrounding your arrest and conviction...in January. Not today." She stared at her hands and made the confession in a hushed, hurried spiel. "Part of why I came to you for help with finding Spence is because... well, because I couldn't forget our kiss. Because I was curious. I wanted to meet with you, talk to you, see if the same spark of attraction I felt in January was still there or if it was just a drunken illusion."

When she peeked up at him, her expression was at the same time resentful, embarrassed and anxious. Roman felt a quickening in his chest, an easing of the tension that had knotted inside him when he learned how she'd dug into his past. Not that he could completely dismiss her actions, but what did he have to lose if he heard her out, let her present her case to him about this Spence person who had stolen some money?

He reached for her lapel again and unfastened the top button of her coat.

"What are you doing?" she asked, pushing at his wrist.

"I think you'd be more comfortable if you took this off. This could take a while. We have a lot to discuss."

Chapter Three

Morgan draped her coat over the back of one of the chairs at the corner table as Roman settled across from her. Her body still hummed in the wake of their core-quaking kiss. What had she been thinking, kissing him again? Hadn't she just spent the last eleven months telling herself that kissing Roman DiMera had been a mistake? She had no intention of getting involved with a man who was a walking billboard, a blatant reminder of the worst day of her life—a day that still gave her nightmares. No amount of kissing skill or sexual allure was worth torturing herself daily with the ink that Roman wore.

Even now she shivered as she stared at the design on his wrist as he rested his hands on the tabletop. But meeting his gaze wasn't any less intimidating. His dark brown eyes reflected his distrust now, but moments earlier they had been ablaze with desire.

Her stomach somersaulted. *Get up. Leave. You can find Spence some other way.*

Morgan swallowed hard, but her mouth remained dry. She'd sworn to her siblings that she could bring Spence to justice. Her family had been through so much this year, and she felt compelled to take the lead on this mission.

"Tell me more about this man you're looking for and what he means to your family," Roman said, as if reading her thoughts. She started at the beginning, explaining how the Truth Foundation had believed Ronald Spence had been railroaded and imprisoned on trumped-up charges. She took out a copy of both his mug shot and a several-months-old image captured on Colton and Colton's security cameras from a visit the thief had once made to their office. She slid the pictures toward him, and he lifted each one in turn to study it.

"Our organization fought to get him released from prison, but it soon became clear he'd lied to us and tricked us to win his freedom. He's suspected of a number of crimes, including murder. Righting our mistake has been priority number one for some time now, especially in light of what's happened in the last few weeks."

"What happened that changed things?" Roman prompted. He slid the photos back to her and leaned forward, his arms resting on the table, his expression intrigued.

"First he pulled a gun on Alexa and our mother. Then—"

Roman tensed. "Good God! Were they hurt?"

"No, thankfully. Alexa disarmed him, and he ran. But our mother had a very scary panic attack and—" She paused to calm her breathing. Just the memory of the attack on her family was enough to raise her blood pressure. "Then last week, he trespassed at Kayla's family ranch, found money that had been previously stolen and hidden there by Kayla's father."

"Who's Kayla?"

"My brother Jasper's girlfriend, who works on his ranch, the Gemini. Her father stole—" She waved a hand. "That's a rabbit hole we don't need to go down. A story for another time. The point is, when Spence learned we were onto him, he tried to scare Kayla and my brother off his trail. That two-faced creep opened fire on my brother!" Morgan paused and suppressed the shudder that always followed the knowledge of how close she'd come to losing Jasper that day last week.

Roman blinked slowly, a stunned look crossing his face as he sat back in his chair. "And is Jasper all right?"

She jerked her chin in affirmation. "He is. As is Kayla, who was with him, but Spence—" Her mouth tightened as fresh waves of fury boiled inside her. "Spence duped the Truth Foundation to win his release from prison. I feel like this whole thing is my fault for having freed him from prison. We found out too late that the man was every bit as deceitful and guilty as he'd originally been charged. Ronald Spence crossed a line when he tried to hurt my family. If his past crimes, deception and theft weren't enough, he made an enemy of all the Coltons when he put Isa, Alexa, Jasper and Kayla in his crosshairs."

"I hear you."

"We had a family meeting and agreed the best way to track him, to stop him before he flees the country with his ill-gotten gains, is to follow the money. He's bound to want to launder it before he makes his next move."

"And that's where I come in?" Roman scratched his neat beard and narrowed his eyes. "You think I can help you discover how and where he's laundering that money."

"Even as we speak, presumably, so we're in a hurry. As I'm sure you know, because of the Bank Secrecy Act, financial institutions can flag transactions of greater than ten thousand dollars."

"Right."

"So it makes sense that he'd try to avoid raising suspicion by keeping bank deposits below that threshold over the course of several days."

"But even that could trigger suspicion. That's a pretty common red flag to regulators—a steady stream of small deposits has the look and smell of dirty doings."

"Exactly. All the more reason to find a business or associate that can run the funds through a legitimate operation to help mask the source of the money."

Roman snorted. "You're preaching to the choir, Colton."

A satisfied grin spread across her face as she leaned forward, her arms folded on the cool wooden table. "My original point, Mr. DiMera. You may not be involved in illegal activity, but you understand how it works. You have connections to people who have connections to other people, and I believe you can point me in the right direction before Spence finishes his operation and leaves US jurisdiction."

"You're sure he plans to flee the country?"

"Again, wouldn't you, under the circumstances?" she returned.

"Touché."

"Say you'll help us."

He made a clicking sound with his tongue, his eyes

speculative. "Why have you really come to me for this favor, instead of, say, one of the many other ex-cons you must know through your firm?"

She opened her mouth. Shut it. Chewed her bottom lip as she averted her gaze.

"Wow. I've rendered you speechless. I'd wager that doesn't happen often." When she pressed her mouth in a frustrated scowl, he leaned across the table toward her and lowered his voice. "I am intrigued," he said, "but..." His gaze traveled over her before stopping at her mouth. "I need something in return."

"Don't be skeevy, DiMera."

"Wouldn't think of it, Colton."

"Then what do you need?"

"I want to hear you admit that you didn't come here today, didn't find me for this favor *in spite of* that kiss in January, but *because* of it."

Her heart tripped. "Wh—I..."

One corner of his mouth tugged up in a cocky grin. "That's what I thought. So I have an offer."

"An offer?"

"A date."

A trill sang in her blood, but she shut it down and quipped, "July 4, 1776."

His brow creased. "What?"

"You asked for a date, I gave you one."

He pulled a wry grin.

"I prefer January 14 of this year."

Her breath stilled. That date... Lorie's birthday. The night he'd driven her home, and—

She swallowed hard. "Try again."

"Okay, how about tomorrow? That'd be December 19, if I'm right."

She frowned. "Okay, you've lost me."

"A date. Tomorrow. You and me."

"Then…you're serious?"

"Do you want my help finding where Spence might launder that cash?"

"That's extortion!"

He gave her a dismissive look. "It's a fair trade. I do you a favor, and you join me for dinner. Happens all the time in business. Just dinner. A chance to talk and get to know one another. Your brothers can vouch for me. They come up here to play billiards all the time."

"If you know my brothers, why not do this as a favor for them? As a friend?"

"Because that wouldn't get me a date with you." His smile was lopsided and devilish, but his eyes were kind and warm. "Do we have an agreement? Dinner out."

Morgan pressed a hand to her stomach, where her breakfast was performing acrobatics. She hesitated, more because she didn't want to seem overly eager than because she was reluctant. The notion of a dinner out with Roman tantalized her. She'd been so invested in her work, in the family's troubles this past year, she hadn't given her social life much attention. And anything remotely romantic? She scoffed mentally. Zilch. *And you want to break the fast in your love life with Roman DiMera? A tattooed, ex-con bar owner?* her buttoned-up, hardworking lawyer brain asked. She studied his square jaw and neat beard, the rumpled hair that curled at his collar, his smoldering eyes and full lips. *Yes, please! Me-yow! Come here, tiger!* replied the part of her psyche that was purely female lust and long-deprived need.

Her animal attraction to him aside, she desperately wanted to do something, to contribute some way to ending the menace that was Ronald Spence for her family. She'd held a maternal, protective role with her siblings for too many years do anything other than step into the line of fire to save them. Compared to a bullet, what was one date? Quickly arriving at a compromise for her internal debate, she asked, "No strings?"

He tipped up one hand as if about to concede, then gave her a sultry smile. "Why don't we…see how the evening unfolds before we make any promises like that?"

Lord help her, but the verbal chess match with him was exhilarating! She'd have to be careful, stay in control of her libido on said date, if she wanted to maintain a professional rapport with Roman. But *was* that what she wanted? A completely sterile business relationship? His kiss was—

She cut the sidetracking thought off. Her gaze flicked to his wrist, the Celtic design inked in green there…

She heard the footsteps, smelled stale cigarettes… and then someone grabbed her from behind and restrained her. A tattooed arm. When the man tugged hard on her purse, she refused to release her grip on the strap, determined not to fall prey that easily. She turned to find a man with a feral glare tugging at her purse. He had a teardrop tattoo by his left eye—gang code meaning he'd killed someone, she'd heard—to go along with the sleeve of ink on his arm. Ice tripped down her spine.

Now, she squeezed her eyes shut and pinched the

bridge of her nose as she shoved the memory away. The past was irrelevant. She had to move on, put the memory of those tattoos behind her, along with the rest of the violent mugging day. But how did she truly move on when just a tattoo could trigger a flashback? Or the scent of cigarettes? Or hearing the Eagles song that had been blaring from the bar down the street as she lay bleeding on the pavement, waiting for help?

"Headache?" Roman asked. "We probably have some aspirin behind the bar if you—"

She blinked her eyes open and shook her head. "No, I'm fine. I just—"

"Hangover?" he suggested, his tone and twitching grin mocking.

His jibe was enough to douse the chilling memory with the heat of righteous indignation.

"*Nooo,*" she intoned, drawing the word out to emphasize her pique. Growing up in a family as large as hers had provided her ample opportunity to practice deflecting sarcasm and teasing. And Roman's none-too-subtle reminder of their last encounter firmed her resolve to keep any further relationship with him strictly professional—the one date she'd promised him aside.

With a dismissive huff, Morgan tapped the file that still lay on the table between them. "Keep this. It's a duplicate copy of relevant information about Spence. Perhaps you could review it and see if any of the names of his associates ring a bell?"

"Whoa, now," he said, turning his palms toward her. "We haven't agreed to anything yet. Before I look at any papers or involve myself in any proceedings, I want to be sure we're in agreement."

Morgan goggled. "What do you mean, besides me saying I'll go out to dinner with you?"

He lifted a hand. "I don't know. But can you blame me for being wary? It's not so much you reneging on our date I'm worried about as the sort of business we might brush up against in your search for Spence. I counted on a handshake agreement in the past that ended up costing me five years in the New York state pen. If your investigation into Spence goes sideways—"

"It won't. We'll be careful."

He arched a black eyebrow. "Forgive me if verbal guarantees don't convince me. I want assurances that I won't be pinned with something. That you don't expect me to break any laws and that my participation is conditional on having my terms met. I get a sniff of anything fishy, I'm out. I can't get caught up in something that could put the Corner Pocket in a compromising position."

"I promise not to put you in a compromising position."

"The bar. I'm perfectly willing to assume a compromising position with you." He tugged a scampish, lopsided grin.

Heat stung her cheeks.

"Mr. DiMera," she started tightly, standing as she struggled to block the sensual images that popped into her mind.

He scraped his chair back and stood as well. "Take a breath. I was just poking at you. Don't overreact."

Her hand tightened around her purse strap. "A little tip… Never, *never* tell a woman she's overreacting. It's condescending and dismissive of her emotions. Whether she is overreacting or not, it will never do anything but escalate her temper."

He pulled a chastened look. "So noted. As long as we're being instructive, I'll just put this out there. I'm attracted to you, Morgan. I think our kisses make it obvious we have chemistry. I think it is equally obvious neither of us knows what to make of that chemistry. You're not the type of woman I typically date. I'm guessing, based on your prickly attitude toward me, that you're not thrilled with the idea that I turn you on, either." He paused, and the lift of his eyebrows asked, *Am I right?*

Morgan firmed her mouth, debating how to answer. Finally, in deference to an amicable and open working relationship—she still needed his help finding Spence—she nodded. "True."

He waved a hand toward her chair, inviting her to stay. With a relenting sigh, she sat.

"I will help you in whatever limited way I can to track down this Spence character, and I think we owe it to ourselves, in light of the attraction we feel, to get to know each other. So I'm asking. Will you have dinner with me tomorrow…no strings attached, but all options mutually agreeable still on the table?"

Morgan stared across the polished table into his alluring dark eyes for several moments. The open-ended way he'd proposed the dinner left a hum of anticipation hovering between them. The promise of *maybe* hot in his gaze. The tantalizing potential, wrapped in a veil of safety and an out clause. She swallowed hard, a secret thrill spiraling to her core, and heard herself answer, "Yes."

Chapter Four

Later that afternoon, Roman stepped off the elevator in a riverfront office building and found the door that read Colton and Colton, Attorneys at Law. He lifted a corner of his mouth, remembering the lively, if round-about, discussion he'd had with Morgan that morning. He had to admit he was anticipating their dinner out more than he'd have expected. If he could get past her apparent biases toward him, he could see them having interesting and electric discussions, engaging in lively banter—and enjoying passionate sex. He may have agreed to limiting parameters for their first date, but he had no illusions that it would be an only date. He enjoyed a challenge, and his gut told him Morgan was worthy a little risk and effort.

He entered the law office, and an older woman with intelligence glinting in her brown eyes glanced up from her computer monitor and greeted him with a smile. "Good afternoon. How can I help you?"

He read the name plate on her desk and replied, "Hello, Ms. Hanlan. I'm here to see Morgan Colton."

"Is she expecting you?"

He twisted his mouth. "Well, yes and no. I don't have

an appointment per se, but I have some thoughts on a project that we discussed earlier today that I'd like to run by her."

The door to the back offices opened, and a tall man with neatly trimmed dark brown hair strolled out, his attention on the file open in his hands. "Rebekah, did we ever hear back on the deposition—" He glanced up and fell abruptly silent when he spotted Roman. "Oh, hi. I didn't mean to interrupt." He snapped the file closed and waved a hand, silently inviting Roman and the receptionist to finish their conversation. The guy had enough facial similarities to his siblings that Roman immediately tagged him as Caleb, Morgan's brother and the other half of Colton and Colton.

Morgan wasn't the only one who could do background checks and general snooping on the internet. He wanted a level playing field as he undertook this fact-finding mission with Morgan. He'd learned the hard way not to enter any relationship, any business deal, without his eyes wide-open and all the cards on the table.

Roman offered his hand to Caleb and introduced himself.

Caleb's face brightened with recognition. "You run the Corner Pocket."

"I do. I own it, in fact."

Caleb grinned. "My brothers and I enjoy shooting a little pool at your place when we have spare time. Your hot wings and jalapeño poppers are some of the best in town."

"I'll tell my cook you said so." He stuck his hands in his pockets and divided a querying glance between

Caleb and the receptionist. "I spoke to Morgan earlier today and have some follow-up information for her if she's available."

Caleb dropped the file on Ms. Hanlan's inbox. "Regarding a case?"

"No. A family matter."

Caleb's eyebrows shot up. "A Colton family matter?"

Roman ducked his chin in affirmation. "She's asked for my help tracking down Ronald Spence and the money he stole."

Caleb squared his shoulders. "Did she?" He shifted his weight. "Huh. And you have something on Spence that would be helpful?"

Roman shrugged. "I guess we'll see. That's what I'm here to discuss with her."

"I'm afraid she stepped out for a minute. She had paperwork to file at the courthouse, but she'll be back any—"

The outer office door opened, and Morgan breezed in, stumbling to a halt when she found three sets of eyes on her. She blinked, and a flush tinted her already cold-pinkened cheeks a shade darker. "Roman?"

"Hello, Morgan. Do you have a few minutes? I think I have that starting point you mentioned earlier." He turned to Caleb. "You're welcome to join us."

Caleb checked his watch. "I wish I could. I'd be interested to know what info you've got, but I have a client meeting in five minutes."

"I'll fill you in later," Morgan told her brother, and as she slid her coat off, Roman stepped forward to help her with it. "Oh. Thank you."

She sent her brother and Ms. Hanlan a guilty glance,

as if his helping with her coat gave away a secret liaison between them. After draping her coat over her arm, she headed toward her office. "This way, Mr. DiMera."

Roman followed, giving her brother a polite nod as he passed. Once ensconced in her office, he took one of the leather chairs that faced her desk and propped one ankle on the opposite knee, getting comfortable. Morgan stashed her purse in a desk drawer and gave his casual position a side glance. He'd swear he saw irritation flash over her face before she assumed a straight-back, all-business pose and set her hands, fingers laced, on the desk. "All right. You have my attention. What have you learned?"

He wanted to chuckle at the tightly reined, professional persona she projected. He'd had a glimpse of the fiery passion that lived beneath that schooled expression and rigid posture. Brushing aside the incongruity, he cleared his throat to answer. "Not so much learned as recalled. I had a bartender for a year or so, Tim Hall, who did time in Nebraska for laundering money he embezzled from his employer. Back in March, he left for a better-paying job working construction for a company across town."

"Hang on," she said, raising a finger. "The guy stole from his last employer and you hired him?"

Roman took a slow breath. The question no longer bothered him. He got it so often, had explained his reasoning for hiring ex-cons enough times, that it was now rote. Beyond the tax credit, which helped his bottom line, his desire to pay it forward and offer a hand up was key to his personal redemption plan. "You of all people, what with your law firm helping clear wrongly accused persons of charges, should know that just because a person serves time, it doesn't automatically make them a lost cause."

"Was Tim Hall wrongly accused?"

"No. He was guilty. He succumbed to a moment of desperation and weakness when his rent and utilities were due, and he had medical bills to pay after his son was hospitalized. I don't excuse it. There's no excuse for breaking the law, but I understood it. He served his time, fulfilled his debt to society, and I gave him the benefit of the doubt. He was a top-notch bartender, and I have no regrets for having hired him."

She held his gaze, and her expression softened as she said quietly, "Champion of the downtrodden. Giver of second chances."

He dismissed her accolades with a small shrug. "I know how much it meant to me when Mr. Kikorama gave me a second chance when I was released from prison. He gave me my first job postincarceration and gave me time to find my feet before I decided to move west and buy the Corner Pocket."

She gave him a smile and an impressed look. "Kudos to Mr. Kikorama. But…back to Tim. He's still in town, you say? You think he, with his history of laundering, will be able to steer us in the right direction?"

"Worth a shot. I can try to reach him tonight after he gets off work—" Seeing her shake her head, he paused. "What?"

"Not tonight. We should talk to him now. We'll find him at work and ask him for help." She rolled her chair back and stood. "Time is crucial. That money could leave the country any moment."

He put his foot on the floor and leaned forward. "What's this *we*?"

She wrinkled her nose as if puzzled. "We." She flapped a hand between them. "You and me. What's the problem?"

"I just don't know if he'll talk in front of you. He's not proud of his past and might be reluctant to be completely open with you there."

"I guess we'll see when we get there." She retrieved the purse she'd just stowed and rounded her desk. "Because I *am* going. This is my family's investigation, and while I will take whatever assistance you can offer, I will not delegate any part of the search for Spence entirely outside the family."

Roman poked the inside of his cheek with his tongue, ruminating on Morgan's stubborn response. "Even if your presence could sabotage any effort to gather information?"

She sighed. "If Tim appears reluctant to share what he knows in my presence, I will, of course, step aside, go outside, wait in the car or…whatever is necessary. But until that point, I take the lead. Understood?"

He rose, chuckling as he followed her out. "Bossy thing, aren't you?"

She spun to face him, her eyes dark with umbrage. "Why is it assertive women are called bossy and assertive men are praised as leaders?"

"Sorry. No offense meant." He took her coat from the rack and held it out to help her don the wrap.

She took it from him and put it on by herself, muttering, "I don't need help."

"Again, no offense meant. Just trying to be poli—"

"For your information, I had to be bossy from an early age. I helped raise my brothers and sisters, especially after our father died in an accident and our mother was grief-stricken and overwhelmed with caring for a large family."

He'd learned as much with his research into her this afternoon, but he let her continue. He was learning nuances about how she saw herself, her worldview, her history that he could never learn from the internet.

"In law school, I had to be aggressive and take charge, or I'd get swept under the rug by men who didn't think I was tough enough to go head-to-head with criminals and judges and opposing counsel."

As he admired her fire, her moxie, her conviction, his mouth twitched in a grin—which she clearly took the wrong way.

"Women have to work twice as hard to get— Are you laughing at me?"

"Not at all. As a son raised by a single mother who busted her ass to provide for us and pay for me to go to college, I have all the respect in the world for strong, capable women."

She narrowed her eyes suspiciously, as if deciding whether to believe him. "Then why were you grinning like that?"

"I was thinking that Ronald Spence had better be looking over his shoulder, because with you on his trail, it's just a matter of time before he's caught and paying for his misdeeds." He opened the office door and waved her through. "After you. Shall I drive or would you like to?"

She twisted those lips that had kissed the life out of him earlier today as she considered his question. "You drive. I'm going to do a little background search on Tim Hall before we speak to him. I like to be prepared."

"So I've heard."

True to her word, Morgan had her nose in her phone the entire trip to the north side of town, where the construction office had told Roman Tim was working that day.

"Do you see any numbers on these buildings?" he asked as he drove slowly down the street his GPS app had guided him to. "Thirty-two eighty-eight should be right around here somewhere."

Morgan raised her head and put her phone in her lap. She squinted at her surroundings like a gopher coming out of the dark into the sunlight. "Where are we?"

"Hines Street. North district." He spotted a faded number on a derelict building. "Wait. There's 3284…" He pulled his car to the curb and parked in the first spot he found. "That'd mean that one with the red brick should be the work site." He cut the engine, and when he glanced at Morgan, he was startled to see how pale she looked and the wide-eyed, wary look on her face. Ten minutes earlier, she'd been brassy and determined. Now he'd swear he caught a flicker of fear in her eyes. What was up with that?

"You coming?" he asked, watching her closely as he unfastened his seat belt and shouldered open the driver's door.

She took a deep breath and jerked a nod, but her expression remained watchful and uneasy as they headed across the street and down the block. She walked close to him. Not that he minded, but her behavior raised questions.

"You okay?" he asked as he dragged open the cracked glass door at 3288.

"Yes. Fine." Her clipped tone and wan cheeks contradicted her, but he made no further comment.

Instead, he followed the sound of voices and hammers echoing in the building that had been stripped down to studs and wiring. They traipsed through the debris of loose nails, empty coffee cups and drywall scraps until they found one of the construction workers.

"Excuse me," Roman asked. "We're looking for Tim Hall. We were told he was working here today."

The man in a hard hat and overalls appraised them with an up-and-down glance. "He in some kind of trouble?"

"No, nothing like that," Morgan replied, flashing a smile. Had he not sensed her nerves sixty seconds earlier, Roman might have missed the slight quaver of her lips that gave away her jitters. "We just want to ask him a few questions. We think he has information that could be useful to a case we're working on."

To anyone else, she likely appeared cool and collected. The consummate businesswoman in her element. He pushed aside his confusion over her jitters and focused on the matter at hand. But he had every intention of quizzing her about her mood on the way back to her office.

"A case? You cops?" the worker asked, obviously concerned by the notion.

"Not hardly. I own a bar. Tim used to work for me."

"I'm an attorney, but I'm not here in an official capacity. Our questions are related to a personal matter."

The construction worker's eyebrow hitched up, and he gave Morgan a somewhat leering look. "I see." His tone clearly implied he thought Morgan and Tim were involved in some tawdry way.

"I highly doubt you do," she said, frowning. "Is Tim here or not?"

The man chuffed a laugh. "Yeah. Back that way." He hitched his head in the direction of the hammering.

As they wended their way through studs and trash, she grumbled, "Why do people always assume that 'personal' means 'scandalous'?"

"Scandal is more fun to speculate about. Watch your step there." He took her by the arm to guide her around loose wires on the floor. Entering a back room, they found three men nailing drywall into place, Tim Hall among them. "Hey, Tim?" Roman called. "You got a minute?"

His former bartender, a short man with a middle-aged pooch belly and a military-short haircut, turned, and his expression brightened spotting Roman. "Hiya, DiMera!" Tim's countenance creased with confusion as he set his hammer down and crossed the room, eyeing Morgan. "What brings you down here of all places?"

"We're sorry to bother you at work. We promise to only take a moment of your time, if we could," Morgan said, then held her hand out to shake his. She introduced herself and looked around the bare, under-remodel room. "Is there someplace private we can talk?"

"Uh..." Tim looked to Roman, as if for some hint of what was going on, reassurance he could trust Morgan or some other missing information that would convince him to cooperate.

"Five minutes," Roman said. "Just a couple questions. Nothing to worry about."

"'Kay." Tim turned to his coworkers. "Back in a minute, Sean."

"Hey, you're not getting paid to chat with friends, Hall," the coworker said with a glare.

"We promise to return him ASAP," Morgan said, giving the man a warm smile that seemed to mollify if not appease him.

Tim led the way to another room, this one with the drywall complete, and faced them with a disgruntled sigh. "Make it quick. I can't afford to lose this job, and Sean's already chomping at the bit for a reason to fire me." Then in a quieter mumble, "The son of a bitch."

Roman crossed his arms and faced Morgan. "You're on, Counselor."

Morgan cleared her throat and squared her shoulders. "Mr. Hall, Roman tells me you have previous experience with, um—" she lowered her voice "—money laundering."

Tim bristled, and he shook his head. "Hey, no. I don't know what Roman told you, but I went straight—"

"I'm not asking you to do anything illegal," she rushed to assure him. "I need your advice. Your...insight."

Tim's expression remained skeptical. "What do you mean?"

"We're looking for someone who might be about to try to wash a large sum of money. We want to find him and the money before either leaves the country."

Tim snorted. "Good luck."

"We need more than luck. We need information. We thought maybe, with your past experience and connections—"

"Whoa! Stop right there. I don't have any *connections* like that in Blue Larkspur," Tim was quick to assert. He shot an uneasy glance toward the door of the empty room. "Look, even if I had information that would help you, I sure ain't gonna talk about it here." He glared at Roman. "I can't believe you brought her here to my work site, man. Not cool."

"I don't mean to imply I think you're still involved in anything illegal, Mr. Hall." Morgan raised a hand toward Tim in a conciliatory gesture. "We simply hoped you had some ideas that would help us. I'd be willing to pay you for your time and any information you could gather."

The construction worker's eyebrow quirked. Yep, money talked.

"The man we are looking for is known to be involved with drug smuggling in the area, if that helps."

Roman cut a startled glance toward Morgan. "You didn't tell me that."

She faced him. "Does it change anything? Mean anything to you?"

"No. I'm just surprised you didn't mention that rather significant detail earlier," he said and frowned, peeved that she'd withheld that part of the equation. He *really* didn't want to get on the wrong side of any local drug dealers or smugglers. He ran a clean operation at the Corner Pocket, and even a hint of his involvement with illegal drug culture could bring the wrong element to his doorstep.

"Any particular drug?" Tim asked, his expression changing to one of wary curiosity. "Meth? Crack?"

Roman wondered if it was the drug element that had changed Tim's mood or Morgan's promise of payment. His former employee had certainly become more helpful when Morgan mentioned payment.

Morgan tipped her head. "A little of everything, I think. Why does the drug matter?"

"Well…" Tim shifted his weight and glanced toward the door, as if worried someone would be listening. He canted closer and dropped his voice. "If you track down the dealers he's hooked up with, you might figure out how they clean their money. A lot depends on who the guy knows and can trust. If he already has channels at work in the drug biz that he trusts, he's not likely to stray too far from what he knows will work."

"Right," Morgan replied, nodding. "That makes sense."

"And I don't use or nothing." Tim hitched his thumb toward Roman. "He knows I don't. But I've heard the guys on the crew here talk. Maybe—and that's a big maybe—I might be able to ask some questions. For the right price."

Morgan's face brightened. "That would be great!"

Tim and Morgan negotiated a mutually acceptable sum in exchange for Tim's information hunting, and she dug a down payment toward the total from her wallet. "I'll pay you the rest when you bring me useful information."

"Deal. But no more meetin' here!" Tim was quick to add as he stuffed the folded bills into his chest pocket.

"You can come to my office when you get off work," Morgan suggested. She dug a business card out of her pocket, and Tim looked at it as if she were offering him poison.

"I have a better idea," Roman said, pushing the card back toward Morgan. "Come by the Corner Pocket tonight, maybe around closing? We'll have a drink, something from the grill—on the house, of course—and we'll talk then? No one to overhear, no pressure. What do you say?"

"Well, a'ight." He scowled then, adding, "But the only reason I'm doing this much is 'cause you gave me my first break when I got out. It meant a lot to me, you giving me a chance, a job. I owe you for that."

Morgan arched an eyebrow, as if deciding whether to comment on the cash incentive she'd just paid, but wisely she kept mum. When she glanced at Roman, he detected a degree of admiration for the loyalty and respect Tim voiced. And perhaps a hint of smugness, too?

"So...closing?" Tim asked. "That's eleven, yeah?"

Roman shrugged. "Sorry to make it so late, but I stay pretty busy through the evening hours, filling in wherever I'm needed. The holidays have had us really bustling lately. By ten thirty or so, things calm down. Fewer ears around, less noise. Maybe we'll shoot a round or two of eight ball?"

Tim braced his hands on his hips and looked from Roman to Morgan and back again. "Okay. I'll come. It's been a while since I whipped your ass at pool." He scratched his ear. "But...not tonight. Tomorrow. I need time to look into a thing or two. No promises it'll pan out, though."

"Give it some thought. You might know more than you realize," she said.

Roman took Morgan's arm and tugged her toward the door. She gave him an I-wasn't-finished-grilling-him frown.

"We're done here," he said, more to Morgan than his former bartender. "Thank you, Tim. We'll see you tomorrow night."

DISAPPOINTMENT STABBED MORGAN as Roman hustled her out of the construction site. She wasn't sure what she thought Roman's friend would offer them but leaving relatively empty-handed felt like a defeat. Defeat never sat well for her, whether in the courtroom or in her personal life.

Her face must have reflected her frustration, because as they stepped out onto the north-side street, Roman nudged her with his elbow. "Chin up. He could still give us something useful tomorrow night."

"You really think so? I got the distinct impression he was more interested my payment and in milking you for a free drink while shooting some pool. He seemed wholly unwilling to give up any valuable tips whether he had them or not." Morgan gave the derelict street and neglected buildings a wary glance.

"Maybe, but even if that's the case, you haven't lost anything except that down payment."

"And time. Which is pretty costly at this point. It's unlikely Spence will sit on that money for long. If he's going to launder it, it's going to happen soon. I can feel it in my bones."

When someone down the street shouted, Morgan's pulse jumped, and she sidled closer to Roman, bumping him as she crowded him on the sidewalk. Though his presence gave her some measure of comfort, there was a reason she never came to the north side of town anymore. Her nightmare had been born here.

Chapter Five

When they returned to her place, Morgan invited Roman to come up for a cup of something warm to drink. After all, he *had* given his time to help put her in touch with a possible lead. To summarily dismiss him now that the errand was complete would be rude.

"Thanks, but no. I meant what I told Tim about evenings being busy at the bar. I need to get back. But…" He draped his hand over the top of his steering wheel and gave her a crooked smile. "We have unfinished business of our own."

Her heart slammed her ribs, his sultry tone conjuring the recent memory of the kiss they'd recklessly shared that morning. "What…business?"

"You owe me a date. Dinner tomorrow. Remember?"

"I remember dinner. I never called it a date."

"Call it what you want, but I'll be by your place tomorrow about seven. That work for you?"

"We're supposed to meet Tim tomorrow night at the Corner Pocket."

He bobbed a nod. "At closing. That's eleven on a weeknight. That leaves us plenty of time for dinner. Maybe even a movie after. Then back to my place to talk to Tim." He twitched his lips in a grin. "I promise to have you home by midnight, Cinderella."

She rubbed her suddenly damp palms on her coat. "Right. Well, a deal is a deal."

He scowled. "Ouch. You wound me, Colton. Don't make it sound like such a chore."

"I didn't mean— That is—" She sighed and gave him an apologetic smile. "Seven will be fine." She started to climb out of his car but hesitated. "How should I dress?"

"I'm not planning to take you to the Burger Shack, if that's what you're asking."

She grunted. "I'm not."

He reached to brush a knuckle along her cheek, and a tingle, whether of surprise or of pleasure, she couldn't say, streaked down her spine. "Work attire will be fine, but…maybe wear your hair down?" He tapped the bun at her nape with a finger. "You're much too young and too pretty for this schoolmarm action."

A startled laugh escaped her, despite the oxygen backing up in her lungs when he touched her. "School-marm?"

He winked. "See you tomorrow."

Morgan's phone rang as she was unlocking her front door, and she fumbled her cell phone from her purse, distracted by thoughts of her wardrobe for tomorrow night. If Roman thought her hair was prudish, what must he think of her dark suits and the rest of her plain business attire? The need to look and feel feminine and appealing swamped her, and with these thoughts swimming in her head, she answered the call.

"Hey, sis. Good time to talk?"

The male voice had her instantly alert and on edge. "Ezra? What's wrong? What's happened?"

"Who said anything was wrong?"

"Well… I just never hear from you unless something has happened. Are you okay? Is it Mom?"

Her brother, recently retired from the Army, had spent a portion of the summer living at their mother's home a short distance outside Blue Larkspur. Until he'd met and fallen hard for single mother Theresa Fitzgerald.

"Mom is fine as far as I know. Certainly on cloud nine lately, thanks to her budding relationship with Theo."

Morgan smiled as she slid her coat off and hung it by the door. "I know, right? She's so cute, the way she gets starry-eyed when she talks about him."

"Did you just call our mother cute?"

"Unless you need your ears checked. If nothing's wrong, then what's up?"

"I need a favor."

"Now I need my ears checked. Did my self-sufficient, former Army sergeant brother just ask little ole me for help?" Morgan's grin spread. As one of the triplets born just after her and Caleb, Ezra had always been an independent sort. She couldn't count the times she'd heard him say, "I can do it myself!" when she tried to help young Ezra saddle a horse or tie his shoes or do his chores.

"If you want me to ask someone else…"

"What's the favor, Ez?"

"Well, Theresa and I are planning to do most of our Christmas shopping for the girls tomorrow, and we need somewhere to hide the gifts until Santa delivers them. They've been rather snoopy lately, and we don't want anything to spoil the surprise."

Morgan pictured Theresa's energetic six-year-old twin daughters, Neve and Claire, and her heart gave a tug. The blonde pixies had melted Ezra's heart and wrapped him around their pinkies. "Of course. But why here?"

"Why not? Your house isn't too far from Theresa's, and I last time I was there, you had all that extra space in the guest bedroom."

Morgan kicked off her shoes and considered the utilitarian pumps. She needed something sexier for dinner tomorrow. "What size shoe does Theresa wear? Do you think she has anything strappy and sparkly I could borrow?"

"Um, what?"

"Sorry. I'm planning my outfit for an outing tomorrow. Yes. Bring the gifts over. I'll hide them for Santa. And ask Theresa about the shoes. I wear a seven."

"Hang on." She heard muffled conversation before he came back on the line. "Sorry, she says she has nothing strappy and sparkly in a size seven. What's the occasion?"

"Just...a business dinner." Well, that was partly true. She wouldn't characterize her dinner with Roman as a date...or, at least, not to her younger brother. "You remember where I keep my spare house key in case I'm not home?"

"I do. And you remember that I told you hiding a key outside wasn't safe? Burglars are smart enough to find keys under flowerpots and doormats."

"Which is why my key isn't under a mat or a pot. It's inside the toolshed in a soup can."

Ezra made a low growling noise of discontent before signing off with, "Thanks, Morgan. Love you."

She blinked her surprise at the last sentiment, startled that her military-tough brother had spoken the endearment. Proof positive that Theresa and her girls—and maybe his recent brush with danger and death—had given Ezra a new perspective on love and family. "Love you, too, Ez."

But she'd taken too long, stunned and touched by his words, and he'd already hung up.

She set her phone aside and stretched out on the couch, propping her bare feet on the cushions. Truth was, her whole family had been rattled by the series of disturbing events over the last year. Far too much peril and misfortune had invaded their lives. The upside of it all was the fresh appreciation for her siblings and her mother, for the love that had found her brothers and sisters. Sighing, she told herself she was not jealous of the relationships and joy her siblings had found. But the still quiet of her home seemed to echo around her. The silence mocked her. And when she closed her eyes, Roman DiMera's face appeared in her mind's eye.

THE NEXT DAY at work, Morgan had a difficult time concentrating. Her mind strayed frequently to the evening ahead. She found herself looking forward to dinner out. It had been a long time since she'd shared a meal with someone outside her family and their significant others. As much as she loved her brothers and sisters, seeing them pair off and find new love had her feeling a bit lonely and left behind. Her friends' busy lives, the holiday rush and her backlog of cases thanks to the extra time she'd devoted recently to family matters and the Truth Foundation projects meant she'd had little social life.

Schoolmarm. Roman's term to describe the knot she kept her hair in for work had pinched when he used it, but she was starting to see that more than her hairstyle was too wound up and boring. She'd been fun once, hadn't she? Had taking on the responsibility of helping their mother with the youngest siblings killed her sense of adventure and whimsy?

She shoved away the contract she was reviewing, having read the same paragraph five times without letting the words sink in and needled by the idea she'd lost some of her spark. Flopping back in her desk chair, Morgan mused on the notion she was dull and too wrapped up in work. Was that why her love life had been lacking? If they were sitting across from her now, her friends, especially Stacy, would encourage her to cut loose, maybe indulge in a one-night stand to expend some pent-up sexual energy and reclaim her mojo.

On the heels of that thought, an image of Roman popped into her brain as he'd looked the day before, when she'd confronted him at the Corner Pocket. When he'd learned she'd dug into his past, his eyes had lit with an intensity and fire that had smoldered with something that had felt a bit dangerous, a little untamed and a lot sexy. She'd have never thought she'd be drawn to a— what was the term Stacy used?—bad boy. Someone with rough edges and a questionable background and a dark, rugged look that told the world he wouldn't conform.

No, geeks and white collars had always been her style. Maybe that was why she was still single, still looking for Mr. Right. When she weighed the last perfectly nice accountant she'd dated against the somewhat mysterious and broad-chested Roman DiMera, it was the ex-con bar owner who titillated her interest and made her blood sing.

"It was that damn kiss," she muttered to herself, turning her chair to stare out the window to her enviable view of downtown Blue Larkspur and in the distance, the mighty Rocky Mountains. But she saw none of it. Her mind was remembering Roman's mouth, the feel of his fingers massaging her nape, caressing her cheek, setting fires wherever he touched her. Heck, even his guiding hand on her elbow when they'd visited Tim Hall at the construction site had made her breath hover in her lungs and her pulse skip like a schoolgirl's.

If she hadn't kissed him, hadn't had that taste of Roman, she'd be far more capable of resisting the allure of this particular bad boy. Any dieter knew, you didn't take even one bite of that tempting chocolate cake. Once the heavenly sweetness was in your mouth, your senses all fired and demanded more. Not until you binged on the whole thick slice of cake and overloaded your tongue with rich fudgy goodness could you satiate the yearning for the sweet treat.

Morgan groaned. *Great.* Now she wanted Roman DiMera *and* a thick slab of homemade chocolate cake!

She slapped closed the file on her desk and jerked open the bottom drawer of her desk to retrieve her purse. As she headed out of the office, she stopped at Caleb's office door. "I'm calling it a day and heading home."

He consulted his watch. "At two o'clock? Are you sick?"

"No. Just…horribly distracted and getting nowhere. I have a business meeting set for late tonight, and I think I'll do better getting in the right frame of mind at home on my treadmill. I do some pretty good thinking there."

When she was putting on her coat, giving Rebekah an update on what little she had accomplished today, her youngest brother, Gavin, burst into the office, buffing the cold from his hands. "Hey, there's my favorite sister!"

Morgan chuckled as he folded her into a bear hug. "You must need a favor."

"What? Why would you think that?" He nodded a greeting to Rebekah with a wink.

"Because I've never been your favorite sister before." She stepped back from the hug and took in her brother's happy countenance. Since falling in love with Jacqui Reyes, he'd exuded a contentment and joy that Morgan, frankly, envied. "In fact, when you were seven, I distinctly remember you telling me you hated me."

"*Pfft.* Not me. Must have been one of the triplets."

"Oh, it was you. I was making you turn off your video game and go to bed. But I forgive you. What favor can I do?"

Gavin's grin turned sheepish. "Well, since you asked…"

Morgan cuffed his shoulder. "I knew it."

"I've got a draft of an epilogue to the latest podcast

series on the wild mustangs that I wanted to run by someone for a set of fresh eyes."

"Why not ask Jacqui? Wouldn't her experience with the Colorado Bureau of Land Management make her a better resource for something like this?"

"Well, she's helping me with the podcast in other ways." He stuck his hands in his pockets and scrunched his face in a way Morgan had seen many times through the years that said he knew he was expecting a no. "What I need is a layman, someone who doesn't know a lot about the topic, to be sure we're explaining things well and have smooth transitions."

"Hmm. Ordinarily I'd have to turn you down, much as I love to help my sibs when I can. Caleb and I have been slammed lately, and this business with Spence on top of the holidays and our normal office backlog…"

"Oh."

"But—"

Gavin's face brightened with anticipation. "Yes?"

"As luck would have it, I was just headed home. I'm too distracted thinking about a meeting tonight to get anything productive done here. So…follow me to my house and you can run it by me while I'm on the treadmill."

"Thanks, Mor. I knew you were my favorite for a reason!"

She snorted. "Yeah, until you want to go horseback riding at the ranch and suddenly Aubrey will be your favorite."

He pressed a hand over his heart. "You wound me."

Morgan tugged on her knit hat and started out. "See

you tomorrow, Rebekah. Come on, brat. If you're good, I'll make you a cup of your favorite cocoa."

Having Gavin with her, getting a peek at his latest journalistic project, proved a welcome distraction from her upcoming date. At five thirty, when Gavin headed home with her feedback and a to-go cup of cocoa, she turned her attention to prepping for her dinner with Roman.

"Not a date," she repeated to herself every time her stomach bunched in anxious anticipation. "Just dinner. Then a business meeting with an informant."

At 6:58 p.m., when Roman's Corvette pulled up in front of her house, she took a slow breath, let it out even more slowly and pressed her thumbs together in the technique she'd learned early in her career to stem pretrial jitters.

She counted to ten before answering her doorbell. *You can't look too eager or let him know you've been ready and watching for him for thirty minutes.*

"So punctual. I like—" she quipped as she opened the door, then lost the rest of her jibe as she saw her date's attire.

Roman wore an impeccable dark gray suit that fit him as if tailored for his broad shoulders and slim hips. His light blue dress shirt was wrinkle-free, and the perfectly coordinated silk tie sported a neat Windsor knot, more symmetrical than any she'd ever seen Caleb manage. His black dress shoes were polished, the scent of his aftershave subtle yet deliciously enticing. He looked, for all intents and purposes, like an attorney she might go up against in court. Or one of the accountants she used to date, except...better. So much better. Because while his suit hid his tattoos, he still wore a neat beard, still had a dark, dangerous intensity in his eyes, still twitched his full lips in a devilish grin that taunted and beguiled her.

"You like...what?" he prompted, when all she did for a stumbling heartbeat was gape like a dork at his transformation.

"I, uh… P-promptness."

He tugged at his sleeve, straightening it. "I consider it rude to keep someone waiting if you have a set meeting time."

She bobbed a stiff nod. "Um, r-right."

He waved a hand toward her dress. "You look incredible, by the way."

She looked down at the light blue, form-hugging sheath dress with an asymmetrical neckline and flesh-colored spike heels she'd dug from the back of her closet. "Oh, thanks."

"I thought I told you office attire would suffice. Surely this isn't what you wear for your clients."

She fumbled with the diamond and pearl pendant she'd added at the last minute. "No. But I don't get too many opportunities to wear this dress, so I thought, why not?" She paused and frowned. "Why? Is it too much? Too dressy?"

He waved off her concern. "It's perfect. And just as I suspected—" he stepped closer and carefully tucked a wisp of her hair behind her ear "—your hair should always be worn down and loose around your face. It's stunning."

A bit startled by his compliment, she chuckled awkwardly and, with a flick of her hand through her hair, said, "What, this old thing? I've had it for years." Her mouth dried a bit as she sent another gaze over his sharply creased suit pants and snug jacket. "You, sir, have surprised me."

"Thought I'd be in my *good* Rolling Stones T-shirt, huh?"

"I don't mean that. I just—"

"I used to work on Wall Street. Remember? Or didn't your digital snooping go back farther than my arrest and conviction? I used to dress like this every weekday for work and on some weekends, if I was wining and dining someone I wanted to impress."

"Well, bravo, sir. You cut quite the dashing figure."

His mouth twisted wryly. "So I clean up well. Is that what you're saying?"

She took her coat from the tree behind the door. "It's not. But you do."

He reached for the wrap and helped her put it on. As she locked her front door, she asked, "Where are we going? I'm famished."

That was a lie. In truth, she'd be surprised if she could eat anything at all.

He named a swanky restaurant in a neighboring town she'd heard of but never tried. She didn't want to be impressed, but she was. When they arrived at the high-end establishment and were seated in a candle-lit corner booth, her nerves edged even higher. This was far cozier and more intimate than a mere business dinner. She opened the menu, saw the price of the meals and did a double take. "Roman, what if we split the—"

"If you even hint to the waiter that we are splitting the check, I will leave you standing on the side of the road and not even feel bad about it," he said without looking up from his menu. "I knew what I was doing bringing you here. I am buying you a nice dinner, and that is the end of the discussion."

"Then this *is* a date," she countered accusingly, but without real heat.

"Did I ever say otherwise?" He snapped his menu closed with a flourish and flashed a cocky smile. "I recommend the redfish with dill sauce and the prime rib. I've had both in the past, and they're excellent. Is red wine all right with you? They serve one of my favorites here, a Beaujolais I'd love for you to try."

"I— Yes. That sounds…nice."

He flagged the waiter, and while he ordered the wine and a stuffed mushroom appetizer, she stared at him, uncertain what to make of her dinner companion. He certainly didn't jibe with the image she'd created of Roman DiMera. Was he trying to impress her? Mocking her for her earlier presumptions about him? The incongruity left her off balance. She liked having things fall in neat categories. Same-shaped pegs to fit in perfectly sized holes. Order. Predictability. Being caught off guard in court was tantamount to disaster. Planning and predictable routines were how she'd managed raising her siblings while finishing college and then law school.

This Roman DiMera didn't match her earlier conceptions, and it caused an uneasy quaking at her core. "Tell me more about yourself," she said, hoping to remedy the uneasiness with a better understanding of the man across from her. "Tell me something a Google search wouldn't. Something about who you really are."

Roman leaned back in the booth and flipped up a hand. "I'm an open book. What you see is what you get."

She narrowed her eyes. "I don't think so. I'd never have pegged the man who met with me in his bar yesterday or went with me to a north-side construction site to be a rare wine connoisseur or have a custom-fitted suit in his closet."

His dark eyebrow arched. "Maybe that's because you weren't looking at the whole picture. Just the slim piece you've seen firsthand. I've never hidden the fact that I worked in finance, any more than I've hidden my stint in prison, my childhood in a rough Philly neighborhood or my college years at Penn State."

She lifted her glass of ice water. "You're right. I concede the point. But my question remains. Fill in some gaps for me. Philly, for example. You say your neighborhood was rough. How so?"

"Well, we didn't have a picket fence or a snotty HOA to contend with. No grassy-lawn subdivision for the DiMeras."

The waiter brought the wine for them to sample, and when they both nodded their approval, he filled their glasses and discreetly disappeared.

"It was just me, my younger sister and my mom," Roman continued. "Dad left when I was five, and Mom worked two jobs to put food on the table and make rent. That was the case for most of the kids I knew, too. Absent or overworked parents. Not a lot of structure or guidance at home. Living paycheck to paycheck. Violence, drugs and crime lived all around us, and I brushed up against my share of it. Nothing too bad, but I did live hard and push the limits, like my friends did.

I got away with too much, in fact. I think that was part of my downfall later, in my twenties."

"Oh? How so?"

"I got cocky. I thought I was… I don't know, smarter than the police, above the law, untouchable somehow. I'd gotten away with so many things as a kid—vandalism, trying pot, truancy, that sort of thing—that I was overconfident. I took chances that deep down, in my truest self, I knew were wrong. I knew were risky. I knew were a mistake. But I didn't listen to my conscience. I rolled the dice with a stock purchase I knew better than to make. I was greedy and full of hubris, and I got caught."

"Insider trading," she said quietly, remembering what she'd read about his conviction.

"Yep." He met her eyes evenly as he took a sip of his wine, and his matter-of-factness needled her.

"So you knew it was wrong, but did it anyway? Why?"

He shrugged. "Like I said, poor judgment, greed… and a coworker pressuring me to join him in the venture that backfired on us."

Morgan had dealt with enough people accused of crimes, both justly and unjustly, that she could read facial expressions, body language, tone of voice quite well. She could usually tell when someone was lying, hear guilt in a denial, knew when someone was withholding critical information related to a case. So it bothered her that, in Roman, she sensed no remorse.

"Now," he said, resting his forearms on the table as he leaned toward her, "tell me something about Morgan Colton that my Google search of you didn't."

She choked on the sip of wine she'd just taken. "You googled me?"

He grinned unrepentantly. "Did you really think I wouldn't after you told me you'd *researched* my past?"

"But…that's so…" She fumbled for the right word, aghast at how violated she felt, even though she understood why he'd done it.

"Yeah," he said, giving her an expression of mock offense. "I know! Right?" His eyebrow quirked up, making his point, and she felt the sting of shame in her cheeks.

"Are you ever going to let me live that down?" she asked.

He made a finger gesture like he was dropping something. "Done. Forgotten."

"Thank you."

"But I still want to know you better. Obviously you come from a large family. What was that like, growing up?"

She chuckled. "Chaos." The appetizer arrived, and once they'd placed their dinner orders, Morgan added, "Our father died when I was nineteen. But you probably knew that from Google, huh?"

He shook his head as he chewed a mushroom. "No, since I didn't really google you."

For the second—third?—time that evening, he'd surprised her. Something shifted inside as she tried to mentally keep up with the serpentine path the evening was taking. His unpredictability was maddening and flew in the face of her need for control and composure.

"Chaos, huh?" He pinned an incisive look on her. "You must have hated that."

Her pulse jumped again. Having him so nearly echo her thoughts, as if she were transparent to him, rattled her further. She cleared her throat. "Sometimes. But the chaos was outweighed by the love and laughter. Despite sharing a bathroom, the TV remote, the best seat in the living room and dealing with constant noise and activity, having eleven siblings has been a blessing. I wouldn't change anything about it."

He smiled. "I only had to share a bathroom with one sister. It didn't bother me much, but she hated it." His expression grew more somber. "How did your father die? If I may ask."

"Car accident on an icy road." She exhaled as the memories of that night washed over her. "I remember it like it was yesterday. Our mother was so distraught. I knew right away I was going to have to do more, make sacrifices and play a bigger role in raising the youngest kids. Alexa and Naomi were only six. Gavin was eight. I had started college already at UCLA, but I transferred to CU Boulder and commuted to class. I took fewer hours each semester than most students and took longer to earn my degree, but Caleb and I wanted to be there for our mother, for the kids."

"That...doesn't surprise me about you." He swirled the wine in his glass as he studied her speculatively. "Everything I've seen of you points to someone who's hyperresponsible, concerned for her family and friends, and willing to go the extra mile to take care of those around her."

"You get that from our—what? Two, three meetings?"

He nodded. "In January, even when you were drunk

as a skunk yourself, you didn't leave the bar until you saw that all of your friends had a safe ride. And I heard you warning one of your friends about the risks of a one-night stand with a stranger."

"Oh...yeah. Stacy," she said remembering. She toyed with the stem of her wineglass. "Do you know that Stacy and Dan, the guy she took home that night, are still seeing each other and happy as clams?"

Roman chuffed a laugh. "No kidding?"

"No kidding." As happy as she was for her friend, Morgan felt a twinge of jealousy. She, it seemed was the only one Cupid's arrows seemed to have missed. She sighed. Maybe she should get a dog. No, she stayed too busy to keep up with the needs of a dog. A cat, then. Didn't old spinster aunts always have a cat?

"You don't look happy about it. You don't like Dan?" Roman asked.

"Oh." She pushed the smile back on her face. "I am. I do. I was just..." She waved him off. "Off down a depressing rabbit hole. But I'm back." She sat taller, determined not to dwell on anything negative tonight. She had a handsome date, good food and a possible lead on Spence. The sooner she and the family wrapped up *that* loose end, the sooner she could relax into the cheer of the holidays.

"Do you have plans for Christmas?" he asked, again spookily echoing her thoughts.

"Um, dinner and gift opening with the family. If it snows—I know, a gosh-awful thing to even mention after that blizzard earlier this month—we might pull out the old sleigh someone found in an auction a few years back. Aubrey, maybe? Anyway, there will be more children around the tree this year, and so I can see the family dusting off old Colton traditions. Cookie baking. Hot cocoa. Snowball fights and singing carols…which can turn into singing some very un-Christmassy tunes as the grown-ups get deeper into their cups, as it were."

"Sounds like a good time." His mouth quirked up but appeared edged with melancholy.

A pang of something—sympathy? Curiosity? Compassion?—tugged in her chest. "What are your plans?" she asked as her head whispered, *Don't you dare invite him to join your family!*

"Working. I'll be closed on Christmas Day so the crew can have the day off, but I'll spend the time getting files ready for tax season or doing a deep clean of the grill or something equally useful but uncelebratory."

A harder tug. *Don't do it!*

She curled her hand in a fist on the tabletop. "Why would you do that? What about your mom and sister?"

"My sister lives in London now. She manages an art gallery there. My mom will be in London with her, because that's where *the grandson* is." He emphasized the words with a comically impassioned expression, relaying the universal significance of grandchildren to which his mother clearly ascribed.

Morgan brightened. "You're an uncle!"

This new revelation, piled on the other surprises of the evening, left her head reeling.

"I am." Warmth sparked in his eyes. "I can bring out the pictures if you like, but it feels so…cliché."

"We'll save that for the next date," she said with a laugh, and when his eyebrows lifted, she realized what she'd said and backpedaled. "Not that this is a date or… that there will be another…"

He wrapped his fingers around her clenched hand and squeezed, a low, throaty chuckle rolling from him. "Geez, Colton, don't hurt yourself backing up there."

Realizing how she'd balled her hand, she relaxed her fingers and flattened her palm on the table. "Sorry. I'm still a little nervous, and all the…*unexpected* things I'm learning about you have my head spinning."

"Not the one-dimensional ex-con you imagined?"

Was that defensiveness she heard in his tone? Or… hurt?

Morgan sat back in her chair and studied Roman while she did a mental accounting of her own prejudice and preconceptions. She had been rough on him based on nothing more than her unwarranted biases.

Chastened, she focused on what was beneath the surface. The fine creases beside his eyes that told of hard work and hard times. The stubborn set of his mouth and square jaw hinted he had more unsavory secrets, while the intensity of his dark gaze hinted at a depth of emotion and character that trumped any past misdeeds.

She knew better than to make snap judgments or follow preformed notions. So what was it about him that had sent her walls up and made her so dubious of him? What was she afraid of? Learning that he was actually a nice guy? Well-rounded and interesting and good-natured?

When she reviewed what she *did* know about him, how he'd graciously driven her home in January and had *not* taken advantage of her, how he'd selflessly agreed to help her look into Spence, how he'd come back from a terrible mistake and built a new life for himself—it all spoke of an admirable arete.

Her cheeks heated, and a guilty gnawing sawed in her gut. "No. You're not what I imagined. And… I've been unfair to you, Roman. I apologize."

Chapter Six

Morgan's apology caught Roman off guard. He settled back against the booth's soft leather and weighed a proper response.

Though their repartee had been edgy and barbed at times, he hadn't taken any of it personally. He'd developed a thick skin on the streets of Philly and during his five years in a New York state penitentiary. A sometimes-prickly Morgan hadn't even registered on his scale. Except to the extent that he wanted her to trust him, wanted her to feel safe with him, wanted her to...well, *want him* as much as he wanted her. He hadn't been able to stop thinking about her and the fire he knew lay just below the surface of her cool facade. Her kiss was proof of that. And just the two kisses they'd shared, months apart, but equally ground-shaking, had shown him that they clicked. They had that mysterious something that made him want to know everything about Morgan...and then make love to her until the sun rose.

Finally he decided on a simple "Apology accepted," determined to let it go and move on. He had her as his captive audience tonight, and he wanted to spend the time learning about her, not hashing out regrets and awkward explanations.

When their dinner arrived, he guided the conversation toward safer topics—first-date fare and musings on local current events. He found her description of the Truth Foundation's work fascinating and explained to her how he'd decided to hire ex-cons who needed someone to gamble on them.

"So we're not that far apart in respect to the incarcerated and second chances, even if we come at it from different angles," she mused, and he was heartened to hear her finding similarities now instead of cataloging their differences. As they savored their meal, Roman saw Morgan unwind by degrees, her muscles finally relaxing, her smile brightening and coming more easily, her contributions to the conversation growing more forthcoming and personal. Each passing moment drew him deeper into her thrall. Not only was she intelligent and quick-witted, but when she loosened the straps of her protective shield and allowed herself to breathe easily, she also radiated a beauty and confidence that mesmerized him. Her eyes had more life, her complexion more color, her humor more zing and her discourse more dimensions and warmth. This version of Morgan was someone he could fall for if he wasn't careful. And fall hard.

By the time their shared dessert arrived, he had her laughing at stories of his mischievous early childhood. "You were a scamp! Your poor mother."

"Now tell me one of the creative ways you got into trouble," he said.

"*Qui, moi?*" she said, feigning confusion, her hand pressed to her chest.

"*Oui, toi.*"

She blinked when he matched her French with his own, then wrinkled her nose in thought. "Don't you mean *vous*? *Toi* is the intimate, more personal version of 'you.'"

He shook his head, and his voice was quieter when he answered, "I meant *toi*. I've had a good time tonight and...would like to see you again sometime."

Morgan set down the spoon she'd used to scoop up chocolate mousse. "Well, I may need more assistance from you as I track down Spence. But... I guess we'll see what Tim has for us tonight and make a plan after that."

He reached for her wrist, stroking his thumb across the tender underside of her arm where a strong pulse throbbed. "You know what I mean."

"I do. But... I'm not ready to make that call."

Seeing her retreat from the repartee they'd been enjoying, he ignored the impulse to try to persuade her now, instead saying, "Come on, Morgan. Your French-innocence act doesn't fool me. Someone with your sharp mind and curiosity surely got into a pickle or two along the way as a kid. Especially with a twin brother to egg you on. Or were you the ringleader?"

"Fine," she said, flushing so hard her ears turned pink. "There was one time I tried to help my mom with the dishes and used liquid dish soap instead of dishwasher powder." She cringed and covered a giggle with her hand. "We had suds all over the kitchen. Gosh,

I must have used the whole bottle. If a little is good, a lot was better, right?"

He chuckled. "Yikes. Hard for Mom to fuss when you were trying to help."

"Mmm," she hummed, her thoughts clearly reviewing her childhood. "And I took a snowmobile out for a spin without permission once, not realizing at age eight that it was a good idea to have a full tank of gas and then allow for some on the return trip. I ran out of fuel far, far from where we were staying and spent the night in the snow. Learned my lesson, though." She sighed and shook her head. "Was I ever so glad to see the ranch hands coming for me on horseback the next morning!" She tipped her head as she looked at him. "For what it's worth, I have a much better sense of direction and time now."

"Good to know. Speaking of which—" Roman dug in the inside pocket of his suit for his phone and woke the screen to check the time. "Huh. We should get going." He angled the phone toward her so she could read the display. "We told Tim we'd meet him at closing."

Morgan glanced at the time, and her eyes widened. "It's almost ten? My gosh!"

Roman signaled the waiter for the bill, paid, and they were back at the Corner Pocket by 10:40. As he escorted her from his private parking place toward the back entrance, he asked her, "Need to freshen up before we meet with Tim? You're welcome to the bathroom upstairs in my apartment."

His question seemed to startle her, but after a brief hesitation, she nodded. "That would be nice. Thank you."

He showed her up the back stairs and keyed open the

door for her, standing back to let her enter first. Thank goodness his housekeeper had been there yesterday, so the place wasn't a complete wreck.

Morgan took off her coat, her gaze traveling around the living room he'd furnished with masculine pieces. A leather couch, a huge recliner, end tables, lamps and a dining table that were high on function and low on decorative frills. Real walnut pieces, not cheap warehouse stuff, but plain in design. Dark, traditional colors—maroon, black and navy.

As she peeled off her coat and gloves, she gave him the perfunctory "Nice place," followed by a smile that seemed genuine enough.

He exhaled. Why did he care so much what she thought of his apartment? Sure, he'd felt judged by her, coming up short by her standards, since they met. But he'd told himself he didn't care what Morgan Colton thought of him. When had that changed?

"Roman?" she said, her voice sounding odd. She pointed toward a window that looked out over the river. "There's a cat over there."

He chuckled as his gazed followed hers to the brown tabby he'd inherited when he bought the building. "That's Rufus."

She chuckled. "You are full of surprises, DiMera. I certainly never pegged you as someone who would get a cat." She strolled over to the window, where Rufus was blinking at them, still groggy from his disturbed nap.

"I didn't so much get a cat as I bought a building that had a cat living there. I didn't have the heart to evict him. The previous owner started feeding him, and he, of course, hung around. He purred and head-bumped his way into a permanent gig. I guess he's officially mine now."

Morgan scratched the cat's head. "You old softie."

"I'm as surprised as anyone, but he's good company and doesn't have to be walked. So…you wanted to freshen up?" Taking her coat from her, he pointed her toward the bathroom, hung up his suit jacket and her coat, and loosened his tie while she saw to her ablutions. He heard her brushing her teeth and paused, wondering if she was using his toothbrush or if she'd dug through his cabinet for a new one. He wandered into his small kitchen and got a glass of water from the tap, poured some dry kibble in Rufus's food bowl, then settled on the couch to wait for her.

"Remind me to get my toothbrush before I go home?" she said as she strolled back into the living room a moment later. "I didn't want to put it back in my purse wet, so I left it on the sink to dry. Okay?"

He flipped up a palm. "Sure." Then, "You always carry a toothbrush in your purse or…is tonight a special occasion?"

She wagged a finger and set her purse on the recliner. "I know what you're thinking, mister. It's not like that. I keep a travel toothbrush in my purse for court days or…this sort of circumstance." She opened her hands to emphasize *this*. "Having a piece of broccoli in my teeth while arguing an appeal to a judge is not an event I wish to repeat."

"That happened?" he asked with a grin.

"Unfortunately. Big piece. Front and center. Very embarrassing." She rolled her eyes, crossed the room to pat Rufus again, then hitched her head toward the door. "Shall we go? I don't like to be late."

"Um, soon. Your story has made me self-conscious. Let me scrub up my teeth before we head downstairs." *And maybe freshen my breath, because I've been wanting to kiss you again all evening.*

Roman returned from his own spiffing up to find her studying the few family photos he'd set out on his mantel. He walked up behind her to peer over her shoulder at the cheesy group pose his mom had picked from their discount-store photo session when he was twelve.

"Look at those braces," she said, pointing to his silver smile.

"Yeah, not the most flattering picture of me but… they earned me these bad boys." He flashed a toothy grin at her, and she laughed.

"Impressive. And broccoli-free. Bonus points."

He clicked his tongue as he winked at her playfully.

"I keep ole metal mouth on display because it's the last family picture we took. Somehow the teen years passed in a blur of acne and overloaded work schedules and not enough money. We haven't taken a family shot since."

She faced him, brow furrowed. "Not even at your sister's wedding?"

Roman inhaled deeply, rubbed a hand over his chin and exhaled slowly. "I didn't make my sister's wedding. I was in prison."

"Oh." Her face fell, and her tone was sympathetic when she added, "I'm sorry."

He shrugged one shoulder. "My own fault."

Her gaze lingered on his face, and he sensed a shift

in the mood. When he eased closer to her, she didn't retreat, so he reached for her cheek. Her hair slipped silk-
ily over his fingers as he moved his hand to her nape and
nudged her forward. Her hands flattened on his chest,
but not to push away. Instead, she slid the fingers of one
hand between the buttons and inside the placket of his
dress shirt and tugged him closer still.

His breath stilling, he dipped his attention to her
mouth. Freshly stained a smoldering shade of plum,
her lips glimmered when the tip of her tongue darted
out to wet them. A pulse of something hot and powerful coursed through his blood, and when she rose on
her toes, he took a nip of her bottom lip before opening
his mouth to taste her more fully. Minty and warm, she
was pure seduction, and he lost himself in the kiss—

Until his phone rang.

Morgan drew back quickly as if caught in some compromising position.

Fisting his hand in frustration, Roman snatched his
phone off the end table and answered the call. "Yeah?"

"Hey, boss," his waitress Penny said. "There's a guy
down here says you have a meeting with him. You know
what that's about?"

Meeting. Tim. Of course.

How easily blue eyes and moist lips could distract
him…if they belonged to Morgan Colton.

He pinched the bridge of his nose, trying to blot
the humming sensation left by her kiss from his head.
"Yeah, yeah. I'll be right down. Get him whatever he
wants to drink on the house. We're on our way down."

Clearly understanding what the phone interruption
meant, Morgan was already smoothing her hair, tidy-

ing her smeared lipstick with a finger and a compact mirror, and heading toward the door.

Roman adjusted his tie and followed Morgan onto the narrow landing at the top of the stairs that led down to the bar. He shoved aside the thrum of irritation at the lost moment, the interrupted bliss. Three kisses. He'd only had three kisses from Morgan Colton, but those three samples of her were enough to know they were not enough. He wanted all of her. He wanted her naked and warm in his bed. An open book, sharing secrets and savoring touches. No protective walls, no preconceptions, no distractions.

And Roman was a man who knew how to get what he wanted. His fresh start in Colorado and the success of the Corner Pocket when the rest of the economy was struggling bore witness to that. His body zinged with anticipation. He'd win over Morgan. It was just a matter of time.

Chapter Seven

"It's about time," Tim grumbled when Morgan and Roman emerged through the employee door that led to the bar's office and kitchen. "I've been here for ten minutes."

Morgan glanced at the neon-lit clock over the bar as she followed Roman across the pub to greet Tim with a handshake. It was still five minutes before closing. They weren't late, but she wouldn't bother pointing that out to Tim. Nor would she dwell on why they were late. She needed to concentrate on what Tim had to tell them, not the mind-boggling talent of Roman's lips. "Thank you for coming," she said instead. "Did you learn anything?"

Roman motioned toward a table away from the last customers finishing their drinks. "Let's talk over here, huh?"

Tim unzipped his black puffy coat but didn't remove it. He took a seat, brushing a few crumbs off the table-top, and Roman pulled out a chair for Morgan. Once they were all settled, Morgan repeated her question, eager to cut through the chitchat and get at the answers she'd waited for all day.

"First things first." Tim divided a look between them. "You got my money?"

"I do." Morgan reached for her purse, then remembered she'd set it on the big chair in Roman's apartment. She'd been so rattled by his kiss that she'd left it upstairs. "And you'll have it, once you fulfill your end of our deal." She squared her shoulders, employing the tone of voice and don't-mess-with-me expression that she'd mastered going head-to-head with criminals and hard-nosed attorneys over the past fifteen years. "I promised to pay you for *useful* information, and I will. You have a down payment. Now tell me what you learned, and if it's valuable, if it proves authentic and helpful, you'll get the rest of your fee."

Tim folded his arms over his chest and scowled. "This one's a piece of work, Roman. Where'd you find her?"

"I didn't find her." He cast her a look that seemed… what? Smug? Impressed? Proud? The warmth in his eyes made her toes curl as he added, "She found me."

After glancing around the nearly empty bar, as if double-checking no one was eavesdropping, Tim leaned forward, his arms on the table. "Well, when you mentioned this guy you're after was hooked up with the local drug scene, I figured I might learn something from, uh…an acquaintance."

"Oh? What acquaintance?"

Tim shifted restlessly. "Look. I'm risking a lot being here. I need some guarantees that nothin' I say ever gets back to…certain people. I trust you, DiMera. You're good people. But I don't know her from Adam." He jerked his chin toward Morgan. "I need some concrete assurances you'll keep what I'm telling you on the down low." He paused and narrowed his eyes. "Or I get up and walk out right now."

Morgan nodded. "I understand your concern. I promise you, I am in a position to protect what you tell me. I keep information clients give me in confidence all the time. I'll treat our interaction with the same respect and utmost privacy." When Tim continued to frown dubiously at her, she added, "I swear."

The wary look remained until Roman added, "I'll vouch for her. She's good people, too. What do you have for us?"

Tim put both hands on the table, and his fingers drummed as he gathered his thoughts. "Okay. So my boss, Henry…he's got a drug connection." Tim shifted on the chair. "He uses. It's not really a secret to anybody who works for him. You can tell on the days he's out of it, or mornings after a bender. Or his wife comes in to cover business stuff for him. She's sober, and honestly, she's the only reason the drywall company's still afloat." He rubbed his chin before continuing, "According to some of the other guys on the crew, Henry got in a bit of trouble with his dealer a year or two back. Couldn't pay what he owed, and so he made an arrangement with the dealer to run money through the drywall business, to clean it."

"Okay," Morgan said, to let him know she was listening. She was accustomed to clients giving detailed backstories, needing to justify or set context for events or actions. She gave Tim the same leeway.

"So this guy I know says the dealer sends a runner up to the drywall office about twice a month. He's this wiry-lookin' kid. Definitely a user himself. He brings this messenger bag with him that's always full when he comes in and flat when he leaves. He thinks the kid's bringing cash from street deals to be processed through my boss's accounts."

"Who is this guy that told you about the runner?" Morgan asked.

Tim's face drained of color. "What?"

"You said a guy you knew saw this runner come into the company office," she pressed. "I need a name."

"I—" Tim muttered a foul word, then flapped a dismissive hand at Morgan and Roman. "He's one of the guys I've met through working on the drywall crew. If he knew I told you his name..." His face creased in another scowl, and he flopped back in his chair, scratching his cheek.

"You have our word," Roman said calmly. "No names you give us leave this room."

Morgan nodded her agreement. "Everyone involved will be protected. It's Spence we want. We have no intention of stirring up trouble for you or your informant or your boss. But I need a name if I'm going to find Spence."

Tim hedged, glancing around nervously, and with a deep breath, he said, "Evan. That's all I know. No last name."

Morgan nodded. "Go on."

"Anyways, Evan got curious one day. Says he followed the kid after he made the cash drop, and he went to this warehouse on the riverfront on the edge of town. He couldn't remember the name of the place, but he said they rent big equipment."

"What kind of equipment?"

"Construction. Backhoes, 'dozers, trenchers, that sort of thing. But he said there were piles of other construction materials there, too. Plywood, spools of wire, siding, vents. A crap load of stuff just sittin' around."

"That's odd," Roman said, his eyebrow lifting.

"Is it?" Morgan divided a glance between the men. "If the warehouse deals in construction equipment, why is it a stretch that they'd have other materials there?"

"Well, they could. Sure. But Evan said the stuff was kinda random and not stored in any organized way. Looked more like someone raided a construction site and stole the stuff from a project and dumped it in the middle of the warehouse."

Morgan waved a hand and sighed. "Okay, I don't want to know if this business is dealing in stolen property or black market or whatever you're implying. We need to stay focused. Do you have any information that links Ronald Spence to this warehouse? Is that what you're getting at?"

"So, yeah. Someone found Evan poking around and got testy. They took him into the office and asked him about his business there. He made up a story about wanting some blow. Said Henry had sent him. They calmed down when they heard he knew Henry, but he was sent away empty-handed. He was told a guy named Ron would find him later that afternoon and to wait for him at a certain address on the north side."

Mention of the north side of town sent a shiver down Morgan's back. She truly hoped that finding Spence didn't mean she'd have to go back to the seedy streets of northern Blue Larkspur. The visit to the construction site to talk to Tim had resurrected enough bad memories.

"Ron?" Roman said and glanced at Morgan. "As in Ronald? Think it was your guy?"

"Could be." She turned back to Tim. "Did he go? Did he meet him?"

"Yeah. Had to. He'd used Henry's name as a cover. If he didn't show, he was afraid it'd look bad, be suspicious. He didn't want the dudes at the warehouse coming after Henry or him later."

Morgan drew a slow breath, her heart pounding with excitement. This was the best tip they'd had in a while about places and cohorts linked to Spence. "Do you think Evan would talk to me?" Immediately, Tim started shaking his head, and she added, "Or to Roman? I need a physical description of this Ron that met Evan. I need more evidence that Spence is connected to this warehouse. I need something solid that says that whatever business is operating from that warehouse location is laundering drug money."

"No." Tim's jaw was set, his eyes hard. "You're not talkin' to Evan. I swore to him his info was safe."

Morgan gritted her teeth, frustration writhing in her gut. "Then…will you go back to him and ask? Get a description of the man named Ron."

Tim skewed his mouth sideways as he pondered this.

"How long ago was this?" Roman asked. "When did Evan say he followed the runner and had this drug deal with Ron?"

Tim shrugged. "Few months back. Sometime this summer." He gave Morgan a speculative glance. "Evan might help you, but he's gonna need some incentive.

You give him the same fee you're givin' me, he'll feel kinder toward you." When she scowled, he added, "Times are tight. A man's gotta feed his family."

Morgan wanted to say no. She hated feeling manipulated, and Tim was pushing buttons that sent her lizard brain into cautionary mode. But he was helping her, at risk to himself and his job, so… "All right. Same deal for Evan, *if*—" she paused to lend the condition more emphasis "—he provides us useful, truthful information. I won't pay for a wild goose chase or fake leads dreamed up to milk me of cash."

Tim stiffened. "You calling me a cheat?"

Roman jumped in quickly, waving a settling hand. "No one is calling you a cheat." He angled a side glance at her. "But you don't want to mess with her, either. She's earned her reputation as a preeminent attorney, and if that weren't enough, she's got the Colton name and a phalanx of formidable siblings to back her up."

Morgan blinked, surprised to hear Roman speak so highly of her.

"Look, I don't know what this *flanks* thing is you're talking about," Tim said with a dismissive flick of his hand. "I just know Evan isn't gonna take risks for nothing. Talking to you is a risk. There's plenty of people who'd be unhappy to know he was spillin' his guts."

Morgan squared her shoulders. "Evan will be compensated for valuable tips. We need a physical description of Ron, a last name, something more substantial and admissible. Now where is this warehouse? I want an address."

He gave her a street name on the north side by the river but didn't have a building number. "Not much else near it. Building next door is abandoned, and the lot on the other side is vacant."

"Which gives them privacy for drug deals and other illicit business," Morgan mumbled, then added, "This is good information, Tim. Thank you. And any more information that leads us to Ronald Spence will be rewarded. I promise."

"Speakin' of…" Tim turned his palms up and wiggled his fingers. "I told you what I learned. I want my money now."

Morgan exchanged a look with Roman. "My purse is upstairs in your apartment."

They both pushed their chairs back, and Roman dug a key out of his pocket.

"You don't need to come. I know the way," she said, taking the key from him.

As she headed through the kitchen to the back stairway, Gibb glanced up from where he was cleaning the grill. "You all done out there? I gotta show Roman something in the storage cooler."

"Almost." As she climbed the stairs, two thoughts occurred to her. First, she was glad she didn't have to climb these stairs every day like Roman did. They were steep! And second, how much, if anything, had Gibb overheard? The bartender had made himself scarce, but that didn't mean he hadn't caught a phrase or two as he was straightening behind the counter. She made a mental note to ask Roman about Gibb.

She found her purse where she'd left it, took the opportunity to use his restroom, then hooked the purse strap over her arm as she locked Roman's door behind her. She carefully maneuvered the stairs again—steep angles, high heels and several glasses of wine called for extreme care—and returned to the floor of the pub.

Tim was pacing by the front door, his coat on, clearly antsy to get going. "Took ya long enough. Geez, did you have to go to the bank or something?"

She cast a glance around looking for Roman. "Where's...?"

At that moment, Roman reappeared from the kitchen. "Sorry. I had to check a problem in the cooler and show Gibb where the circuit breakers were. Any problem getting in upstairs?"

"No." She opened her purse, took a bank envelope out of a side pocket and extended it toward Tim. "It's all there."

He thumbed through the bills counting. "Forgive me if I check, just the same. Trust isn't something I do so much anymore." Once he was satisfied the full amount had been paid, he tucked the envelope in his coat pocket.

"When can you meet us again?" she asked.

Tim looked confused. "Again?"

"You said you'd talk Evan, get more on Ron and the warehouse. The sooner the better. Can you come back tomorrow night?"

Her informant's face darkened. "Pushy thing, aren't you? If I get a chance to talk to Evan, then, yeah. I can meet again tomorrow. But no promises. And...not here again. I don't want to set no patterns."

"All right." Roman spread his hands, palms up. "You name the place."

"How 'bout, if I get anything, I'll call you. Arrange a place then." Tim took a couple steps backward toward the door.

Morgan agreed to the terms, and after thanking Tim again and bidding him good night, she and Roman returned to his apartment to get her coat. "Quite the mercenary, that one. I thought you said we could trust him."

Roman chuckled. "I said I thought he could help you. Not that he wouldn't be expensive. And for what it's worth, I think his caution is a good thing. We don't need him giving the wrong people the idea we're a threat."

She let a growl of frustration rumble from her throat. "Yeah, well, given the right information, there's no saying I or one of my siblings might not be a threat. I hate the idea of an illicit drug trade going on right under our noses."

Roman placed a warm hand low on her back, guiding her toward his door. "One battle at a time, darlin'. Let's catch Spence first, then we'll turn to fighting the other crimes in the community, huh?"

"Let's? Are you thinking we're a team now or something?" she asked, trying to ignore the warmth in his tone and how his use of the term *darlin'* tripped pleasantly to her core.

He clapped a hand to his chest, his expression playfully wounded. "You wouldn't kick me off the team before the mission is complete, would you?"

"Mission?" She chuckled. "We're not spies, Roman."

"Call us what you want, but there's still evidence to be gathered. People to track down. Business to finish. Don't cut me out now, Sherlock!"

She hesitated as they reached his door. "Are you serious? I mean, I appreciate the introduction to Tim and use of your bar for the meeting tonight, but I think I can take it from here. Caleb can help me with the follow through on the warehouse and any further interviews with Tim."

He unlocked the door and pushed it open but didn't move. He met her eyes and tilted his head as he returned a weighty gaze. "I had been teasing, but…it sounds like you're ready to write me off completely." His attention dipped to her mouth, and his tone grew husky. "And we have more unfinished business than just your search for Ronald Spence."

Sweet sensations curled in her belly, and his sultry grin revived the erotic tingle in her blood. She swallowed hard before she could speak again. "Do we?"

"Really, Counselor? You and I both know the kind of energy that sparks between us when we kiss is not common or to be ignored. Aren't you even a little curious to see where this heat between us might lead?"

Her senses were still humming from good food, wine and conversation, and the imprint of his kiss lingered on her lips. Of course she was curious. But curiosity didn't mean she had to be reckless and follow her primal impulses. Plain sense said she and Roman had little in common, and she still had a voice in her head that insisted she have some semblance of a relationship with a man before she slept with him. Even if that man cleaned up surprisingly well, had impressed her with his savoir faire and had charmed away her initial doubts about his past. "I'm not looking for a fling."

"And yet you've found the opportunity to have one… if you decided to follow your desires."

"What I want isn't the point. It doesn't matter."

His head jerked back, and he stared at her like she had three heads. "What do you mean, what you want doesn't matter?" His eyes narrowed. "Surely you don't think I'd force anything on you without your full consent?"

"No, nothing like that. I just mean there are more things to consider than just what I want. Practical matters…"

One dark eyebrow cocked up, and he challenged, "Such as?"

"Well, I—" Though she tried to think of a valid reason to give him, her thoughts were still somewhat muzzy from the wine. From Roman's intoxicating proximity. "I don't know…" She shook her head, and the floor tilted. She reached for the lapel of his jacket to brace herself, and he drew her closer, an arm circling her waist.

"When was the last time you put your own needs, your own wishes and desires ahead of anything else? Not your job, or your family or any perceived responsibilities to someone else. Just Morgan."

She screwed up her face as if that was the most ridiculous suggestion he could make. "What? I do plenty for myself."

"Such as?"

She grunted, somewhat perturbed that he was pressing the issue. She grew more irritated when she couldn't think of an example. "I, uh… Well, I don't know. But people count on me, and it would be unprofessional to ignore my clients' needs. And if I hadn't helped my mother after our father died—"

His snort interrupted her.

She scowled. "Excuse me?"

"You've been taking care of other people your whole

life." He tucked her loose hair behind her ear, pressed a kiss to her jawline. "What if, tonight, you let me take care of you?"

The soft brush of his beard on her chin was a sensual treat she hadn't expected. When he moved his lips to trail along the tendon in her neck, the tickle of facial hair against her skin made her breath stick in her throat. She couldn't form a coherent thought when his teeth nibbled lightly on her shoulder.

"A hot bath, a foot massage…an orgasm or three?"

Her pulse pattered, and her heavy eyelids blinked open with a tantalized start. "Three?"

"At least. More if you desire." The seductive tone of his voice slid through her like warm chocolate. So sweet and tempting. So promising.

If she didn't break away from his embrace, his kisses, she would give in. She could feel her resolve crumbling.

And then he released her and stepped back. Straightened his tie. "But if you really want to go home, I'll get my keys and drive you now." He walked through his apartment door and bent to scoop up Rufus, who was trying to sneak past him and get out, then disappeared inside with his cat, leaving her body humming and frustrated.

"I—" She swallowed hard. "But—"

After setting the cat on the couch, he took her coat from the closet where he'd hung it and plucked a set of keys from a wooden bowl on a table by the door.

Her hand shot up to his chest, blocking his progress when he tried to leave. "Roman, wait. I…"

He said nothing, only met her eyes with a patient gaze. She set her jaw and scoffed a laugh. How could he look so calm and collected when she felt like she'd fly apart if she didn't ravish him this instant? And how had he flipped things around on her, changed her mind so completely without showing his cards?

She grabbed him by the Windsor knot and hauled him in for a hungry kiss. "Damn you, DiMera. You know what I want. I'm not going anywhere until I get it."

Without taking his hot gaze from her, he tossed the car keys back in the bowl and kicked the door shut with his heel.

Chapter Eight

"Are you sure?" Roman asked when, after several minutes of kissing on his couch, Morgan stood and tugged him toward his bedroom. He meant what he'd told her about needing her full consent before he'd take her to bed—though at this point he wasn't sure even an hour in a cold shower could ease the ache for her that had been building all night. He was certain of one thing—Morgan Colton had no idea how beautiful and desirable she was. Even when buttoned up, she was attractive, but when she let her hair down, literally and figuratively, she was a knockout. That she was intelligent and kind sealed the deal. He could easily fall for this woman. *Except...*

He shoved the *except* from his brain. Right now, he didn't want to analyze anything other than the creamy shoulder Morgan bared as she slid her dress off. Then her round hip and long, sleek legs. Good grief, but the girl had gams, even when she stepped out of her high heels and rolled her foot to stretch her ankle.

"I remember something about a foot massage?" she said, crooking a finger as she scooted across his bed and propped herself against his pillows.

Roman ditched his dress shirt and suit pants in re-

cord time and sprawled across the mattress to the alluring woman wiggling her toes at him. "Indeed. I am
a man of my word."

A seductive-sounding moan rolled from her throat
as he took the foot between his hands and stroked his
thumb down her arch. Fire shot through him, just hearing her sighs of pleasure, but he was determined to be
patient. Be thorough. Indulge Morgan in every grain of
seduction and pampering he knew she'd denied herself
in the past while taking care of everyone else.

When he finished with the first foot, he gave equal
attention to the other, then her calves and upward until
he reached her hips. He raised his head to gauge her
willingness for something far more erotic, but her eyes
were closed. "Tell me you did not fall asleep on me?"

Her eyes blinked open, and she tugged her mouth in
a crooked, wicked-looking smile. "No. But I am becoming more…hmm, *relaxed* by the minute."

"I see. Well, maybe this will energize you." He
hooked his fingers into her panties, skimmed them
down her legs and bent his head to kiss her intimately.

Morgan gasped and arched her back. Her fingers
wound into his hair, and he stopped long enough to
ask, "Okay?"

"Better than okay. Don't you dare stop!"

He didn't. He followed the guidance of her groans
and gasps, sighs and wiggles until she pulsed with a
climax.

When he moved to cover her with his body in the
wake of her pleasure, she wrapped her arms around his
neck and smiled contentedly. "That's one."

"Mmm-hmm." He stroked his palms over her bare

skin and nibbled her ear, her neck, her bottom lip before kissing her deeply.

When he stretched out full length beside her, she
stroked his bare calf with her toes and smiled lazily at
him. "May I return the favor?"

His body quickened, and heat raced through his
blood. Gritting his back teeth, he ruthlessly forced his
libido back like a lion tamer containing a raging beast.
He hadn't been with a woman in…well, a really long
time, and his man parts were reminding him of this
fact with a powerful ache. "Soon. I promised to make
tonight about you, and that's a promise I aim to keep."

"Still, fair's fair. It would make me happy to—" she
drew a finger down his chest "—do something nice
for you."

She did. Embarrassingly easily. But it *had* been a
long time since…

And the night wasn't over. He could still prove his
endurance later…

"C'mere, you," he said, tugging her back into his
arms after he'd caught his breath. He lavished her with
lingering caresses, gentle nips, teasing licks, skillful
tweaks until she was writhing, begging for release. He
kept her teetering on the edge for a while longer, just
because he could and he knew her climax would be all
the better for it.

"Roman! Please!" She dug her fingernails into his
shoulders, her body quivering.

With a sure stroke of his hand, he sent her tumbling
into oblivion. She cried his name and clung to him as
she arched into the wave of pleasure.

"Two," he whispered in her ear as her gasps and moans ceased and her limbs grew limp.

"Damn skippy," she whispered.

She dozed after that, and he watched her nap, studying the fan of her dark eyelashes against her cheeks. Her almost model-like bone structure. He caught wisps of her hair between his fingers, rubbed the silky strands. Inhaled their fruity scent. It reminded him of summertime…of fruit stands by the roadside the only time they'd driven to Hilton Head beach when he was ten.

Peaches. Sweet and juicy and fresh-picked from the trees that lined the South Carolina highways. His mother had saved all year to take them on that road trip, wanting to show her kids the state where she'd grown up, the beaches she'd visited as a kid, the orchards where she'd had a summer job…and gotten pregnant with Roman. The memory of that trip created a mellow warmth in his chest. His mother had made so many sacrifices to give him and his sister a good childhood, despite their meager means. He'd had love and a safe home. He'd gone to college…and blown it with one stupid, risky investment. His arrest and conviction had crushed his mother, and he would spend the rest of his life making it up to her.

Morgan stirred then, and her blue eyes found his. "Hi."

"Hi yourself."

"I fell asleep?"

"Mmm-hmm."

"Sorry. Not a commentary on your performance, I swear."

"Good to know."

"But I'm rested now and ready for…three." Her lop-sided grin was somewhat wicked. And totally enticing.

He kissed her, and they twisted themselves in the sheets as the foreplay progressed. When, at last, she rolled to her back, bring him on top of her, she whispered, "Now."

"Patience, Peaches." He levered away reluctantly, only his nagging sense of responsibility strong enough to stop him at that point.

"Peaches?"

"You smell like peaches. I guess it's your shampoo or body wash. But I like it. A lot."

She acknowledged him with a coy smile and a breathy hum.

He snapped on a bedside lamp so he could see in his bedside drawer and find the box of condoms he kept there. A new box. Unopened. He tore at the cardboard impatiently and ripped a plastic packet off, opening it with his teeth. He sheathed himself quickly and, when he turned back to Morgan, caught the odd look on her face.

"You okay?"

Her finger traced the shape of one of his tattoos. A flame on his chest. One of his smaller ones. One of his first, meant to represent "hearts on fire," the motto he and his Philly friends had come up with for living life at full speed. With passion, daring and no regrets.

She twitched an unconvincing smile. "Yeah. I just… hadn't seen this one in the dark."

He paused as he took her in his arms again. "Do my tattoos bother you?"

"N-no." But she'd taken several beats to answer.

Haltingly, at that. Then her smile returned to her eyes, and she dragged his head close to kiss him again. "Now, where were we?"

"About…here." He cupped her cheek and returned the lingering kiss, inhaling the sweet scent of her skin and nestling between her legs.

"Roman?" she said, angling her head to glance at the lamp. "Can we turn the light back off?"

"What if I want to look at you when I'm inside you? See your face when you reach…three." He wiggled his eyebrows.

"Oh. Well…" Her smile was dimmer now, but she gave a small nod. "If that's what you want."

Clearly it wasn't what she wanted, and he had sworn tonight was about her wishes, her pleasure. He stretched to reach the switch and snap off the light, resisting the urge to ask why she wanted it dark. Though he had a funny suspicion as to why.

He groped playfully on the pillow and across her face once the light was off, as if he couldn't see anything. "Peaches, where are you?"

"Right here." She captured his head between her hands and raised her hips against his.

And then he was inside her, moving with her, and all else was wiped from his mind. His world narrowed to that moment, to Morgan, to the feel of her body gripping him, her sighs tickling his ear. The wait had been worth every second. So intense were the sensations that washed through him, he almost cracked a tooth clenching his jaw, holding back his release until she shuddered and arched her neck with a cry of ecstasy. He held her tighter and let go of the tension coiled inside him. He lost himself in sensation, her face before him, his heart feeling as if it might judder through his chest.

Hearts on fire. Hell yeah. It had been a long time since he'd felt this level of elation, energy, passion for life and promise for his future. Was this love? Maybe. Whatever it was, he knew Morgan was at the root of it, and he wanted this feeling to stick around. If only he could be sure she did. And there was that nagging *except* again.

"Three," Morgan said with a sigh. "Oh my."

"I am a man of my word, Peaches."

Morgan lay limp and quiet and satisfied beyond her wildest dreams. Gary Bilkin, her first at age seventeen, had been bumbling and inept. And her last lover—geez, that had been more than five years ago?—had been so unimpressive, she couldn't even remember his name now. But Roman... Ah, *Roman.*

"I'm not going to ask where you learned to do that, because I think the answer might make me jealous." She rolled on her side to face him, and her foot found something soft and warm at the end of the mattress. Rufus. When had the cat come in and settled on the bed? Not that she'd had any bandwidth left to notice anything besides the delightful things Roman was doing to her, with her. She rubbed Rufus with her toes, then gave all her attention to the human beside her. She trailed her fingers over the soft, short hair of his beard. Recalling how that beard felt against her breasts, her thighs, her belly made her insides quicken and her breath catch. She'd considered herself a woman of modest needs and self-control before this evening. Now, after one taste of the elixir that was Roman, she was insatiable. Greedy for more.

He propped on one elbow, his cheek on his hand, a position that emphasized his impressive biceps. "Really? You're not willing to consider the idea that I could have natural talent without having a sordid history?"

"As long as it is history, and you're not cheating on a secret wife or something, I don't think I need to worry." She stroked a hand over the expanse of his shoulder and muscled chest, her fingers still restless to learn every inch of his warm skin.

He chuckled, and the sound was rich and mellow. She felt the vibration from his chest, and the sensation tingled up her arm and settled in her core. She absorbed the feeling into her flesh, making it part of her, locking it away like a treasure. She gazed at him through the wan light in the room, memorizing the dark features of his face, his eyes, his lips. *Her lover.*

And how do you feel about that? her lawyer brain asked.

"I know so little about your history," she mused aloud.

"What? Your Google search of me was incomplete?" he said in mock surprise.

She found a single hair on his chest and plucked it.

"Ow!" He rubbed his free hand on the offended spot.

She pressed a kiss to his lips. "Tell me about your sister. Are you close?"

"I love her a lot and was always very protective of her, but we weren't best friends or anything. We lost touch during the years I was in prison. She—" he twisted his lips in thought "—was furious with me for being so stupid, taking risks and flouting the law. And for how I'd hurt Mom with my actions." He sighed heavily and rolled to his back, folding one arm behind his head. "Not as furious as I was with myself, though."

"Why did you do it, then?" Morgan scooted closer so she could drape herself over his side and peer into his face as he spoke. "You used insider information to buy stock. Right?"

"Yeah. My gut was telling me it was a mistake. My conscience was screaming not to do something so unethical. But my buddy at the firm, who had all the bells and whistles of a lifestyle built on lucrative investments, was egging me on, appealing to my hedonistic side. The greedy itch that wanted the high-rise penthouse and vacation home on Martha's Vineyard and a private jet parked at Newark. He swore I could have it all if I followed his lead in investing."

"Was he caught in the same sting that you were?"

He gave a mirthless laugh. "Yeah. But he had more money for better lawyers and got off without serving time."

"Ugh!" She put all the disgust with the ways the legal system could be contorted unfairly behind her groan. Now she flopped back on her pillow but laced her fingers with his, wanting, needing to feel the connection to him. "That sort of unfairness is why Caleb and I established the Truth Foundation."

"You've mentioned it before. The Foundation is for people wrongfully convicted? Is that right?"

"In a nutshell. But we do more than that now." She took a breath, squeezed his hand and delved into the murky history behind the Truth Foundation. "We—

Caleb and I, primarily—spearheaded the formation of the foundation after we learned the truth about what our father had been doing."

"Your father?"

"Mmm-hmm. Judge Benjamin Colton of Lark's County. Except that an intrepid reporter's investigation uncovered that he was less than honorable. He was taking bribes and kickbacks from private prison facilities, letting the influence of money sway his judgments. He was sentencing people, young and old, to far harsher punishments than were justifiable. And worse, he looked the other way when innocent people without sound representation were wrongfully convicted."

"Your father did this?" The shock and distaste in Roman's tone were humbling.

"Shameful, I know. Restoring some honor to the Colton name was one of the reasons Caleb and I started the Truth Foundation. At first, our goal was to find the people wrongfully convicted and give some justice to the poor souls our dad misused for his personal gain."

"Was your father convicted of any of this?"

"No." She explained how Ben had been killed in a car accident before he could be brought to trial, and how the kickback scandal, the loss of her husband and the loss of income were overwhelming to her mother. "That's why I dedicated myself to helping raise my youngest brothers and sisters. Along with odd jobs to help with expenses."

"Did he not have life insurance?"

"That was awarded to the victims' families after a civil suit. Mom couldn't stand to benefit from others' pain.

"Anyway, you see I really have no right to judge

you for one mistake you regret when my family is trying to live down dozens and dozens of mistakes our father made."

He was silent for a moment before he said, "I'm not sure I regret what happened to me."

Morgan had to replay his words in her head to be sure she'd heard him correctly. Her pulse jumped, and she twisted to face him. "What are you saying?"

"I regret the wrong I did but not having to serve time. I grew up in prison. When I started my career on Wall Street, handed a top-notch financial job right out of Penn State, I was still the irresponsible, risk-taking, immature thug I'd been on the streets of Philly. The cocky guy with frat boy sensibilities. Prison knocked some sense into me. Straightened me out and forced me to look at my priorities."

"And what are your priorities?" she asked, almost hesitantly. A man's values and focus were so telling. Far more so than externals. Suits or jeans. Fine wine or domestic beer. Beards or tattoos.

"I want to be able to face the man in the mirror. Leave the world a little better than I found it. Give someone a hand up without expecting anything in return."

"Is that why you hire ex-cons?"

"Partly. Ex-con doesn't mean unskilled or unworthy. People make mistakes. All people. And who am I to judge?" He tipped his head toward her. "What would you say was your worst mistake?"

A startled laugh burst from her. "Wow. Um…let me think."

"Geez, if you have to think about it, it couldn't have been that bad."

"Maybe I'm trying to decide which of many I deem the worst."

He turned his face toward her, his brown eyes glinting with mischief. "I find that hard to believe. Not my Peaches. Let me guess. Straight As? Never had a speeding ticket? Never fudged an excuse to get out of jury duty?"

My Peaches. She liked hearing the endearment more than she wanted to admit. Endearments signaled a level of relationship she hadn't brought herself to acknowledge with Roman. She savored the sweet thrill of the pet name for a moment longer before addressing his challenges. "Yes to the As in high school, but I made a B once in college."

"Horrors!"

She snorted in response to his mocking tone. "Mmm-hmm. Music history. Darn that Dvořák. No speeding ticket and, sadly, no jury duty. I wouldn't fight that. I'd love it! I'd never get picked, though. One side's lawyer or the other would likely boot me based on my law degree."

The conversation continued for hours. Even when sleep tugged at her, she fought it, too fascinated by the stories Roman told of Wall Street, his childhood and the roadblocks he'd faced getting the Corner Pocket up and running. For her part, she regaled him with more details of the cases she and Caleb had taken on through the Truth Foundation, righting the wrongs Ben Colton had inflicted on clients, and life with eleven siblings. "Let me tell you, we are not cheaper by the dozen. I don't know how our mother kept us all fed. Especially the boys. They ate like…well, teenaged boys!"

No response came from beside her. She angled her head to look at Roman, whose dark eyelashes were fanned below his closed eyes. "Roman?"

Still no answer, no indication he'd heard her. His breathing was deep and steady. Stretching to reach his phone on the bedside stand, she checked the time, disturbing Rufus in the process. The cat chirped a meow and blinked slowly.

"Sorry, fuzzball." She woke the phone screen—3:52.

Wow. Time flew and all that. She returned the cell phone to the bedside table and kissed Roman's cheek softly. "Sleep tight."

Rufus resettled, snuggling up against her legs. Morgan did much the same, curling against Roman's warm strength. And like Rufus, she was asleep in minutes.

Chapter Nine

When Morgan woke the next morning, the bed beside her was empty, and she could hear the shower running in the adjoining bathroom. She stretched lazily, feeling the tender ache in her limbs and other places that bore witness to the previous evening's activities. She smiled to herself. Three. He was a man of his word.

She tossed back the covers, shivered a bit as the cool apartment air nipped at her and considered hopping in the hot shower with Roman. But the sound of the water cut off, and with a pang of disappointment, she shifted her plan to having a bite of breakfast ready for him when he came into the kitchen. Borrowing a robe from his closet, one redolent with his masculine scent, Morgan traipsed into the kitchen to start a pot of coffee and scramble a few eggs. If he had bread, she'd make toast.

Rufus greeted her in the kitchen with a leg rub and plaintive meow. Morgan tried to recall where she'd seen Roman get the cat's food last night. As if answering the question for her, the tabby rubbed his cheek on the knob of a lower cabinet and meowed again. "That's right. Thanks, Rufus. Good kitty."

After a quick scratch behind his ears, Rufus trotted

over to his food bowl to wait while Morgan found the bag of food and fumbled it open. She poured some into the waiting bowl, and the cat tucked in.

"You're welcome." She resealed the bag, returned it to the cabinet and turned her attention to the humans' breakfast.

Breakfast. Good grief. What had she done? Raking her hair back from her eyes with one hand, she exhaled a long, slow breath. She'd slept with Roman DiMera. Bar owner. Ex-con. Risk taker. In their pillow talk last night, Roman's stories of his misspent youth, wild college days and the illegal stock purchase that had landed him in jail all pointed to a man who was no stranger to taking a gamble. Damn the torpedoes and full speed ahead.

But she shied away from even a hint of risk. Stability and certainty were cornerstones to the law practice and home life she'd built for herself. She craved safety.

Morgan opened Roman's refrigerator and stared into it without really seeing. So why had she fallen into bed with him when she'd so specifically told herself doing so would be a mistake?

She thought back to his promises of comfort, pampering, pleasure. His appeal for her to consider her own needs instead of always taking care of others. And he had pampered her, pleasured her—three times!—and made her feel…well, safe. She blinked, and her pulse tripped. Roman, who for all intents and purposes was a living, breathing risk with a capital *R*, made her feel safe. How was that for irony?

She took out the carton of eggs and milk, and as she went about the mundane tasks of starting coffee and finding a bowl to crack the eggs into, she found her-self humming. Dvořák's New World Symphony, of all things. Because she'd been reminded of the music dur-ing their late-night conversation? Probably. Who knew how the human brain worked?

She considered, too, how, at one point, when she'd discovered the tattoo on Roman's chest, she'd jolted for a moment. She'd somehow blocked out thoughts of tat-toos—his and...*others'*—last night. Maybe because of the dark. Or her slight inebriation. Or the distraction of the pleasant things he was doing to her.

She sighed as she cracked an egg and tossed the shell in the trash. Would Roman's tattoos forever be a trigger of her worst day? She shivered, thinking of the parade of ink Roman's body bore, most covered up by his winter clothing, but still there, stirring bad memo-ries at the oddest times.

She picked up another egg, but instead of cracking it, she stared without seeing, awash in a fresh flood of memories.

Her shoes beat a staccato rhythm as she hurried down the shadowed street, eager to get back to her car. She should never have come to this side of town alone. She'd been warned. Caleb had offered to come with her, but she'd been too stubborn. Too self-sure. Too... foolish. *Call it what it was. Bad judgment. She tucked her purse more securely under her arm and pushed her pace faster. She was practically running.*

The sound of heavy feet thudded behind her. The scent of cigarette smoke found her, and before she could turn and look over her shoulder, an arm snaked around her waist from behind. An arm covered in tattoos. Her

*purse was tugged, hard, but she clung to it for all she
was worth. "No! Help!"*

*The grant check to pay for her last semester was in
her purse, and without it how...?*

*Her purse slipped with the man's next yank, but her
fingers dug into the strap for all she was worth.*

*Something hard smacked the back of her head, and
she blinked against the black spots that swam in her vision. The arm around her dragged her backward then.
She stumbled and almost fell as he forced her into a
dark side alley. She fought, twisting and screaming.
Tried to stomp the man's foot with her heel, to kick back
at him, desperately attempting to wiggle free of his py-
thon grasp. When she got one arm free, she clawed at
the man's tattooed arm with her fingernails.*

*"Stop it, bitch!" he snarled. His fingers on her other
arm dug deep into her flesh, and he slung her to the
ground with a tooth-rattling jolt. Stunned as she was
by the fall, her attacker was able to snatch the purse
from her. The loss of the means to pay for her last semester of college was wrenching. She pressed a trembling hand to her mouth to catch the wail of despair
that rose in her throat.*

*That's when the attacker hesitated. He'd been pre-
pared to flee with his stolen booty, but he'd spotted the
ring she wore. A large ruby surrounded by diamonds.
An antique passed to her from her maternal grandmother. A ring worth far more to her because of the
sentimental value, even if the jewels were themselves
quite valuable.*

He stepped back to hover over her. "Gimme that ring!"

*She shook her head. Fisted her hand. "No! Please!
It's my—"*

He lunged toward her, grabbing her hand. She tried desperately to keep her hand balled, to jerk her arm from his grip. The whole time that she battled him, her vision was filled with that beefy, tattooed arm. Then, with a terrifying dark glare over his shoulder at her, he backhanded her. "I'm taking that ring if I have to cut your finger off to get it!"

Terror roiled from her in a piecing scream, and like a woman possessed, she fought. And was battered and bloodied in return. At some point she was knocked out, and when she came to in that dark alley that smelled of garbage and urine, her grant money, her ring, her earrings and a simple gold chain necklace were all gone. Along with her sense of safety. She'd pulled herself to her knees to sob, when—

A tattooed arm slipped around her from behind, across her collarbone, and she was tugged backward.

She screamed. Batted at the encumbering arm, dropping the egg she held— Egg?

"Morgan, easy. It's me!" A male voice. The arm loosened, and she spun around still struggling, still slapping...

And blinked hard as the alley melted into a homey kitchen.

Morgan drew a shuddering breath and covered her face with her hands, her whole body shaking. Tears flooded her eyes, and she hiccuped as a sob tore from her.

"Hey, I'm sorry, Peaches. I didn't mean to scare you." Roman put a hesitant hand on her elbow and gently nudged her forward. "Morgan, honey, what...? I'm so sorry."

She shook her head and swiped at the moisture

dripping onto her cheeks. "I'm… I'm okay. I just—"
Another hiccup cut her off, and she leaned into the welcome warmth of Roman's offered embrace.

"You sure don't seem okay. Geez, you're shaking all over. Did I really scare you that badly?"

"It's only… My head had gone to a bad place, and when you grabbed me—"

"Hugged you. It was hardly a grab."

She levered back to look up at him. "Because of the where my thoughts went, it felt more ominous." She took a step back from him, noticing his state of dress—or undress, as it were. He had jeans on, but that was all. His feet and chest were bare. The flaming heart tattoo that she'd discovered last night was on full display, along with the few on his arms, his wrist. Fresh on the heels of her walk down Nightmare Lane, it was all a bit too much. She averted her eyes from him, unable to even savor the masculine beauty of his well-formed shoulders and muscled arms.

Instead she ripped paper towels from the roll by the sink to clean up the egg that had broken when she dropped it. She felt a bit like that egg. Fragile. Shattered. A mess. How could she build a relationship with a man who conjured her worst fears simply because of his body art? Why couldn't she get past his ink?

And did she want to? Did she want a future with Roman?

SOMETHING MORE THAN Morgan being startled out of deep thoughts was going on here. That much Roman knew. And based on how Morgan couldn't hold his gaze, could barely look at him, he had to wonder if in the sober light of day, she'd considered everything she'd learned about him last night—all the myriad ways they were different, the sum of his somewhat checkered past—and regretted sleeping with him. She was clearly having second, even third, thoughts about him.

Crouching beside her, he took the wad of paper towels from her. "I'll do that. You take a minute to catch your breath. Can I get you anything?"

"I, um…" She stood and tugged on the belt of the robe she'd borrowed. "Really, Roman. I—I'm okay now." She dragged fingers through her hair. "But if you don't mind, I will get a shower. Then, uh…you'll have to drive me home. Remember?"

He tossed the soiled paper towels in the trash and nodded. "Right. Whenever you're ready."

She disappeared into his bedroom, and the shower came on. Turning back to the bowls on the counter, he finished cracking eggs, toasting the bread and frying some bacon. The least he could do after scaring her so terribly was feed her a nourishing breakfast.

Rufus rubbed against his legs, reminding him Rufus needed feeding. His thoughts elsewhere, he got the cat food bag from under the counter. Why had Morgan been so scared of him? What bad place had she gone to?

She'd seemed fine last night, seemed to enjoy their dinner…when he'd been decked out in his best Wall Street attire. But under the sheets, when the business suit and tie had come off, they'd spoken of their pasts. She'd come face-to-face with the real Roman DiMera, bad choices, blemished life and all. And this morning she'd balked. In the harsh light of day, she'd seen him for the inked bar owner he was and retreated. Hard and fast.

He stewed over her withdrawal, her drastic reaction to him this morning, and couldn't reconcile it with the warm and willing woman who'd purred her satisfaction in his arms last night. When Rufus bumped his furry head against Roman's leg, his thoughts focused enough to recognize that Rufus already had food before he poured more. Morgan must have done that. Rufus would have demanded it. The corner of his mouth twitched. "You beggar."

He turned back to the bowl of eggs and sobered again as Morgan's wide, fearful eyes flashed in his memory. Damn it!

He didn't need a mercurial, fickle woman in his life, no matter how much he liked Morgan. From what she'd told him during their pillow talk before sleeping, the Coltons were like lodestones for drama and conflict of late. He didn't want anything like the tumult she'd described the family going through this past year coming close enough to taint the Corner Pocket.

Selfish? Maybe. But he'd worked too hard to build the bar from nothing, dragged himself out of the quagmire of his own folly and imprisonment to make a fresh start to put it at risk.

Self-protective? That, too. He didn't want to lose his heart to a woman who couldn't accept him and his past. Disappointment arrowed through him, sharp and merciless. Morgan was symphonies, a big family and law and order. He was hard rock T-shirts, the streets of Philly and second-chance employees. He needed to forget about Morgan Colton and move on.

A hollowness opened in his chest, imagining his life

without Morgan. He'd quickly become fond of her and her sharp wit, sexy kisses and engaging conversation.

He shook his head to clear it. *Don't be an idiot!* he could hear his sister Adrienne telling him, echoes of his youth when he'd brag about his wild exploits with his friends. Thank goodness Adrienne had fallen in with a good crowd, had found a loving man and happiness. Was it so terrible that he wanted the same happiness? He'd finally gotten his life on track, and he was staring down forty without a family of his own.

After prepping the eggs, he returned to the bedroom to finish dressing. He was pulling on his shirt when he heard the shower water stop.

Ten minutes later, Morgan reappeared in the kitchen, wearing the same clothes from their dinner the night before, her face free of makeup, her wet hair slicked back from her hot-shower-pinkened cheeks. She padded across the room in bare feet and sent him a bright smile. "There. Much better."

He set plates loaded with the food he'd finished preparing on the table. "Perfect timing. Breakfast is served."

Her expression grew sheepish. "I'd intended to be the one serving up hot food to you. Before—" She sighed.

He sat at the table and picked up his fork. "Yeah. Before. Do you want to talk about this bad place you went? Is there anything I can do to help?"

After pouring herself a fresh mug of coffee, she joined him at the table, put a napkin in her lap and met his eyes. "I really don't want to talk about it now. Maybe someday, but…not over this terrific breakfast."

After the openness they'd shared last night, her deferral stung a bit. Further evidence of withdrawal, of Morgan erecting defenses around herself.

Roman slathered a piece of toast with butter and strawberry jam. "Why don't you tell me more about Ronald Spence, then?"

"Spence?" She pulled a face. "He's another topic that will ruin a meal." Morgan wiped her mouth, then lifted her mug of coffee. "But I do owe you a better case history, thanks to your assistance connecting me with Tim, helping me get that lead on the warehouse where Spence might still be doing drug business and cleaning his money."

She drummed her manicured fingernails on her mug. "So last night I told you how we learned our father had been taking bribes and kickbacks and handing down wrong and overly harsh sentences. When Spence first appeared on our radar, we considered him one of the men our father had wrongfully convicted. We took on his case through the Truth Foundation to get him released from prison earlier this year."

Roman groaned.

"Exactly," she said, raising her mug to acknowledge his moan of dismay.

He opened his mouth to reply just as Rufus jumped up on the table and made a stealthy grab for a bite of eggs. Scowling, he lifted the cat back to the floor and returned his gaze to Morgan. He could imagine how Morgan must feel about her family's mistake, helping Spence when the man was actually duping them.

"In fact, we have every reason to believe he's responsible for ordering a hit on a man in prison," she continued as if not having noticed the feline's antics or, at least, not being bothered by them. "The murdered man took the fall for Spence's crimes, and still Spence thought he needed to silence him. Of course, Clay Houseman's murder—he's the guy Spence had killed—sent a chilling effect to others connected to Spence. No one would talk. We had a hard time substantiating our suspicions that Spence was dealing again. But he sent warnings to the family. He's behind a good bit of the bad stuff I told you my family has suffered of late. He even tried to kill our mother and our sister Alexa before he went into hiding."

If someone had tried to kill his own mother and sister, he'd be apoplectic. "No wonder you're out for his blood."

"Well, not blood if we can help it. Just getting him back behind bars would suffice. To correct our overzealous attempt to right our father's wrongs." She sipped her coffee, then cradled it as she added, "Then he must have heard about the money hidden at Kayla's family ranch, and that's when he faced off with her and my brother Jasper earlier this month."

"Got it." He chewed a bite of bacon as he thought. "An all-around bad guy. And where are the police in all of this?"

"Oh, they're involved at various levels. Of course. How could they not be when our mother is romantically involved with the chief of police?"

Roman blinked and tugged a corner of his mouth in a grin. "She is?"

Morgan nodded, cracking a small grin of her own. Then, sobering a bit, she continued, "But while the police are aware of Spence and are helping, we have members of our family—and their significant others—with experience and skills in finding people. And we have the personal connection to make it a priority." She set the mug on the table and flipped up a palm. "That's really where we are at this point. Finding Spence. When we do, we'll let the police or FBI or whoever claims him step in and arrest his sorry ass."

"Which is why you came to me for tips as to where a man of Spence's character might launder fifty thousand stolen dollars."

"And you were a great help. Thank you." She took a last bite of toast and pushed her plate away. "It's getting late. I need to get back to the hunt. Back to the office and clients, and I plan to follow up on that warehouse."

Roman, too, gobbled down the last bites of his meal, matching her sense of urgency to get the day started. Morgan hustled back to the bedroom, returning with her shoes and purse.

He rinsed both plates and their mugs but left them in the sink to deal with later. Morgan was clearly ready to go.

"Well, time for the walk of shame," she said, hiking her purse strap onto her shoulder and straightening her back as if preparing to march to the gallows.

Her characterization was a gut punch to Roman and further confirmation of her feelings about their ill-advised relationship. "Why is it a walk of shame? Are you ashamed of what happened last night?"

She blinked. "Wow. No one could ever say you weren't blunt."

"I've said before, I don't go for a lot of bull—malarkey. Just say what you mean and be done with it." He

cocked his head and narrowed his gaze on her. "So…
are you ashamed?"

She huffed and pulled a dismissive face. "No!"

He hated to admit how much he'd wanted her to deny
it, wanted to hear her say their lovemaking had been…
making love for her, too. That they'd planted the seeds
of a possible relationship, if they could find a way past
all their differences. But hearing her denial didn't mean
he fully believed it. Actions spoke louder than words,
and he'd seen her wariness, her backpedaling, her *fear*
this morning.

She waved a hand, and her mouth opened as if she
were fumbling for words. "I just… It's an expression.
Maybe *awkward* is a better word? It's the morning-af-
ter march in the clothes from the night before and—"

"I know what the expression means." He crossed
the room to her and stroked a hand down her arm. He
ducked his head a bit to meet her eyes straight on. "I'm
just wondering how you really feel about walking out
of here, past my employees and early-morning vendors.
Do I need to sneak you out the back door?"

She pinched her lips, twisting her mouth in delibera-
tion. "Your employees are here already?"

"Penny won't be in for a little while yet, but Hector
does food prep, and Gibb meets deliverymen and cleans
bathrooms, that sort of thing. I actually need to get
down there and do my part." He stepped toward the door
as she pulled on her coat. "So…front door or back?"

She kicked her chin up as if in challenge. "Front,
thank you."

"All righty, then." He held the door for her and ushered her down the stairs. She might have been putting

on a good front to spare herself more questions or soul-searching, but her response heartened him just the same.

His good mood lasted until he reached the bottom of the steps, where the sound of angry voices in the kitchen could be heard.

Chapter Ten

"Cameras don't lie, man!"

"Maybe not, but they can deceive. I didn't steal nothing!"

Morgan frowned and cast a worried glance at Roman. "Uh-oh. That doesn't sound good."

"Not at all." He mustered the resolve to dive into the middle of his employees' argument and strode into the kitchen, where Gibb and Hector were squared off, chests puffed out belligerently and expressions taut with fury.

"Hey!" His shout brought both men's attention to him. "What's going on?"

"He stole the tip money and—" Hector said at the same time Gibb shouted, "He's accused me of stealing—"

Roman whistled loudly to silence them both. "One at a time. Hector?"

"The cash from last night's tip jar is gone. I always count it and divvy it up in the morning, first thing. But the jar's empty." He aimed a finger at Gibb. "Security footage shows him takin' the money. Red-handed."

"I didn't steal nothing! I put in as much as I took out. I swear!"

Roman cut a glance to Morgan. "Mind if I deal with this before I drive you home?"

"By all means." She slid her coat off her shoulders and draped it over her arm. "It needs settling."

He plowed fingers through his hair and waved the men back to his office, where they could watch the security feed on his computer. On his desk was the zippered bank bag used to carry the day's take to the bank each night. Last night, he'd given his office key to Gibb and delegated the night-deposit job to the bartender. Now, Roman lifted the empty bank pouch and asked, "Any problems with the deposit last night, Gibb?"

His bartender sent him a startled look, then his face drained of color. "I didn't make a deposit. I—I thought you did."

Roman fought the surge of irritation that coiled inside him. "No. I gave you my keys, asked you to take the deposit and lock the place up, remember?"

"And I locked up like you asked." Gibb dug in his pocket and brought out the loop with the three pub-related keys. The office door, the front/back doors and the desk drawer where employee files, Roman's handgun and other valuable items were kept. As he handed the keys back to Roman, he said, "But there wasn't no money in the deposit bag, so I figured you'd decided to make the deposit yourself, in the morning."

At the office door, Hector spit out a foul curse word. "He stole the day's take, too!"

Gibb spun around, his face growing red. "I didn't take nothing! Maybe it was you!"

"I wasn't even here, you asshole! I left at nine. You know that. If it wasn't you, maybe Penny took it."

"Yeah, and maybe Santa took it. Or his elves." Gibb's tone was snide, and his face was growing more florid.

Hector stiffened, his hands fisting. "You son of a—"

Another whistle sliced the tension and silenced the shouting men. This time it was Morgan who'd loosed the shrill sound. The men all turned toward her, and she held up both palms in a gesture signaling for calm. "Gentlemen, I think we need to look at the security footage. We can resolve this easily enough if the thief was caught on camera."

Tipping a nod of appreciation toward her, Roman sat down at his desk.

"What about Penny?" Morgan asked. "She should have a fair chance to defend herself from accusations."

"She starts at noon," Roman returned. "She'll get a chance to speak up if she's implicated."

Gibb or Hector, or both, had already called up the saved security feed from the night before. Roman hit Play. He reviewed the feed from behind the bar first, including the spot behind the counter where the accumulation of each day's tips was stored in an oversize jar. Typically, the sum was counted the following morning and divided evenly among the hourly workers who were on duty the previous day.

Together the four of them watched the comings and goings of the limited staff with reason to be behind the bar. Then, around the time stamp of 10:30 p.m., Gibb approached the jar, lifted it and plunged his hand inside. With his hand fisted around a number of bills, he pulled his hand out, then carried the jar and cash just out of camera range.

"See!" Hector snarled, waving a finger toward the computer screen.

Gibb's head hung low, and his mouth was clamped in a grim line. "It's not how it looks. I needed small bills, ones and fives, so my kid would have lunch money today. I put in the same amount I took out. Two twenties! I swear!"

"Then why was the jar empty this morning?"

Roman rubbed his temple. "It does appear rather damning, Gibb. And the night deposit? Where is that?"

Gibb's mouth remained tight. "I don't know," he grumbled through clenched teeth. "Maybe you should watch that part of the footage and see for yourself who took it?"

An uneasy roiling had already started in Roman's gut. He'd known he was taking a chance hiring ex-cons, and Gibb had a history of theft. Had he trusted Gibb with the deposit and locking up last night as a test? His gut had told him Gibb had turned his life around, was sincere in his desire to make a clean start. But the security footage seemed to contradict that.

The black-and-white images of the office were far duller. The office remained empty except for Roman popping in once in a while. He fast-forwarded through hours of this nothingness until the camera captured him retrieving the keys for Gibb to lock up. Shortly after that, the feed ended. Static snow crackled on the screen. Roman frowned. "What the hell?"

"What happened?" Morgan asked.

"Good question. It's like someone cut off the cameras."

Hector grunted and faced Gibb with an accusing look, his arms crossed over his chest. "So no one could watch him steal the deposit money."

Gibb shoved Hector. Hard. Called him a vile name.

Hector shoved back, and Gibb threw a punch. The tussling men knocked a stack of files onto the floor and crashed into Morgan. Lifting a hand to her cheek, Morgan squawked in pain and stumbled out of the way.

Rage filled Roman, not just for seeing Morgan injured, but having his employees scrapping like junkyard dogs. He grabbed a fistful of Gibb's shirt and hauled him away from Hector. "Enough!"

Gibb's chest was still heaving with rage as he poked a finger at Hector. "You got a lot of nerve accusing me. I bet it *was* you took it all."

"I wasn't here!" Hector repeated.

Roman wedged himself between the men and faced Gibb, his fists balled in anger. "I said enough! Get your things and get out of here."

Gibb twitched, narrowing a stunned look on Roman. "What?"

"You heard me. Get out. I told you when I took you on that I had a zero-tolerance policy. You step outta line once, you're gone."

The bartender's face grew florid. "I didn't steal nothing! You got no proof!"

"I have some pretty suspicious circumstances, though. But more important, you just hit a coworker. That alone is grounds for dismissal."

Gibb shot a dirty look from Roman to Hector and back. "You're firing me? Days before Christmas? Are you freaking kidding me?"

Roman exhaled a slow breath. He felt awful. Not just for letting Gibb go and the timing, but because Morgan had witnessed the whole sorry incident. But he'd made a determination long ago that he'd hold a firm line with his employees. No excuses, no third chances, no debate. "I'm not kidding. Get your things and go."

He turned to Morgan, who was still holding her cheek, her eyes wide and skin wan. "I'm so sorry. Let me look." Peeling her hand from her face, he found a small cut and the earliest stages of bruising on her high cheekbone. She was trembling, and her obvious upset roused a protectiveness in him that he hadn't felt since he'd defended his sister's honor on the streets of his old neighborhood. "Hector, get the lady some ice, and both of you apologize profusely for injuring her."

The two men shot sheepish glances at Morgan and muttered apologies, which she accepted with far more grace than Roman could muster at the moment. When they were alone, Gibb presumably gone home and Hector retrieving the cold pack for Morgan, Roman took her in his arms and held her close. "Geez, Peaches, you're still shaking."

"Adrenaline, I guess. I wasn't expecting to be caught in a street fight this morning. Not here, anyway. Maybe later today at the north-side warehouse, but…"

He stiffened and leaned back to look into her eyes. "Excuse me? You're going to the warehouse? The one Tim mentioned last night?"

He saw something akin to fear flit through her gaze before she visibly gathered her composure and bobbed a nod. "I need to see it for myself. Maybe ask a few questions. Maybe have a look around the—"

"No."

"What?"

That old protectiveness flared again, burning hot in his gut. "No way. I can't let you go down to a known drug-dealer hot spot and poke around. It wouldn't be safe."

A shudder raced through her, one Roman felt beneath his hands as he gripped her arms and saw in the drift of shadow over her countenance. She drew another deep breath and pulled her shoulders back. "I—I didn't say I was looking forward to it. But why get the tip from Tim if I'm not going to follow up? If Spence is operating through that warehouse, I only have days, maybe hours, to find him before that money he took leaves the country. Before he's got the funds set up in untraceable accounts and can flee somewhere the US can't extradite him."

Roman chewed the inside of his cheek, stewing for a moment. "Can't you send your brothers? You said one of them was an FBI agent, right?"

She shook her head. "No. I mean, Dominic is, but he's retiring in January. Besides, he's in Denver, and—"

"Caleb, then." His grip tightened as his sense of urgency grew. The thought of her in danger—and his gut told him that warehouse was crawling with all forms of danger—made him sick to his stomach. "If you can get away from the office to investigate Spence's possible connections to this warehouse, then so could he."

She folded her arms over her chest. "Watch it there, Mr. DiMera. You're starting to sound sexist. I hope you aren't implying that I as a woman am not as qualified—"

"Peaches, I have no question about your abilities in

any area," he said, allowing his tone to imply all the double entendres she cared to think, "but I cannot in good conscience let you head into a viper's nest alone. And you certainly can't go looking like you just attended an evening at the symphony." He motioned to her date-night attire, and she surveyed her dress as if just remembering she was still in her best clothes.

"Well, I would change into something else first, naturally."

"Such as?"

She snorted as if the answer were obvious. "My regular clothes. Something less dressy, of course."

"Jeans? Sweatshirt?"

"I—" She hesitated.

"Do you even own jeans?"

"Yes!" Her expression shifted, and in a mumble, she added, "They don't fit, though. I lost weight this year because of all the worry over the stuff my family's been enduring. I haven't taken the time to shop for more."

Hector returned then with the ice pack, which he offered Morgan with another apology for his part in injuring her. Roman took it and held it to Morgan's face, meeting her gaze.

She covered his hand with hers, trying to take the cold compress from him. "I can do that."

He tucked a loose wisp of her hair behind her ear. "I know you can, but you're always taking care of everyone else. Let me take care of you."

Her gaze clung to his as if mesmerized, and he remembered he'd used much the same words last night. Heat filled his veins, remembering all the ways he'd taken care of her, and the flush in her cheeks suggested she was remembering as well.

She let her hand fall away from the ice.

He cleared a strange thickness from his throat before announcing, "I'm going to come with you to that warehouse. You do what you have to do, but I'm coming, too. To watch your back."

She opened her mouth, as if to protest, but instead sighed. Smiled. "Okay. I accept. I would appreciate your assistance."

"Wear the jeans you have, though, even if they're too big." His mind clicked in fast forward, planning. "In fact, wear all baggy clothes that look like you've lost weight, like you're not eating well and not taking care of yourself."

"Why would I do that?"

"Because it's a good cover. You can't go down there looking like the gorgeous and successful attorney you are. You'll ring all kind of warning bells, and no one will talk."

"So what do you suggest?"

"I have a ratty old sweatshirt you can wear, and we can use makeup to make dark circles under your eyes. We need to maybe get some grease from the kitchen so your hair looks like you haven't washed it in a week or two."

"Whoa! What?"

"We want you to look like you're an addict looking for your next hit. Desperate. Strung out. Unkempt." He nodded to her dressy, button-front wool coat. "Leave that at home. It reeks of money and prestige. Power. Everything the shady warehouse managers want to avoid. Drug dealers and distributors prey on the weak and desperate."

She lifted her chin. "I'm aware. Unfortunately. Far too much experience with drug abusers and dealers in my line of work."

He scratched his head as he studied her. "You ever do any acting?"

"Acting?"

"Yeah. Plays in high school or whatever."

"Not really. I was the angel that spoke to the shepherds in a Christmas pageant when I was about twelve."

"Hmm. Well, you're going to have to employ some top acting skills to convince them you're an addict. Your current demeanor and body language are far too confident and assertive. Can you tone it down? Way down? You have to convey a literal and figurative stink of desperation."

"Literal?" she asked her gaze narrowing. "Roman, what are you—?"

"Come on," he said, catching her hand. "We have some prep to do."

Chapter Eleven

Two hours later, Morgan surveyed Roman's handiwork in her bathroom mirror and paled. "Good grief, Roman. It's…shocking. Humbling."

To give her an aroma of body odor and neglect, he'd taken her for a strenuous jog around her neighborhood, after which he'd showered and she'd not. A small amount of the stale grease from the pub was streaked through her hair with a comb, and dark smudges were applied with a matte eyeshadow under her eyes. The small cut and bruising on her cheek, courtesy of Gibb and Hector's brawl, added to her decrepit appearance. She'd donned his oldest sweatshirt after he'd rolled it in the soil of her back garden, her baggiest jeans and the holey tennis shoes she wore in the garden when she wasn't in boots. She removed all her jewelry and nail polish, and he ruined her manicure with a few ragged scissor snips.

"It's like reverse Pygmalion," she mumbled, then cringed when she caught a whiff of herself. "I hope this works, because this is—" She shuddered.

"It's perfect. You dress down well, Peaches."

She met his gaze in the mirror when he used the

moniker he'd given her. She'd never admit it, but she rather liked the nickname, the special bond it implied. That he could look at her in her current state of mess and stench and use the pet term was heartening.

"All right. Let's do this." She headed out to his car and hesitated before climbing in. "Are you sure you want me in your car?"

He lifted her hand and kissed it gallantly. "In my car. In my bed. In my life. I've grown rather fond of you, Morgan Colton."

She grinned. "I'm going to remind you that you said that when your Corvette still reeks of stale grease and horse poop next week."

On the drive to the north side of town, they worked on a scheme, a line of attack for Morgan to pursue. She needed some confirmation that Ronald Spence used the warehouse accounts to launder his money. "They aren't just going to volunteer information like that."

"No, but if you can keep them busy, distracted, I might be able to find some proof of his activity in the files or—"

"You can't take anything. That's theft."

"Trust me, Peaches, I have no intention of going back to prison. Not even for you. I'll figure something out. You just…keep the baddies distracted. Okay?" He patted her knee, then pulled the car into a parking spot several blocks from the warehouse.

She pulled two photos from her purse and held them up. "Just to refresh your memory, this is Spence. If you see him, sound the alarm. I can't risk him seeing me, recognizing me. He could show signs of an injury, thanks to the bullet Kayla put in him. We're pretty sure she hit him, but we don't know where or how badly he was hurt."

Roman arched an eyebrow. "She hit a moving target in the dark? Mighty impressive. Am I going to get to meet this Annie Oakley sometime?"

Morgan shrugged. "I suppose. She lives at the ranch, so…"

She let the sentence trail off, realizing that for Roman to meet Kayla at the ranch, he'd have to visit the Gemini. Which meant the whole family would learn she'd brought him there. Which would lead to questions about *why* she'd brought him, and who he was to her and—

She cut the thought progression off there. She didn't even know what Roman was to her. How could she answer any questions from her family?

She fisted her hands and determinedly refocused her thoughts. Now was not the time for that debate. She needed to focus on the task at hand.

"Hmm. Those eyes are rather chilling, huh?" Roman mumbled as he studied the pictures of the stringy-haired, lean-faced man another moment then handed them back. "Okay. You ready?"

They walked together the first couple of blocks, then split up. The only way Morgan was able to keep from panicking as she traveled the final two blocks alone was knowing Roman was following her at a discreet distance. Every shout, passerby and car horn made her jump, and she battled to keep nightmare memories at bay. She had to stay focused on her mission today.

Despite all her self-talk, by the time she stumbled into the gravel parking lot beside the warehouse, she had a genuine sheen of nervous sweat and anxious twitters working for her. She clenched her teeth and put herself in the mind-set of addict Abby Johnson, the name she'd chosen for the persona she'd assumed. Mustering every grain of her courage and acting skill, she pushed through a door into the warehouse, intentionally leaving it open so Roman had a window inside. Within moments, one of the warehouse workers spotted her, confronted her.

"Hey! Who are you? What are you doing in here?" The man wore a hard hat and held a cup of something that steamed with a white cloud in the cold air.

She fought her instinct to stand straight and meet the man's gaze boldly, head high. Instead, she tried to shrink, to cower and avoid his eyes. "I… I'm looking for someone. I just need some…" She ducked her head and fidgeted with the frayed edge of Roman's sweatshirt. "I was told to ask for R-Ron. Is he around h-here? Ron?"

The man scowled. "Ain't no one works here named Ron. Get lost, huh?"

She moved closer, taking a few quick, shallow breaths. "Wait! I know he prob'ly doesn't work here. But my old man said…" She cast a glance around as if looking to see who was listening. She spotted Roman approaching the edge of the parking lot before he slipped behind some dumpsters. "Please. I need a hit. M-my old man said Ron could hook me up." She dug in the pocket of her jeans and dug out some crumpled money. "I can pay."

The man eyed the cash. Sighed. "Wait here."

ROMAN MOVED CLOSER and found a spot in the shadows behind a metal barrel where he could peer through the door Morgan had left open. He arrived in time to see the first man she'd approached return with two other men. Big men. Men who didn't look happy to see her. His cold hands fisted in his pockets. He'd charge in there and take every one of them down if they hurt Morgan.

He couldn't hear more than mumbles from Morgan... which fit her fake-humbled persona. One of the men jerked a nod and sent a sharp glance toward the open door. He stomped over to close the door while the other two men seized Morgan under her arms.

Roman hunched down behind the barrel, praying he wouldn't be spotted. Once the door closed with a metallic clang, he moved down the wall to a high window and peeked around the edge. Everything in Roman quailed when saw the men drag Morgan into the front office and shut the door. If not for the office's large window that looked out into the cavernous warehouse, he'd have busted down the door and swept Morgan away from the site, their fact-finding mission be damned. But through the window, he could keep tabs on what was unfolding, even if he couldn't hear what was being said.

After a moment, he sneaked back to the door Morgan had used and cracked it open, slipping inside. He kept close to the wall as he sidled deeper into the warehouse, sneaking closer to the office, hoping to overhear something. Sweeping his gaze from one corner of the dim warehouse to the next as his eyes adjusted to the lower light, he kept watch for workers who might spot him and sound the alarm.

Business was slow, though. Whether because it was near Christmas or because they typically worked a skeleton crew, he couldn't decide. He saw no sign of the building materials Tim had mentioned. Perhaps those stockpiles had been a fluke? He heard a door squeak and shrank back behind a vending machine as a guy in coveralls left a room to the right of the door where the men had taken Morgan, climbed in the cab of a truck and drove away. A woman exited next, her purse over her arm, coat in hand, and disappeared in the other direction down a short hall.

The door the woman had exited through remained open, and curiosity bit Roman hard. Staying below the edge of the large window of the main office, he duck-waddled to the open door, rose to his feet and peered inside. The desk inside held a double computer screen and was cluttered with folders and stacks of papers and surrounded by metal file cabinets. The fluorescent tube light overhead hummed—the only sound he heard other than the rumble of indistinct male voices from the next office.

He gritted his teeth, praying Morgan was all right, then slipped into the empty office and quietly closed the door. He moved to the desk and scanned the files. Rolled the computer mouse to wake the screens. As he scanned the headings on the computer tabs that were open, the woman returned.

Roman thought a foul word but kept an outward appearance of calm.

She blinked at him and frowned. "Can I help you?" Her tone was far less hospitable than the words suggested.

He decided in an instant that his best tactic was to act as though he belonged there. As though he were somehow the one with the upper hand. He might even learn something useful.

"You make a habit of leaving the computers and all these records unguarded?" he asked, his tone rough as he swept a hand around, motioning to the room as a whole.

She bristled, but her eyes reflected a note of concern. "I—I was just going out for a smoke, but I left my lighter." She aimed her thumb to the next office. "And the guys are—"

He slammed his hand down on the desk, cutting her off. "I don't want your excuses!" Shoving to his feet, he pointed to the computer. "The boss is not going to like knowing you left that up. And, make no mistake, I will be reporting back to him how you let records of the whole operation sit here, exposed, vulnerable to any Joe that walked in off the street."

For a moment, her expression grew contrite, but soon her suspicion returned. "Any Joe like you, you mean? Who are you?"

He drew his shoulders back and narrowed his eyes. "Someone with very little patience today. Boss wants a report on his money. What's the holdup?"

She grew even warier, backing toward the door and casting a glance toward the next office as if looking for backup.

Roman's pulse kicked, and in three long strides, he crossed the room and swung the door shut. "Damn it, this is serious! You've jeopardized the whole operation, and I want answers! The boss wants answers!"

"Tony never said anything to—"

Roman barked a dark laugh. "Not Tony, idiot!"

She shifted her weight and put her purse and coat on a chair beside the desk. "Then who are you talking about?"

He dragged a hand over his mouth, his beard scraping his palm, and debated the risk before him. Was the gamble worth it? There'd been a time in his life when he wouldn't hesitate to roll the dice, to flout caution. Some days he wondered how he'd survived the streets of Philly in one piece. But his hubris had caught up with him on Wall Street, and he'd paid the price. A voice of caution whispered in his ear. If he blew this, he was risking not just his own life, but Morgan's, too.

The woman stared at him, growing more suspicious with every second that ticked by without him answering. When she made a move to leave the office, he shot an arm out to hold the door closed. "Spence."

The name tumbled out, and the next moment, a chill washed through him. If he'd just blown not only his cover, but Morgan's… If he'd rung warning bells that couldn't be unrung…

If—

But the woman tensed, and the color drained from her face. "B-but there aren't problems with his— It's all on schedule. He knows the money has to settle before it can be moved."

A tingle raced through Roman, and he bit the inside of his cheek to contain his smile. *Holy cheese on a cracker!* Did the woman just give him the proof the Coltons were looking for?

Keeping his tone rough, low and tight, he said, "He just needed to know if there'd been any problems. He ain't heard from no one."

"Because he said not to. That he was being watched and didn't want to g—"

"Why do you think I'm here? Because he can't come outta hiding before the money clears and he can get outta town."

The woman twisted her mouth and rubbed her hands on her slacks. "Yeah. Okay."

"So will the whole fifty K clear regulations on schedule? He can't afford any holdups, you know."

She nodded. "Everything will still be done by the twenty-third. We staggered the deposits, spread them out like he asked. And Carl will have his new passport ready to go on the twenty-third, too. The warehouse will be closed for the holiday then, so he can come get the passport any time that day. He can be out of the country by Christmas Eve like he wanted."

Roman kept a tight rein on the surge of relief and victorious adrenaline that pumped through him. His gamble had paid off better than he could have imagined. The temptation to pump the woman for more information hovered like low-hanging fruit, but every good gambler knew that sometimes the smartest move, even when you were winning, was to lay down your cards and walk away from the table. Now was that time. Before the men next door caught wind of him.

Jerking a nod, he backed toward the door. "Boss wants this kept quiet. I was never here. Right?"

She nodded weakly, her eyes still reflecting a hint of suspicion and ill ease.

He ducked out of the office and hesitated. He had to signal Morgan somehow, get her free of the attentions of the men and get them safely away from the warehouse without triggering any alarms. He eased to the edge of the large window and peered into the main office. Three men had Morgan surrounded. Two had their arms crossed. One leaned close to her, his arms braced on the arms of the chair where she sat. All had their backs to the window. But Morgan's gaze flicked repeatedly from man to man then to the window, both keeping her pretense of the jittery drug abuser and monitoring events outside the office. Roman let her see him once and hitched his head toward a bay door of the warehouse. *Let's go.*

Suddenly Morgan started screaming and twitching. For a moment, Roman jolted, a heartbeat away from rushing to her aid, before he realized she was creating a diversion, allowing him to get out of the office unseen. *She's quite the actress after all.*

Hurrying out of the warehouse, he slipped behind a parked truck and watched the bay door for Morgan's exit. A movement across the lot caught his attention, and he saw a man with unkempt, stringy hair shuffling toward the alley on the far side of the warehouse. The man, a cigarette pinched between his lips, had a limp and held one hand on the thigh of his injured leg as he disappeared from view.

A fresh bolt of energy charged through Roman. He hadn't seen the man's face, just a rear view as he disappeared, but the hair, the limp... Could it have been Spence himself? If so, what had Spence seen and heard? Had he spotted Roman? Morgan?

He considered following the man, but Morgan stumbled out of the main door of the office end of the warehouse, shouting curses and flailing angrily at the men who ushered her roughly out of the building. She headed in the direction they'd come, toward his parked car. He followed, keeping her in sight but not approaching her until they were several blocks away from the warehouse and he could be sure they hadn't been tailed.

When he felt safe catching up to her, he called her name and jogged up behind her. She continued walking, fast and head down, toward the street where they'd left the Corvette. When he got close, he snagged her arm and tugged to stop her.

Morgan screamed and spun, flailing an arm at him and slapping at him.

"Whoa! Morgan, stop!" He fought to trap her wrists. "It's me."

She blinked hard, her face whey-colored, and she released a shuddering sigh. Then another.

"Sorry, Peaches. Didn't know you were still in character," he said glibly, but he soon realized she wasn't recovering from her start easily. She was still quaking, her eyes moist and her bottom lip trembling. "Morgan? My God. Did they hurt you?"

She shook her head and fell against him, clutching at his shirt. "N-no. I just…need a minute. You scared me."

Again. As he had that morning. A gnawing guilt bit him, along with a growing need to know what had happened to Morgan that made her so edgy, so easily spooked. Because he had a sense that this was no average tendency to startle, but a symptom of some sort of PTSD.

"I'm so sorry. I called out. Didn't you hear me?"

"I— No. I was…thinking. These streets…this part of town just…spooks me. Reminds me of…" She exhaled sharply. "And the men in the office stirred up memories…"

"Oh, Peaches. You're okay now. I gotcha." He hugged her tight, more certain now that Morgan was struggling with trauma, something she didn't trust him enough to share with him. He held her for a moment, then escorted her, tucked under his arm, the last block to the Corvette. Even in the state she was in, stinking and messy, having her snug against his body gave him a feeling of completeness, the satisfying click of two magnets with opposite charges locking together and forming a strong connection.

"I have news that I think will cheer you up," he said, giving her a light squeeze.

She tipped a querying glance up at him, and her blue gaze punched him hard in the gut. No amount of makeup and disguise could mute the beauty of her eyes. The clear intelligence, caring warmth, bright openness. "Tell me."

"We have the right warehouse. Spence is laundering his money through them. And someone named Carl is getting him a new passport, which he's to pick up the day the last of the funds settle. Three days from now, on the twenty-third."

Her steps slowed and her eyes widened. "Picking up? As in coming to the warehouse to get?"

"That's my understanding," he said, unable to hide the grin of success that burgeoned in him.

She grabbed him by the sleeves, her back straightening to the erect posture he knew and loved.

Loved? Roman's heart quaked a bit realizing he was forming deep attachments to Morgan.

Confidence and joy filled her eyes, and she chuffed a small laugh. "Then we know where he'll be, and we can catch him in the act. We can have him arrested when he shows up on the twenty-third!"

His smile dimmed. He sensed another dangerous trip to the warehouse was in the offing. "Well, yeah. But I hope you don't think it will be as easy as that. He might send someone else to pick up the passport. And we don't know exactly when. It could be at 3:00 a.m. for all we know."

"Doesn't matter. This is our best lead yet, and the Coltons will not miss this opportunity to nab that SOB. Come on! I can't wait to tell Caleb what we've learned." Head high, she hurried the rest of the way to his Corvette.

Chapter Twelve

Buzzing with excitement, Morgan began forming ideas for how to stake out the warehouse and catch Spence when he showed up on the twenty-third. What a Christmas present that would be for the family! Having Spence off the streets again, correcting the error they'd made, finding justice for all the harm he'd done to her family this year. She couldn't wait to tell Caleb!

And she owed it all to Roman. Not only had he extracted the information from the woman at the warehouse, but his introduction to Tim had been the key to finding the warehouse to begin with.

She studied his profile as he drove, the sun peeking out from clouds now and then to highlight the strong lines of his face and shine diamonds in his dark brown eyes. Her attention was drawn to his lips when he twisted them in thought.

"Do you want to go home or by my place to clean up before going to your office?" he asked.

"I probably should but...no."

He cut a surprised glance her way.

"The office is closer than either, and I really am too excited to wait. It's been such a stressful year thanks to Spence. I can't wait another minute to tell Caleb the good news."

He chuckled. "You look like a kid on Christmas morning while Dad fumbles to set up the camera. Itching to tear into presents and told to wait."

She scratched her scalp. "Itching is right. A shower is definitely next on my agenda, but give me five minutes at the office. Please?"

"Your wish is my command, Peaches."

She sniffed her arm. "Rotten peaches, more like."

He wrinkled his nose. "No argument there, but I'm not complaining. The disguise worked. Right?"

She nodded as he turned in at the parking lot beside her office building. Hurrying inside, she showed Roman up to the offices of Colton and Colton, secretly praying none of her most important clients were in today. What would they think if they saw her looking like this? She chuckled to herself, imagining Mrs. Hempshaw's snitty reaction. She might be their longest-standing and most affluent client, but the older woman was too tightly wound and judgmental in Morgan's opinion.

"What's so funny?" Roman asked as they plodded up the stairs.

"Just imagining the horror on an elderly client's face if she saw me in this state." When she pushed through the front office door, Caleb and Rebekah looked up from consulting on a file and gave her matching looks of shock and dismay.

"Something like that?" Roman laughed and motioned to her brother's stunned look.

"Good God, Morgan! What happened to you?" Caleb circled Rebekah's desk and hurried over to her.

"I can explain."

When Caleb got close, he drew up short and wrinkled his nose. "Oh my God, you stink!"

"I know. Believe me, I know, but I was too hyped to go home and shower before I told you my news." She grinned and glanced at Roman before she launched into her explanation. "We did a little undercover investigating today at a warehouse down on the riverfront."

Caleb shifted his attention to Roman, offering a hand to shake. "Hello, Roman. You're the rest of the *we*, I presume."

"Guilty."

"We got a tip about drug deals happening at this warehouse on the north side of town," Morgan said and hesitated when she saw Caleb frown. "Don't worry. I didn't go alone. Roman was with me and—"

The door opened again, and the mail carrier stepped in with a stack of envelopes and a puzzled look for Morgan.

Caleb took her elbow and tugged her toward the back offices. "Let's finish this conversation in my office, huh?" He twisted his mouth, then said, "Or your office. I'd rather you didn't perfume my space with your funk."

She flapped a bent arm at him like a chicken wing, fanning her collective odors toward him. "What's wrong, Caleb? I smelled your stink often enough after your sporting events, and in the highly aromatic pre-teen and garlic-love years."

Her brother only grunted.

She glanced over her shoulder to Roman. "Coming?"

"Right behind you, Peaches."

Caleb's eyebrow lifted. When they reached her office, her twin stood back to let Roman enter but kept a grip on Morgan's arm. "We'll be right back. I just want a quick word with my sister about…family matters."

Concern spiked in her chest. The past year had brought so many crises and near misses that the hint that something else had happened instantly alarmed her. "What family matter?"

Her tugged her toward his office, then, seemingly having second thoughts, guided her to the file room and closed the door. In a low voice, he said, "Okay, *Peaches*. Spill."

"I'd rather explain what we learned with Roman present. He was as much a part of learning—"

"Not your warehouse adventure. Your relationship to Roman DiMera. And that bruise on your cheek. I'm guessing it's not makeup like some of the rest of this." He waved his hand in a general, all-encompassing motion.

She went on full alert. "What are you asking?"

"Tell me honestly. Did DiMera do that to you?"

She touched a hand to the small cut and frowned at her brother. "Heavens, no! He was mortified when it happened. An accident at his bar this morning."

Caleb studied her silently as if deciding whether to believe her.

She grunted. "Is that all?"

"No. What's with Peaches?" His expression lightened, and a teasing glimmer lit his eyes. "Teaming up for undercover fact-finding? Is there something you want to tell me?"

She couldn't mask the smile that sprang to her lips

or the happiness that bubbled up in her chest in a swell of warmth. "What?"

He snorted. "Don't be coy. What's the deal?"

"Who says there's—" she started, but the ache in her cheeks from smiling was such a giveaway that she didn't finish the sentence. "Okay, yes. He and I might be…sort of… I don't know what to call it. We had a really nice dinner date last night and—" She nibbled her bottom lip, deciding how much to confide in her brother. If he were Rachel or one of her youngest sisters, she might confess all, but Caleb had always been so protective of her as the oldest brother and her twin. It felt awkward telling him all the ways Roman had made her feel cherished and giddy and…wanted.

"And?" His tone implied he knew exactly what she was leaving out.

Morgan felt her cheeks heat and glanced toward the bulletin board where an out-of-date calendar hung. She walked over to unpin the paper calendar and flip to the correct month, glad to have something to do with her hands. "And…none of your business."

"Will the family be seeing him at Christmas dinner?"

Her brother's question sent her mind off in multiple directions. Morgan had pressed down the impulse to invite Roman for Christmas with her family at their dinner last night. But that was before…well, *before.* Did she want Roman as her date for the Colton holiday celebration? It would alleviate some of her sense of being the only member of the family unpaired at the moment. Even their mother had found love again with the dashing chief of the Blue Larkspur police department, Theo Lawson. She dreaded the idea of being the only single one at the gathering, like some spinster aunt from a Brontë novel. But what would her family think of her bringing Roman?

She faced Caleb with a furrow in her brow. "Can I ask you something?"

He spread his hands. "You know you can."

She drew a deep breath. "I do like Roman. A lot. But…" She brought a fingernail up to bite, but the stink of the warehouse on her hands stopped her before she put the finger in her mouth. Dropping her hands to her sides, she stood taller and blurted, "Roman is an ex-convict. He served time for illegal stock investments."

Caleb's face remained impassive. "And?"

"And what?" she asked, her voice edged with frustration. "He was in prison for five years."

"So he's paid his debt to society?"

"Well, yeah."

Caleb shrugged. "And?"

"Would you stop saying 'and'? Caleb, he's an ex-con!" Her voice rose, and she quickly reined her tone in. Roman was just down the hall, and she didn't want him to know she was discussing his history with Caleb.

"Uh, how about… So?"

"It doesn't bother you that he was convicted of a crime?"

"A white-collar crime. That he's paid for. It's not like he murdered someone or is a serial rapist." Her brother tipped his head and studied her. "What does he say about his conviction?"

"That his actions were the biggest mistake of his

life, and he learned a lot about himself and life while in lockup. That he grew up in prison."

"Seems to me you're the one with an issue about his past," Caleb said.

She drew her shoulders back, prepared to deny it, but instead said, "I did, at first. But he's…" Her gaze dropped to her ratty tennis shoes as she mulled her feelings. "He's not what I expected."

"Do you love him?" her brother asked, bringing her head up.

A spurt of adrenaline charged her heartbeat. "We just met! We're not *there* yet. I don't even think you could say we have a relationship. I just…"

Caleb lifted a shoulder and moved to the door of the file room. "Okay, *Peaches*," he said, chuckling warmly. "Tell yourself that if it helps you sleep at night. I'll have the family set another place at the table on Christmas, though."

She stuck an arm out to keep the door closed another moment. "Then it doesn't bother you that he's…an ex-con? A bar owner? He's hardly my type."

"And where has *your type* gotten you in twenty years of dating?" Her twin met her eyes evenly. "If he makes you happy, then I'm rooting for you. I want you to have what I've found with Nadine. If Roman is the one, then you don't need my blessing or anyone else's. Just be happy, Morgan, and don't overanalyze it." He leaned in to kiss her cheek, then coughed and fake gagged. "But for the love of God, take a bath!"

WHILE ROMAN WAITED on the brother-sister discussion to conclude, he took the time to explore Morgan's office, learning a little about her based on what she surrounded herself with day to day at work. One wall was nothing but shelves full of law books and journals. She had a few decorative items on display—a painted horseshoe, a beautiful old clock in a polished wood case that had stopped with the hands reading 1:36, a gavel mounted on a marble slab engraved with First Court Win and a date. Unlike in her home, she had no family pictures out. He didn't for a minute let himself misconstrue this as a lack of affection for her family. Quite the opposite.

After numerous meetings with his own lawyers in New York, Roman was familiar with the precaution attorneys often took, not advertising to office visitors the people who meant the most to them. Persons of questionable ethics and dangerous leanings could use knowledge of her family against Morgan, so naturally she protected them and herself by keeping her loved ones private.

He inhaled deeply, and the scents of the books, the leather chair behind her desk, the wood polish took him back to the days surrounding his trial and conviction. But over those familiar scents was the hint of Morgan's peach shampoo, the floral scent of her hand lotion, the hint of mint from the candies in a bowl on her desk. A sweet and feminine complement to the stodgier odors.

From the next room, he heard the low murmur of voices, Caleb and Morgan in their private confab. He wondered what had concerned Caleb enough that he'd wanted a sidebar with his sister. Her twin hadn't looked too happy to learn they'd gone to the north side of town and snooped around the warehouse. Not that he blamed Caleb. Roman had worried plenty of times about his own sister being out alone the streets of their Philly neighborhood. Especially after dark. Or was it something else that had bothered Morgan's twin?

Roman moved to one of the office chairs and was just settling in when he heard Morgan raise her voice.

"Caleb, he's an ex-con!"

Roman stiffened, his pulse stuttering at the tone of Morgan's words. He had no doubt he was the ex-con she meant. He'd almost convinced himself she'd moved beyond that detail of his past, that they could find an equal keel based on the present, based on their mutual attraction, based on the new, easier—even light-hearted—rapport they'd established. But her voice was edged with distaste, with distress, with disconcertion.

Roman heaved a slow sigh, unable to dislodge the ball of irritation and disappointment in his chest. He was still stewing a few minutes later when Morgan led her brother in and sat behind her desk. Caleb gave him an odd look as he braced his hip against his sister's desk and folded his arms. "So you two are working under-cover these days, huh? Where? What did you learn?"

"A good bit, as it would happen," Morgan said. She opened a drawer of her desk and removed a package with pop-up face wipes. She began cleaning the dirt and makeup off her face, wincing slightly when she swiped over her purpling bruise. "In a nutshell, we visited a warehouse across town that we confirmed is used for drug deals and laundering money. Spence's cash, among others."

Caleb divided a look between them, his posture stiffening. "Spence? How…" He shook his head a bit and waved a hand. "Back up a bit. How did you learn all this? About the warehouse and—"

Morgan removed a small plastic bag with the drugs she'd procured with her ruse and dropped them on the desk.

Her twin stopped short, and, pushing away from the desk, he gawked at her illegal booty. "Good God, Morgan! What did you do?"

"These need to be flushed," she said, pointing at the bag. "Pronto."

"Flushed?" Caleb scowled at the bag, then his sister. "They're evidence of drug dealing. We should call the cops on the people who—"

"We can't. Not yet, anyway," Roman interrupted. "We don't want to sound any alarms until we can catch Spence there on the twenty-third."

"What's happening on the twenty-third?" Caleb asked, shifting his attention to Roman. "And how the hell was my sister able to buy drugs from these scumbags? Is that the reason for this appalling getup?" He waggled a finger in her direction. "Were you with her when she was dealing with these lowlifes?"

Roman scratched his chin. "Sort of."

Caleb's expression darkened. "You let my sister go in alone? What were you thinking?"

"It wasn't my idea. But have you met your sister? Have you ever been able to dissuade her from an idea once she gets her teeth in it?"

Morgan's twin twisted his mouth and sent her a frustrated sigh. "No." Dropping into the chair beside Roman, Caleb said, "Back to the twenty-third. What's going down then?"

"If we're lucky, that's when we'll catch Spence with his hand in the proverbial cookie jar. But we're going to need help." She tossed the small collection of dirty wipes into her trash can. "I want to have a family meeting tomorrow. Early, if possible, so we have more time to make our plans and preparations."

"Plans for what, exactly?" Caleb cocked an eyebrow. "Dressing in dirty rags to buy drugs?"

She returned her brother's withering glance. "No. That's what the meeting will decide. Looking at all our options and choosing a path forward. Roman will come with me and tell you word for word what the woman in the warehouse office told him, and we'll go from there."

Caleb rubbed his chin and gave Roman a narrow look. "And why is he involved in any of this to start with? Is the Corner Pocket a part of this somehow?"

Roman opened his mouth to defend the reputation of his bar, but Morgan beat him to it.

"Not at all. No connection. And Roman is only involved because I asked him for help. Because…well, never mind. That's none of your business."

Caleb gave a harrumph and pulled out his phone. "Significant others, too, or just the sibs?"

"Um, sure. Dane and Philip especially could have valuable insights with their backgrounds in law enforcement. We can crowd everyone at Mom's or the main lodge at the Gemini. Which do you think?"

"Mom's works for me if she's willing. Ten a.m. sound okay?"

She dipped her chin in a nod. "I'll call the girls, and you call our brothers. Tell them it's urgent. Attendance is mandatory."

Caleb chuckled. "How long do you think you'll keep up this bossy act? The youngest kids are grown adults now with lives of their own. You can't mother and boss them anymore."

"I don't—" Morgan stopped short and frowned. "Old habits die hard. Strongly suggest their attendance, then. I want everyone's input. We've all been affected by Spence in one manner or another, and even if, say, Aubrey and Naomi don't participate in whatever we come up with for the twenty-third, they deserve a voice in planning."

Roman followed the back-and-forth between the twins as if watching a tennis match and felt like a third wheel. He imagined himself at the Colton family meeting tomorrow, and his discomfort grew. He'd be the outsider in a sea of inside jokes, established bonds and decades of history. Should he opt out? Part of him wanted to, but another louder voice wanted to see this project he'd started with Morgan through to fruition.

Or did he just want another excuse to spend time with her?

"All right. Ten tomorrow at Mom's, assuming she's prepared for such an invasion of troops."

Morgan rose from her chair and bent to take her purse from a desk drawer. "And now I am going home for a shower. I can't stand this grimy version of myself any longer."

"Please do," Caleb quipped, grinning and fanning his hand in front of his nose.

Roman shoved to his feet and let Morgan lead the way out the door.

Caleb stepped close to him as they exited Morgan's

office and in a lower voice said, "I understand you and Morgan have a started seeing each other outside this investigation. That your relationship is more personal than just looking for Spence." Caleb's expression darkened. "I also saw the bruise on Morgan's cheek. She had an explanation for it…sort of, but—"

Steel entered Roman's spine, and he fought to keep his expression impassive, friendly. "Is this the conversation where you threaten creative ways to torture me if I hurt her or break her heart?"

Caleb looked mildly amused but also met Roman's gaze with an unflinching stare. "It is."

Roman bobbed his head. "Unnecessary. I have no intention of hurting Morgan in *any* way. I feel terrible that she got that bruise, but it was not my hand that put it there."

"That's what she said. But as her brother, I had to make that point. You understand, right?"

"I do." He gave Caleb a friendly smile. "Your threat of bodily harm is noted for the record, Counselor."

As CALEB AND Roman lingered behind her in a private confab of stern faces and serious tones, Morgan headed to the reception area but stood well away from Rebekah's desk, self-conscious over the fug that hung around her. She walked to the window and paused.

A movement in the parking lot below snagged her attention, and in her peripheral vision, she caught the barest glimpse of a lanky man smoking a cigarette. Or so she thought. When she shifted her gaze to the spot where she thought she'd seen the figure…nothing was there. But was that a trace of smoke hanging in the air?

Morgan's heart beat faster. Could that have been Spence? She leaned closer to the window and searched the parking area more fully. Too much of the lot was hidden from view by evergreen trees or a bad angle from the window. Dang it! She'd have sworn—

"Ready?" Roman asked behind her.

She sighed. Was her brain so full of Spence and catching him that now she was imagining she saw him where he wasn't?

"Ready." She turned from the window and followed Roman down to his Corvette. As they crossed the parking lot, she scanned the street, the space between cars, the shadows beneath trees. Nothing. No one. Just a bird fluttering from a bush to peck seeds from the ground. The sparrow raised its head and chirped, and the tiniest of white breath clouds escaped its beak.

Morgan's shoulders drooped. Not cigarette smoke, then. Just the frozen earth sighing in icy vapors. She shivered just the same as an uneasy feeling crawled up her neck. Eyes watching her? Remnants of her confrontation with the drug dealers at the warehouse? The specter of what lay ahead of the twenty-third? She couldn't say, but neither could she shake the feeling.

"You okay?" Roman asked.

"I… Yeah. Just my imagination running wild."

Roman opened the passenger side door for her, and she slid inside the car. The sooner they got Spence off the streets, the sooner she could rest easy, once and for all.

Chapter Thirteen

Morgan had never enjoyed a hot shower more. As the warm water streamed over her, she pictured not just the grease and stink of her disguise washing away, but the cloying, jittery feeling that had plagued her since setting out on the fact-finding trip to the warehouse that morning. The north side of town. Memories of being attacked. Hallucinations of Spence lurking at her office. She tipped her face to the showerhead and let it all wash down the drain.

Her muscles relaxed a bit, and she let her thoughts stray in a different direction as her stress and anxiety eased. Roman. His buff physique, wrapped only in a towel. The spicy scent of his soap clinging to him this morning. Had it just been this morning? She missed him and the tantalizing twining of their bodies already. Regardless of how she defined what he was to her now or where the relationship might go, nothing said she couldn't enjoy a bit more of the sweet pleasure they'd shared the night before. Three glorious—

A thump cut into her daydream. She cut the water off and strained to listen. Silence. Nothing but the drip of the shower, the whir of her central heat, the tick of the old analog clock she'd hung in the bathroom to keep her on schedule in the morning.

Shaking her head, Morgan decided it must have been a delivery to her front porch. She'd resorted to last-minute online shopping by and large this year, and it seemed every time she got home, another box awaited her on her porch. She considered turning the hot water back on, returning to the erotic woolgathering the noise had interrupted, but she knew she had a lot of plans to make before she presented her case to catch Spence to the family tomorrow. She wanted to think it through. Analyze the contingencies. Prepare for counterarguments. She chuckled to herself. You could take the lawyer out of the courthouse, but not the courthouse from the lawyer.

She dried off quickly and stepped into her bedroom to dress in something warm, fuzzy and soft for her private strategy session. Once snuggled in flannel jammies and her favorite robe, she strolled out to the kitchen to make a cup of hot tea. She paused in the hallway, sniffing the air. Was that…smoke?

She darted to the kitchen to make sure she hadn't left a burner on, and the smell followed her. Not overpowering. Not obvious…but *there*. Cigarettes.

Again, Spence and his chain-smoking habit popped into her mind. Had Spence been here? In her house? She checked her front door and found it unlocked. Damn! Hadn't she locked it behind her when she came in from the office? She couldn't remember.

She retraced her steps to the back of her house, checking every room, every closet, every nook and cranny. No one was hiding. She was alone.

Then, spying her dirty clothes on the bedroom floor, she lifted them and sniffed. Mingled with the other noxious scents was the hint of cigarette smoke. One of the bosses at the warehouse who'd interrogated her before selling her the drugs had been smoking. Had she just been smelling her dirty shirt and jeans?

Morgan rushed to the laundry room and stuffed the garments into the washing machine, dumping floral-scented detergent in without measuring. She slammed the lid shut and stood there shivering. Unsettled.

A tattooed arm snaked around her from behind and dragged her into the alley—

"Stop it!" she chided herself. Plowing both hands into her damp hair, she gritted her teeth and growled her frustration. This Spence business…the fistfight between Hector and Gibb this morning…the terrors her family had faced in recent months… Roman's tattoos…

She'd been bombarded by triggers and upheaval of late. Was it any surprise she was feeling so jittery? Imagining monsters lurking in the shadows? In the past, her own force of will had been enough to hold the demons at bay. But lately…

"It's just your imagination running away."

She took a deep breath. Exhaled. But didn't feel any better.

She was at loose ends. More and more she felt herself unraveling. She just didn't feel safe anywhere, anytime, in any way. Except when Roman held her.

Morgan wrapped her arms around herself now and clung to that thought.

Tonight she wouldn't dwell on the fact that one man

could both frighten her and make her feel so safe, so secure. Such contradictions were a problem for another day.

THE NEXT MORNING, Morgan stopped by the Corner Pocket on her way to the family meeting. She knew Roman could find her mother's home with the use of a GPS app on his phone, but she wanted to arrive with him, to smooth any possible wrinkles if one of her overprotective brothers decided to give Roman a hard time. Because by now, she was certain, Caleb would have let her brothers know about Roman's history and that, despite her assurances and explanations, she'd had a mysterious bruise on her face the last time her twin had seen her. She had to give Roman high marks for his willingness to run the Colton-brother gauntlet today in order to help her catch Spence.

Hector, a broom in his hands, answered her knock on the front door of the Corner Pocket and sent her to Roman's office. "You remember where it is, right? You can go on back."

She did and she found Roman with a stack of files on his desk.

"Knock, knock." He glanced up and smiled broadly, a grin that sent her heart scampering and a gooey warmth to her belly. "Hector sent me back. Ready to head out to the meeting with my family?"

"I am. Let me just put some of this away." He tapped half of the stack of files straight and slid them into an open file drawer. "With Gibb gone, I'm more short-handed than ever. I was looking through the applications I've taken in recent months to see if anyone stood out."

"And did they?"

"A couple looked promising, if they haven't found other employment." He moved to tidy the rest of the stack, but a couple of files slipped from his fingers and fell on the floor. He grunted and buzzed his lips in frustration.

When he bent to retrieve the papers, she crouched to help. The first file she picked up read Tim Hall. "Huh. Tim's file."

Roman took it from her. "Man. I wish I could pay him enough to get him back on staff. He was a hard worker. Good bartender, too. Mixed a mean Irish car bomb. The drink, I mean."

She laughed. "I assumed as much."

As he shuffled the pages of the file, Roman stilled and his brow creased.

"What is it?" she asked.

"Tim's original job application. It's here in his file."

Morgan moved closer to look over his shoulder. "What about it?"

"Tim said the other guy from the drywall crew who gave him that information was named Evan, right?"

"Yeah. That's right."

Roman tapped the top page of the file. "Look at this. Tim's full name is Timothy *Evan* Hall."

Morgan confirmed as much, reading the neatly printed job application. Her heart seemed to slow as the name registered. "That's…*interesting.*"

Roman hummed darkly.

She folded her arms over her chest, adding, "I don't much believe in coincidence in my line of work. I'm more a proponent of the 'if it looks like a duck and quacks like a duck' philosophy." When he looked bemused, she added, "Then it is a duck! You've never heard that expression?"

"Uh, no. That one didn't find me on the streets of Philly or in the pen. Ducks, huh?"

"Forget the ducks." She pointed at the file. "Did Tim lie to us? Did someone else named Evan go to that warehouse, or is he this Evan person?"

"And does it matter?"

"What do you mean, does it matter?" she asked, agog. "Of course it matters. If he lied about his source, who knows what else he lied about!"

"But the woman I talked to yesterday confirmed they were laundering money for Spence. That's all we need to know."

"And you saw him—"

"I *think* I saw him." He held up a finger as he corrected her. "I saw someone with a limp. Right size and height. But I didn't get a good look at his face."

She lifted one shoulder. "So maybe Tim did lie to protect himself, but what—"

A loud crash and shouts from outside the office stopped her midsentence. The harsh tone of the voice sent a chill slithering through her.

Roman frowned as he glanced toward the office door. "That doesn't sound good. Wait here."

As he headed out to the floor of the pub, she considered hanging back for all of a second before falling in step behind him. The yelling grew louder and the words clearer as she made her way out through the kitchen toward the public area.

"What's going on?" Roman called to Hector as he pushed through the swinging door.

"Gibb is happening," Hector, who stood near the front door, replied. He jerked his head toward the inner doors, where Gibb was clearly visible through the double doors' glass inserts. The ex-employee's face was contorted with rage, and as they watched, Gibb lowered his shoulder and rammed the vestibule's inner doors.

Roman grumbled a curse. "Gibb, stop! Go home. Don't do this!"

"He was waiting outside when I went to unlock the doors," Hector explained. "He lit into me. I shoved him off and barely got the inner doors locked behind me. But that bolt ain't gonna hold if—"

Even before Hector could finish speaking, the wood around the inner door bolt cracked.

Morgan gasped, and Roman shot her an irritated glance. "I thought I told you to wait in the office."

"You did. But you're not the boss of me." She held up her phone. "Should I call the police?"

"Not yet. If I can talk him down, work things out without involving the cops, then—"

The wood finished splintering, and Gibb burst through the broken doors. He aimed a finger at Hector. "You sorry piece of garbage!"

"Gibb, stop this! If you go home now, I—"

The enraged man swung toward Roman now, visibly shaking with his anger and adrenaline. "Go home and do what? Rot?" he shouted. "Without a job, how do I pay the bills? How do I look my wife in the eye? How do I buy Christmas presents for my kids?"

"You shoulda thought of that before you stole from us!" Hector snarled.

"Hector, can it! Let me—" Roman started, but Gibb picked up the chair closest to him and slammed it down, smashing it, then threw the remnants toward Hector.

Morgan yelped as sharp bits of wood flew past her.

"I didn't steal nothin', you sorry bastard!" Gibb fisted his hands and looked ready to charge Hector.

"Hey!" Roman held up both hands and took a step closer to Gibb. "Settle down!"

"Settle down? You'd like that, huh? Sweep it under the rug like it ain't nothing?"

Gibb's sour expression darkened further. "You fired me without cause, man, and ruined me in the process. I didn't steal nothing!"

"We saw you on the video!" Hector said.

"Hey!" Roman aimed a finger toward Hector. "I said let me handle this."

Morgan edged closer to Hector. Maybe she could help by getting the cook to return to the back of the pub. She put a hand on the man's arm, but he shook it off.

"You didn't watch the whole thing, or you'd have seen whoever took the money for real. It wasn't me!"

Hands still up in a conciliatory manner, Roman tried again to appeal for calm. "Gibb, if you'll just take a breath and—"

"And nothing, DiMera! You know I ain't gonna find another job at Christmas…and with my record! My parole officer already came round the house and put me on notice!"

"I fired you because you assaulted Hector. I didn't

call the cops because I wanted to give you a chance
to—"

"Screw your chance!" Gibb roared and threw another chair.

Roman rushed forward to grab Gibb, and Morgan
gasped, "Roman!"

Hector joined the fray, trying to restrain Gibb, and
had to duck as another chair was swung.

Having seen enough, Morgan scuttled back a few
steps and tapped in 9-1-1 on her phone. The emergency
operator answered, and Morgan opened her mouth to
ask for police to be sent when something hard smacked
the side of her head. She blinked and clutched the throbbing spot even as she felt herself wobble. Knees buckling, she sat down hard on the floor. When she looked
at her hand, she had blood on her fingers.

"Hello? What's your emergency?" the operator repeated.

"I, um…can you send the…police?" Why was it suddenly so had to concentrate?

"…address?" she heard and shifted her gaze to the
men groping and scuffling near her. Gibb had now
seized a pool cue and swung it like a baseball bat.
Roman ducked and grabbed the other end, trying to
wrench it from Gibb's grasp.

"The Pocket… Corner. The Corner Pocket." She
moved her hand to her head again, found a goose egg
swelling there.

Hearing grunts and curses, she turned her attention
back to the struggle unfolding before her. With Hector's help, Roman finally had Gibb pinned against a pool

table, his arms behind his back. "Find something to tie his arms until the cops get here," he called to Morgan.

Feeling dazed, she set the phone down and climbed woozily to her feet. She shuffled her feet slowly, her head throbbing, and tried to decide what could be used to tie Gibb. Where to find it? She moved to the front door, where tinsel garland draped around the frame, and pulled the shiny decor down. She carried it to Roman, who looked at her offering as if she had rocks for brains.

"Garland? Morgan, he—" Roman stopped, his eyebrows knitting as he frowned. "Morgan? You're bleeding! What—" He jerked his gaze toward Hector. "You got him? Morgan is hurt."

Hector nodded, and Roman released Gibb and took Morgan by the arms. "Sit down. Let me look at you."

She obeyed, but already her fuzzy thoughts were clearing, even though her head still ached. She found a clean napkin on one of the tables and pressed it to her head. "It's not as bad as it looks."

"I've heard that before." He peeled her hand away from the wound to examine for himself. "How did this happen?"

She shrugged and pointed toward where she'd been standing. "I don't know. I was over there and something hit me."

He crossed the floor to the spot where she'd left her phone and spoke into it. "Hello? Yes, we do still need the police. And an ambulance." Bending, he picked up the broken-off leg of one of the smashed chairs. He raised his eyes to meet Morgan's as he returned to her side, holding out the makeshift club for her to see.

"Roman, no ambulance. I'll be fine."

"Yes," he said to the operator. "There's a woman with a head injury."

She shook her head. Mistake. Dark spots danced in her vision, and she winced.

"Right. Thank you." Roman hung up the phone and sat across the table from her. "This is why I asked you to stay in the office," he said, his tone more concerned than chiding. Facing Gibb, he waved the broken chair leg for his ex-employee to see. "You did this. You hurt Morgan. Again!"

Gibb's chest rose and fell, still winded from his outburst and likely still seething over his firing. His expression softened a degree as he looked to Morgan. "Sorry, ma'am."

"Should I call your family and tell them we're not coming?" he offered.

Morgan lifted her chin—too fast. *Ouch.* "No! We're still going. We have to go! We called the meeting. We're the ones with the information about Spence and—"

"You're injured." His fingers gripped her wrist gently. "You should rest."

"It's a goose egg, Roman. Do you know how many of these I've had over the years? Living with rowdy brothers. Learning to ride a horse. Being a general klutz who all too often forgets to close cabinet doors." She smiled at him. "I appreciate your worry, but I am not missing the meeting with my family." She took her phone from him and checked the time. "Dang it! If we wait for the police, we'll be late."

Roman glanced over his shoulder, where Hector all but sat on Gibb's back. "I can't let this go like last time.

I gave him a chance, and he came back to destroy property and wound my best girl."

He gently brushed her loose hair back from the tender spot on her temple. Her heart swelled hearing him call her his *best girl*. She bobbed a slow, careful nod. "Okay. But we are going. We only have two days until the twenty-third. No time to delay."

The police arrived then, and Roman went to talk to them while Morgan called Caleb. "We'll be a few minutes late," she told him. "There's been an…incident."

"What kind of incident?" Caleb's timbre was instantly alarmed. She guessed that would happen when you'd had enough of these emergency notification calls in one year. "I'll explain later. It's in hand now."

Later proved to be close to an hour and thirty minutes behind when they were supposed to have arrived at her mother's home. The rest of the family had already gathered and were well into second and third cups of coffee and hot tea when her mother answered their knock.

Isa hugged her oldest daughter, greeted Roman warmly…and immediately noticed the purpling lump on Morgan's forehead. "Gracious, darling! What happened to you?"

Caleb, followed by Jasper and Gavin, entered the foyer. Roman helped Morgan remove her coat and passed it along with his to Isa's waiting arms.

"Yes," Caleb said darkly, narrowing his eyes on Roman. "Why does my sister have another bruise on her face?"

Roman squared his shoulders and straightened his back. "A former employee showed up at my business this morning as we were leaving. He caused some problems, and the police were called. I'd asked Morgan to stay in my office while I dealt with the disturbance, but as you can see, she didn't. She got caught in the crossfire."

"Crossfire? Has someone been shot?" asked her sister Naomi, appearing from the back of the house with her fiancé, Detective Philip Rees, at her side.

"Not literal crossfire, just…" Morgan sighed, and as the murmur of her siblings' and mother's concerns and questions rose, she lifted both hands and shouted, "Hello?"

When they quieted, she looped her arm through Roman's in a show of unity and support. "I'm fine, and Roman is innocent of all the bad things you're thinking right now." She wagged a finger at her brothers, who were all glaring at their guest. "Can we go in the den? I'll explain it once, to everyone, so I don't have to repeat myself, and we can get down to the real reason for this meeting."

"Roman, may I get you something hot to drink? Coffee, hot cocoa? Something else?" Isa asked, the consummate hostess. "I made cinnamon rolls for everyone, and there are plenty left."

"That sounds great. I'd love one. And black coffee." He followed her to the kitchen, and Morgan couldn't resist tagging along, muffling a grin. Isa was an artist, a darned good one. But not a cook.

Isa tried, though. Bless her. A burned-sugar scent hung in the kitchen. A bad omen.

When Isa turned with the plate of sweet rolls and a mug, Roman took one glance at the spots under the icing—as black as his coffee—and blinked. To his credit, he managed to maintain a smile and accepted one of the proffered rolls, even taking a big bite. Isa winced at the crunching sound.

"I'm afraid I got distracted this morning, and the rolls are a bit overdone."

"Mmph," Roman mumbled around his full mouth. He washed the burned cinnamon roll down with a swig of coffee and smiled politely. "It's fine. Thank you."

Morgan's heart tugged, seeing her mother's embarrassed expression, and she quickly changed the subject to something she knew would brighten her mother's mood. "How are the wedding plans coming, Mom?"

"Swimmingly. We've reserved the lodge at the Gemini for Valentine's Day, and I have met with the florist and the photographer. I'm planning a trip to Denver in a couple weeks with Rachel and Naomi to start dress shopping. You're welcome to join us. I'd love your input!"

Morgan clasped her mother's hands between hers. "Sounds wonderful. Let me know when, and I'll clear my schedule."

"Wedding plans?" Roman echoed, setting his plate aside discreetly. "Congratulations, Mrs. Colton. Who's the lucky man?"

Her mother blushed—no doubt where Morgan had inherited the tendency—and her seventy-two-year-old mother looked years younger. Happiness was the best beauty product, Morgan thought.

"Theo Lawson. He's the—"

"Chief of police," Roman finished for her, his tone startled.

"You know him?" Isa asked.

"Well, not personally. I hear he's a good man. Fair. I have a number of…acquaintances who have spoken of him. I employ ex-cons at my bar—a few were probably arrested by Chief Lawson."

Isa's eyes widened. "Oh. I see."

"Hey, what's the holdup?" Ezra said, sticking his head in the kitchen. "We're all waiting on you, Morgan."

She gave her brother a raspberry, childish as it was. Some things between siblings never changed. "I was introducing Roman to our mother. Keep your pants on, soldier." She met her mother's gaze. "Sheesh, you can take the man out of the Army, but you can't take the Army out of the man, huh?"

"Shall we?" Roman asked, nodding his head toward the kitchen door.

"Brace yourself. My family can be a lot to take in, and they seem to be multiplying."

With a hand at the small of Morgan's back, Roman ushered her into the den, following her siblings. Instead of sitting, Morgan assumed a post in front of the fireplace where all her brothers and sisters and their significant others could see and hear her. The room, spacious as it was, was crowded with bodies. For the briefest moment, Morgan, ever the planner, considered how they would fit everyone around the table at Christmas when a half dozen or so more adults, plus several children, were added to the family's numbers. She was happy for the swelling ranks of Coltons but…good grief! Where would they put them all?

"Morgan?" Caleb prompted. "You called this meeting. So…" He waved a hand, urging her to begin.

"Right. Well, first of all, for those of you who haven't

met him, this is Roman DiMera. He owns the Corner Pocket, a bar and billiards place in town."

Roman lifted a hand in greeting, and the Coltons called back a variety of welcomes. She dispensed with the business of her injuries quickly. "I'm fine," she assured them all after explaining how the bump happened.

Caleb seemed appeased, but Jasper and Dominic exchanged a skeptical glance. She sighed. She'd reassure her brothers again later. On to the business at hand.

"The reason we're all here is… I need your help. Roman and I have done some groundwork, some investigating in the last few days, and we have a strong lead on Spence."

Many of the bodies in the room sat taller. Chins came up. Eyes widened. The room buzzed as her siblings responded with gasps, questions and side comments. Morgan raised both hands to call for quiet. "At least we think we know where he will be, if only for a few minutes, in two days." She explained how she and Roman had learned about the warehouse from Tim, had carried out their recon, and Roman's encounter with the uneasy financial secretary.

"Roman even thinks he might have spotted Spence on the property before we left. He apparently heard the commotion I caused to untangle myself from my…well, *meeting* with some of the male warehouse workers and was fleeing the scene. With a limp."

"A meeting?" Rachel repeated.

"Our sister bought drugs from the lowlifes at this north-side warehouse," Caleb announced.

"What!" Isa cried.

More gasps and comments rose, including Alexa's

new love, Dane Beaulieu, who covered his ears and sang, "La la la la! Former vice here... I didn't hear that!"

Beside him, Philip swiped a hand down his face. "Not my jurisdiction, but... Come on, Colton!"

"Well, it *is* my jurisdiction!" her sister Rachel cried in dismay. "Morgan, what were you thinking?"

"It's been flushed! I had to have a believable cover, and—"

"And let me tell you about this cover she devised," Caleb said, chuckling and holding his nose. "She looked a fright and smelled like an unmucked stall."

Sniggers and guffaws filled the room until a shrill whistle rent the clamor. Morgan clapped her hands to her ears, the high, loud trill making her head pound. She, like the rest of the occupants of the room, fell silent and glanced at Roman. He removed his fingers from his mouth, having gained everyone's attention, and said, "We need a plan to catch Spence when he returns to the warehouse for his fake passport. If we miss him, he and the money will be out of the country by Christmas Eve, and your family may never have the justice they seek."

Morgan smiled at Roman, grateful for the way he brought the meeting back into hand. Back on point. "We need to stake out the warehouse. Wait for him. Watch for him. And we'll need the right personnel in place or close by to take him into custody and make the arrest when he shows up." She made eye contact with the members of her family with specific ties to law enforcement, positions of power and military or other defensive training. Dominic, who was still with the FBI....for now. Detective Philip, former Vice Dane, DA Rachel, former Army sergeant Ezra, and US Marshal Alexa to name a few. Her family had no shortage of talent and connections. "We have two days to form a plan, a surveillance schedule. This is likely our last and best chance to catch Spence. We can't blow it."

Chapter Fourteen

A subcommittee of sorts—the siblings that planned direct involvement with the operation—huddled in one corner. The rest of the family had returned to work or lingered in the kitchen with Isa. Morgan cast a glance around at the capable people she called family and sighed with confidence. This was really happening, and she had every confidence it would work.

"So Morgan and Roman will take first shift watching the warehouse," Dominic said reluctantly, the FBI agent having been appointed to take the lead on the operation. Their mother's fiancé would be advised of the plan and asked to have his officers standing by. Alexa, a US marshal, would also have a team ready to help.

Despite the objections of her brothers, Morgan had insisted that she would take the first shift watching the warehouse and waiting for Spence to show.

"I just don't like your involvement, Morgan. You're not trained for this work," Ezra pointed out.

"I'm not talking about confronting Spence. But we've said the law enforcement support will have to stay far back from the warehouse to avoid being spotted. You'll need eyes closer to the building. That's where I come in."

"The north side isn't safe," Caleb said. "You, of all people, should know that."

Morgan bristled slightly at her brother's obvious reference to her attack. She raised her chin. "I'll have Roman with me. I'll be fine."

Roman turned a startled look toward her but said nothing. They hadn't verbalized the plan for him to be a part of the Colton operation to catch Spence, but she couldn't imagine him not playing a role. When he smiled at her, warmth spread in her belly.

Dominic cast side glances to his brothers and Alexa, seeking their agreement, before sighing and saying, "Fine. But you don't engage Spence or anyone else at the warehouse. If you see him, you call in backup. Promise me that, or I will pull you from this. I swear, I will."

She gave Dominic a level glare. "You were happy for my help when I decked Henry Willis on the playground."

Her FBI agent brother arched an eyebrow, and their siblings chuckled. "That was third grade. And, while I still appreciate it," Dominic said, "it's irrelevant to this conversation."

"Just want you to keep things in perspective. I respect your position and training, but you're not the boss of me. We wouldn't have these leads on Spence without the investigating that Roman and I did."

A muscle in Dominic's jaw flexed as he clenched his back teeth and narrowed his eyes on Morgan. She didn't flinch. She'd been matching wits with her rough-and-tumble brothers and stubborn sisters her whole life.

"Point taken," Dominic replied. "But you're still not to engage Spence. It's too risky."

"All right. You have my word," she said. "We'll only surveil. No contact with Spence or anyone in the warehouse."

"Philip," Caleb called to Naomi's fiancé, who was standing near Morgan. "Does she have her fingers crossed behind her back?"

Philip leaned back and glanced behind Morgan. "Clear."

"Is she groping Roman's butt?" Dane asked, and the gathered family all chuckled.

She held both hands up. "No." Then with a wicked smile added, "I'm saving that for later."

"Yeah, you are," Alexa said, nudging her older sister with her elbow and a gleam in her eye. "Look at her blushing!"

"What kind of security system did this warehouse have?" Ezra asked.

"You planning to sell them one?" Dane quipped. "You heard he's starting a private security firm, right?"

Morgan blinked. "You're what?"

Ezra affirmed it with a nod. "It was time for a change. I can run the company remotely and be at home at night with Theresa and the girls." He poked his thumb toward Dominic. "After he retires in January, Dom's going to join me in the security biz."

Morgan's mouth dropped open as she turned to Dominic. "Why didn't anyone tell me all this?"

Dom shrugged noncommittally. "I think we just did."

"Joking aside, Dane raises a good point," Roman said

and went on to elaborate on what he'd seen and made note of securitywise at the warehouse.

Morgan could feel the moment when, after deciding on a working plan of action for surveilling the warehouse and Spence's arrest, her brothers' attention shifted to Roman. As if they all, as one, turned their gazes on him—a pack of wolves, working in unison to sniff out the new man in her life.

As the meeting broke up, her sisters, who'd been waiting in the kitchen to pounce, pulled her aside, wanting the scoop on Roman, while her brothers cornered Roman with friendly but no-nonsense expressions. Caleb seemed to be keeping the interrogation under control. While she knew Roman could hold his own, she still cringed internally for him. Seven overprotective Coltons versus one well-meaning bar owner. Uneven odds.

She kept Roman at the edge of her vision as her sisters grilled her, all seeming to talk at once.

"Are you bringing Roman to the family celebration on Christmas Day?"

"How did you meet him? You don't play pool or frequent bars."

"I may be engaged, but *hubba hubba*! He's good looking, Mor."

"You've already slept with him, haven't you? You're blushing!"

"Dead giveaway every time!"

Thirty minutes later, she pried herself and Roman from her family. "I really do have a full schedule today, and Roman is shorthanded at the Corner Pocket, thanks to the dustup with his employee."

"I'll be in touch with all of you about specifics for the twenty-third. Everyone knows their assignments before then?" Dominic asked.

A round of hugs and goodbyes later, she and Roman finally pulled away from the house. Roman was uncharacteristically silent in the car, and Morgan, too, found herself lost in ruminations, ranging from her mother's upcoming wedding to, predictably, the upcoming stakeout for Spence.

Then Roman coughed, snapping her out of her preoccupied thoughts. "Roman? You all right?"

"Hmm? Oh, yeah. Just dry air. Throat tickle." He flashed a crooked smile.

"I meant that you're awfully quiet." She reached for his hand on the steering wheel and covered it with hers. "The Coltons are a lot to take in. And my brothers were—"

"I'm not worried about your brothers. They were only reacting the way I would in their place, the way any brother worth his salt would."

"Then you're going over the plan for later in the week?" she guessed.

He turned his palm up to squeeze her fingers and kiss her knuckles before returning his hand to the steering wheel. "No. It's a good plan. We've got some of the best minds around from all walks of law enforcement backing us up, thanks to your large family. I think we're good there."

She angled her body more fully toward his. "Well, your furrowed brow and silence say you're upset and thinking about something. Anything I can help with?"

He brought his Corvette to a stop at a crossroad and

tapped a finger restlessly while waiting for traffic to clear. "I keep thinking about something Gibb said this morning."

"Gibb?" She didn't even try to hide the surprise from her tone. "Roman, I know you feel bad about how that unfolded, but the man stole from you and assaulted Hector and—"

"Did he steal from me? He swears he didn't. And that's where all this started."

"We watched the security camera playback. We saw—" She stopped searching her memory for exactly what they saw. Gibb had stuck his hand in the tip jar. Brought some money out. But was it all the cash? Was he making change for his kid's lunch money, like he'd claimed? And then the video feed had mysteriously cut out for a while. "Oh no. Did we jump to conclusions based on circumstantial evidence?"

"When I get back to the bar, I'm going to rewatch that footage." Roman pressed his mouth in a hard, determined line and bumped his fist on the steering wheel before pulling away from the stop sign.

"*We* will rewatch that tape," Morgan said, her tone brooking no argument. "If you can help my family, then I can help you. Two sets of eyes are better than one. Right?"

"Sounds like a prudent plan. One I should have th—"

His reply was cut short when an old-model white sedan roared past them, swerving into the side of Roman's Corvette. The scrape of metal was punctuated by Roman's pithy shout at the other driver. The sedan hovered beside them, then purposefully swerved into them again. On purpose.

Roman fought the wheel when they hit a patch of ice, pumped the brake and corrected the spin of the Corvette as the other vehicle sped away.

Shocked by what had transpired, Morgan only gaped at Roman, adrenaline making her tremble from the inside out. "He...he *tried* to run us off the road!"

Roman pulled his car onto the shoulder, emergency lights flashing, and stopped. "That's my take on it."

Morgan squeezed her hands into fists, fighting for her composure. "D-did you get a look at the driver?"

Roman shook his head. "Too busy keeping us from crashing in the ditch. You?"

"No. Tinted windows. And it happened so fast, I—" A shudder rolled through her, and to her dismay, a sob rolled up and broke from her, unbidden.

Roman's brow creased, and sympathy pooled in his dark gaze. "Peaches, what is it? We're okay. No one's hurt...other than my 'Vette. But scratches will buff out. And I have insurance."

She leaned her head back on the seat and closed her eyes. A soul-deep shaking rattled loose a cry from her core. "I just want to feel safe again! I'm so tired of being scared!"

Despite the gearshift and armrests, Roman moved as close to Morgan as he could, pulling her into an awkward-angled hug. "Honey, what do you mean? You're one of the bravest, most self-assured women I've ever met. What do you mean you're scared? Scared of what?"

"Just...anything. Everything. I can't forget...him. The memories...haunt me, and... I don't ever feel completely safe. Things like this—" she waved a hand down the road where the sedan had raced away with a roar

"—only serve as triggers. They rattle me and undermine my sense of security all over again."

Roman's hand plowed deep into the curtain of her hair. Cradling her nape in his wide, warm palm, he dragged her close enough to kiss her temple. "I'm going to move the car from the shoulder. Park in a lot somewhere quiet where we can talk. And I want you to tell me everything. Can you do that for me? I want to understand. I want to help. I want… I want you to feel safe. With me. In life. Always."

She drew strength and comfort from his touch, his presence, the glow of compassion in his gaze. Morgan nodded, and Roman held her hand as he drove a short distance to the parking lot of an elementary school that was closed for the holiday break. Once the engine was off, Roman sent her a side glance. "Think I can come around to your seat? I very much want to hold you, but bucket seats and gearshifts are not conducive to snuggling."

She glanced at the low-slung passenger seat and snorted wryly. "I'm not sure there's room for two but… I very much want you to hold me, too."

He exited the driver's side and rounded the fender, taking cursory note of the scrapes in his paint, and then opened the passenger-side door. He scooped her into his lap as he wiggled inside, and she curled against him. He closed the door against the chilly air and wrapped her in a tight embrace. "Why are you scared all the time? What happened to you, Peaches?"

Morgan drew a shuddering breath and began. "My last year of college, I… I ran an errand on the north side of town. Alone."

His eyebrow lifted as if he could see where she was headed.

"Caleb warned me not to. Offered to go with me, but I was Ms. Independent, self-sufficient. I was invincible." Her tone held her disdain for the attitude she now viewed as having contributed to the attack. "I'd conquered college and was helping raise my siblings." She sighed and felt the burn of tears in her sinuses. "I was cocky and stupid. And I was…attacked. Robbed. And beaten. The man responsible was never caught."

She explained how the man had approached from behind, snatched her purse, demanded her jewelry. She scoffed and shook her head. "And even knowing the threat he was, I refused to give him the ring. I put sentimentality over safety. In the end, he took the ring and the rest of my jewelry, and I ended up with a bloodied lip and bruises all over my body. So much for my hubris."

She peeked up at Roman to gauge his reaction. His face was pale, and his dark eyebrows were drawn together in a deep furrow. "Oh, honey, I'm so sorry. That's horrible!" He squeezed her tighter. "But before you say another word, I have to clarify something."

"Wha—"

He grasped her chin between his fingers and thumb, his gaze direct and stern. "You did nothing wrong."

"Well…but if I'd—"

"No!" His firm tone cut her off. "Regardless of whether you were overconfident or it was ill-advised to go to that part of town alone or any other fault you try to put on yourself… You. Are. Not. To. Blame. You didn't ask to be attacked. You are not at fault."

"But—"

He silenced her with a kiss, and when he raised his head and she opened her mouth to comment, he repeated, "No! The bastard who hurt you is the only one responsible for the attack. What he did to you is unconscionable and entirely his fault, and if you don't see that, can't grasp that fully and own that truth, then…" He took a breath, his eyes full of pain and compassion. "Then you need to talk to a counselor, Peaches."

Morgan inhaled slowly, weighing his suggestion. "I've always considered myself too…" She waved her fingers vaguely as she searched for the right word. "Competent, too capable to need a counselor, but…" She sighed and snuggled closer to him, curling her fingers in the front of his shirt. "I know that plenty of capable people need therapy, but just telling you about it has helped."

"I'm not a professional, though. And while I care, while I would do anything to help you with your pain and fear and bad memories, I can't do what a licensed therapist can. There's no weakness in admitting you need someone to talk it out with and get coping strategies."

She nodded. "I know you're right. I just…"

"Make it your New Year's resolution. Or my Christmas present. But do it. Please, Peaches."

She raised her mouth to his and pressed a whisper-soft kiss to his lips. "I promise."

He laid his cheek on the top of her head, his arms still around her. "Thank you."

"Roman, there's something else you should know." She felt him tense and hated that she had to tell him.

"The man who attacked me…the main detail, almost the only thing I could remember later to tell the police, the thing that still haunts me when I remember him and the attack…"

"Yeah?"

"His arms, his neck, his cheek were covered with tattoos. Tattoos…are a trigger for me."

Beneath her, beside her, he went still. "Oh, Peaches."

Chapter Fifteen

Hell! He was a walking, talking, freaking *inked* reminder of Morgan's worst nightmare. Roman's gut swirled with acid. No wonder she'd appeared so reticent, so repulsed by him. While, on the one hand, he was glad it wasn't him personally, how did he rectify the fact that his tattoos were a painful reminder of Morgan's trauma? How did they move forward?

For the rest of the drive back to the bar, the questions, recriminations and implications clattered and ricocheted in Roman's head like pool balls scattering after a break.

"I know that look," she said. "I didn't tell you to make you feel bad. But I thought it only fair to explain what I couldn't before."

He forced a grin. "I know."

"And it's not your problem to handle. I'll find a way to—"

"Not my problem? My ink is a harsh reminder to the woman I love of a brutal attack. I'd say it's a problem. One we need to resolve together. I won't put this all on you."

She was staring at him with a strange look on her face. His gut redoubled its gnawing. "What?"

"You said 'the woman I love,'" she whispered.

Roman swallowed. He'd been thinking as much for a day or two, but he hadn't meant to say it. He hadn't wanted to overwhelm her while so many things were happening with Spence, the holidays, Gibb...

Their relationship was still so new. He hadn't wanted to rush her or confuse her or...well, *this*! She was clearly freaked out. And coming on the heels of her painful recounting of her attack, she was especially raw and vulnerable. Morgan Colton, *vulnerable*? He'd not have thought so a few days ago, but he had learned even someone as confident and capable and accomplished as Morgan could have scars and insecurities. Knowing what he did now about her past made him want to protect her all the more. Made him admire her for her ability to hold her demons at bay when they'd visited the warehouse earlier that week. No wonder she'd seemed so jittery.

"Roman?" Morgan's voice roused him from his tumbling thoughts.

"I, uh... I know. It's too soon. I meant it only as...an expression. I care about you and don't want to hurt you."

Morgan curled her lips in as her mouth grew taut. Her nose flared as she took a long, deep inhalation and nodded her head. "I understand." She waved a finger toward the road. "We should get going. Things to do. Motions to file. Appeals to review." She flashed a quick smile. "Everyone wants their case wrapped up before Christmas."

"Right. And I want to take another look at that security video. If Gibb is right—" He didn't bother finishing the sentence. She knew. He hoped he had been wrong about Gibb, even if that meant he'd have to eat a whole lot of crow. But if not Gibb, then who had taken the money form the tip jar and the nightly deposit?

When they returned to the Corner Pocket, Hector and Penny had the slow lunch crowd well in hand. Roman spoke briefly to a regular who was sipping a beer at the bar, then Morgan followed him back to his office.

"I thought you had to get back to work. Motions and appeals and Christmas, oh my! Yeah?"

She grinned at his *Wizard of Oz* reference. "Oh my, indeed. But I have time to help you first. I owe you that much after all the time you've taken away from your bar when you were already short-staffed."

"Thanks. Maybe with your lawyer's eye for details, you'll catch something I missed."

She pulled a face. "The key is not to assume anything. Try to keep an open and impartial mind-set. I know you're as personally involved in this as you can get. But let the facts speak. Not personal biases or preconceived ideas of what happened."

He grimaced and waved a hand at the computer. "Roll the tape. Let's just see what's what." As the video started playing on his computer screen, Roman leaned close, studying every detail of the scene unfolding. Tension swam through him, and he balled his hands in his lap. Waited.

"Hmm," Morgan muttered after a few moments.

"What?"

"Take a look." She tapped the screen. "At the edge of the picture. That's us. In all the hullabaloo, I'd forgotten that was the night we talked to Tim and learned about the construction warehouse."

He grunted. "Yeah. Been a busy and eventful few days, huh?"

They reached the time frame on the tape where Gibb put his hand in the tip jar, drew out a wad of cash. His body blocked most of what he was doing with the jar, but he definitely cast a suspicious-looking glance left and right before he stuck some bills in his pocket as he moved out of frame. A bit later, he returned the jar to the shelf under the counter. Roman hit Pause. Tried to zoom in. "Can you tell if the jar is empty?"

Morgan frowned. "No."

Buzzing his lips with frustration, he let the feed play again.

Penny strolled by the jar and jammed some cash in without pausing as she hustled to the kitchen.

"There. That's significant." Morgan pointed at the screen. "If the jar was empty, wouldn't Penny have noticed? And if she added money to the jar after Gibb supposedly emptied it, then there should have been some bills in there the next morning."

"So the theft happened after Penny put her tips in," Roman said, nodding his agreement. They continued watching until the feed ended, the picture going blank.

Roman pinched his nose. "And curtain. Damn it."

"Wait. Rewind a bit."

He did, and they rewatched the final seconds before the screen blanked. The time stamp read 11:19 p.m. Just after closing time. She reached past him and hit Pause. "Help me reconstruct what was happening then. Why didn't we see what happened to the camera?"

"It could have been a technical malfunction. Look…" He switched screens. "The office camera went out, too."

"No. Too big of a coincidence. Someone cut the feed to cover their tracks. I'm sure of it."

"But…" Roman dragged a hand down his chin, scratching his beard, lost in thought. "We were both there, on the bar floor, talking to Tim. How did we not see—?"

"Not at 11:19. By then the bar was closing." Morgan closed her eyes as she mentally reconstructed the events of the evening. "We had finished our discussion with Tim and… I went back to your apartment to get my purse so I could pay Tim."

Roman lifted his eyebrows, his pulse picking up. "You did, didn't you? Huh." Another memory surfaced, and he frowned. "While you were upstairs, Gibb and I dealt with a short in the cooler. I showed him where the circuit breakers were."

"He could have hit the circuit to the security cameras," she said, finishing his thought.

But something nagged. "No. I had the cameras set up on a separate power source, so they'd stay on in case of power failure. The feed would have to be manually cut."

"So we're back to someone intentionally turning off the cameras." Morgan gave him a level look. "Gibb knows where the power switch to the security system is, right?"

Roman clenched his back teeth, not liking where this was going. "Yeah. I'd think all my employees do. It's a pretty standard system."

Morgan visibly tensed. "All your employees?" She pressed a hand to her mouth. "Rewind a bit."

Once more they watched the feed, and just before the

video cut out again, Morgan gasped. "Roman, what was Tim wearing that night when he talked to us?"

"Tim? But we were with him—" He stopped short, realizing they'd just said they'd left Tim alone in the dining room while Roman fixed the cooler and she retrieved her purse. His stomach flipped, and a sinking feeling dragged at him. He rocked back in the desk chair and scraped both hands down his face, searched his memory. "I don't recall what he was wearing. He… never took off his coat."

"And the coat was…?"

He narrowed his eyes on Morgan. "Black. That slick, puffy kind."

"Would I be wrong if I guessed the power switch is just below the main camera on the bar floor?"

"No."

Morgan reached past him to back the feed up a few frames. "Look. There!"

She pointed to the very bottom edge of the screen. For the briefest moment, part of a hand and arm could be seen. The arm wore a puffy black coat.

"Tim!" Roman snarled.

"He had opportunity while we were gone upstairs and to the cooler. As a former employee, he'd know about the security system and remember where the tip bowl was kept."

"And he'd know the end of the day meant Penny would have put the day's take in the cash bag on my desk. My office wasn't locked. Gibb was supposed to make the deposit for me."

"While most of that is circumstantial, we have this." She pointed to the blurry still image with the hand and coat sleeve. "Not much, but maybe enough to confront him. We did leave it open to having another meet-up to see what else *Evan* could learn for us."

Roman nodded, his whole body tense with rage. "That son of a—"

"Poor Gibb. It seems as if he was telling the truth," Morgan said.

Roman's blood chilled, and sour guilt pooled at the back of his throat. "Oh, man. I have some major reparations to make."

Morgan reached for his hand and laced her fingers with his in solidarity. "You were justified in letting him go. He did hit Hector and smash up the bar."

"After being wrongfully accused and fired. I won't press charges if he'll apologize to Hector. Regardless of his provocation, I can't condone his resorting to violence."

Morgan leaned forward to kiss his cheek. "Don't beat yourself up."

He ground his back teeth together and shook his head. "But I should have done a more thorough investigation the day all this came up. I should have listened to Gibb. Believed him."

Morgan grimaced. "I had you distracted with catching Spence."

He grunted. Grinned. Stood and pulled her to her feet. Wrapping her in an embrace, he bent his head to kiss her lips. "You had me distracted in more ways than that. But I was still remiss."

She touched her forehead to his. "Speaking of remiss, I have neglected my responsibilities at the office long enough. I must go. But I want to be with you when you confront Tim."

He nodded. "And I will confront him. What do you say we get past this Colton family operation on the twenty-third first, huh? One thieving jerk at a time."

WITH THE PLAN for catching Spence set, Morgan spent the next day working cases she'd neglected, doing the Christmas shopping she put off and catching up on the random bits of her life—picking up dry cleaning, grocery shopping, her yearly visit to the gynecologist—she'd let pile up while she focused on tracking down the thieving, murdering drug dealer that had been a thorn for her family this year.

As she sat at her office desk, crossing items off her to-do list, she paused when she reached the item "doctor." Should she talk to her gynecologist about birth control while she was at his office? Abstinence had been her primary method of birth control for years, but if she was going to continue seeing Roman...

Was this relationship going somewhere? Was she grabbing at the first kind and handsome man to warm her bed because she wanted what her siblings had found? Because at almost forty, she felt like her chances for marriage and children were slipping past her? Roman was a lot of good things, but he was so many things that were outside her comfort zone. An ex-con. A risk taker. A rule breaker.

And his tattoos...would they always be a source of anxiety and a disturbing reminder of the attack?

You need to talk to a counselor, Peaches.

Morgan exhaled a slow breath and tapped her pen on her desk. A therapist? She'd thought about it over the years, of course. But wouldn't talking about the trauma only keep it fresh in her mind? She'd been doing well enough suppressing the memories...until she'd seen Roman's tattoos. Until the search for Spence had led her back to the north side of town, near the very place where the attack had happened. Until the recent spate of dangerous and troublesome events in her family's lives had unsettled her sense of peace and well-being. She'd spent most of the last twelve months one jolt away from a panic attack.

So much for being the most organized, competent and put-together Colton sibling.

Make it your New Year's resolution. Or my Christmas present. But do it.

A shudder rolled through Morgan. There was another way to deal with the demons that had resurfaced— shove them back in the dark corner of her brain where they'd lived since she was in college. And cut ties with Roman. Go back to the guarded, careful life she'd been successfully living for almost two decades. Her tried-and-true routine and suppression had a certain appeal. It was safe. Predictable. Comfortable.

But so lonely.

Propping her elbows on her desk and her head in her hands, Morgan groaned.

"Headache?"

She glanced up at Caleb, who stood at her door, frowning. "No. Well, sorta. But trying to decide some things, too, and I'm...stuck."

"What, no pro and con lists? Isn't that your usual method of deciding a course of action?"

She sent her brother a withering look. "I'm not that bad."

"Oh, but you are," he said with a light chuckle. "I've seen your court notes and calendar. All the side notes and lists. Charts."

"Charts won't help this time." She sat back in her chair and stared at her lap.

"Sounds serious. Is this about the plan to catch Spence tomorrow?" Caleb walked deeper into his office, tucking the file in his hand under his arm.

She shook her head. "No. More personal."

Her twin cocked his head to the side. "Mmm. Can I help?"

She said nothing for long seconds, before, "Do you like Roman?"

"DiMera?"

"No, Polanski." She pulled a face. "Yes, DiMera. I don't know what to do about him."

"What's to decide? I thought you two were an item now."

"Well, no. And also yes. But…going forward, I don't know if…"

Caleb lowered himself into one of the chairs across from her, his eyes narrowing. "What did he do?"

"Nothing. It's not him. Not really. We're just so… different. And he's…"

"An ex-con. A bar owner. Yeah, we've been over this." He slapped the file on her desk and folded his arms over his chest. "Is there some new issue? Because, honestly, the Morgan I saw at Mom's yesterday at the family meeting was the happiest Morgan I've seen in a long time. And I could tell by watching DiMera that he's crushing hard on you, too."

"He said he loved me. Sorta. Then he backpedaled when I asked him about it."

Caleb dragged a hand over his mouth. "Look, I'm no relationship expert. If you want advice for the lovelorn, you should talk to one of our sisters. Or Nadine. I know she'd be happy to listen and is good with this kind of stuff." He leaned forward, flattening a hand on the wooden surface of her desk. "But I'll tell you this. I care about your happiness. You deserve the best. You deserve someone who thinks you hung the moon. If you love Roman, if he makes you happy, then don't overthink it. Be happy. Be in love. That's what matters. I almost let Nadine get away. But thank God we found a way past our issues and gave our love a chance, because she is the best thing that ever happened to me."

Morgan gave her brother a gentle smile. "I can see that. And I'm so happy for you." She bit her bottom lip. "So Roman's past doesn't bother you? You don't see a problem for the family, for our law firm or The Truth Foundation?"

He laughed. "Our firm and the Foundation have built their reputations on second chances. On giving ex-cons a fair shake. On giving good people caught in the justice system a hand up. I see no conflict of interest. In fact, your relationship with Roman is very...*on brand*."

Morgan sputtered. "Listen to you with your marketing terms. Nadine teach you that?"

"Naw. I was talking with Gavin yesterday about his podcast and how he'd sell it." He took the file back off her desk and headed back to the door. "My point is simply this. Don't be an idiot. If you care about Roman, then it doesn't matter what I think or anyone else. Don't blow it by being too… Morganish."

She arched an eyebrow. "Morganish? What does that mean?"

With a sly smile, he patted the door frame as he exited. "Good luck. I'm headed to the courthouse. Back around four. Don't work too late. We have an early morning tomorrow, and everyone needs to be at their best."

Right. Tomorrow. The stakeout at the warehouse. Hours of sitting with Roman waiting for Spence to show. Morgan sighed and let her shoulders drop. How was she supposed to get any sleep tonight?

AFTER ANOTHER FIFTEEN minutes of stewing—Morganishly?—over Roman, and the plan to catch Spence, and Roman again, Morgan decided Caleb was right. She was overthinking everything. She stuck her to-do list under her desk calendar for later and grabbed her purse out of the bottom desk drawer. She needed what she thought of as ranch therapy. The Gemini was a working dude ranch that offered little luxuries to guests at the day spa. Morgan could think of nothing better than a hot stone treatment and a massage.

As she left the office, she gave Rebekah a message for Caleb that she'd taken his advice and was gone for the day. The look Rebekah gave her said their office assistant was worried about Morgan's odd behavior of late. Bad enough she kept showing up at the office with new bruises and smelling to high heaven. Her unusual hours the past week or so had Rebekah curious and disoriented. Morgan couldn't stand to think she'd caused her any distress and paused long enough to offer Rebekah some consolation.

"If I promised you everything will be back to normal after the holidays, would you believe me?" Morgan asked as she donned her coat.

"I wish I could," the older woman replied. "But after the tumult this year has brought your family, I can't say I'd believe you."

"Well, you needn't fret over me. I promise I'll be back in my routine soon." She flashed what she hoped was a reassuring smile and pushed open the office door. "If you want, why not take off early today?"

Rebekah shook her head. "Too much to do. I'll stay and hold down the fort, at least until Caleb gets back from the courthouse. But thanks."

In her car, Morgan called her brother Jasper, co-owner of the Gemini Ranch with his twin, Aubrey.

"Am I in trouble?" Jasper said as he answered the call.

"Trouble? Why would you ask that?"

"Because it seemed any time you wanted to talk to me growing up it was because I'd done something wrong or so you could nag me about homework or chores."

Morgan scowled. "That's not true!" She bit her lip. "Is it?"

"Probably not. Just yanking your chain, sis. What's up?"

"I was wondering if I could take a horse out this afternoon. Solo. Riding is a source of comfort to me. A great way to clear my mind and focus my thoughts. I need that right now."

"Sounds serious. Is this about tomorrow? Spence?"

"In part. I just need…clarity." Morgan stretched her neck, tipping her head from side to side. "And maybe a massage. You wouldn't know if there are any openings at the spa before dinner?"

"Don't know, but I'll check and get back with you. It's on the house. Call it a Christmas present."

"You don't have to—"

"I know. I want to." Jasper cleared his throat. "And I will ask Kayla to have Misty saddled and ready for you. Are you sure you don't want company? I could spare an hour or so if you wanted me to—"

"Thanks, but no. I'm sure. I just need some time in the saddle to clear my head. I'm on my way home to change, and then I'll be right out to the ranch. Maybe an hour?"

"You're on."

She hung up with Jasper and set her phone aside, wending through afternoon traffic to her house. As she unlocked the back door and hustled inside, the reek of smoke, something burning, met her nose. Frowning, she checked the stove, the toaster, the oven. Nothing was on. Had she burned her breakfast and forgotten? No. She sniffed again, recognizing the acrid scent. Not burned food. Cigarettes. Again.

A chill raced through her and, setting her purse on the kitchen counter, she took out her keys and readied the pepper spray she'd carried since her attack in college. She moved room by room. Checked closets. Under beds. No one. She sniffed again, and the scent was much less noticeable. She raised an arm to smell her coat. Had she brought the scent in on her clothes by darting inside the gas station after refueling her car? There was a hint of used oil from fried food and…maybe cigarettes. Her shoulders drooped, and she dropped heavily on the side of the bed. Was she so stressed about tomorrow that she was hallucinating sights and smells? The shiver that ran from her head to her toes had nothing to do with cold. Her fears, stirred by Spence, by recent events, even by Roman's tattoos, were making her life untenable. If she couldn't concentrate, couldn't sleep, was imagining things…

You need to talk to a counselor, Peaches.

She sighed. Right. Maybe. But today, she would rely on her own version of therapy. Nature. Horseback. Fresh air. It had been too long.

The drive to the Gemini Ranch took about half an hour from her house, and between the additional tourist traffic and some construction on the highway, the trip had Morgan twisted tighter than ever. Kayla met her in the parking lot and escorted her to the stables. "Wow, such personal service! Do all guests get this top-notch treatment?"

Kayla laughed. "We try, but the truth is, when Jasper said you were on the way, I promised him I'd pull out the red carpet for you. He says you're kind of tense or have some deep thinking to do?"

"Hmm, yeah. Life's been intense, and I want to both put tomorrow out of my head and get a sharper focus on it at the same time. Which of course means my thoughts have been spinning like a lasso lately."

"Anything I can help with?" Kayla waved to a couple guests who were crossing the ranch property with ski boots under their arms.

Skiing. That was another thing she hadn't done enough of lately. She wondered idly if Roman could ski. She could always teach him if…

"I may not have any new insights, but I'm good at listening. Sometimes all you need is to talk a thing out, and you realize you've had the answer all along," Kayla said, and Morgan refocused her attention on Jasper's girlfriend.

"Thanks, Kayla. I appreciate the offer."

The younger woman tucked a wisp of brown hair that had escaped her ponytail behind her ear. "Would this pensiveness and reflection have anything to do with the handsome bar owner you brought to the family meeting?"

Quickly, Morgan swung her gaze to Kayla. Too quickly. Her reaction to the question was obviously all Kayla needed to know.

"I see," the ranch hand said with a laugh. "I'm sorry. I'm not minimizing your confusion, but having seen that expression you're wearing all too recently in my own mirror, I should have known right off it was a man that had you tied in knots."

"I— It's not— Well, it's more than one man, actually," Morgan admitted with a sigh.

Kayla's eyes rounded. "Well, well, well. More than one man?"

Waving Kayla's presumption away with a flick of her hand, Morgan said, "Not like that. One man is Spence. I'm just determined that everything go according to plan tomorrow, and I've rehearsed the day in my head, looking for trouble spots, a hundred different times. And it boils down to one huge unknown. Will Spence really show? How will he react? Am I putting my family in harm's way for no reason?"

"Your family, the ones involved with the scheme for tomorrow, are skilled law enforcement and military. They know what they're doing."

"Yeah, but Spence is smart. He's eluded us for months. What if he gets wind of our operation somehow or gets spooked before we can nab him? What if—?"

"Oh, wow," Kayla chuckled wryly. "Jasper was right. You are hyperanalytical." The younger woman cringed as soon as she spoke. "What I mean is—"

Morgan touched Kayla's arm. "Caleb called it 'being Morganish' just this afternoon. Apparently, he thinks I've taken fretting and analyzing to a whole new level. And he's right. I will tear a problem apart a hundred different ways and try to put it back together completely solved." Her footsteps slowed briefly as it occurred to her that she was being Morganish about Roman, too. They reached the stables, and Morgan pulled open the sliding door to the stalls. Warm air from the ceiling space heaters rolled out to greet her along with the scents of hay and horses. "Too bad life doesn't work that way, huh?"

"Well, I can tell you this. Tomorrow is in good hands. I believe that the Coltons, working together, are unstoppable. Have faith." Kayla led her to a stall where a stocky, young-looking guy stood absorbed in his cell phone. "Ethan, phone."

The ranch hand straightened and jammed the cell phone in his back pocket. "Oh, right."

"Is Misty ready?"

"Um, no. I'll saddle her now." Ethan scurried off to find a saddle, and Kayla rolled her eyes.

"He's actually a good worker when I can get him off that phone. Lord knows who he's texting all the time." Kayla stroked the dapple-gray mare's nose. "Anyway, I've always found a ride in the pastures can change my perspective and refresh me."

"That's what I'm hoping," Morgan said, putting a saddle blanket on her favorite mare herself.

"As for the *other* man you're pointedly *not* talking about but clearly torn over," Kayla said with a half smile.

Morgan grinned and shook her head. "You are perceptive."

"Maybe it's just because I've so recently jumped headfirst into a relationship with Jasper, but I highly recommend giving love a chance. Even if it seems confusing or unlikely or full of roadblocks, love is worth it. After all he's told me you've done for your family, you deserve a wild, wonderful affair of your own." The attractive hand smiled as she handed Morgan Misty's bridle. "No analysis needed."

Morgan thanked Kayla with a grin and a nod as they stepped back to allow Ethan to put on the saddle he'd collected and cinch the girth. "I can see why Jasper fell in love with you."

If possible, the brunette ranch hand's face brightened even further. "Aw, shucks," she said playfully. Then, checking her cell phone, she settled a bit. "So sunset is in an hour and ten minutes. I needn't tell you how fast it gets dark in the foothills after the sun goes behind the mountains, right?"

Morgan took out her own cell phone and set an alarm, just in case she lost track of time. "I will be back in one hour. Jasper is setting up a postride massage for me in the spa, and I do not want to be late for that."

Kayla motioned to a portable mounting block. "Need this?"

Morgan firmed her mouth a tad. "I'm not that old—" Sticking her foot in the stirrup, she hoisted herself up with minimal struggling and settled in the saddle. "Oof. Yet."

Clicking her tongue to Misty, she headed out of the stable and onto the ranch property. Ethan ran ahead of her to open the gate that led into the upper pasture and toward the rise of mountains. The old familiar rhythm and cadence of rider and horse flowed back to her. She'd never been as proficient at riding as Jasper and Aubrey, but she did love having the brisk wind from the Rockies in her face and the reins in her hand.

She took her favorite path out to a point high above the ranch with a sprawling view of the many guest cabins and outbuildings, lit like a mantel-top Christmas village.

"I wish Roman could see this," she whispered to Misty, who chuffed and rattled her bridle in response. And what did it mean that her first thought upon encountering something so splendid and beautiful was to share it with Roman? She grinned to herself, imagining Roman in a saddle. Bad-boy bar owner playing cowboy… She'd pay to see that. And in her core, she knew Roman would be up for it. Because he didn't shy from trying things, taking risks…and because he'd move mountains to make her happy. He'd proved that in the last few days. Not just their exquisite lovemaking, either. His attention to detail on their dinner date. His generous donation of his time and energy to help her track down Spence.

A short distance down the trail, a crackling noise, like rocks clattering when disturbed, warned her something—or someone—was there. Misty pranced sideways uneasily.

Morgan stroked the mare's withers. "Whoa. Easy, girl. What are you sensing?"

The ranch had no shortage of wildlife—from the cute and furry pika to the more lethal bears and mountain lions. Not common, but possible. And wouldn't that be just her luck to cross path with a hungry, agitated puma?

When she reached the area where Jasper and Kayla had reportedly had their shootout with Spence, Morgan swung down off Misty's back and walked the field, searched the icy grass, looking for…she didn't know what.

You're dwelling. You're supposed to be clearing your mind, and instead you're combing a frozen pasture for closure you won't find here. Only capturing Spence, seeing him sent to prison for his crimes, will do that.

"I should go in, shouldn't I?" she asked Misty, and the horse blinked her dark eyes. "I'll take that as a yes." She eased back to Misty's left side and raised her foot to the stirrup. Heaved herself into the saddle. "Now can you help me decide what to do about Roman?"

The mare snorted and tossed her head, and Morgan imagined she heard the horse say, *To do that, you have to talk to the man himself.*

With a sigh, she gave the reins a small flick. "Misty, how'd you get so smart?"

Chapter Sixteen

Roman arrived at Morgan's house early the next morning, well before the sun—and most people—were up. She bundled herself in layers of warmth and tucked her knapsack of accoutrements into her back seat. By agreement, they were taking her vehicle. Roman's classic Corvette was far too conspicuous, while her sedan was common.

"Although if we really wanted to blend," Roman said as he climbed in the passenger seat, "we should be in some old beater with rust spots. Know anyone with a car like that we could borrow?" His tone was light and teasing, but Morgan brightened.

"As a matter of fact, I think there may be one near that description parked somewhere in a barn or something at the Gemini Ranch. One of the ranch hands drove it for a while long ago, I think, but—"

"I wasn't serious." Roman closed his door and fastened his seat belt. "I'm sure we'll be fine. The plan isn't to stay in the car after all, but to park and go on foot closer to the warehouse to watch the back and side door."

Morgan nodded as she cranked the engine. The

motor took a moment to catch in the cold air. "I remember the plan. But if you ask a Colton if they have a fill in the blank—" she waved her hand as if signaling the word *blank* as well "—there are enough of us with diverse interests that chances are good someone in the family will have a thingamabob or whatsit you can borrow. Crampons? One of my outdoorsy brothers. A springform pan? One of the indoorsy sisters or in-laws. Ammunition of a certain caliber—"

"I get the point," Roman said with a sideways grin.

"I only mention it because…" She twisted in her seat and rummaged with one hand in the knapsack she'd brought. Bringing out a box that rattled, she placed the supply of nine-millimeter cartridges on Roman's lap. "Dominic asked if you owned a gun. I told him you did. I'd seen it in your office one day and thought I remembered it was a nine-millimeter. Was I right?"

Roman bent to dig at his feet in the small duffel he'd brought. He pulled out a black pistol and held it for her to see. "You were. But it's already loaded. I swear, if we need any rounds at all, something's not gone to plan today. And if I need more than one clip to protect us with all the backup standing by today, we're seriously screwed."

"Hmm. Point taken. Dominic just wanted us prepared." She replaced the box of ammunition and pulled out a thermos. "Can I interest you in coffee instead?"

Again he rifled through his bag and brought out his own thermos. "It seems great minds think alike."

"Indeed." She put her thermos back for later and nodded toward her travel mug. "Top me up, please?" Turning back around, she shifted into Drive and set out.

"Is your java request an indication of how you slept?" he asked as he unscrewed the top of his insulated bottle.

"Sorta. I've never been able to sleep well when I had a lot on my mind."

Roman acknowledged that with a grunt. When he finished filling her travel mug, he capped the thermos and stashed it. "I went to see Gibb last night."

She shot him a side glance. "Oh? How did that go?"

"Well, I took an *I'm sorry* ham and gifts for his kids with me. Those got me in the door without getting punched. I explained what we discovered, leaving out who we suspect. No point giving Gibb any ideas…"

"Smart."

"Long story short, he'll be back at work after the first of the year, and he agreed to both apologize to Hector and take a few classes at the Y on anger management."

Morgan blinked and sent Roman a startled look. "Really?"

"His wife suggested the second condition. Apparently, his temper has gotten him in trouble before." Roman shrugged. "Anyway, I slept better knowing I'd righted that wrong, at least in part. Injustice in any form is an anathema to me." He cut a side glance toward her. "Ironic, I know."

"What's ironic about it? Plenty of people find injustice hard to stomach."

"Well, you know, seeing as how I was dealt my own dose of the justice system's punishment." He drew his dark eyebrows together. "Not that I didn't deserve it. I did the crime, so it was only right I serve my time. And I got my head straight in prison. So all in all, it was a blessing in disguise."

Morgan reflected on that. "You have a healthy outlook regarding your prison time. That's good."

He gave a small shrug. "That doesn't keep others from seeing me as menace to society. Based on the dark looks I received the other day, I got the feeling your brothers were none too happy with my past."

"Did someone say something to you?" She turned a concerned look to him. "Because Caleb assured me he likes you just fine."

Roman jerked his chin toward her, his expression startled. "You talked to Caleb about me?"

"Don't sound so surprised. He is my business partner and twin, for Pete's sake. We talk about almost everything." Morgan navigated across the river bridge that took them into the heart of the north-side district. She suppressed the shiver of ill ease that coiled in her core. She was fine. She was with Roman. Her family was close with backup. This plan would work. *Please, oh, please, let this work!*

She cast a quick glance to Roman and saw his unsettled expression.

"Really, Roman. He likes you. The only reason I asked him his opinion was…well, to put it in his terms, I was being too Morganish. Yes, my brother made my name into an adjective. I don't think he meant it as a compliment, either. He thinks I'm a ridiculous overthinker and a picky over-planner and—"

His hand covered hers on the steering wheel. "Well, I find your Morganishness endearing and useful."

She shot him a grateful smile. "You say that now. But Caleb has lived with it almost forty years, and it apparently is tedious to him." She sighed. "And if I'm honest, he's right in a way. I am…doing a lot of thinking…struggling with certain aspects of our relationship." She drove slowly down the dark street where, despite the early hour, a few people already stirred. Garbage collectors banged dumpsters. A pawnshop owner unlocked his front door. The lights in a mom-and-pop diner glowed through the front window. They were a comfortable walking distance from the warehouse now, and Morgan scanned the street for a parking place she deemed safe.

"What…sort of thinking are you doing?" Roman asked slowly, hesitantly. His tone was quiet, and she heard a note of hurt or caution.

"I— This isn't the best time to get into it. But surely you know that there are things about you, about…us that…" She paused long enough to take a beat, a breath. "That, well…scare me."

"Scare you?"

She nodded. "We're so different. And I have some things to work through before I can— It's difficult for me to— Roman, I can't— Geez. How do I explain without sounding…cruel. Harsh. I just…"

He gave her a tight, forced smile. "It's okay. No need to explain." But the look on his face said he didn't understand, that he felt rejected. That wasn't what she'd intended at all.

Her heart sank. She'd messed it up, distracted as she was by the upcoming stakeout, her driving, her skittish mood, being in the heart of the north side's dark streets. Her feelings about their relationship deserved her full attention. She would broach her reservations, her fears with him later. Right now they had a job to do.

A criminal to catch. And by God, she intended to have Spence in custody by the end of the day or die trying.

She swallowed hard. Bad choices of words. She knew how dangerous this plan was, how deadly Spence could be. She parked her car and drew a long, deep breath for courage. She, Roman and her family were venturing into a den of vipers, and she prayed no one got bitten.

ROMAN CAUGHT MORGAN by the arm as they neared the warehouse and tugged her into a side alley. She stiffened, flinched.

"Slow down, Peaches. Let's approach from a more protected angle."

Her throat worked as she swallowed, and her answering nod was jerky.

Damn, but she was tense, he thought. And no wonder, considering what had happened to her when she was in college. Considering what they were up against today. She had reason to be scared.

There were things about him that scared her.

His gut curdled at the memory of her confession. Her admission echoed a truth he'd been trying to find a workaround for, but so far, he kept running into a brick wall. He *scared* her. How do you build a relationship with that elephant in the room?

You didn't.

Acknowledging that reality gnawed inside him and slashed at his heart. With effort, he shoved the emotion away to stay focused on the job at hand. His reason for being here today was singular. Yeah, Spence was a bad guy that needed to be off the street. But the Coltons had a whole host of qualified law enforcement and military muscle in their ranks to capture the drug-dealing murderer. He was along for the ride to protect Morgan, who would not be dissuaded from being part of the takedown.

Roman understood her need to be on hand, to have a part in seeing Spence brought to justice. If someone had harmed his family, he'd want to be the one to slam the jailhouse door. So Morgan was marching into battle, and his intention was to be her shadow, to have her back and to step in front of a bullet if needed to keep her safe. Period. And then, for her mental health, for her own good, he would step aside and give her the out she needed to leave this ill-suited relationship without guilt.

He linked hands with her as they hustled through the pink-gray first light of morning to a position behind the warehouse, where they could watch the back entrance. Shrubbery hid them on one side, and a large garbage bin shielded them from the front. They each had an earpiece and tiny lip mic, provided by her well-equipped brothers, with which they could communicate with the backup team. They took turns peering around the edge of the trash receptacle and any activity behind them.

"There's Alexa," he said, nodding to a shadowy figure barely visible in a second-floor window across the street.

Morgan nodded. "Yeah. Probably. And if I'm not mistaken, the homeless man we passed sleeping on Third Street was Dominic."

"Roger that," said a male voice in his earpiece.

"Good morning, Dom," Morgan said with a grin. "Is there a way to turn this mic off so you're not eavesdropping on our conversation before we need you?"

"No convo. You need to stay quiet, attentive. Got it, sis?" he replied, sternly.

Morgan sighed. "Aye-aye, Captain."

"Roger that, boss," Roman added, hearing a few chuckles over the earpiece from the other team members who were listening.

Not that Roman had planned to have any painful, personal discussions with Morgan that would be a distraction from their surveillance, but the reminder that her family was listening confirmed that any conversation about their future—or the lack of it—had to wait.

And so, in silence, he and Morgan waited and watched. Someone in a truck with a logo on the door arrived at about seven o'clock. Soon after, more employees arrived, and the back bay door was raised so that an eighteen-wheeler could leave with a backhoe and a bulldozer on a trailer.

When Morgan yawned, Roman held his coffee out to her in a nonverbal offer. She nodded, and he poured some hot java into her travel cup. She smiled her thanks. Sipped. And returned to the tedious watch.

Two more hours passed, during which Roman tried not to think about these silent, tedious minutes being his last minutes with Morgan. A clean break with her would be easier in the long run for both of them. Each time a subtle winter wind stirred and carried the fruity scent of her shampoo to him, his chest tightened with grief. When she shivered, he tucked her closer under his arm to keep her warm—and willed himself not to break cover by shouting his frustration and regrets.

Then, as his phone's clock said the noon hour was approaching, a familiar face showed up in the side alley by the warehouse, skulking through the shadows as if trying to keep out of sight. Roman tensed, his heart thumping as he narrowed his gaze, confirming what couldn't believe he was seeing. He muttered a curse word under his breath.

"Roman?" Morgan whispered, her expression alarmed. "What?"

"Team one, report," came Dominic's voice in his ear.

"Not Spence. But potential trouble," he said.

When Morgan tried to peer past him to the alley, he caught her and dragged her back. She glared at him, mouthing, *What?*

Roman gritted his back teeth and cast another glance to the man lurking in the side alley. "Our informant, Tim Hall, is here."

Chapter Seventeen

"Who?" Dominic asked through Morgan's earpiece at the same time she sputtered, "What the heck is he doing here?"

"Shh," someone else warned through the comm, even as Roman raised a hand telling her to hold on while he sneaked another look past the shrubbery.

Morgan scuttled to the other side of the trash bin and looked for herself. Sure enough, the compact man with a buzz cut she'd most recently seen on the security camera footage playback in Roman's office was pacing in the alley next to the warehouse. Tim blew on his hands and cast furtive glances toward the street. He seemed to be waiting for something. Or someone.

Roman muttered something dark and unholy under his breath as he shifted onto his heels and put his back to the dumpster. "This changes everything."

"This changes nothing," came Dom's low voice in her earpiece.

"What do you mean?" she asked Roman.

"He's my former employee. He has a family. I feel responsible for him." Roman dragged a hand down his face and rubbed his beard. "I can't sit here and let him get caught in the crossfire of…*whatever* happens when Spence shows up."

"DiMera, I don't know what you're thinking, but don't do anything rash. Stick to the plan," Dominic warned.

"You don't owe him anything, Roman. If we're right about our suspicions and what we saw on the security recording, he *stole* from you. He lied to you."

"That's our suspicion, yes. But I haven't confronted him about it yet. And whatever else he was or is, he was a good employee."

"Maybe so, but you heard Dom." She put a hand on his arm. "This changes nothing."

Roman's expression was conflicted. Clearly he was invested in Tim Hall and the man's well-being. He didn't just give lip service to his employees. How much more would he be involved with someone he loved? Her heart tugged with pride and affection for the man she'd come to know. Roman was good to the core. Whatever else he was or the choices he'd made in the past, she was sure of his integrity and kindness. Somehow she could find a way forward with him, couldn't she?

Roman shook his head. "Even if he's here looking to buy drugs or make some sort of backstreet deal, he still should be warned away before Spence arrives."

She heard Dom's grunt of disapproval. "DiMera…"

"What are you thinking? You can't show yourself."

Roman squeezed his eyes shut, and a muscle in his jaw flexed. Her heart ached seeing his struggle.

"I don't know who this Hall person is, but the plan remains the same. Everyone hold position." Her brother's voice was firm, commanding.

Morgan squeezed Roman's arm through the layers of his coat and clothing. When he met her gaze, she tried to silently impart her support, her sympathy, her plea for cooperation with a sad smile. A look. A shake of her head.

In response, Roman heaved a deep sigh, caught the back of her head with his hand and gave her a hard kiss. Then, pulling his gun from under his coat and shoving it in her hands, he whispered fiercely, "Stay here. I'll be right back."

Morgan was so startled by his departure that she could only gape as she watched him stride across the blacktop of the warehouse parking lot with wide, quick steps.

Dominic bit out a curse word. "DiMera, stop! Stand down!"

"Roman, no!" she said into her lip mic. She watched, crouched down, her stomach knotting, as Roman snatched the earpiece from his ear and shoved it in his pocket.

Above the buzz of adrenaline in her head, she heard her siblings' moans and sighs and curses.

"Morgan, what the hell?"

"I know! I'm sorry. I— What do I do?"

"Nothing." Dominic's tone vibrated with fury and frustration. "No one move. Just…hold position and wait for my orders."

If this went south because of Roman, the man she'd brought in from outside the family, she would never forgive herself. If something happened to Roman because she'd brought him in on dangerous business, she'd also never forgive herself.

Trembling with anxiety and her own irritation that Roman had broken ranks, Morgan kept watch. All her natural instincts, her inborn need for order and security, told her to follow Dominic's directions, to stick to the plan she and her siblings had drawn up. To obey the rules.

But another voice in her head screamed at her to race after Roman, to guard his back, to help him with whatever new course he'd chosen. If she loved Roman, didn't she need to trust him? Support him? Protect him?

"Dom, I'm sorry," she whispered into the comm. And tucking the gun into her knapsack, she scurried out of hiding to follow Roman.

ROMAN MADE HIS way to the side alley as quickly as he could, doing his best to approach from an angle that would keep him out of view of security cameras or anyone watching from a window. His nerves jangled, and his heart was thumping a furious cadence as he slid into the shadows. He'd half expected to have been shot by now, either by someone edgy in the warehouse…or by one of Morgan's siblings for having defied Dom's orders. But his conscience wouldn't allow him to let anything happen to Tim while he sat back and watched.

Not all his experiences from the streets of Philly were mischief and risks. He'd learned a respect for friendship, loyalty, a brotherhood with those caught in the snares of life. Sometimes all a man needed was a chance. A break. An opportunity to make good.

Yeah, Tim had probably stolen that money from him. Yeah, the betrayal stung. But did Tim deserve to get shot because he was in the wrong place at the wrong time now? Not to mention the fact that Tim's presence could blow the operation. Roman knew he'd be excoriated for breaking cover and defying Dom, but he had to do something to keep Tim out of harm's way. To get the Coltons' plan back on track.

Although he'd tried to be as quiet as possible in his approach, Tim, obviously hearing his footsteps, whirled around as Roman reached the end of the alley. His ex-employee's body language was all nerves and caution—tense face, jerky movements, wary eyes.

Roman approached with hands up. "Easy, Tim. It's me, DiMera."

Tim blinked and cast his gaze about in confusion. "What the hell? Why are you here?"

"I could ask the same of you."

The soft patter of footfalls behind him drew Tim's attention, and even without looking he knew with a sinking certainty that Morgan had followed him.

Tim's face darkened as Morgan reached Roman's side. "Why is she with you?" His scowl grew black. "I don't know how you found me, but I've told you all I know. If you don't get out of here now—" he pointed toward the street "—you'll ruin everything for me."

"What will we ruin, Tim?" Roman asked. "Who are you meeting?"

Tim shifted his weight from one foot to the other and glanced away from Roman. "No one."

"Then why are you here? What are you up to, man?" Roman pressed.

"None of your business," Tim snarled. "You need to get lost. You can't be here!"

"Funny," Roman said, shoving his hands in his pockets, "I was going to say the same to you. You need to clear out of here, or else—"

"Or else what?" Tim cocked his head and narrowed his eyes.

A good question. What lengths was Roman prepared to go to? What options did he have?

"It's a free country," Tim grated. "I don't work for you. You can't tell me where I can or can't be."

"Roman, please," Morgan whispered, inching close to him. "We should go. Don't blow this for us."

"Are you buying drugs?" he asked Tim and heard Morgan's frustrated sigh. He could imagine what her brothers were saying through the comm in her ear.

"What?" Tim pulled a face.

"Maybe with the money you stole from the Corner Pocket? From the tip jar?"

"Now is not the time for this," Morgan muttered under her breath. She tugged on his arm. "Please, Roman."

His former employee said nothing, but his expression remained hard and angry.

"Despite your best efforts, we caught enough on the security video to identify you as the one who cut the cameras off."

"You're lying. You ain't got nothing on me." Tim cast another uneasy glance down the alley and rolled his shoulders. "If you know what's good for you, you'll scram. Now."

"I haven't called the cops on you...yet. But if you don't return the money, I'll have no choice."

Tim's gaze sharpened. "*She* put you up to this? I did

you a favor, telling you about this warehouse, and this is how you repay me?"

Roman aimed a finger at Tim. "I did you a favor hiring you when no one else would, and this is how you repay *me*?"

Morgan tugged harder on his arm. "Roman! Do this later. Please!"

Tim's attention focused on Morgan and he frowned. "Hey, what's that in your ear? Are you wired?" He bristled and cast a panicked glance around him. "Are you working with the cops?"

Roman raised a hand to calm the other man. "No one is here to arrest you, but you need to clear out before you get caught up in something serious. Something that has nothing to do with you."

"I know! I know!" Morgan said, presumably to her brother, who was no doubt blowing a gasket.

Roman figured he'd be lucky if he didn't end up in jail for Christmas for obstructing the Coltons' operation. The operation might be unofficial, but they could probably convince Chief Lawson hold him for a while on principle.

"Look, I will turn a blind eye to whatever you're doing here now, and deal with your theft from the bar another day, if you leave the premises *right now*." Roman squared his shoulders and took a step closer to Tim. He took full advantage of his height to tower menacingly over the shorter man. "I know you may not believe it, but I don't want anything bad to happen to you."

"Is that a threat?" Tim asked hotly.

"Oh, for God's sake!" Morgan huffed and shoved past Roman. "He's not threatening you, you jerk! He's trying to save your sorry ass! But I am threatening you. I have numerous connections to law enforcement and the judiciary, and I will see that you go to prison for theft or dealing drugs or violating parole or… Geez, pick your poison, pal…if you don't get the hell out of here, now!"

Roman would have laughed at the wildcat Morgan had transformed into had the situation been less dire. As it was, the acrid scent of a used ashtray reached him and registered a split second before he heard a scuff of feet. At the end of the alley behind them, a revolver clicked as it was cocked.

Spinning around, his attention darted to the lanky man with unkempt dark hair and a cigarette dangling from his lips. His blood ran cold. Roman mumbled a curse word, then, "Too late."

Chapter Eighteen

A chill raced through Morgan hearing the ominous tone of Roman's words. She didn't have to look to know Spence had arrived. Had seen them. In the next instant, Roman was shoving her behind him, putting himself between her and Ronald Spence.

While holding his gun on them with one hand, the stringy-haired man shook a cigarette out of a pack, then crumpled the dark blue package labeled Smitty's and dropped it on the ground. He lit the new cigarette from the one already in his mouth and flicked the old butt away.

When Spence took a few steps deeper into the alley, Morgan held her breath. Her throat was frozen with fear, seeing the weapon trained on them, but she managed to scrape out, "Dom, he's here."

"Spence?" Dominic asked in her ear. "But how—?"

Her brother didn't finish the moot question. Instead, he started barking orders while Morgan watched Spence limp down the dark alley, his eyes taking in the trio before him.

Tim chose that inopportune moment to draw his

own weapon. "Hey, where's my green? You owe me ten K, Ron."

"Alexa, get down there! Ezra, take the west side! We need that alley surrounded! Move!" Dom shouted through her earpiece. She took courage and strength knowing her family was close. They had her back. If they got here fast enough…

At the moment, she and Roman were caught between Tim's gun and Spence's.

Roman's hand curled tightly around Morgan's arm, now tugging her away from Tim, his attention divided between the two armed men. "Both of you put the weapons away. No one needs to get hurt."

When Spence locked his gaze, his *gun* on her, her gut flipped.

"Morgan Colton. Well, this is a surprise. I thought I'd missed my last chance to kill one of Ben Colton's children before I left town."

Gritting her teeth, she straightened her back. "Oh, you won't be leaving town. Not if my family has anything to say about it."

"But they don't. As of last night, all my money is in untraceable overseas accounts, and by tonight, I'll be joining it in South America. So I win."

"You don't go nowhere 'til I get my money!" Tim growled. He took a few steps closer until Spence leveled the gun in his hand at his accomplice. Tim extended his own weapon, and Morgan shivered. Would they get caught in a volley of shots between these two? She thought of Roman's nine millimeter in the knapsack slung over her shoulder. Could she get to it without calling too much attention to herself? She moved a hand slowly toward the drawstring opening while Tim groused.

"We had a deal. Now you cough up the coin."

"Patience. I have to handle this problem first." Spence's gaze returned to Morgan, and she stilled, her hand near the opening of the small backpack. "Your father screwed me over for profit. He was paid to hide evidence that would have cleared me, and now I have my revenge."

"But you were guilty," Morgan said.

Spence brushed off her argument with a negligent shrug as he strolled closer. Stopped about ten feet from her. "Your papa still did me wrong. Killing you is just the icing on the payback cake, doll face." He flashed a gloating grin. "Thank you for your help getting me out of jail, by the way. You and your brother were most helpful."

Acid burned in her core. She flicked a glance to the pistol in Spence's hand. "If you shoot any one of us, I promise you will not make it out of this alley alive. This block will be swarming with law enforcement any moment. Your best move is to lay down your weapon and surrender peacefully."

"Do what the lady said," Roman demanded, his tone like steel.

Spence hesitated, his eyes narrowing speculatively, clearly deciding if he believed her or not. He snorted. "Bull."

But he was clearly rattled by the notion that a net was closing around him. His attention turned to Tim suddenly. "Enough of this. Where's my passport?"

"Where's my money?" Tim asked, striding closer.

Roman gripped Morgan's arm harder and eased them backward, closer to the brick wall behind them. "If bullets fly," he whispered in the ear without the comm piece, "lie flat."

She gave a small nod toward the knapsack, trying to send him a message with her eyes about where the gun was. But Roman's full attention was on Spence. Then, as she moved backward, her foot hit a discarded soda can. The clank sounded like cannon fire in the tense alley.

Tim twitched. Discharged his gun.

Immediately, Spence returned fire.

Morgan screamed, as much from surprise as fear. With a yank, Roman pulled her down. She flattened herself on the ground, and Roman covered her with his body.

More shots rang out, and a male shout of pain echoed below the ear-shattering concussion of blasts. She angled her head in time to see Tim fall, clutching his gut. Spence ran forward, rifled Tim's pockets until he found the probably-forged passport, then ran at a limping lope to the end of the alley nearest the river.

With Roman's weight on top of her, she struggled to free her arms and dig his pistol from the depths of the backpack. When it was out, she aimed at Spence. Not a kill shot. She just wanted him delayed until her backup arrived. Pulled the trigger…and missed.

"Damn! Dom, where's my backup? He's getting away!"

"Coming. Stay down!" Dominic's voice shouted in her ear. "Alexa, report!"

"I see him. In pursuit. But he's got a sizable lead," her sister said.

"Roman, let me up! We have to follow h—"

Roman's groan cut her off. When he rolled aside, she wiggled out from under him. He was clutching his left arm. Blood spread on the sleeve of his coat. "Roman!"

"I'm fine. Tim…"

She raised her gaze to where Tim lay in a heap, his hands pressed to his stomach. His pallor was wan, his eyes bright with anguish. She rushed to the man's side. "Tim?"

His lips moved, but no sound came out.

"Someone call an ambulance! Tim and Roman are down!" Realizing she still held Roman's pistol in her right hand, she set it on the ground. Pushed it away as if it were alive and could bite her. Adrenaline shook her from the inside out. Noises tangled and blurred. Her siblings filling her ear with staccato orders and reports. Her own heavy, panicked breathing. The shuffle of feet behind her as Roman moved up and knelt beside her and Tim.

And the squeal of tires.

She jerked her chin up, following the sound of peeling rubber. "Spence." Even if she couldn't see the vehicle, it was easy enough to conclude.

Roman made a dark, angry noise in his throat and snatched his weapon from the pavement. Surged to his feet and hurried to the end of the alley near the street.

"Roman?"

"Stay back!" he shouted.

The roar of an engine grew louder, and a white sedan with the passenger side heavily scraped, sped down the street. An arm emerged from the driver's window. With a gun. The muzzle flashed as it was fired.

The seconds that followed could have been hours, could have been an instant. Morgan watched, as if from outside herself.

Roman charged toward the car. Aiming his pistol with his right arm he took aim. Fired.

Alexa appeared, running full out. Assumed a shooting stance in the path of the car. Her weapon discharged. More blasts answered.

Sprinting toward the street, Roman continued firing at the driver of the vehicle.

The white car swerved. Alexa tried to jump out of the way. But the front fender hit her. She was spun around. Went down.

"Alexa!" Morgan screamed in horror. "Dom, Alexa is down! Spence hit her with his car!" she choked out as sobs tightened her throat.

Arriving police officers opened fire as the sedan raced away. Swerved suddenly. Hit a power pole.

Her siblings swarmed the street from different directions. Ezra and Philip, with a few members of Alexa's team, closed in on the white sedan, guns at the ready. Dominic and Dane rushed to where Alexa's prone form lay on the street. Unmoving.

Then Roman staggered and dropped to his knees before toppling onto his side.

Ice filled Morgan's belly. She stared, numb. Her mind blank, as if filled with static. Her limbs paralyzed.

Finally Morgan managed to draw a shaky breath and clambered to her feet. She stumbled the first steps, in such a rush to reach her loved ones, she didn't have her feet under her before she charged forward. "No!"

She reached Roman first. His eyes were pinched closed, his mouth pressed in a taut line of pain. "Roman?"

He squinted up at her. "I'll live. I—" Sitting up slowly, he reached for his jeans with his right hand, pulled up the torn leg and winced at the huge raw scrape.

Her gasp was half sympathy for the bloody, painful-looking injury, and half relief that she wasn't staring at bullet wound. Like his arm…

Shifting her attention to his left shoulder, she tugged at the sleeve of his coat. "Your arm—"

"Will be fine. Alexa…" He knitted his brow and turned a concerned look to the other side of the street.

Dominic's back blocked her view, and she could hear her brother's deep voice calling, "Alexa?"

Dane's more pained and panicked voice beseeching, "Alexa, baby, please answer me!"

Morgan's stomach swooped, and tears filled her eyes. "Oh God, please!"

Roman hitched his head toward her fallen sister. "Go."

And she did. She raced to kneel across from Dominic at Alexa's side. Her sister's head was bleeding, and she was unresponsive. Dane clutched Alexa's hand, his expression stricken, and Morgan joined Dominic in calling softly to her sister. "Please, sweetie. Open your eyes."

When Morgan reached for her sister's shoulder, Dominic barked a brusque, "No! Don't move or jostle her. She could have a back or neck injury."

Morgan snatched her hand back as if burned. Tears spilled on her cheeks, and she put an arm around Dane's shoulders. "She…she'll be all right," she said, as much to convince herself as to buoy Dane.

The distant wail of sirens signaled the approach of the local police. Or an ambulance. *Please, God, let it be an ambulance!*

Morgan cast a glance down the street to the white sedan that her brother, Philip and a number of other Blue Larkspur police officers were swarming. No one looked especially tense, as if the danger had passed, yet she didn't see any sign of Spence in handcuffs. She shivered, knowing what that could mean. She replayed the image of the scraped white car rolling past the end of the alley, Roman firing, Alexa— She cut off the recollection and squeezed her eyes shut…where another memory burgeoned. Two days earlier as they'd left her mother's house…

"Dominic," she whispered, her voice hoarse, "that white car…it's the same one that tried to run me and Roman off the road two days ago."

Dominic raised a sharp look to her. "What!"

"I'd dismissed it as a random drunk driver or—I don't know. So much has happened, and we got distracted talking about the attack on me in college and…" She released a tremulous sigh. "But it was Spence. One more tick mark in the charges to bring against him when—"

"No one will be bringing charges against him," Philip said as he approached behind her. "He's met his final justice." Philip crouched beside Dominic, a deep furrow of worry etched in his brow.

"He's dead?" Morgan asked, a tangle of emotions knotting in her chest.

Philip bobbed a quick nod. "Multiple gunshot wounds. How's Alexa?"

"She's—" Dom started but fell silent when Alexa groaned.

Morgan's breath caught as her sister's eyes blinked open.

"Alexa!" Dane leaned closer. "Can you hear me?"

"Mmm," Alexa grunted. "Dane?"

"I'm right here. Don't try to move," Dane said, tears in his voice. "Help is coming, love."

"Where are you hurting?" Morgan asked. "Besides your head…"

"I don't… I'm not…" Alexa moaned again, then frowned. "Everywhere."

Knowing that Alexa was conscious, that Spence was dead, lifted a huge weight from her. But the day wasn't over. And Roman—

She shifted her attention back to the man she'd fallen for so completely in the past several days. Knowing her sister was surrounded by loved ones, she rose and scanned the street for Roman. He was back in the alley, crouched beside his wounded former employee.

Roman was covered in blood.

Chapter Nineteen

Tim's blood was on his hands. Literally and, quite possibly, figuratively as well. If Tim lived—and that was unlikely at the moment, Roman realized with a slash of guilt—the whole messy business of Tim's theft from the Corner Pocket, his involvement with Spence and any other crimes could be sorted out later. Right now, Roman was determined to save his former bartender. He held a wadded shirt against Tim's gaping gunshot wound with both hands.

Roman grimaced. He'd heard gut shots were especially painful. "Hang on, Tim. Help's coming."

When he heard the patter of running feet, he glanced up to see Morgan returning to him. His heart twisted. This morning's horrible business was over, and Morgan was safe. Everything else was a side note for Roman, but he knew Morgan well enough to know she'd take the weight of all the injuries upon herself. And he was the one to blame. He'd broken ranks, put his agenda, his desire to keep Tim safe, over the Coltons' carefully laid plans.

But Tim had been involved. If he'd let the scene play out instead of charging in, he'd have seen Tim's transaction with Spence play out. Why hadn't he trusted the Coltons to keep Tim safe? Why had he thought Tim was his responsibility?

"How is he?" Morgan asked, her voice reflecting the knowledge that Tim's condition was grave. She lowered herself carefully to her knees and studied the sucking wound in Tim's stomach with wide, horrified eyes.

He met her gaze with a mournful look. Shook his head subtly. "I'm sorry. I blew it. This is on me—"

"Morgan!" Ezra rushed over to them, dropping into a crouch. Her brother gave Tim a pitying glance before gripping Morgan's shoulder. "Are you hurt?"

"N-no. But Roman is. And Tim." She cast a look over her shoulder to where the ambulance was arriving as three EMTs hustled out to swarm her sister. "And Alexa."

Ezra nodded, his face taut with worry. "I know." He glared at Roman, then, "What the hell were you thinking?"

Roman straightened his back and faced the accusation in Ezra's stare.

Before he could defend or accept the fault for his actions, Morgan said, "Back off, Ez. He was protecting a friend! He didn't know Tim was involved. He thought Tim might blow the operation, scare Spence away."

"Instead, he nearly blew it." Ezra arched an eyebrow. "Lucky for you, Spence didn't get away."

Roman frowned. "He's in custody?"

"Spence is dead. He caught multiple bullets from the local cops and was likely dead before his car crashed."

"You're sure he's dead?" Morgan asked, her skin almost gray from shock.

Ezra scoffed a humorless laugh. "Sis, what part of 'multiple bullets' left any doubt?"

Ezra's sarcasm chafed Roman, but he figured everyone was edgy, so he said nothing.

Morgan closed her eyes and sighed. "I just…want to be sure. He's caused so much trouble for so long… I've been imagining I can smell his cigarettes in my house, that I'm seeing him lurking in the bushes at work—"

"You what?" Roman asked sharply. "You never said anything to me."

"I didn't want to add any worry on top of everything else I'd piled on you. It's just that I've felt so unsettled lately, so…scared by recent events that I let my mind conjure things…"

"Just the same," Ezra said, "I want a chance to search your house before you go back home. In case Spence was there. In case he booby-trapped it somehow."

Roman saw the shiver that gripped Morgan. "I'm coming with you when you do," he told Ezra, though his focus was on Morgan. "I need to know she'll be safe."

Morgan opened her mouth as if to argue, but one of the EMTs arrived, and Roman moved aside so the medic could attend Tim.

The EMT assessed Tim's dire situation in a glance and shouted back toward his coworkers, "Lower abdominal GSW! This man needs transport, stat!"

MORGAN STALKED THE corridors of the hospital, waiting for information on Alexa and Roman. She'd been assessed as well and treated for mild shock.

Roman finished with the doctor first. His leg scrape and the bullet graze on his arm were both disinfected, bandaged. He was discharged with a prescription for an antibiotic, which Morgan insisted he fill right away at the hospital pharmacy.

"You should go home and rest," she told him.

Roman lifted his eyebrow and narrowed a look on her. "I could say the same for you."

"I'm not going anywhere until I have word on Alexa."

Roman nodded. "I figured as much. And I'm not going anywhere until Tim is out of surgery."

"He's not your responsibility, you know. You aren't to blame for his bad choices," Morgan countered.

Roman's expression hardened. "I'm staying."

Morgan dropped her protest. She admired Roman's loyalty, even if she thought it rather misplaced. It boded well for their relationship...if—

A doctor shoved through the swinging doors to the emergency room waiting area and, en masse, the whole of the Colton clan stood from chairs or shoved away from walls where they'd been leaning.

Rachel reached the doctor first. "How's Alexa? What did you find?"

"Alexa will be fine with bed rest and TLC. X-rays show she has a small fracture to her iliac crest and another hairline fracture to the parietal bone."

Morgan turned to the woman beside her, Gideon's new wife, Sophia, who was also a doctor. "What does that mean?"

"Cracked hip and a concussion, back here." Sophia patted the back of her head, then called to the ER physician, "Any signs of intracranial hemorrhage or hematoma?"

The other doctor turned his head to meet Sophia's

gaze. "Only minor bleeding under the skull. Most of the visible blood when she came in was from the external wound where her head hit the pavement when she fell."

"Will her hip fracture require surgery?" Sophia asked, and the family, as if by unspoken unanimous vote, parted and nudged Sophia to the front of the cluster of bodies.

"No. I don't believe so, but I've put in a referral to a specialist to see her tomorrow. We'll be keeping her overnight for observation. All in all, she was very lucky. Given the scenario described to me, her injuries could have been much worse. Apparently, she drank her milk as a child and teen. Alexa has strong bones."

Isa lifted her chin and turned to Aubrey. "See? I told you kids you needed your calcium."

"For now, Alexa is asking to see Dane. One additional person can stay with her, but the rest of you need to clear the waiting room, please."

With a buzz of conversation and sighs of relief, her family began to disperse.

"Doctor?" Roman said, fighting his way through the cluster of Coltons to catch the physician's attention before the other man could disappear through the swinging doors again. "Do you know anything on Tim Hall? He arrived when Alexa did with gunshot wounds. Went into surgery almost an hour ago."

"Are you family? Privacy laws prevent me from discussing his condition with anyone not listed on his HIPAA release."

Roman firmed his mouth in disappointment and shook his head. "No. I'm a friend. I just… Can't you at least tell me if he's going to survive?"

"I'm sorry. I can't." The doctor's expression was apologetic. "If you'll excuse me, I need to get back… to him." With a subtle lift to his eyebrows, the doctor whisked through the swinging doors to the treatment area.

"So…at least you know he's still alive. That's something, isn't it?" Morgan asked.

"I guess." He glanced across the room where the family was slowly exiting, returning to their cars. Morgan followed him as he approached Ezra. "I'm going to take Morgan home now, if you want to join me in searching her house."

"What's this?" Ezra's fiancée, Theresa, asked. "Honey, you've had a difficult day, too. You should come home with me and rest."

Ezra put a hand on Theresa's cheek and gave her a quick kiss. "I will. Soon. But I need to do this first." Then to Roman, "Let's go."

Chapter Twenty

"Tell me what's been happening. What are we looking for?" Ezra asked as he crossed Morgan's yard.

"Probably nothing. I probably imagined something that wasn't there, but…"

When she let her sentence hang, Roman picked up the thought. "But there's been enough worrisome things happening for the family lately that it can't hurt to be sure."

"Specifically, what have you experienced?" Ezra pushed as they stopped on her front porch.

"A few times in the last week I've smelled cigarette smoke in my house. I don't smoke, and neither does anyone I've let in recently. When I search the house, it's empty. Nothing gone. Nothing moved."

Ezra grunted and took her house key from her trembling hand to unlock the front door.

"You should wait here while we search," Roman said, catching her arm when she moved to enter.

She scowled at him. "No. It's cold out here, and I won't be ruled by what is probably a figment of my imagination."

"But—" Roman started, then groaned as she stepped inside her foyer.

All three of them paused and sniffed the air. The faintest scent of sour smoke still lingered. But maybe she was trying to find something that wasn't there?

"Do you smell it now?" Roman asked. "I don't smell anything except…you. Fruit. Peaches."

She strolled deeper into her home. "A hint. Not as strong as before." She rubbed her arms and sat on her couch. "Ezra, am I losing my mind?"

Ezra took another deep breath, his nose up like a hound dog tracking a scent. "I smell it."

Morgan's heart tripped. Both with relief that someone else could verify the odor she'd been smelling, but also with concern over what it meant.

"DiMera, check the attic. Something could be smoldering in the electrical system. I'll search down here. Morgan, check all your outlets for excessive heat."

They all set about their tasks and reconvened in her living room twenty minutes later. Ezra shook his head. "I don't know. It smells more like tobacco than wiring. I see no sign it's electrical, but call an electrician tomorrow, just in case. Are you sure you haven't had any workers in the house that smoked? A plumber or food delivery?"

Morgan shook her head. "No one, except you and Theresa to wrap gifts last week."

Ezra moved toward the front door, stopping in the foyer. "We didn't smoke or smell anything then."

"Oh, and Gavin came over to preview his podcast a few days ago. But I was with him, and he didn't smell like smoke."

"I don't know, Mor." Ezra stopped and faced her, concern denting his brow. "I don't think it's your imagination. I smell it, too. Just a hint. Keep your doors locked," he said as he took a step backward and knocked into her umbrella stand. Ezra spun to catch the large open-topped urn she used for storage and righted it. "Oops. Sorry. No harm, no f—"

Ezra's face creased, darkened. He stooped to reach into the bottom of the umbrella stand. "What are these doing in there?"

He pulled out two pieces of trash.

Roman stepped closer to take a look. "Well, I can explain the used Kleenex with the cough drop. Morgan threw that in there last January."

A rusty flash of memory spun through Morgan's mind. Drunk. A cough drop. A kiss...

"I brought her home when—"

She cleared her throat loudly to cut Roman off, flicking a side glance to her brother. "Never mind that. What else was in there?"

Ezra held out the crumpled blue wrapper of a cigarette pack that read Smitty's.

Morgan gasped.

Roman moved to her side. "Do you recognize it?"

She nodded. "That's the imported brand that Spence smokes...smoked. He chain-smoked them. But how—?"

She cut the question off as the obvious answer came to her and settled heavily in her gut. She hadn't been imagining the smell of cigarettes.

Roman stiffened as the truth crystallized for him as well. "Good God, Spence was in your house. Likely more than once."

"He tried to run us off the road," she said numbly.

"He said he was glad to have another chance to kill one of Ben Colton's children."

A nearly convulsive shudder shook Morgan, cold terror pooling in her gut.

Roman wrapped her in his arms and drew her close. "But he didn't. And you're safe now. Spence is dead."

She peeked up at Roman, then to Ezra, who nodded. "Very dead," her brother said. "But just in case he left a parting gift, I'm going to have another look around."

AFTER ANOTHER THOROUGH search that turned up nothing further, Ezra left for home.

Roman faced Morgan with a narrowed gaze. He wished he could read her mind, tell where her head was, but her expression remained oddly blank. "Do you want me to stay here tonight? I'd stake my life it's safe. We've gone over everything, but if—"

"No." She wrapped her arms around herself as if cold. "I mean… *I* don't want to stay here until I can have the place cleaned from top to bottom. Aired out, sanitized. It gives me the creeps to think of him here, touching my things. I know it's an overreaction, but I want all traces of *him* gone. I…can't—" She closed her eyes, and finally her face crumpled. She choked on a sob. "I just want to feel safe again, Roman."

His heart broke for her, and he reached out to take her in his arms. "Come home with me. You can stay as long as you want—"

Her vigorous head shake cut him off, and she sidestepped his embrace. "No. Not your place, either. I—I think I'll go back up to the hospital. I want to take a turn sitting with Alexa."

He sighed his disagreement. "You need to rest. You've had your own shocks and stresses."

"Then I'll go to Caleb's or Aubrey's or…"

Anywhere but your place. She didn't say as much, but it was in her eyes. Her words from that morning, the talk they never finished… *There are things about you that scare me.*

"Right," he said, backing toward the door, his tone resigned. "I'll just see myself out. Take care of yourself, Morgan. You know where to find me when…if you change your mind."

"Roman, I—"

He paused at the door, waited for her to finish her sentence, to ask him to stay, to initiate one of her soul-searing kisses.

Instead, she sighed. "I'm…sorry."

"Yeah. Me, too, Peaches."

Chapter Twenty-One

"Hello?" Morgan tapped softly on the hospital room door and peeked inside. The scene was not what she'd have predicted. But when had the Coltons ever been predictable? Alexa was awake, staring at the ceiling, and Dane slumped in a chair, snoring. On the foldout cot, Sophia was curled in a ball with a hospital blanket pulled up to her chin.

"Hi," Alexa said from the bed. "Why at you here at this hour?" She motioned to the wall clock that read 6:58 a.m.

"Checking on you, of course."

"I'm fine. Just achy. And a little nauseated. Makes it hard to sleep."

Morgan moved into the room and sat carefully on the edge of the bed. "I'd have thought the meds they gave you would have put you out."

"I guess I'm the exception. I'm wired. And itchy." Alexa scratched her arm as if in demonstration.

"Okay, Dane I get," Morgan said pointing to the sleepers, "but why is Sophia here instead of Mom? Or Naomi?"

"Because our sibs insisted Mom go home and sleep in her own bed and come in later this morning."

"Good."

"And Dane thought if anything happened overnight, he wanted Sophia here to translate medicalese and look over the nurses' shoulders."

Morgan pulled a face. "I bet that went over well with your nurses."

Alexa flapped a hand. "Sophia's been great. Calming Dane without stepping on any professional toes." Her sister tipped her head. "You okay? Why aren't you home tucked up in bed? Or better yet, tucked up with your hunky bar owner?"

"Long story."

Alexa spread her hands. "I'm not going anywhere, and I enjoy a good story."

"This one is something of a horror tale." She gave Alexa an abbreviated version of how she'd sensed Spence in many ways over the last few days, and how they'd found the cigarette wrapper in her house.

Alexa frowned. "That is creepy." She blew out a breath and shook her head. "Am I glad to have that guy out of our lives!" Then, with a frown at Morgan, she said, "'Fess up, Morgan. You're not here because Spence was in your house. What's going on with you? Jasper said you were all kinds of melancholy yesterday at the ranch and that you were talking about clearing your head."

"I wasn't melancholy!"

Alexa's expression was unconvinced. "You sure seem that way now. And defensive."

Morgan gritted her back teeth. Stared at her lap. Finally she said, "I don't know what to do about Roman."

"Do? You can start by thanking him for helping us catch Spence." She smirked then. "After that, I'd recommend you take that fine-looking man to bed and not let him up for a long, long time."

"I second that," came a groggy voice from the cot.

Alexa chuckled, then pressed a hand to her head. "Ooh, it hurts to laugh."

Morgan sent Sophia a sheepish grin. "Sorry to wake you."

Sophia sat up, keeping the blanket wrapped around her. "You two didn't. His snoring did." She cut a scowl toward Dane. "I kept dreaming I was chasing a locomotive. But they say weird dreams are a part of pregnancy." The smile Sophia wore shifted to an "oops" grimace.

A beat passed as Morgan replayed Sophia's words. "Hang on…pregnant?"

Alexa gasped. "Oh, Sophia! Say it's so!"

Sophia pressed a finger to her lips and shushed them both. "We were trying to keep it a secret until the end of my first trimester. After Christmas. Until all the mess with Spence was wrapped up."

Morgan flew from the bed to hug her sister-in-law. "That's so wonderful! When are you due?"

"Mid-May." Sophia divided a smile between them. "Please don't say anything to anyone. Gideon wants to make the announcement to everyone in January."

Alexa drew her fingers over her mouth. "My lips are sealed."

Morgan nodded. "I promise."

Sophia took Morgan's hands. "Now what's this about not knowing what to do with Roman?"

With a sigh, Morgan returned to the end of the hospital bed and looked for the best way to explain. "I guess for you to have the whole picture, I should let you in on something that happened to me when I was twenty."

She told Sophia about her attack, recapped recent events for both women and explained how Roman's tattoos had been a trigger for bad memories. She told them she planned to contact a trauma counselor, realizing she hadn't put the attack behind her as she'd believed. "In recent weeks, with so much turmoil and tragedy in the family, I've had this feeling of danger looming over me. I just don't feel safe anywhere. And this morning when we figured out Spence had been in my house—" She shuddered. "And if you could have seen the look on Roman's face when I told him I didn't want to go to his place... I know he thinks I'm rejecting him because of his tattoos or all our differences. Maybe our differences are part of why things feel unsettled between us—"

"Morgan, I know you're looking for a nice, tidy answer. But emotions and falling in love and past trauma—none of that is neat or tidy," Alexa said. "Relationships just aren't black-and-white. They're not even shades of gray. They're green. And yellow. And bright pink. They're swirled colors and beautiful rainbows."

Morgan blinked at her sister and chuckled. "Is that my sister or the painkillers talking?"

Sophia laughed quietly. "I actually like that way of putting it." Sobering, she met Morgan's eyes with her warm hazel gaze. "You need to deal with your past. I think it's clouding how you look at everything else, including Roman."

"Answer this for me, Morgan," Alexa said, and wagged a finger. "No deliberating, just gut feeling, instant answer. Okay? What would your future be like if Roman weren't in it?"

Morgan's heart wrenched, and her soul seemed to wither. "Bleak. Lonely. Horrible!"

"Well, there's your answer," Sophia said.

"If you don't want a future without him," Alexa said, "fight to keep him. Show him you love him and want him in a way he can't dispute. Then allow yourself to be happy."

THE NEXT DAY, Christmas Eve, Roman puttered around the Corner Pocket, wiping down glasses and debating closing the bar since so few people were coming in. If he closed, though, he'd officially have nothing to do except dwell on the fact that a future with Morgan seemed remote. She hadn't wanted him last night when she'd been upset about finding Spence had been in her home. He didn't need the unfinished conversation to know he represented all things scary to her. Risk. Rule breaking. His tattoos…

His cell phone beeped, signaling an incoming text, and he checked the screen. It was from Morgan. Meet me at my office in an hour.

He considered refusing. What was the point of belaboring the issue? But he supposed a clearly defined breakup and closure would be better for both of them.

"Let's call it a day," he told Penny, and his waitress couldn't take her apron off fast enough. Hector had the kitchen cleaned up and turned off quickly, and he locked the door behind them. He killed thirty minutes upstairs in his apartment, feeding Rufus and changing into clothes that didn't smell like beer and chili. Then, though he'd be early, he set off for the offices of Colton and Colton.

The door to the law office wasn't locked, and Roman let himself in, calling, "Hello? Morgan?"

"Back here!"

He found Morgan sitting behind her desk, talking with Sophia. The two women were giggling like teenagers over some private joke.

"Knock, knock. Am I interrupting?" He waited at the door until Morgan waved him in.

"Speak of the devil!" Sophia said, her grin widening. "Good to see you again, Roman."

"Likewise. How are things in the—" He wracked his brain for Sophia's profession. Was she the social worker? The DA? Then he remembered her quizzing the ER doctor the day before. He snapped his fingers and pointed at her. "Pediatrics game treating you?"

Sophia chuckled. "Lots of runny noses and coughs this time of year, but nothing our office can't handle. How's the bar and billiards game treating you?"

"Lots of holiday toasting and rounds of eight ball this time of year, but nothing my staff can't handle. Today was slow, though, so I closed early."

Morgan rose from her chair and started around her desk to greet him. She swayed on her feet and had to brace herself with a hand on her desk. "Whoa. Who made the floor move?"

Roman frowned. "Peaches, are you...drunk?"

"No! Well, not exactly."

"But I think you should drive her home, just the same," Sophia added. She checked her phone and gasped. "Gosh. Look at the time. I better get going. I still have to make my pies for the big Colton gathering tomorrow." She rose and gave Morgan a hug. "I'm serious. No driving yourself for several more hours."

Morgan grinned and drew an X with her finger on her chest. "Cross my heart."

Sophia gave a little wave as she hurried out of the office.

"What's going on? Why can't you drive if you're not drunk?" Then adding Sophia, a doctor, into the mix, a new concern swelled in him. "Are you ill?"

She pushed away from the desk and stumbled a couple steps to him. Looping her arms around his neck, she smiled up at him. "I have something to show you. I did something today. Two things, really, and…well, consider it my answer to the question about where I see us going, what I think of our future."

Roman arched an eyebrow. "That sounds…intriguing."

Morgan levered away from him and returned, unsteadily, to her desk chair, where she opened the bottom drawer of her desk to get her purse. She dug in it, pulled something out. She circled the desk again—this time he met her halfway and caught her around the waist to steady her.

Now he could see a mix of anxiety and doubt in her blue eyes, and his pulse hammered. "Morgan, spill. What's going on?"

She raised her closed fist, turned it over and opened

her fingers. On her palm lay a key. "I want you to have this. It's a spare key to my house."

He lifted a corner of his mouth. Leave it to Ms. Practical to think of such a detail. Then she added, "I know living over the bar is handy and all, but…well, I hope soon you'd consider making this the key to *our* house." A dent formed at the bridge of her nose, and it seemed her eyes darkened. "Will you move in with me?"

With his thumb, he rubbed the wrinkle on her brow. "Well, the apartment over the bar *is* terribly convenient for work." He leaned in to kiss her nose. "But your house is more convenient to the woman I love. The woman I want to spend my future with, so…" He hesitated when he realized what it was about her eyes that seemed off to him. Her pupils were bigger than seemed right. When he added this fact to her wobbly gait, his smile faded. "Why are your eyes dilated? If you're not sick or drunk…what's going on?"

She patted his chest and licked her lips. "I took a painkiller that made me a little loopy."

He scowled. "Because?"

She stepped back from him, propped her bottom on the edge of the desk as she raised her shirt and tugged down her skirt a few inches, exposing a red, raw-looking place on her hip. When he looked closer, he noticed something darker in the red and swelling. "What the—?"

"I got a tattoo!" she said and laughed.

"You what?" He leaned in to look closer and, sure enough, the conservatively dressed, mother hen, type-A lawyer was sporting ink. A small heart around the initials *RD*.

"I survived the application process…barely, but when I was finished, I *hurt*! I took a something left over from that time last year when I broke my arm. Don't worry. I didn't drive. Sophia was with me."

Roman blinked, met Morgan's eyes, bent to look at the tattoo again. The significance of her decision was not lost on him. "You got a tattoo."

"The place was next door to the hardware store where I had the key made, and it seemed like a sign. Once the idea came to me, it just felt…right. Symbolic." She touched the tattoo lightly, winced, then canted forward to drape her arms around his neck. "The ink is permanent, just like my love for you. As is my promise to talk to a counselor about my PTSD from the attack. I want nothing negative to stand between us."

Warmth filled Roman's chest, and after giving her a big kiss, he tucked his shoulder under her arm to brace her and hitched his head to the door. "Come on, Peaches. Let me drive you back to *our* house."

Epilogue

Morgan poked her head into her mother's bedroom, where Theresa, Hilary, Sophia, Aubrey and Rachel were already gathered and chattering excitedly as Isa finished applying her makeup. Aubrey rose from the settee where she'd been sitting and crossed to Morgan with a broad smile on her face.

"Oh, thank God! Quick, Morgan, talk to me about something that does not involve swollen ankles, birth canals or morning sickness!"

Morgan laughed, but when she glanced from face to face of the other women gathered with Aubrey, she realized the pregnancy hormones had to be off the charts in the room. Poor Hilary was so large in the late stages of her pregnancy with twins, she wasn't sure how Oliver's wife could even walk.

Rachel, who already had one-year-old Iris, had announced at New Year's that she and James were expecting another baby in July. For most couples, two children under two would be too much, but James had opened his own law firm, so he could set his own hours and spend more time at home with Rachel and Iris.

Sophia was well into her sixth month of pregnancy and rubbed her rounded belly with a loving hand.

Besides Aubrey, only Ezra's new wife—as of a tiny private New Year's Eve ceremony—Theresa wasn't currently pregnant, but she was, even then, regaling Hilary with tips and her own stories of giving birth to twins.

"After having my girls, I found the best thing for stretch marks was coconut oil and staying hydrated. The skin needs moisture and elasticity to heal. Bonus that coconut oil smells like a tropical vacation!" Theresa said.

Morgan put a hand on Aubrey's arm and squeezed. "It's okay, sis. Pregnancy isn't contagious."

"It's not that Luke and I don't want children, but do I have to talk about pregnancy acne and squashed bladders before I get pregnant?" Aubrey asked, rolling her eyes.

"Sorry." Sophia raised her hand and flashed a sheepish grin. "I got it all started by telling the bride she didn't look like the mother of twelve and grandmother to a growing number of little ones."

"And I asked how the mothers-to-be were feeling," Isa added, dusting powder on her nose. "It took off from there. Aubrey, dear, don't let morning sickness or swollen ankles dissuade you. I had twelve babies and never regretted a minute of any of my pregnancies. You'll make a wonderful mother when you and Luke are ready."

The bride paused in her preparations and grew pensive. "I do hope we will be in town when all these babies come. Theo and I have gone a little overboard with all our travel plans." Isa had recently put her house on the market and would be moving with Theo to a new home in town where they could make a fresh start. "It's just with him retiring… Well, we want to see the world while we can. Time waits for no one."

Morgan couldn't help but think of her own chances for becoming a mother. At forty, she was past the safest years for childbirth. But more and more women were having babies after forty, and Sophia could help connect them with the best obstetric doctors. Or, like Caleb and Nadine, who were poised to adopt the three foster children they'd recently been caring for, she and Roman could adopt a child.

She gave her head a small shake and cleared her mind of those thoughts. Roman had only moved into her house two months ago. One step at a time. Even though her counseling was going well and she had no regrets about any of her recent changes, she could be patient.

She looped her arm through Aubrey's. "Shall we talk about your wedding plans, then? May might seem far off, but it'll be here before you know it!"

"Thank you for scheduling it for the end of the month. The last thing I'd want is to go into labor during your ceremony!" Sophia said.

"That makes two of us," Aubrey said with a wink. Turning to Morgan, Aubrey said, "We know it will be at the ranch, and we are hoping by then Luke's family can join us. Beyond that I haven't gotten far, but I plan to grab a minute with Mom's caterer before they pack up and go home. I'm thinking about a barbecue after the ceremony. Thoughts?"

Rachel covered her mouth and looked rather pale. "Please. No talk of food right now. I'm queasy enough as it is."

"And I could eat a whole rack of ribs and gallon of potato salad," Hilary said. "It's hard work growing twins. I'm starving!"

"Same here," Sophia added.

"Well, we can't get these hungry mothers to the reception until I've said 'I do.'" Isa snapped her compact closed and stood. "I'm ready if Theo is."

"We'll go check on the groom," Morgan volunteered and tugged Aubrey out into the hall with her.

"I hope I didn't sound too harsh. You do know I'm tickled pink and baby blue about all my current and future nieces and nephews, right?" Aubrey asked, a tiny furrow in her brow.

Morgan put an arm around her sister's shoulders and gave her a side squeeze. "Of course I do! Even talk of something as joyous as babies can be overwhelming for someone not yet in that stage of life. Just two months ago, I was more than a little envious of all of you finding your husbands and wives. It was both easy and hard to smile when one of you talked about how in love you were."

"But now you have Roman."

Morgan could feel the power behind the smile that lit her face. "But now I have Roman."

"And may I just say, *hubba hubba* and *mrow*! He's is quite the catch, sis. You always were a high achiever." Aubrey bumped her with her hip and waggled her eyebrows. "Although he's not the kind of guy I pictured you marrying."

They'd reached the room where the men, including Theo, were getting ready, but Morgan hesitated, facing her sister. "Honestly, me, neither. But love and fate are odd things, hmm?"

Aubrey nodded, then cocked her head. "Um, are you planning to marry him, then?"

She lifted a shoulder. "The jury is still out."

Aubrey gave her a shrewd look. "Meaning he hasn't asked yet?"

"Precisely." Morgan squared her shoulders. "But I have no intention of letting him get away, and he's assured me he's not going anywhere. And my Rome is a man of his word."

Aubrey pulled her close and kissed Morgan's cheek. "Oh, Morgan. I'm so happy for you!"

At that moment, the door to the men's dressing room opened, and Luke filled the doorway. "I thought I heard the voice I love."

Aubrey leaned in to kiss her fiancé. "The bride is ready. How are things at this end of the hall?"

"We're a go!" someone called from inside the room. The clamor of male voices in the groom's room was as loud and jubilant as the bride's, so Morgan couldn't be sure which voice was whose.

"Then let's round 'em up and move 'em out!" Aubrey called over the men's voices. "C'mon, Morgan. Let's corral the rest of our herd to their seats."

Within minutes, under Morgan, Aubrey and Alexa's direction, the family was in place, and the processional music began. Roman looped his arm around Morgan's waist and held her near his side as she watched her mother, beaming with happiness and love, take her place beside Theo. Morgan savored every minute of the ceremony, frequently brushing away tears of joy. Once the vows were said, the rings exchanged and the newlyweds introduced, a cheer went up that could have shaken the foundation of the Rockies.

The reception was an equally loud and boisterous affair. Morgan circulated the perimeter of the dance floor, where Jasper and Kayla were showing everyone their best moves, and she made a point of spending a few minutes with each of her siblings and their partners. If the past year had taught her anything, it was how fast life could change, for good or ill, and family should never be taken for granted. Besides, she wanted Roman to have a chance to get to know her family better. She'd teasingly told him there'd be a test at the end of the day, and he'd taken on learning the family roster as a challenge.

"So that was Naomi and Philip. I remember them because Philip was on-site at the warehouse the day we caught Spence," he said, sotto voce. "Their wedding is…this summer? He's with the PD in Boulder, and she's…" He snapped his fingers trying to recall.

"A TV producer. Her twin, Alexa, is the US marshal."

"I remember Alexa," he said, his face sobering. "Hard to forget when you see someone struck by a car during a gun battle."

"But she's fine now. How could she not be with Dane doting on her?"

Hands linked, she led him to the spot where the triplets congregated with their significant others. Oliver and

Hilary were snuggled on a couch with Ezra and Theresa, Dominic and Sami standing facing them.

"Hey! That's close to us!" Theresa was saying to Sami, a bright note in her tone as Morgan and Roman approached the circle.

Dominic noticed his oldest sister and moved to wave them into the gathering, holding out a hand to shake Roman's. "Hey, man. You're getting quite the indoctrination to the Coltons the last couple months. First Christmas à la Colton, which is a holiday on steroids, then a family wedding seven weeks later. Whew!"

"It's eye-opening, for sure. But a blast," Roman replied with a smile.

"Morgan, Sami was just saying she and Dom have bought a house close to us. Isn't that exciting?" Theresa said.

"With the FBI officially behind me, a wedding in the works and my new career with Ezra's thriving security firm taking off, I thought it might be time to try homeownership," Dominic said. "I mean, if you're going to make changes in your life, why not every aspect?"

The group laughed. "All in, Dom!"

Jasper approached from the dance floor, Kayla on his heels, and caught Morgan's arm. "Hey, Peaches…"

Morgan gave him a withering glare. "Roman is the only one who gets to call me that."

"Not a good idea to tease your sister when you're about to ask a favor," Kayla said.

Morgan raised her eyebrows. "A favor?"

Kayla nodded. "Jasper and I really want some time away from the ranch. Time to relax and…well, I got a good deal on a cruise to Cancún."

"Sounds awesome! And you want me to join you? Done!" Morgan said with a laugh.

"Actually, we were hoping we could leave Bandit with you and Roman."

"Bandit?" Roman asked.

"Their Australian shepherd. Service dog dropout."

"Oh. Um, why can't one of the other hands feed him?" Roman asked.

"Well…truth is—" Jasper rubbed the back of his neck. "He's kinda spoiled. He gets really lonely."

Kayla grimaced guiltily. "We've been letting him sleep in the room with us, and if we aren't there…he tears stuff up."

Morgan's eyes widened. "Tears stuff— You know I have to work, right? Is he going to rip up my house?"

"No problem. I'll take him into the bar with me. He can keep me company." Roman smiled like he'd just been given a prize. "I always wanted a dog. What do you think, Peaches?"

"To getting a dog or babysitting theirs?" But she needn't have asked. Roman could ask for anything, and she'd give it to him if she could. She faced Jasper. "Yes. Write up comprehensive instructions, and I will keep Bandit." Facing Roman, she added, "We'll talk about it later. We need to see how Rufus reacts to Bandit first."

"Daddy! Daddy! Come dance with us!" Two blonde darlings in flower girl dresses scampered up and grabbed Ezra by the hands. Morgan saw the pride and love at being called Daddy by Theresa's daughters, Neve and Claire, beaming from her brother's face.

"Duty calls," he said as he let the girls lead him away.

"Show them the worm!" Oliver called from the couch.

As Ezra took the dance floor, Nadine joined him with the three foster children, who—with a few more signatures and formalities—would officially become her and Caleb's family. Ten-year-old twins Romeo and Juliet showed some snazzy moves, while their sister, Portia, six, largely spun in circles until she fell down laughing. James, who seemed all the happier for the chance to be home more, swayed rhythmically to the music with a cooing Iris on his hip.

When Oliver and Dominic joined Ezra, Nadine and the children, Morgan sidled away, tugging Roman's arm. "Quick, before we get drafted to dance."

He followed, lifting an eyebrow. "You don't dance?"

"Not without more liquid courage or a slow song to keep things simple." She led him toward a table where two seats were open.

Roman craned his head toward the DJ, and a speculative gleam winked in his gaze. "I can arrange both. Before we leave this party, Peaches, I want you in my arms dancing."

She demurred with a "hmm" before leaning toward Gavin, in the chair next to her, to ask, "How was the podcast on the wild mustangs received? Do you have any ratings numbers or download figures back yet?"

Gavin's face brightened before he sent a side glance to his fiancée. "Uh, I promised Jacqui I wouldn't talk about work."

Jacqui sent him a grateful smile. "You can brag on the podcast's success for five minutes. You deserve that much after all the hard work you put in. Just don't bore people with it all afternoon."

Eyes bright, Gavin said, "It was big. Huge numbers. I'm being courted by Spotify for a regular gig!"

Morgan squealed and hugged her brother. "That's fantastic!"

Roman pulled out the chair next to Morgan and shook Philip's hand. "Detective Rees. How are you? I don't think I've seen you since the big shindig at Christmas."

"Hey, DiMera. Good to see you. Yeah, between a new case and helping Naomi plan our wedding, we've been busy bees. How's your arm? Everything healed up after Spence winged you?"

Roman patted his arm. "Good as new. Other than a new scar to add to the collection. What's the new case ab—"

The loud ding of a spoon against a champagne glass silenced the room and the music from the speakers. Caleb stood at the microphone near the head table and motioned for silence. "Family, friends, people who crashed because they knew a good party when they saw it—" Caleb paused for the chuckles to quiet. "Raise a glass with me, if you will, to the newlyweds."

Around the room, champagne flutes, hot chocolate cups and beer mugs lifted. "We are so happy to welcome Theo to the family, and we—"

Isa Colton *Lawson* put a hand on Caleb's shoulder to stop him.

"Mom? What's—"

She took the microphone from his hand and said, "Thank you, Caleb. I appreciate your welcome to Theo and the good wishes I know you planned to offer us as we make a fresh start together. Everyone has been so kind, so gracious, so loving and supportive for months now as we put this day together. I thank you all. But I don't want today to be just about me and Theo. Today is Valentine's Day, a day to celebrate love. We chose this day for that reason. But not just because of our love for each other—" She held out her arm, and Theo wrapped her in a side hug. "But because of all the love in this room." She swept a hand, motioning to all the couples at tables and children clustered on the dance floor.

Isa took a moment, took a deep breath. "Raising twelve children was not easy, especially when I lost your father so early. But... I couldn't be prouder of how my Colton dozen turned out. This past year has tested us, refined us, strengthened our love, reinforced the bonds that have held our big, boisterous family together for so many years."

Morgan blinked and found moisture trickling down her cheeks. She grabbed a clean napkin and dabbed at her eyes, feeling her heart swell with joy. Roman pulled her close and kissed her temple.

"And somehow," Isa continued, "in the midst of what seemed like endless trouble and tragedy, our family was blessed with not just twelve beautiful, talented, loving partners, but a new generation of Coltons—" She extended her arms toward the kids waiting patiently on the dance floor for more music. "Grandchildren! And more on the way!"

The children gave a cheer, recognizing they were the center of attention at that moment.

"So today we celebrate love of *all* forms, and twelve new beginnings!"

Theo leaned into the microphone and said, "Thirteen. Don't forget me, love."

A rumble of laughter filled the room, and Isa gave her new husband a kiss. "I could never forget you, my sweet." She kissed Theo and finished her speech, lifting a wineglass and saying, with emotion thinning her voice, "The Coltons are strong. Resilient. And so blessed. I raise my glass to you, my family, my loves, all of you!"

Gideon gave a whoop, and beside Morgan, Roman surged to his feet, his drink held high. "To the Coltons!"

Flutes clinked, couples kissed and Morgan leaned into Roman, smiling with a happiness that radiated from her soul. "Welcome home, hon. I love you."

"Then marry me, Peaches."

Morgan blinked, grabbed his suit lapel and kissed him. "I have time on my schedule next Saturday."

"Is that the lawyer way of saying yes?"

She chuckled and kissed him again. "It is."

* * * * *

COMING SOON!

We really hope you enjoyed reading this book.
If you're looking for more romance, be sure to
head to the shops when new books are
available on

Thursday 5th
January

To see which titles are coming soon, please visit

millsandboon.co.uk/nextmonth

MILLS & BOON

THE HEART OF ROMANCE

A ROMANCE FOR EVERY READER

MODERN

Prepare to be swept off your feet by sophisticated, sexy and seductive heroes, in some of the world's most glamourous and romantic locations, where power and passion collide.

HISTORICAL

Escape with historical heroes from time gone by. Whether your passion i for wicked Regency Rakes, muscled Vikings or rugged Highlanders, awa the romance of the past.

MEDICAL

Set your pulse racing with dedicated, delectable doctors in the high-pres sure world of medicine, where emotions run high and passion, comfort love are the best medicine.

True Love

Celebrate true love with tender stories of heartfelt romance, from the rush of falling in love to the joy a new baby can bring, and a focus on t emotional heart of a relationship.

Desire

Indulge in secrets and scandal, intense drama and plenty of sizzling ho action with powerful and passionate heroes who have it all: wealth, stat good looks…everything but the right woman.

HEROES

Experience all the excitement of a gripping thriller, with an intense ro mance at its heart. Resourceful, true-to-life women and strong, fearless face danger and desire - a killer combination!

To see which titles are coming soon, please visit

millsandboon.co.uk/nextmonth

JOIN THE
MILLS & BOON
BOOKCLUB

* **FREE** delivery direct to your door

* **EXCLUSIVE** offers every month

* **EXCITING** rewards programme

50% OFF
YOUR FIRST
PARCEL

Join today at
Millsandboon.co.uk/Bookclub

JOIN US ON SOCIAL MEDIA!

Stay up to date with our latest releases, author news and gossip, special offers and discounts, and all the behind-the-scenes action from Mills & Boon...

 @millsandboon

 @millsandboonuk

 facebook.com/millsandboon

 @millsandboonuk

It might just be true love...

GET YOUR ROMANCE FIX!

Get the latest romance news,
exclusive author interviews, story
extracts and much more!